Sat - Aug 09, 2014

W9-BPM-619

Solomon's Song

Roberta Kells Dorr

MOODY PUBLISHERS

CHICAGO

©1989, 2014 by
ROBERTA KELLS DORR

All rights reserved. No part of this book may be reproduced in any form without permission in writing from the publisher, except in the case of brief quotations embodied in critical articles or reviews.

Interior design: Ragont Design
Cover design: Brand Navigation, LLC
Cover images: Woman: Shutterstock / 45457591 / © Ivan Feoktistov
              Man: Shutterstock / 79845391 / © CURAphotography
              Pattern in Horizontal Bar: iStock LP / 6836464 / © naelnabil
              Solomon's Crown: iStock LP / 18598022 / © talymel
              Solomon's Shirt/Armor: iStock LP / 11610880 © Valentin Casarsa

Library of Congress Cataloging-in-Publication Data
Dorr, Roberta Kells.
    Solomon's song / Roberta Kells Dorr.
       pages cm
    Originally published: San Francisco : Harper & Row, c1989.
    Summary: "The sadness and the tenderness of life are felt so acutely in the presence of beauty, and love is revealed more in our sorrow than in our joy. -Solomon, from Solomon's Song. The wisest of all kings, beloved son of King David and his wife Bathsheba, builder of a prosperous empire, lover to many wives and concubines-King Solomon was once merely a son of David with no guarantee of ever taking the throne. On the cusp of adulthood, with no direction in life, Solomon found himself infatuated . . . in love with a lowly shepherdess, a young maiden chosen for his father to serve David in his later years. Overhead clouds ceased to discharge life-giving rain, and the anxious people looked to King David for relief from the famine. In their weakness they turned from Yahweh and sacrificed to foreign gods. But the David's eldest son, Adonijah had a plan, one that could cost the Benjamites their lives. Revenge. Solomon was still Bathsheba's eldest son and with it came certain family expectations. His mother wanted nothing less than the throne for her eldest living son. He must marry a princess first, and then he can marry any common woman he desired. Solomon s struggled against family expectations and his chief rival, his own brother, Adonijah; he fought against the most disappointing aspect of his quest to become ruler. 'Love is nothing, when pitted against strength and power.'"—Provided by publisher.
    ISBN 978-0-8024-0955-3 (pbk.)
    1. Solomon, King of Israel—Fiction. 2. Bible. Old Testament—History of Biblical events—Fiction. 3. Israel—Kings and rulers—Fiction. I. Title.
PS3554.O694S6 2014
813'.54—dc23

2013034186ISBN

We hope you enjoy this book from River North Fiction by Moody Publishers. Our goal is to provide high-quality, thought provoking books and products that connect truth to your real needs and challenges. For more information on other books and products written and produced from a biblical perspective, go to www.moodypublishers.com or write to:

River North Fiction
Imprint of Moody Publishers
820 N. LaSalle Boulevard
Chicago, IL 60610

1 3 5 7 9 10 8 6 4 2

Printed in the United States of America

To my daughter, Debby
who like Shulamit
has a special love for
plants and animals

Love is as strong as death;
jealousy as cruel as the grave

(KING JAMES VERSION)

Prologue

*T*he sound of a flute rose and fell with a lonesome, wistful insistence, giving voice to the moonlight and making the unseen listener grieve with a sorrow deeper than tears. Leaning over the parapet, the king saw that the musician was a young shepherd boy, who probably felt only the poignancy that always seems entwined with a jasmine-scented night.

"How is it," Solomon wondered as he watched the slow movement of the branches on the palm trees that lined the courtyard below, "that the sadness and the tenderness of life are felt so acutely in the presence of beauty, and love is revealed more in our sorrow than in our joy?"

The shepherd's notes grew faint as the boy moved down the path toward the valley. The king turned from the parapet with a sigh and walked through the curtained doorway into the richly draped and carpeted room where his young scribe still sat crosslegged on the floor, writing the day's accounts.

The boy must have been startled by the king's silent, brooding look. He let the stylus fall from his hand and bounded forward to kneel before Solomon.

"There's no need to be distressed," Solomon said gently as he stooped and lifted him to his feet. "Let's be done with the matters of the court and the problems of the day. Tonight is a special night—a night to ponder old memories and then lock them away for some future date, some future time."

He motioned for the boy to bring out a parchment in gold-embroidered wrapping from under the cushions by his bed. "I'll sit here and listen while you read to me the story of the most beautiful girl in the world, the song of a love that was stronger than death and jealousy more cruel than Sheol, the most glorious song I've ever written: The Song of Songs."

Solomon sat down and leaned back among the cushions where his face would be hidden by the shadows, so that the young scribe couldn't see the emotion that came and went on his face or the tears that flooded his eyes. As the scribe read, Solomon remembered the beloved face and gentle hands of the Shunammite maiden and all that had passed between them. He remembered her words to him:

"Come, my beloved, let us go out to the vineyards.
Let us get up early and go out to see whether the vines have budded,
Whether the blossoms have opened, and

Whether the pomegranates are in flower.
There I will give you my love."

The scribe read well the words of the maiden just as she had said them and as Solomon, remembering, had recorded them. Solomon could see her dark hair caught carelessly in the folds of coarse linen that framed her face, making the small, curled tendrils that escaped more dear.

She was always shy, leaving her eyes to say much more than her lips. From the very beginning there had been some mysterious, wordless flow of feeling between them that made him feel completely accepted and loved. There was no part of her, except her eyes, that he remembered as being separate and distinct from any other. Like a rare jewel cut by a skilled craftsman, she was perfect in every way.

"Your neck is stately as an ivory tower,
Your eyes as limpid pools in Heshbon by the gate of Bath-rabbim.
The king is held captive in your queenly tresses!"

How true the words had proven to be!

The scribe read on and on from the scroll that had been written by the king's own hand on the finest of parchments. The king heard only fragments, however, for suddenly the room seemed peopled with voices from the past. Once again he could picture the day just as it had been and the events that led up to the first time he saw her.

The pain of remembering such lost joy and happiness was almost unendurable. Yet he couldn't turn back from it. This was the night for remembering, and he was a man who faced life squarely and didn't shrink from the pain, lest he also lose something of the joy.

1

*I*t was his eighteenth birthday. It should have been a day of festivity and rejoicing, but because of the famine that held the land in a death-like grip Solomon expected no celebration. Instead, he chose to ride out and observe for himself the plight of the people.

His close-cropped dark hair outlined a strong, tanned face with eyes that were often described as deep and quiet. His mouth was full and sensuous with an inclination to smile, showing strong white teeth and a firm, well-shaped jaw. Solomon was young and handsome, as were all of David's sons.

Today there was no laughter as he rode with his younger brother Nathan down the ridge toward his father's lands at Bethlehem. He saw the devastation of three years of drought, and his expression was grim and troubled. In every village he saw men and women with large, frightened eyes, children with distended abdomens, cattle frail and emaciated. The fields of barley that were usually bright green at this time of year stood in dwarfed brown spears.

In the palace they had heard that the people were close to rioting. Solomon could see that this was true. "We've already lost the barley harvest," they complained to him. "We must have rain by Passover or we'll lose the wheat also. The king must *do* something."

When Solomon reached Bethlehem, he found the situation even worse. The great stretch of fertile basin that had been the pride of Boaz, then Obed and Jesse, was now a swirling dustbowl. The men of the village sat in small, dispirited groups at the city gate, their faces dark, their eyes hopeless, and their mouths twisted with bitterness. The women listlessly ran their hands over silent grindstones or rocked the whimpering babies.

"Water must be the strongest thing in the world," Solomon remarked to Nathan as they rode back to Jerusalem. "Without it a whole nation can be brought to starvation and death."

Nathan was always amused at how his brother loved to analyze everything. He himself was a student of the Law, and his lessons with the prophet Nathan didn't leave room for such fanciful speculation.

"I don't agree at all," Nathan said. "Water is necessary for things to grow, but to do that it must disappear into the ground—and then it's no longer water."

"You're right," Solomon's eyes were wide and alert as he mulled over the problem. "Then," he asked, "what is the strongest thing in the world?"

Without hesitation Nathan replied, "Why, rocks, of course. That rock over there will never go away or change. It was there when our father Abraham passed this way."

Solomon gave his brother a playful push. "It isn't fair. I spend so much time trying to understand things, and you know the answers without even thinking."

Nathan nodded. "Things are seldom fair. I'm free to do as I wish; you can't."

"You're right. Just yesterday I had a quarrel with our mother. Now she wants me to marry a princess from Rabbath-ammon."

"She wants to put you ahead of Adonijah for the throne."

Solomon made a dismissive gesture. "I've heard that the princess is plain and has a sharp tongue."

"Perhaps," said Nathan. "But she *is* a princess. Mother's even planned a surprise for your birthday so you can travel in style to get your bride."

Bride. Solomon stiffened as he gave his mule a brisk flick with his prod, making him lunge forward down the path.

* * *

Back in Jerusalem Bathsheba, Solomon's mother, was finishing preparations for her favorite son's birthday. She had not only prepared a celebration but had commissioned old Tobias, an Egyptian craftsman, to build a palanquin of intricate and cunning design. The celebration would be a relief, she reasoned; it would be good for them to forget for a few hours all the concern over the lack of rain.

Almost everyone in Jerusalem had been involved in planning for the special day or making the unusual birthday gift. Some of Bathsheba's maidens had carefully woven a golden canopy, while others had decorated the seat and back with fine needlework. To everyone's delight, the palanquin had been finished on time and stood waiting for Solomon's return from Bethlehem. Excitement mounted as the maidens anticipated the final unveiling, which would reveal a panel of black ebony with a needlework insert that carried their secret and daring message.

* * *

By late afternoon a group of young women had assembled in the tower room above Jerusalem's South Gate. They primped and gossiped and even laughed in a way that hadn't been heard in months. From time to time they excitedly glanced out the high, narrow window that looked down the Kidron Valley toward Bethlehem.

They were just beginning to get impatient and fretful when a young girl named Yasmit screamed, "He's coming!" She grabbed her tambourine and pushed through the shrill laughter and nervous giggles to get to the door first. Others quickly followed, while a few clambered up to look out the window so they too could see the flying banners and bright swords of the young men who rode with the prince.

Yasmit looked back and grabbed her younger sister's hand, roughly pulling her down the steps as she whispered, "Hurry! I want to get close enough to really see the prince."

"I hope you're not going to do anything foolish," her sister admonished as they moved with the young women into the open space before the gate.

There was the usual fanfare of trumpets as the gates opened and Solomon came riding through, looking rather dusty but still regal and handsome. At first, seeing the young women, his face registered surprise. Then he pulled the reins taut and broke into a merry laugh. Quickly he urged his mule on and rode before the maidens up the narrow streets to the open courtyard before the palace.

The women sang as they beat a steady rhythm on their tambourines and kept time with their slapping feet on the cold stones of the cobbled court. "He is strong and handsome; his eyes are tender and warm." One voice, the voice of Yasmit, rang out higher and more strident than all the rest. Boldly she reached for the bridle of Solomon's mule and led him to the place where Tobias stood with some of the palace guards beside a large covered object.

Laughing boyishly, Solomon dismounted and greeted Tobias with a warm handclasp. "What's this?" he bantered, pointing to the bulky form.

"My lord—" Tobias didn't finish his sentence, for at that moment there was a stir off to one side as a tall figure, richly dressed, rode into the midst

courtyard. He forced his mule through the shrieking women and
ted.

It was Adonijah, the crown prince and oldest son of David by his wife
Haggith. He ignored Solomon as he faced Tobias with cold contempt. "Old
man, by what right do you make such a commotion in the king's courtyard?"

Tobias cringed, but Solomon stepped forward boldly. "It's not the king
who is disturbed, but you, my brother. Our father loves festivals and encour-
ages surprises."

"A festival?" Adonijah looked at the women crowded around the strange
covered object. "A surprise? What surprise can there be that I know nothing
of?"

"I'm eighteen today," Solomon said, smiling at Adonijah's obvious discomfort, "and my friends have made something for me. There seems to be
some mystery about it. Come," he ordered the old man with mock sternness,
"let's see your workmanship."

With a nod Tobias motioned for the maidens to remove the covering
and reveal the new palanquin. Solomon was speechless. He bent down and
examined its silver posts and golden canopy. He ran his hand over the warm
cedarwood and traced the etching done on the silver casings. Then he noticed
the seat of fine woven purple, embroidered with his own seal.

The young women and their parents grew silent as Solomon inspected
the finely wrought ebony back and to read the words embroidered on the royal
purple fitted into the center. At first he read them silently, then he smiled and
read them aloud for all to hear: "With love from the maidens of Jerusalem."

He glanced around. His eyes were twinkling and his mouth curved into
the half-smile that all of them found so irresistible. "Thank you, thank you," he
said, as the tambourines again began to shake and the dance became hurried
and insistent.

Suddenly, amidst the joyful noise and general uproar, Yasmit pushed her
way to the front and brazenly looked into the prince's face. "Do you wish for
love?"

"I've never been in love, so I don't really know." Solomon's eyes crinkled
with amusement. He was obviously not moved to return her ardor, though
he was flattered as always by the unsought attention he drew from women
wherever he went.

"I've been in love often and have found it to be the most pleasant of experiences," Adonijah said, looking at Yasmit and giving her a bold challenge with his eyes. For a moment she looked from Solomon to his older brother; then, most deliberately, she turned from Solomon. "Let him have the love of the maidens of Jerusalem," she snapped. "I'm looking for something more warm and personal." The last words were said with a tilt of her head and a sly, suggestive timbre to her voice.

Abruptly the merrymaking stopped as everyone waited to see what would happen next. They weren't disappointed. Yasmit sidled over to Adonijah and let him put his arm around her. Then, pulling back, she glanced at Solomon to see if he had noticed the smug, victorious look Adonijah had flashed in his direction. Satisfied that he had, she turned and elbowed her way through the crowd until she was lost from sight.

There was a stunned, awkward silence and then the festivities started again, but things were somehow spoiled for Solomon. Secretly he cursed his brother's interference. It had taken the edge off the celebration, just as Adonijah had intended it should.

To everyone else, however, the festivities were a wonderful success. For one brief afternoon they were able to forget the empty feed bins, starving cattle, and their own gnawing hunger. For one brief hour they danced and sang, pretending that their lives were free of worry and care and that tomorrow some miracle would rescue them.

Solomon lingered in the courtyard until it was time to change his dusty clothes and meet with his father and friends for evening prayers. He hurried through the arched gateway past the guard station and was about to pass the cramped quarters of the scribes when he was accosted by Adonijah, who stood blocking the way. "My brother," he said, "I've been waiting for you."

Solomon was cautious. He had always dreaded meeting Adonijah alone. When they were children, the older brother would grab Solomon's arm and twist it behind his back, or trip him in the courtyard as he whispered, "Your mother is an adulteress!" Such antagonism never failed to send Solomon into a towering rage.

Adonijah led a reluctant Solomon away from the men at the gate into the shadowed entryway to the throne room. "Don't look so suspicious." he chided. "It's only some business that concerns our father."

"If it concerns our father, what business is it of ours?" asked Solomon. He didn't like the smooth, practiced way that Adonijah was talking.

"Our father is getting old." Now Adonijah's voice was low. He looked around as though making sure their conversation couldn't be overheard. "When a king no longer takes an interest in his harem, he's too old to rule."

"But my mother—" Solomon started to object.

"I don't know about *your* mother, but mine hasn't been called in years."

"The king is busy with his plans for the temple." Solomon turned to leave but was stopped by the harsh grip of Adonijah's right hand.

"There have been no children born in the harem for over a year—and no royal bastards." Adonijah's eyes glinted with malice.

Solomon was always surprised that Adonijah could transform himself, as he was now doing, from a laughing, relaxed prince to a tense, vindictive plotter. No wonder David and even his own mother, Bathsheba, had never suspected a darker side to this prince.

"It's the king's business, not ours," Solomon said as their eyes met and held in silent hostility. To his satisfaction, it was Adonijah who turned away first.

"It may not be our business, but there are people who plan to make it theirs. This is the third year that both the barley and the wheat crops have failed. People are blaming the king."

"It's only the worshipers of Baal who believe a king must be fertile for the rain to fall and the seeds to come to life. What do such beliefs have to do with the king of Israel?" Solomon had often heard such superstitions mentioned among the servants and common laborers, but that was because many of them were Canaanites, Jebusites, or Gibeonites, and they didn't worship the God of Israel.

"You're so simple," Adonijah mocked beneath his breath. "There are many who have lost faith in Israel's God. They're ready to put the king to the test to see if he's really too old to rule."

"And if they find that he is too old?"

"Why, if the king is too old to be attracted to a pretty young girl—everything will be settled logically. The crown will be given to one of his sons."

"And I suppose you plan to be that son?"

"No, no, not so fast. First there must be a test."

"Test?"

"Yes, a harmless test to see if our father is still a real man. We'll urge the king to search out a young maid to warm him in his bed. We must word it all very carefully, of course. He'd have nothing to do with a heathen superstition."

"I don't understand," Solomon said.

"It's very simple: if he can resist the most beautiful young girl in Israel, then the people will decide that he's too old to rule." Seeing that he had succeeded in disturbing Solomon, he smiled with satisfaction. Then, adjusting his robe over his left shoulder and fingering the deep fringe at its edge, he turned and hurried out through the guard room into the courtyard.

Solomon glanced down at his own firm, brown arm and flexed the muscles where Adonijah's fingers had held him. He was almost as tall as his brother, and stronger, so he no longer feared physical harassment. Now it was something else—something harder to get at and more difficult to understand.

Solomon had been aware of the increasing pressure of the people on the king to find the cause of the famine. At first they had thought some major sin had been committed, but this idea had lost favor because in spite of their many sacrifices and long prayers, the famine had continued unabated.

Now it was evident that a growing number were beginning to believe in the old Canaanite superstitions. "The Canaanites were on the land centuries before we came," they reasoned. "It may be that some of their old earth gods really do have some control over the rains."

It sounded so reasonable, so very logical, that nature would follow the example of the king. Or was it the other way around: that the king fell prey to the same blight that fell on the land? Whichever way it was, they speculated, if one problem could be solved, the other would follow automatically.

Solomon knew that no one would dare speak openly to the king of such a pagan superstition. Instead, they would use some ploy to bring a beautiful young girl and test the king's virility. Solomon didn't like it at all. With Adonijah involved, certainly nothing good could come of it.

Solomon pulled back the heavy curtain that separated the throne room from his father's private quarters. He noticed with relief that his father looked quite calm and controlled as he stood before his men, leading them in their evening prayers. The men faced north toward the tabernacle at Gibeon to pray. They had done this ever since King Saul had taken Gibeon and placed the tabernacle of the Lord over the old High Place of the Canaanites.

He watched his father's face with growing concern. It was obvious that the unrest and accusations weighed heavily upon him. Lately Solomon had noticed the king's deepening facial lines, the increasing pain from his old battle wounds, and the way he rubbed his knees "to get the knots out." This bothered the young man.

Solomon moved farther into the shadows. He loved to hear the deep, resonant tones of his father's voice calling upon God. David always prayed as though he were standing directly before the heavenly throne, pleading the cause of his people.

Solomon turned his eyes from the men who stood praying and looked over the familiar room with its immense cedar beams and cold stone floors. It was just three steps up from the throne room, and yet it seemed to be another world.

It had always pleased Solomon to notice how the distinctive smell of pine and incense mingled in these private quarters with the strong odor of spikenard. Now he realized that new odors had been added; he could clearly distinguish the pungent odors of eucalyptus balm and strong medicinal teas, which had been prescribed for the king's health.

Once the room had been cluttered with every sort of musical instrument, various pieces of armor, and captured weapons of unusual make and design. Now that his father's attention was centered on building a temple to the God of Israel, however, the room had acquired a very different look. There were samples of stone from nearby quarries, panels of wood carvings, charcoal sketches on fragments of curling parchment, and swatches of brightly colored woven material packed in chests, stuffed in niches and even spilling out over the commodious bed onto the stone floor.

Solomon had never seen the room empty. There were always groups of people sitting or standing about waiting for the king. Even when David wasn't at home or was tending to business in the throne room, his room was still filled with people. Some were his friends and simply wanted to be a part of the excitement that always surrounded the king. Others came with urgent business too personal to be mentioned before the court at large.

No matter how many people were waiting to see him, David always singled Solomon out with a special twinkle in his eye. His brothers, sons of David's many wives and concubines, were also welcome, but most of them preferred to spend their time with young friends or in their own bulging harems. Only Adonijah, the oldest of David's sons and rightful heir to the throne, spent as much time with his father as Solomon did.

The prayer ended and Solomon slipped out through the curtained doorway without being noticed. Adonijah's earlier words were still bothering him. Just what he intended to do wasn't evident, but Solomon had no doubt that he would soon learn more. To his surprise, however, it wasn't Adonijah who next mentioned the subject to Solomon, but rather the king himself.

✳ ✳ ✳

It was late at night. The visiting tribesmen had left, and only a few of David's retainers still lingered around the glowing coals of the brazier that stood in the center of the room. David was propped up in bed with his harp, trying to remember the words to a new song that had come to him that day. The harp twanged repetitiously as David searched vainly for the lost words.

"My son," he said, putting down the harp and reaching across the cluttered fur throws to greet Solomon with a firm handclasp and conspiratorial wink. "My bed is the only warm spot in all Jerusalem. I'm not sick; I'm just cold." He settled back among the cushions. "I must remember not to complain so of the cold. I can't seem to rant and rage as I used to about the weather without my counselors taking it all too seriously."

"What is it now, Father? What are your counselors wanting you to do?"

"Why, all of them, old and young alike, are insisting on finding a young maid to warm me in my bed." He was obviously amused at what he thought was foolish concern for his welfare, but Solomon, knowing their true intent, stiffened and turned away.

"Do they have some maid in mind?"

"No, they have no one person. They just say that we must find the most beautiful young girl in all of Israel. They're determined about it too. They've brought it up every day for a week."

"Father—" It was obvious that David hadn't been told the real reason behind the counselors' insistence.

"Don't worry, I've tricked them." David smiled as he sorted through several parchments on his bed. "Yes, I've tricked them. Outsmarted them." As he chuckled, the faint battle scar on his cheek creased the brown leather of his face.

"How do you mean, 'tricked them'?" Solomon tried to seem unconcerned as he reached out for the sketch his father handed him.

"I told them that I would accept no one who wasn't picked by your mother, Bathsheba. Now *that* is an example of wisdom, my son. I'm not upsetting the counselors, and I won't be upsetting the harem—at least not your mother." He smiled. "This idea isn't totally foreign to our tradition. Sarah picked the maid who was to be given to your father Abraham. Even with those precautions there was trouble. I'll not put up with such trouble now that I'm beginning to have some peace."

"And my mother?"

"She has agreed, but she wants you to ride with her. She says that you can use the trip to check on your vineyard at Baal-hamon, to see if the drought has killed the vines."

Solomon dropped the parchment and stared in amazement at his father.

"Everything is being arranged," David added, without looking up. "The villages to be visited, the heralds to announce your coming, and the gifts, rings, bangles, and fine linen to be given to the young maid who is chosen. It will leave me in peace and give your mother a pleasant change. I've left it to her own discretion whether she chooses someone or not."

"Father!" Solomon's voice was tinged with alarm. "Aren't you afraid things may not go as you've planned?"

But David was already studying another design and didn't seem to hear him.

With a tender glance, Solomon noticed that his father's gray hair was rumpled, his crown lost somewhere among the parchments on the bed. His shoulders were hidden in the bulky folds of a huge red-fox-fur robe; only his lower arms and hands were visible. Solomon noticed, too, that David's forearms, no longer round and firm, were long and sinewy, and in the dim light the hand holding the parchment looked unusually gnarled.

When the king was standing before the throne, or singing in his strong, clear voice with his eyes flashing, he didn't seem old at all. But here, bending over the parchments, his eyes dim, he suddenly *was* old, and Solomon couldn't endure it. "My father—"

"Yes?" David responded absentmindedly, mulling over the old parchments. "Did you get the palanquin your mother ordered for you?"

"Yes."

"Perhaps you can take it on your trip around the country. Try it out before you ride off to get your own bride."

"I had hoped to be riding a chariot into battle rather than going on such a frivolous mission."

"Be glad, my son, that there is peace. Never complain of peace."

Later, as the king was preparing for bed, he again detained Solomon. "There's something I forgot to tell you. Adonijah begged to go along on this little expedition. I thought it very generous of him."

Solomon again stared at his father in disbelief. That Adonijah should make the suggestion was preposterous, but that both his mother and father should accept his offer as generous was unendurable.

Solomon wanted to shout the truth, confide in his father, expose the treachery of his brother's crafty planning, but he saw that it was useless. His father, motioning for the servants to remove the torches, had no suspicions. It was too late; he should have told him long ago. David would never believe him now. He would only be shocked that Adonijah's own brother should make such accusations.

With a last look at his father, he bowed respectfully and felt his father's hand resting on his head in quiet benediction. The opportunity to speak was gone; he left the room without a word.

2

*W*ithin the week, messengers were sent throughout the land to announce the queen's visit. She would be coming, they said, to find the most beautiful girl in the entire country to warm the king's bed. The announcement temporarily served to take everyone's mind off the prolonged drought and caused a flurry of excitement among the young virgins and their mothers.

There was a great deal of primping and practicing of niceties as the search got under way, much speculation about where this young maiden might be found. However, by the time the queen had visited village after village without choosing a maiden, copious tears were shed, numerous recriminations were issued, and finally a general consensus was reached that the queen didn't intend to find a new bride for the king after all.

Despite all of this, when two months later the king's messengers brought news of the queen's impending visit to the northern village of Shunem, in the heart of the Jezreel Valley, they found Bessim and his sons enthusiastic.

"In a good year we grow the finest grapes, the sweetest dates, and the most desirable girls in all Israel." Bessim, chief elder of the village, boasted as he sat crosslegged on a low divan and leaned across the narrow table that separated him from the king's men.

Bessim had invited them to eat the noon meal with him and his sons, and he intended to take the occasion to glean as much information as possible.

"When can we expect the queen and the young prince?" he asked, pulling off bits of choice meat and placing them on each messenger's flat circle of bread.

"They should be approaching the fortress of Megiddo now, and then it will be just a short ride to Shunem," said one.

Though Bessim plied them with other questions, they were interested only in talking of the drought at home and marveling at the differences in the Jezreel Valley; they were amazed that the drought had barely touched Bessim's fields. When they had finished the hearty meal they rose, declining the formalities Bessim always offered such distinguished guests. "We must meet the royal party tonight back at Megiddo," they said, begging to be excused.

For a moment Bessim stood in the doorway, pronouncing the usual blessing on his departing guests; then he returned to the table, where he motioned for his sons to eat. Out of respect for their guests, they hadn't eaten. Now, without question or discussion, the sons moved quickly to fill the places beside their father. Eating ravenously, they tore apart the fowls and pulled at the roast lamb until, in a very short time, the table was strewn with bones and bits of discarded fat and skin. No one talked until they had all licked their fingers, wiped them on their robes, and then passed the wineskin one more time.

Bessim knew that they were waiting for him to speak. He made a great show of raising his own wineskin and drinking deeply, then wiping his mouth and belching loudly. He leaned back and looked around at his sons. They could see that he was unusually pleased about something.

"A pretty girl, the king wants." Bessim adjusted his belt and smiled, rubbing his fat hands together with pleasure. "That we should be able to give him here in Shunem. Now if he had said he wanted one who is rich or one who is clever or one who is strong, I would have had to say that I'm saving all of these for my own sons. But one who is pretty? Those are the ones who are good for nothing, and we're ready to part with one for His Majesty's sake. Eh? What think you, my sons?"

The young men looked from one to the other, reluctant to voice an opinion. At last Nefer spoke; he was the boldest, and the one to whom Bessim was most inclined to listen. "We would agree, but—well—what say you to giving our sister to the king? She's fair enough and worthless enough."

Bessim frowned, his eyes narrowing to thin slits, and the sons knew he was displeased. "That's impossible. I wouldn't part with her for any amount of money. She's the delight of my heart. How could you even think to suggest such a thing?"

"It would be such an honor," Nefer countered cautiously.

"You're talking foolishness. Why, her breasts aren't even developed." Bessim looked around the room at his sons, daring them by his lowered eyebrows to pursue the matter further.

"If she has no breasts, we'll build on her false turrets of silver," Nefer joked. They all laughed. "You must remember, Father, that she's already beautiful. A beautiful woman can become a door that opens to whoever tries the

19

latch. Isn't it better that we marry her to the king while she's too young to trouble us in this way?"

Bessim moved uneasily and drummed his fingers on the table. He had indeed noticed that Shulamit was unusually beautiful and spirited. To have her safely married would give him a certain peace of mind, but he couldn't endure to part with her. She was like a bright shaft of sunlight in the dark house, and the only child of his favorite wife.

No, he decided, he wouldn't part with her yet. "If she's a door," Bessim said, looking at his sons with a frown, "we'll enclose her with cedar boards."

The sons laughed at their father's solution, and Baalak suggested, "If you don't lock her behind your cedar boards while the queen is here, you'll surely lose her."

"You're right," Bessim answered with all seriousness. "We must move fast. Where can we hide her?"

"Perhaps it isn't *where* but *how*," Urim ventured. "If you were to dress her like a shepherdess and send her out with the sheep?"

Bessim couldn't think with his sons pressing him with ideas, so he waved them off. "Bring Shulamit to me," he shouted. "The whole day is being wasted with idle talk."

Unhappy that they weren't to see the disappointment on their sister's face when she heard that she was to miss the festivities, they filed out of the room content that they had at least won their point. Shulamit wouldn't be attending the celebration for the queen.

All this time Shulamit had been sitting quietly in the small enclosed garden that stretched out in back of the fortress. She came here often to enjoy a few moments to herself. The women of Bessim's house weren't used to leisure; there never seemed time enough in any day to finish the many tasks essential to keeping the great household moving smoothly.

Siva, Bessim's first wife and mother of his seven sons, was in charge. She managed everyone and everything, hardly having time to sit with the other women except on the Sabbath, at religious festivals, and at the feast of the New Moon each month. It was her nature, however, to be busy; she became cross and ill-tempered when she found herself with nothing to do.

Ramat, Bessim's second and favorite wife, the mother of Shulamit, wasn't expected to work with the other women. Bessim had decided that she should be free to pursue her various talents as she pleased. Those talents consisted of her ability to weave delicate patterns on the large family looms and her exceptional understanding of plants and animals. Shulamit often helped her mother, and while that pleased Bessim, it only served to make the brothers jealous.

Now, while the brothers were looking for her, Shulamit sat beside the spring in a patch of warm sunlight, eating her noon meal of bread and smoked cheese and drinking fresh, foamy goat's milk. As she ate, she watched with enjoyment pigeons playing in a small pool of water that had leaked from the irrigation ditch.

She loved this small walled garden. Every season it was different. Now it was early spring, and the almond tree was at the height of its white, fluted loveliness. The garden's lush greenness was a welcome retreat from the cold mustiness of Bessim's fort, the raucous noise of the busy household, or the screaming hawkers and rude, jostling donkeys outside the high wall.

In summer it was almost impossible to see the garden walls, but now, with the vines and trees just beginning to put out their young leaves, the wall was clearly visible. Two sides were made of rough stones held together with mud, but the third and fourth sides were made up of the back side of Bessim's fortress and one of its wings. In the fortress wall there was one window rather high up; the only door opened into a sheepcote beneath the west wing.

The garden contained a well-cared-for collection of rare herbs, trees, and vines that Bessim had acquired over the years from traders coming from Arabia and Egypt on their way to Damascus. Though it was a singularly beautiful garden, Bessim hadn't designed it for beauty. In fact, he had simply ordered its construction so that his choice fruits and vines wouldn't be plundered by the envious villagers. "If a man wants fine fruit, he'll have to care for it and protect it from greedy eyes and hands," he often said.

Bessim knew from experience that not everyone was successful with these precious plants. He was well aware that without the almost uncanny knowledge of Ramat, who carefully nurtured the sprouting seeds and expertly pruned his trees and vines, his garden wouldn't have flourished.

Shulamit loved this time of year. There seemed to be a daily change in the garden itself, while overhead in the patch of blue sky could be seen large flocks of storks and egrets winging their way north. It always thrilled Shulamit when they came down with a great flutter and flap to drink from the irrigation ditches or the spring-fed clay trough.

She could hear faint and faraway sounds coming from the fortress and blending with the shouts, laughter, and muted conversation that drifted in from the far side of the wall. She could hear Siva's shrill voice scolding children, then lecturing servants. Then she thought she heard her own name being called. She sat tense and quiet, listening. There it was again. She didn't intend to answer.

"Come, my pet," she murmured softly. One of the pigeons was about to reach out for the bit of bread she offered when suddenly there was a shout from the fortress window. In a flurry of feathers the bird disappeared.

Startled and angry, Shulamit jumped up. "Now you've done it!" she shouted at her brothers as she stood, hands on hips, glaring angrily up at them. "I almost had a baby pigeon eating out of my hand, and you had to come and spoil it."

"Our father is waiting for you. Haven't you heard us shouting?"

"Of course I heard the shouting, but I'd never have a moment to do anything if I ran every time someone shouted." She tossed her thick, curly hair back with one hand and rolled up her sleeves. "I'm not going anyplace until I've given the pigeons their water." She turned to pick up the water jar but felt it being lifted from her hands. She whirled around to face Urim and Baalak, who grinned tauntingly.

"Abishag, our father wants you," Urim said, laughing as though he knew some secret and was enjoying it very much.

"I'm going," she said, pouting as she paused to search their faces for any hint of the reason for their pleasure. Usually they were angry when Bessim called her or showed her any favoritism. "I'm going," she said again, "and don't call me Abishag."

"Abishag, Abishag, Abishag," they chanted after her. The brothers thought it was a very good joke on Bessim that his favorite wife had given him only a girl. They could never remember who had called her Abishag first, but Abishag, meaning "our father's error," was the name they used most often. Secretly the servants and the townspeople had also picked up the name as a way of taunting Bessim. He had boasted so of his virility in producing sons that they enjoyed this joke that nature had played on him. Of course, no one dared to call his favorite child by this ugly name in his presence. To him she was always Shulamit.

Carefully she rinsed out her milk bowl and set it on a shelf above the spring. Then, wiping her hands on her bright woolen skirt, she ran over to

22

the carob tree and quickly climbed out on the limb nearest the fortress. Grasping the rough stones in the opening, she pulled herself up on the ledge and squeezed through the narrow window into the fetid darkness of the fort. For a moment she stood with her hands clamped over her ears to shut out the voices of her brothers, who were still calling the despised nickname, and then she hurried down the hall.

She paused before the door to the reception room to pull the almond blossoms from her hair, straighten her robe, and adjust her waistband. Bessim was always impatient with her for not being more careful of her clothes. "Young ladies should look neat, smell sweet, and speak softly," he always admonished.

Cautiously she pulled aside the heavy homewoven curtain and stepped into the room where her brothers had been eating such a short time ago. A low wooden table with benches on each side ran the length of the long room. In places there were cushions and armrests, but near the door where she stood the worn, bare bench-boards were visible.

The table was piled with carcasses of two lambs, and several empty wine-skins lay almost covered with curling pieces of bread. By the dim light that shone through the window slits, she could see her father sitting crosslegged at the far end, with eyes closed and hands folded over an enormous stomach in his typical after-dinner attitude of relaxation.

As she stood in the doorway for a moment watching him, she noticed that his great stomach rose and fell evenly and from time to time his head nodded and jerked as he dozed. It was forbidden to wake Bessim once he had fallen asleep and was snoring. Everyone knew that at such times the kind and jovial man could become almost violent.

Shulamit hesitated and then slipped into the room and perched on the end of the table. Softly she began to warble the notes of the nightingale. The delicate tune rose and fell as though the small bird were actually sitting on one of the cedar beams above their heads or was shooting skyward just outside the slits in the far wall.

Bessim smiled in his sleep, rubbed his eyes, and finally, with a leisurely stretch, opened them and looked around. "In my dream I was in a meadow, and I thought I heard . . ." Suddenly he saw Shulamit at the far end of the room, smiling at him. "Shulamit!" he shouted, holding out his arms.

"Abba," she cried, running to him and hugging him joyfully.

"Ah, my little Bulbul, what would your old father ever do without you?" Bessim surveyed the table before him and salvaged a fresh piece of bread on which he placed dainty pieces of meat picked from some of the untouched ribs. He pulled and twisted, selecting the tenderest slivers for Shulamit. All the while he was telling her of the messenger's arrival. "Of course," he admitted, "it would be an honor to be chosen as the most beautiful woman in Israel and to marry the king, but this is too soon for you. Your beauty is still the beauty of a child."

"I'm not a child anymore, Abba," she pleaded. "See? If I turn so, isn't my nose like the ridge on Tirzah? Aren't my eyes like the Egyptian dancers we saw at the festival last spring? And if I take off my mantle, unwind my headpiece, and let my hair fall loose—am I not beautiful, Father?"

Bessim looked at his daughter, her black hair curling about her face and rippling down her back, and was shocked to see that she was indeed more beautifully mature than he had thought. He shook his head and licked his fingers, wiping them on his sleeve while he struggled to regain his composure.

Shulamit knew her father well, and she could tell that he was preparing to say no. Impulsively she jumped up, sending meat and other cluttered remains of the dinner flying as she cleared a space on the table. Grabbing her mantle, she tied it quickly around her hips as she had seen the village dancers do. She struck a pose and then began slowly moving both hands and feet in steady rhythm to the harvest tune she hummed.

"No, no!" he shouted, flinging his arm up over his eyes so that he wouldn't see the small feet beating out the rhythm with such sureness, her hips swaying, her eyes coy and tempting. "It's enough; I've had enough!"

The dance ended abruptly. Shulamit sank to her knees in mock submission and bowed her head to the table, then sat back smiling. "See? I'm thirteen and already a woman ready to be chosen for the king."

Bessim held his head in his hands and fairly shouted, "No, no! I'll not agree. You're too young." He raised his head and spoke more calmly. "Besides, your brothers are right: you have no breasts. You're still a little girl."

Shulamit looked down at her barely rounding breasts and frowned. "But Abba, I've seen you pinching young serving girls who look no more rounded than I am."

"Pinching, maybe, but marrying, never." Seeing the look in her eyes, Bessim quickly changed the subject. "The choosing will take time. I've sent for the mothers to come with their daughters soon after sunrise tomorrow."

"Abba, please?" Shulamit was close to tears.

"And you, my young nightingale," Bessim continued as though he hadn't heard her, "will don some peasant clothes and take the sheep out to the fields. I'll not take a chance on your being chosen."

Shulamit's eyes filled with tears, and her lower lip turned out in a pout. "Abba, you know I love to go with the sheep, but it's cruel to send me out when there will be music and singing and the queen herself visiting us."

Bessim was adamant. He called for Sama, one of the young girls who at times tended the sheep. She was Bessim's daughter by one of the servants.

When Sama came shyly into the room and did obeisance to Bessim, he brushed her aside impatiently. "Here, Sama, go with my daughter and change clothes with her. She's to be a shepherdess for the next few days, and you will be allowed to take her place and sit in the receiving room with the queen." Shulamit turned her back to hide her tears, while Sama stood beaming with pleasure.

Quickly, before Shulamit could show any further disappointment, Bessim rose and went out through the curtain to climb to his own private room in the tower.

3

$\mathcal{T}$he last caravan stop before Shunem was the checkpoint called Megiddo. During the time of Egypt's glory, this outpost had been strong and well-fortified. Since then it had passed through many hands and had fallen into considerable decline. Now, under Israel's control, it was garrisoned by some of David's men. They were stationed here, as others before them had been, to extract revenue from caravans that traveled through this pass on their way to Damascus.

The queen and her entire entourage had spent the night in the captain's crowded quarters. The captain had been gracious and hospitable, but as he wasn't accustomed to playing host to such refined company, the queen was eager to leave as early as possible. Before daylight she was up and seated on a camel, in her howdah, ready to start on the next stage of their journey.

When they were all assembled, it was discovered that Adonijah and one of his friends were missing, along with two mules. One of the gatemen eventually volunteered the information that the young prince had left the night before, saying that he was riding to Beth-shan.

Solomon was annoyed. Beth-shan was a center for the worship of Anat, and Adonijah would undoubtedly have spent the night drinking and sporting with the temple prostitutes. "Adonijah has a way of spoiling everything," Solomon muttered to himself as he signaled the trumpeter on the ramparts of the fortress.

Immediately the officer raised his trumpet and blew the familiar staccato notes of the salute to the princes of Judah. Quickly the banners were unfurled, goodbyes said, and saddles checked for the last time. Solomon tapped his mule lightly and moved to the head of the procession. Then silently, like shadows, the small caravan wound out through the crumbling stonework of the gate and onto the path that would lead them to the village of Shunem, across the valley.

In the predawn darkness there was no sound other than the steady clipping noise of the mule's feet on the hard-packed, stony path. Solomon's companions were now only dark shapes moving in and out of the mist, and his mother's howdah could barely be seen.

Finding the most beautiful girl in Israel hadn't been an entirely pleasant experience for the young prince. Though it had freed him from the confines of the court, it had plunged him into the strange world of hopeful young virgins whose ambitious mothers all wanted their daughters to "warm the king's bed."

"'Warm the king's bed', indeed," Solomon thought with disgust. "Why don't people come right out and say what they mean?"

* * *

Soon after sunrise the caravan arrived in the Jezreel Valley, where the narrow strip of green along the banks of the Kishon almost overwhelmed their drought-parched eyes. Water trickled in irrigation ditches and bright green clumps of oleander and marsh grass sprang up in lush abundance along the river.

In a normal year the river overflowed its banks, flooding the valley and leaving large areas of land that couldn't be cultivated. With the drought, however, the river kept within its narrow banks, and some of the rich marsh-land had been reclaimed. Small green shoots of barley were already visible in marked-off plots along the water's edge.

Impulsively Solomon pulled his mule to one side and dismounted. He walked to the streambed and knelt at its edge. He paid no attention to those gathered around him but seemed totally absorbed in the stones beside the water.

His companions knew better than to bother him, but Bathsheba wasn't so patient. She saw no reason to detain the whole caravan for a passing interest in some common stones.

Parting her curtains, she leaned out of the howdah and tried, in her most insistent tone of voice, to discourage him. "My son," she said, "there's nothing of interest in those old brown stones. Our country is unusually blessed with stones. It's one blessing we could well do without."

"But this is interesting," Solomon said, jumping to his feet and coming over to where her camel was kneeling. "We think of a rock as being very strong," he said, fingering the two rocks he held in his hands. "We build our fortresses of them, and even city walls. If a rock falls on us, it could crush us, and one small stone from my father's sling was able to kill the giant Goliath.

Nathan convinced me that there's nothing stronger than a rock, but now I see that I was right all along: there's something even stronger."

Eagerly he returned to the streambed and worked to pry a large stone loose. "Mother, don't be impatient," he said. "This is very important. I've made a real discovery."

Bathsheba frowned. Even in her impatience to be off, she couldn't help being curious. "What can possibly be stronger than a rock?"

Solomon stood up and held out the large rock he had dislodged. "It's water: water is stronger than rock. We've always thought of water as being weak and powerless—something to wash with and drink. This morning it was a soft mist hanging over the stream, and yet it's stronger than the rocks."

There was a murmur of disbelief, but he continued. "See this rock? It's round and smooth on top where the water has been flowing over it, but the underside, which has been buried in the sand, is irregular and even jagged. It's the water flowing over the rock that has worn off the sharp edges."

No one moved. The very idea of something as ordinary and as gentle as water being stronger than a rock was astounding to them. How did he think of such things, they wondered? Who ever heard of anyone asking such strange questions and getting such unusual answers? Why did he ask them? No one else had bothered. What did it matter, after all, if water was stronger than rock? What could a person do with such a strange bit of information, other than wonder about it?

Solomon threw the stone back into the stream and wiped his hands on his short tunic. Then suddenly he reached down and tugged at a reed growing along the bank. He held it out for them to see the small, hair-like roots with moist earth still clinging to them. "Without water nothing can live—neither plants nor people. Without water everything dies. Yes, water really is the strongest thing in the world."

Bathsheba had observed everything with amazement. "He's like my grandfather Ahithophel," she thought. "I hope he'll also have some of the common sense of his father, or he may fare no better than his great-grandfather."

"Come," she urged all of them, "we must be on our way to Shunem."

Solomon turned to one of the guards. "Bring up the queen's white mule," he said. "We'll ride into Shunem together."

* * *

By the time Solomon and Bathsheba were mounted and ready to ride, the sun was well up over the distant mountains and the fog that hung over the riverbed was beginning to lift, giving the road that wound round to Shunem an almost magical quality.

Morning dew sparkled on the bushes and reeds near the river, and in the air was the pungent, earthy smell of spring. "It's obvious that the people of this valley have suffered very little from the drought," said Solomon. He gave his mother a happy, boyish smile. "See, the path to Shunem is paved in light. Perhaps we'll find the maiden here."

Slowly the village emerged from the dark shadows, bright and sparkling like a crowned bride nestled in a hedge of cactus and ancient olive trees. Behind the village and a short distance to the right rose the dark pine forests of Mount Moreh.

"Moreh," Solomon reminded his mother, "means 'teacher' and rhymes with Torah. They both come from the same root." Bathsheba didn't answer, but she was again surprised that he was so knowledgeable.

The riders paused only once more, and that was at the second crossroad that wound off to the right and up the valley toward Mount Gilboa. This was where Israel had suffered her greatest military defeat, and Solomon had decided that while he was in the region he would go to the site of the battle and try to determine for himself why Saul had lost.

Because this road also led up the valley to Beth-shan, Solomon had half-expected Adonijah to meet them there, but he was nowhere in sight. "He hasn't missed an opportunity to embarrass and annoy me whenever possible. No doubt he'll return at the most inopportune moment." With that he turned his thoughts to the village of Shunem and the new experiences they might encounter.

Solomon had always heard his father and the tribesmen of Judah speak of this whole area as the north. From what they said, he had concluded that in the north the people were more prosperous, less religious, and more likely to follow foreign gods and customs. But no one had ever bothered to tell him how rich the land was in comparison to Judea's stony ridges, or how blue the sky was as it spread over the land like a great inverted bowl. He motioned to his aide. "Who are we visiting in this village?" he asked.

"A man named Bessim. He's said to be very rich and powerful. He has seven sons, and with their aid he controls the whole valley. No caravan can pass Shunem without paying a handsome tribute to him."

* * *

It was noon before the caravan drew up in front of the village gate and paused. Something was wrong; the village was strangely quiet, as though they weren't expecting royal guests. As Solomon surveyed the crumbling wall and closed gate, his mule moved restlessly, kicking up the dust in small puffs.

There was an oddly overgrown look about Shunem. Yet the fortress, which could be seen through one of the breaches in the wall, had a look of permanence and strength that made one believe the stories of Bessim's wealth.

Solomon motioned for his trumpeter, and as the clear, vibrant blast of the trumpet echoed over the moss-covered wall, the whole village seemed to spring to life. Faces appeared on the ramparts of the fortress and at openings in the wall. Within minutes there was an answering trumpet blast from the depths of the fortress and slowly—very slowly—the large, unwieldy gates began to open.

The gateman, a very old man, struggled to place two large stones against each gate to hold them open. Then, seeing the prince and his whole retinue clearly for the first time, he shuffled forward and knelt in the dust.

"Welcome, welcome," he said, rising and squinting at the standards flapping in the breeze. "Don't blame my master. It was my fault—all mine. I wasn't told. I didn't know there would be *two* princes."

"Two princes?" Solomon was puzzled.

"Yes, my lord. A prince much like yourself—with regal bearing, papers, and trumpets, but no standard bearer—arrived some time ago and now sits with the ladies of the house. They wait to hear which one he'll choose to be the consort of our king."

"Adonijah!" Solomon muttered. "As usual he's pushed in ahead, trying to gain some advantage. He wants to make me angry and spoil the whole occasion. But I'll not let him have the satisfaction of knowing how he's angered me."

Within minutes Bessim arrived with profuse apologies. "My lord, Prince Adonijah neglected to mention that you were coming. I regret that we've already dispensed with the welcome, the young maidens dancing and the blessing of the sheep for our festive meal."

"Where is it that you would have us go?" Solomon asked as he waited for his mother to dismount.

"I'm sorry, but the prince is already viewing the maidens."

"Never mind the prince," Solomon said, looking over the courtyard with apparent calm. "My mother is the one who is to choose the maiden." He clenched and unclenched a strong, well-formed hand around his riding prod.

"Unload the baggage," Bessim called to his servants rather nervously as he led the way to the stairs.

"Don't be disappointed if no one is chosen from Shunem," Solomon warned as he followed Bessim up the stairs. "We've visited all of the villages on the ridge, and my mother found no one she could accept." He glanced at his mother with tender amusement and then turned and mounted the last three steps into a large workroom, made bright and cheerful by light coming through an aperture in the ceiling. Solomon noted that the room was filled with women working at various tasks in preparation for a feast.

Bessim stopped to catch his breath and reached out to place a restraining hand on Solomon's arm. "I'm sure that it's difficult for your mother with so many beautiful women to choose from."

Solomon pulled away without answering, and Bessim again grasped his arm to get his attention. "Here in Shunem we have the most beautiful maidens in all Israel!" He leaned forward and spoke in a low, confidential tone. "The women of Shunem are round and well-shaped, with no ugly hair on their bodies." Bessim's eyes had grown large and watery, and he sucked in his breath in a manner that annoyed Solomon.

Bessim winked and laughed raucously as he added, "One of our women could bear your father many sons."

He spoke so loudly that Solomon looked at his mother to note her reaction. He thought he detected a slight reddening of her cheeks and a quick intake of breath that gave away her true feelings.

Impatiently he turned back to Bessim and spoke so that the women couldn't hear him. "It isn't necessary that she be strong enough to bear sons for my father. My father is old and complains of the cold. It's for this that his physicians have suggested we find a young maiden."

Bessim stuck his hand in his wide sash with his thumbs out and nodded. "I know. I know," he said. "That's what they *say,* but we all know what's *hoped.*"

Solomon could see the dangerous red spot glowing on his mother's cheek and knew that she despised the gossip that surrounded his father. "It's only the worshipers of Baal," he said, "who believe a king must be about the business of producing children or else the crops will fail and the rains cease."

Bessim nodded and looked from Solomon to Bathsheba. "Well," he said, "one wife choosing another has been done before." With a shrug he led the way to a far door and knocked with the confident air of authority.

The sound of laughter and music ceased. The door opened and Bessim pushed forward. "Prince Solomon and his most revered mother have honored us with their presence," he announced to the roomful of young girls and their mothers.

Solomon saw Adonijah, looking smug and triumphant on a dais at the far end of the room. It was obvious that he was well pleased with his little prank.

Slowly Adonijah rose as they approached him. "I shouldn't have left you in the care of my brother," he said, bowing low over Bathsheba's hand. "I've been in an agony of worry over your whereabouts." As he straightened up, his eyes met Solomon's with a challenge.

Obviously flattered, Bathsheba kissed him fondly on both cheeks and let him lead her to the seat of honor, while Solomon bit his lip to keep from making a caustic remark.

The women of Shunem, meanwhile, were looking at Solomon. Their greedy, lustful eyes seemed to take in every detail of his dress and demeanor; his closely cropped curls, aristocratic nose, and warm hazel eyes were all observed and admired.

He wasn't embarrassed. He stood and observed them with ease, his feet planted wide apart and arms relaxed holding his tooled-leather riding prod lightly. Then, with charming nonchalance, he joined his mother and Adonijah.

With the royal visitors assembled on the dais, the women began again to clap enthusiastically. The drummers beat with new vigor and the Canaanite singers from Beth-shan broke into a high, lilting chant.

Glancing around, Solomon noticed that the room was long and narrow, its width determined by the length of the cedar beams that made up the ceiling. The thick walls were pierced by narrow openings that let in both air and light. It was a fortress that could withstand attack as long as its food and water held out.

The room was now so crowded with women that one couldn't see the carpets or mats on the floor. The prospective brides seemed to be constantly arranging their mantles, fingering their necklaces, or adjusting their earrings. Their chalklike, powdered faces, with dark-circled eyes, were much like those Solomon had seen in the other villages, and he was soon bored with the whole artificial display.

"How ironic," he thought. "At my age my father would have been either defending or attacking such a fortress as this. He would have been shooting arrows from those windows and calling commands from the battlements, while I, his son, sit here idly waiting to choose one of these women as a bride for my father."

He looked around at all the eager young faces so willing to please and realized how tired he was of the whole procedure. He didn't care who his mother chose, just so the selection was over as quickly as possible.

He stood up. Behind the dais there was a curtained door. Perhaps he could excuse himself and wander around a bit. "My mother," he whispered, "I've seen enough dancing and drumming. I'll be back shortly."

Before Bathsheba could voice her disapproval, he had disappeared through the curtained door.

* * *

On the other side of the curtain he was surprised to find himself facing two young boys. By their clothing he guessed them to be Bessim's younger sons. He held out his hand, but they turned and fled, tripping over their own feet and bumping into each other as they hurried out the opposite door and down the steps to the lower court.

Solomon looked around with interest. It was obviously a guardroom, and perhaps a sleeping room for some of Bessim's sons. There were clothes, rumpled and dirty, flung out across the floor in a tangle, along with old bones and dried bread from some recent meal.

To one side was a long narrow window. Solomon stooped down and, shading his eyes from the bright sunlight, looked out. The view was breathtaking. Before him spread the Valley of Jezreel, and beyond that rose Mount Gilboa.

"The Philistines," he reasoned, "would have been camped here in Shunem, and over there, across the valley on that spur of the mountain, must be where Saul made his last stand and was defeated."

For a few minutes he stood studying the terrain, and then he straightened up impatiently. He was determined to get out in the fresh air and go exploring. Without concern for the consequences, he reached down and searched among the clothes scattered about until he found a short tunic and some scuffed sandals. His princely robes would have to be exchanged for simpler garb if he was to leave the fortress undetected.

Deftly he stuffed his embroidered robe, jewel-encrusted shoes, and circlet crown into one of the wall's many niches. In a minute he had the borrowed tunic secured with a worn girdle and toggle-pin and was ready to make his escape.

In seconds he was out the door and feeling his way down the dark steps to the lower floor. He came out into a room very much like the one he had left. Here again the only light came through a narrow slit in the wall. Gently, so as not to be heard, he pulled aside the curtaining vines.

To his surprise, he was looking directly down into a walled garden. It was obvious that the drought hadn't touched this green, walled paradise—and never would, as long as the spring of living water continued to flow.

For a moment he enjoyed the subtle fragrance of early mint and thyme. Although there was very little breeze and no clouds, it was a chilly day; only the sun's warmth penetrating his rough tunic gave any hint that spring had actually arrived.

The light was bright, but his eyes dimly perceived a stir and flutter of flashing white wings. He could hear the soft bleating of a young lamb, and over all rose the insistent cooing of some doves.

Carefully he pushed the vines farther aside and leaned way out. He had to check himself to keep from whistling in surprise. There, beside an old, moss-covered trough filled with water, was a young girl. Her hair was uncovered so that it fell about her face and shoulders like a rich mantle that stirred provocatively with the breeze.

As he watched, one of the pigeons lighted on her shoulder while a smaller one swooped down and perched on her fingers to get at the seeds she held. When he had eaten, she raised him so that she could lightly kiss his sleek, white head and then sent him winging to the roof. "She's beautiful," he thought, *"more beautiful than any of the young girls I've seen in the places we've visited."*

He wondered briefly why she wasn't in the room with the other beauties of Shunem. He shaded his eyes against the sun so he could see her more clearly. He smiled, noticing for the first time her roughly woven dress, its long sleeves tied at the back so that her brown arms were exposed and free. "Ah, she's a shepherdess."

He felt a subtle surge of excitement that was new to him. His old daydream of dressing as a shepherd and going out into the fields to live simply, as his father had done, suddenly returned with a vigor that surprised him.

A flight of pigeons winging their way to the roof passed close to the window, and Solomon glanced down quickly to see if he had been observed.

Still undetected, he sighed with relief. "It would be an interesting adventure to surprise her by dropping down into the garden," he thought. The idea pleased him; without another thought he squeezed himself into the opening, balanced himself carefully, and then jumped. For a moment he seemed to be suspended in space and then, missing the path by an arm's length, he tumbled into a tangled mass of thorns on a climbing rosebush.

Through a blur of pain Solomon saw the girl jump to her feet, her hair blowing about her face in a dark cloud and the pigeons circling about her for a moment before they flew up and over the garden wall. In spite of the sharp pain in his arm, Solomon noticed that it was a picture of loveliness he would not soon forget.

"Who are you?" the girl asked with wide, startled eyes.

Solomon jumped to his feet, rubbing one hand vigorously against his thigh to deaden the hurt of the thorns. "I'm—" He hesitated as he glanced down at his clumsy shoes and worn tunic. "I'm with the royal party and I'm sorry to be intruding in this way."

4

*S*hulamit laughed. She wouldn't normally have laughed, but the sight of a rather dignified young man untangling himself from a thorn bush was just too funny.

In spite of the ordinary clothes, it was obvious that he wasn't rough and crude like her brothers. His hair was expertly trimmed; his arms and legs were brown and well formed; the hand he was rubbing on his tunic to dull the hurt was firm and muscular, without the usual broken, grime-caked nails and callouses; and he was cleaner than any young man she had ever seen.

"It's not as bad as I thought," he said as he examined the long, ugly scratch on his hand.

"Oh, I'm sorry. I didn't see that you were hurt." She reached out for his hand and gently touched the bruised area around the scratch with her finger. He didn't draw back.

"It must hurt a lot," she said.

"It's all right, really nothing at all," he said, pulling back his hand to examine it again. "But you have bigger thorns on your bushes here in Shunem." He looked directly at her and smiled the sort of smile that had won him the reputation of being David's most charming son. She found herself looking into the most penetrating hazel eyes she had ever seen.

His look was oddly disturbing. "If one of my brothers had tumbled into the thorns like that, he would have really cursed," she said. "A scratch from a thorn can hurt as much as a knife wound."

"You're a strange girl. First you laugh and embarrass me terribly, and then you treat a little scratch as seriously as though it were a battle wound." His eyes were warm with approval. "I've had some blows and real wounds. No one but my mother has ever taken much note of them." He smiled again, a slow, winning smile that seemed to be for her alone. This time she enjoyed his obvious admiration.

"By the looks of you, I'd say you've had things a bit easy." She broke the magic spell with her saucy words. "Come, I'll take you to my mother. She has a cure for everything." She turned and started toward the far side of the garden, but Solomon didn't follow her.

"Come on!" she coaxed. "It was our thorn bush, so I feel responsible for you." She pushed aside the thick growth of new jasmine leaves and tugged at a latch that was hidden in the vines. There was a hollow, scraping sound as the door swung back on leather hinges.

Without further objection, Solomon followed Shulamit into the dark enclosure. She could tell by the way he stopped and caught his breath that he wasn't at home in stables or sheepcotes. "This is where my sheep stay at night," she said, reaching around him to push back two old ewes who were trying to squeeze past him.

"Stand right there." She pushed the door closed, enveloping them in a blackness that was rich with the characteristic odors of dung, moldering stone, and damp wool. Slowly she became aware of the heady odors of spikenard and musk surrounding the young man and briefly wondered how the servant of a prince could be so lavish with such costly ointments.

"The steps are to the right." she said, feeling her way along the rough stone wall. "You have to wait a moment before you can see. My mother's rooms are in the west wing, just above this sheepcote."

There was another scraping, grinding sound as she pushed open the heavy door at the top of the stairs. The pleasant fragrance of baking bread greeted them. "Mother?" Shulamit called, "I've brought you one of the guests."

All they heard in response was the sound of someone half-humming a simple harvest ditty. Shulamit drew aside the curtain covering the doorway to reveal a woman squatting beside a clay dome on which she was baking flat, rounded loaves of peasant bread.

"Mother," she said again, "one of the young men who came with the prince fell into our rosebush and hurt his hand."

Ramat turned and looked at Solomon. She rose slowly, dusted the flour from her full, loose-hanging robe, and then with both hands brushed back a dark cloud of hair that fell to her ankles. She handed the forked stick with which she had been turning the bread to Shulamit and reached for Solomon's hand.

Shulamit could see that the young man was fascinated by Ramat and by the strangeness of Bessim's fortress. He seemed surprised that part of the wall on the north side was gone, leaving the room open to the sky. She saw his eyes follow the curving smoke as it wound up and out the opening at the top of the stairs that led to the roof.

"He can't be very important and wear those ill-fitting clothes," she thought, watching him talk to her mother. But remembering the heady odor of spikenard and musk, she reconsidered. "Maybe he's a special friend of the prince." Certainly his manners and bearing told a different story than did his clothes.

"Shulamit!" her mother called. "You've let the bread burn." Shulamit hurried to remove the offending dough and then waved dried grasses and branches to drive out the black smoke.

When the treatment—a poultice of aloes wrapped in preserved grape leaves—was finished, Ramat turned to Shulamit. "The young man wants to see where the battle of Gilboa was fought," she said. "Take him to the roof, where he'll have a full view of both Mount Gilboa and Mount Moreh. I'll bring you some fresh bread and goat's milk in a moment."

Solomon thanked her profusely and then followed Shulamit up the winding stone stairs to the roof.

This part of Bessim's house wasn't as tall as the rest of the fortress, but it was taller than the other houses around it; thus it was possible to stand on the roof and look out beyond the village, across the Valley of Jezreel, to the slopes of Gilboa.

Shulamit was surprised that Solomon's entire attention was immediately focused on the distant Gilboa. As she came closer, she could hear him quoting the lines of the lament written by King David for his friend Jonathan. "Ye mountains of Gilboa, let there be no dew nor rain upon you, neither fields of offerings."

When he paused, Shulamit picked up the words almost without thinking: "For the shield of the mighty was violently cast away, the shield of Saul not anointed with oil."

Solomon turned, his eyes shining with admiration. "It's strange to hear a girl quote lines that are usually sung by men of battle. How— ?"

"I have many brothers and I've heard them sung and quoted often."

"While I'm here I want to ride over to Gilboa and see if I can discover for sure why Saul lost the battle. If El Shaddai, the God of Hosts, was fighting for Israel, how could they have lost?"

"My father says it was because Samuel had died and could no longer advise Saul."

"I'm not sure that's why he lost. There must be other reasons."

Shulamit realized that he wasn't talking to her. His whole attention was drawn to the distant mountain. He didn't even bother to shield his eyes or to gather in his rough cloak as it snapped in the breeze.

She noticed how his eyes narrowed as he looked from one side of the valley to the other, estimating both the distance and the terrain. "I have a mind to go to Endor also. I'd like to see just how far Saul had to walk to consult the witch."

"That's a long way. Just from here to the Mountain of Blood it's five miles."

"The Mountain of Blood? Is that what you call Gilboa?"

"That's what the shepherds call it, and they're reluctant to graze their sheep on its slopes."

"From Gilboa to Endor . . . ?"

"That's even longer. There are many paths through the forest, but you'll need a guide."

"You seem to know the way." His words were clipped, with an air of command about them that surprised Shulamit.

"Aie," she answered, slipping into the dialect of the local shepherds. "I know it well."

"Your mother, would she let you go with me?"

Shulamit laughed. "Having met you, she would surely think such a venture was dangerous. And my father is very strict."

"You would be like a sister to me. I swear it. Now tell me, where do you feed your sheep? Where do they usually graze?"

In spite of the calm, almost uninterested way Shulamit had answered his questions, she could sense a disturbing turmoil going on in both her head and her heart. Used to the roughness of her brothers and the coarseness of her father, she was unprepared for the warm, tender feelings that this young man aroused in her. "Every day it's a different place." She tried to steady her voice so that he wouldn't notice her confusion.

"Where do you stop at midday to rest the flock? How can I find you?"

"I don't know," she said, thinking again of her father's disapproval and her brothers' anger if they should hear of her meeting a young man out in the fields.

"Surely it's better for you to tell me yourself than for me to wander like a vagabond among the flocks of the other shepherds looking for you," he urged.

She blushed at his insistence. It would be impossible for him to leave with her in the morning, but what would be the harm of his meeting her at their noon resting place—just by chance? "It's really quite simple; follow the trail of our flocks to the shepherds' tents beside Harod's Pool. We go there to rest in the heat of the day."

Suddenly the smell of warm bread filled the air and Ramat's quick footsteps could be heard mounting the steps to the roof.

"Come, sit over here in the shade and have a bite," her mother invited. "It'll be a long time before the evening festivities begin, and you may get hungry." Solomon sat down on the cushions under the laced branches of the grapevine.

Shulamit noticed that when Ramat handed Solomon the gourd of warm goat's milk, he hesitated briefly. It was almost as though he had been going to ask her to taste it first, as a prince would do. After accepting the food, however, he ate and drank with real relish.

Later, when Solomon was ready to leave, he stood for a moment beside the lower door to the sheepcote and looked down at her with the same intensity that she had seen before. "Remember, tomorrow follow the trail of your sheep. It shouldn't be too difficult." She nodded her assent and watched his eyes brighten with anticipation.

Without another word he climbed the tree and disappeared through the narrow window back into the main fortress.

✳ ✳ ✳

Solomon found his way to the upper chamber and changed back into his own clothes unnoticed. Bathsheba, though irritated by his long absence, was glad to see him back. The day had been exhausting, and she was tired. She excused herself from the evening's festivities and impulsively asked Solomon to join her, leaving Adonijah with Bessim to represent the royal family.

The guest quarters were small and cramped, but his mother had transformed them with colorful mats, cushions, and wall hangings, giving them a semblance of home. The magic was completed by incense burners, which gave off a delicate fragrance.

Solomon waited for his mother to reprimand him, but as they settled down among the cushions and prepared to eat, he saw with relief that she was genuinely tired and didn't intend to question him.

Absentmindedly, she tore off a piece of roast quail, dipped it into the clabbered cream, and nibbled at it. When more food was urged upon her, she waved the servants away. "I'm too tired even to eat," she sighed. "I think I shall faint if I have to spend one more day looking at all these silly, eager women."

Solomon felt sorry for her. "If you don't want to pick someone, you don't have to," he said gently.

"I know those counselors of David's. They're determined to have their way. If I don't pick someone, they will."

"Well, *let* them pick her then. That may be better than wearing yourself out like this."

She folded one end of her sash and creased it into a pleat with a strong downward stroke. "I've made up my mind. I don't intend to look any further. I'm going to pick someone here in Shunem."

"Did you see anyone today?" Solomon was suddenly interested.

"No, but I've thought of a test—a very simple test that will lead me to the right girl."

"A test?"

"Yes, I'm going to suggest that our host prepare a feast on the day after tomorrow to celebrate the New Moon, and I'll choose her then." She stood to her feet and lovingly rumpled Solomon's hair. "I'll need a day of rest tomorrow, so you may not see me before evening." Without further comment she turned and followed her maid up the drafty steps to the east tower.

Solomon idly surveyed the array of food spread out before him. Cheese, dates, and a skin of Bessim's wine would make a fine feast for the next day. He placed his selection in a tote bag and then impulsively added extra, thinking that his little shepherdess might be eating with him.

He chuckled, remembering her. When he fantasized about being a humble shepherd, there was always a beautiful young shepherdess who loved him passionately.

Because most of his life had been spent in Jerusalem, only occasionally had he ridden out to his father's lands for sheep-shearing or a new-moon festival. However, as one of the princes of Israel, he had little chance of ever meeting a shepherdess.

Briefly his thoughts turned to Adonijah. He knew that if his annoying brother had even the slightest suspicion that the loveliest maiden in all of Shunem wasn't preening and grimacing in that stuffy reception room, he would be mad with jealousy. The very thought of Adonijah sobered Solomon. Adonijah had such an uncanny ability to sort out everything and to appear just in time to spoil things. He decided that he would have to be careful not to arouse Adonijah's curiosity.

✳ ✳ ✳

While Solomon and Bathsheba were sharing their evening meal in the guest chambers, Adonijah was engaged in a boring conversation with Bessim. There seemed little hope of escape until a servant appeared. "There's a messenger at the gate asking for Adonijah," he said. "He's ridden from Jerusalem in great haste and insists he must see him in secret." The servant bowed hastily and was gone.

"You can see him on the roof," Bessim said as he rose and directed him to the stairs. "That's the only place in this house where a man can be alone."

The messenger bowed low before Adonijah as he entered the room. "I have news from your friend Eon," he said.

"Good news?" Adonijah asked.

"Eon said to tell you that the king has determined the cause of the famine."

"I don't understand."

"Israel has suffered from famine because of the sin committed by Saul against the Gibeonites."

"And who came up with that idea?" Adonijah scoffed.

"My lord, it was the king himself."

"The *king*?"

"Yes, my lord, the king."

For a long moment Adonijah said nothing, then he turned to the messenger and asked, "And what does my friend Eon suggest that I do?"

"Come back to Jerusalem as soon as possible."

Adonijah sat down and restlessly drummed his long fingers on the armrest while he thought of all the various angles. "Yes, yes. There's nothing else to do," he conceded.

Later that night, when Adonijah went back to sit with Bessim, he mentioned quite casually that he would be leaving the next day. "I've been called back to Jerusalem on important matters," he said. "However," he added, "I'll be back to celebrate the Feast of the New Moon."

* * *

Solomon had worried that Adonijah would awaken the next morning and insist on going with him. As it turned out, Adonijah had accepted Bessim's hospitable offer of one of the young Canaanite dancing girls for the night and hadn't even returned to their room. Those of Solomon's men who had spent the night stretched out on the hard, straw-stuffed mats around the room were all so tired that they didn't notice when Solomon rose quietly to leave.

Again Solomon wadded his own clothes into one of the niches in the wall, donned the simple tunic and crude sandals he had "borrowed" the day before, and slipped down the stairs and out to the stable.

Although many of the stable hands were already working, no one seemed to notice as he rode past on one of the gray mules; he looked more like one of the servants than a prince.

Outside the gate he was puzzled. There were no sheep tracks on any of the roads leading from the gate. He looked up and down the valley but could see no sign of the shepherds or their sheep. He was just beginning to think that they hadn't come through this gate at all when he caught sight of a narrow path winding in and out around the plots of ripening barley. Here at last he saw a narrow, hoof-pocked trail, still fresh enough to have been made that morning by the sheep.

He urged his mule along at a fast clip and just managed to come to the Pool of Harod before any of the shepherds arrived at their tents for the noon rest.

It was a quiet pool, with rushes and oleander bushes growing in dark green clusters at its edge. Further back, tall palm trees made a shaded bower. The barley that grew in small irrigated plots was obviously unaffected by the drought. No one in this region could be starving. Bessim had actually laughed when he heard that there was no wheat for bread in Jerusalem. "Buy from the Egyptians," he said. "Their gods are kind to them. They never lack food."

Quickly Solomon tethered his mule and threw himself down beside the pool. He glanced around, breathing deeply of the fresh air and reveling in the greenness of the place. He knew very little about plants, but he recognized some of them as ones he had seen long ago in Lodebar with his mother.

Suddenly he noticed a splash of white. Something was already in bloom. He jumped up and climbed over the rocks to see better. It was a lone almond tree growing right out of a fissure in one of the rocks beside the spring that fed the pool. It was the only touch of white in the otherwise total greenness of this little paradise. He gently touched the ruffled flowers and marveled at the way they grew out of the seemingly dead, leafless branches.

He was so absorbed that he didn't hear either the mule's approach or the crunch of footsteps behind him until a voice broke into his reverie. "So, my secretive brother. What brings you here?"

Solomon whirled around to face a smugly triumphant Adonijah.

"It's more in order to ask how you knew I was here." Solomon's eyes flashed with anger, but his voice was calm and controlled.

"That's easy. I watched you ride out, and since I was planning to come in this direction myself, I decided to follow you. I'm sure you haven't come all this way to contemplate the almond tree and its mystery."

"The mystery of the almond tree is something we could all do well to contemplate."

"How ridiculous. There's no mystery, except to dreamers and poets."

Solomon broke off a small branch from the tree. "You remember our father telling us the story of Aaron's rod?" he asked. "It was an almond rod that he placed before God's Holy Ark in the tabernacle, along with the rods of all the others who thought they had just as much right as Aaron to be God's priest. You remember the outcome? The next morning only Aaron's rod was changed at all. His had budded and even had almonds on it."

"And what do you make of that?"

"Well, it would seem that it is God who makes the final decisions as to who is going to lead his people." Solomon looked directly at Adonijah, fearlessly and resolutely challenging him.

With a sudden, quick movement, Adonijah grabbed the offending almond branch and ground it into the grass under his heel. "Don't get any fancy ideas about yourself from that little story. In the first place, I wonder how many people actually saw the almond branch with buds on it. Who were the judges?"

"All of Israel saw it. If they hadn't seen it for themselves, would they have been so willing to let Aaron lead them? God does things like that, Adonijah, whether you happen to like it or not."

"I can see that you're quite taken with the little story. Well, don't expect anything special like that for yourself. Neither God nor the people of Israel will choose the son of Bathsheba to be their king."

Adonijah had touched a raw nerve, and Solomon's reaction was instantaneous. His eyes flashed as he seized Adonijah's arm in a viselike grip. "I've waited for this moment when we would be alone and I could even some old scores."

Adonijah winced and tried to pull away. "What old scores? I don't know what you're talking about?"

"You're surprised. You hadn't realized that I've grown so strong. I've been spending time with Benaiah and some of his house guards."

Adonijah struggled to pull away again. "Don't make an issue of a little teasing. I hear some of the shepherds coming, and they mustn't see the sons of David at odds with each other." He paused and for the first time seemed to notice that Solomon wasn't dressed in his princely robes. "They wouldn't even recognize you dressed in that ridiculous outfit."

Solomon's grip loosened, but his eyes still held Adonijah's with a steady glare. "For today I've chosen not to be a prince. It will go hard with you if you give away my secret, so see that you don't."

5

*S*olomon released Adonijah from his grip as the first of the shepherds came in sight. They had been out on the hillsides since dawn; now they came to water their sheep and rest during the heat of the day.

Solomon turned to Adonijah. "There's no need for you to stay. You have important business."

"This gets more interesting," Adonijah said, touching the hilt of his short sword and smirking. "I intend to stay until I see just what you're doing here and why you're dressed in those odd clothes."

Solomon had no time to reply. At that moment Shulamit and some of her maidens could be seen making their way through the cyprus trees toward the pool, leading their flock of sheep.

Shulamit glanced in surprised recognition at Solomon; then her eyes fastened on Adonijah with wonder and respect. She knelt in the grass and kissed his outstretched hand, then backed off while the others came forward to repeat the gesture.

Solomon noted with disgust that because Adonijah was dressed as a prince, the maidens were totally in awe of him. He looked down at his own nondescript clothes and realized that they had assumed he was one of the servants waiting on the prince. For a moment he was angry; however, because the illusion served his purpose, he decided to go along with it.

Bowing in an exaggerated manner before Adonijah, he motioned toward Shulamit. "My lord," he said, "this is a young shepherdess and her friends from Shunem. I'm sure they would be greatly honored by a word from a real prince." He could hardly resist a tinge of sarcasm in his voice.

One after the other the girls bowed again and then backed away with such a look of awe that Solomon began to be genuinely annoyed. It frustrated him further when Adonijah singled out Shulamit and proceeded to speak privately with her. Worse, she seemed to be completely entranced.

"My lord," he said, taking Adonijah firmly by the arm, "this young maiden is going to show me the way to Gilboa. We mustn't detain you any longer."

"Oh, well," Adonijah said, "I have to get back to the main road to meet my friends. I've been called to Jerusalem for an emergency." When he saw Solomon's look of relief, he immediately reconsidered. "Perhaps I could stay a *while* longer. Here, boy," he said, motioning to Solomon, "hold my mule until I'm ready to go."

Solomon had rarely managed a mule all by himself. He took the leather bridle reluctantly and gripped it with such force that the veins in his hands stood out like blue knots.

As usual, Adonijah had interrupted what could have been a very pleasant time. Solomon doubted that there was any emergency in Jerusalem. He thoroughly expected Adonijah to be with them the rest of the day.

In the meantime Shulamit had spread out a mat of woven reeds in the shade of an oleander bush and was already arranging a comfortable seat for the prince. It was obvious as Adonijah sat down that he was enjoying himself. Every now and then, sampling slivers of goat cheese or encouraging Shulamit with his flattering remarks, he would shoot Solomon a sly glance.

"Naive woman," Solomon thought. "Why can't she see that he doesn't mean a word he's saying?" Solomon wanted to dismiss Shulamit as a little fool, a simple country girl with none of the allure of the more sophisticated women he was used to, but, to his dismay, he found this impossible. Instead, she seemed to become more and more attractive to him.

Casually she led one of the goats out from the larger flock and, perching herself easily on a protruding rock, proceeded to fill a brown clay pot with milk from its udder. Then she began making a fire in some dry straw and nettles. She was so preoccupied that she didn't see the mocking glances Adonijah flashed Solomon from time to time.

He noticed how her hair hung free and rippled in the breeze. He tried vainly to be critical; he told himself that her hair had obviously never been washed in henna, nor had her feet been bathed in milk. "How very primitive of these northern women to go about without covering their hair," he thought.

Usually Adonijah noticed only women of experience and sophistication, but here he was, sitting on the grass and watching Shulamit with obvious delight. Of course, Adonijah had feigned interest in this same way many times before, but it had never made Solomon angry. This was something new he was experiencing—something quite unusual.

"It's getting late," Adonijah said finally, standing up to brush himself off. "The business in Jerusalem is urgent. I must be on my way." As he took Shulamit's small hand and raised it to his lips, his eyes rested on Solomon.

With a smug smile Adonijah took the reins from Solomon, mounted his mule without a word, and rode off through the oleanders out to the road that led to Tannin and on down the mountain range to Jerusalem.

"Isn't he wonderful?" Shulamit exclaimed. "I can't believe I've actually talked with a prince!" She looked after him with undisguised admiration.

"He's nothing but a pompous bore," Solomon exploded. He strode impatiently over to Shulamit and sat on the grass where Adonijah had been just a few moments before.

Shulamit was amazed. "How can you talk about the prince that way?"

"Just because he kissed your hand and wagged a tongue dripping with honey, doesn't mean he's—"

"He did kiss my hand." She no longer had a sharp edge to her voice as she held out her hand and looked at it with displeasure. Some of her nails were broken, and the skin was red and slightly chapped. "I can't imagine why he kissed my hand, when it's so ugly. These broken nails and . . ."

She pulled up her sleeve and looked critically at her deeply tanned skin. "I'm glad he didn't see my arms. I wouldn't *ever let* him see them."

Solomon noticed that they were as tanned as those of the shepherds and vinedressers. Usually this would have disgusted him, but to his own surprise he said, "But your hands are well shaped—not big and ugly, like some I've seen."

She flashed him a questioning look to see if he were sincere and then glanced back at her hands and arms. "But see how brown I am? It's from being out in the sun too much, working in the vineyard and herding sheep."

She pulled her sleeve back down and stirred up the fire to heat some broth. For several minutes both were silent.

"Can you keep a secret?" she asked eventually, gazing up at him with a penetrating look.

"Of course."

"Well, I'll tell you something I would never think of telling anyone else. But if you tell—" The scathing look she sent him convinced him that she had the capacity to be quite angry if really aroused. "If I hadn't been so brown and scruffy from working outside, I would have insisted on being in there with the rest of those silly women. But I look so awful." She tossed her head with a proud, defiant movement that Solomon found most endearing.

With a shrug she turned and bent over a pot of steaming broth, and for once Solomon was at a loss for words. He realized that for all her jaunty air, she was hurt by not being allowed to sit in the room with the other women and be given the chance to win. "To win," he thought with a shudder, "would mean to lose her."

She raised the ladle to her lips and tasted. "It needs more mint," she said, jumping up and dusting off her skirt.

"Where will you get mint out here?"

Shulamit laughed. "Mint grows everywhere."

"You don't have to grow it in a garden?"

"See? It grows wild here in the rocks by the pool." She bent down and pinched off the tops of several deep-green plants and threw them in the pot.

Within minutes she declared the soup ready and began ladling it into gourds. Solomon remembered his cheese, dates, and wineskin just in time to bring them out and add them to the circles of bread that Shulamit had placed on a woven reed mat at the edge of the pool.

After the first taste Solomon decided that he had never been served anything so delicious, nor had he ever eaten in such a relaxed and jolly atmosphere.

He noticed with interest that one of the shepherds had led several of his sheep down into the pool to wash their mud-caked feet and undersides, while another one was checking a very young lamb for thistles and burrs. Solomon laughed as the shepherd pushed two of the sheep up out of the water. "How beautiful they are," he said impulsively, and then improvised. "The water is so blue and the grass so green that the sheep look like white clouds rising out of the water."

"Do you make up poems very often?" Shulamit asked him in obvious delight.

"Sometimes. Do you?"

"What you just said would make a very nice song. Listen!" she said. She quickly put a merry country tune to the words, and Solomon had to admit it did sound rather nice.

She looked up at the sun and realized that it was getting late. "We'll have to hurry if we're to make it up the mountain and back before it's time to start home. I'll tell my maidens to do their best to keep the sheep from loitering."

"We're going with all these *sheep?*" Solomon asked.

"Of course," Shulamit said, looking at the animals with pride. "They're quite well behaved, even though they're miserably stupid."

"I really don't know much about sheep," Solomon said. "But my father used to be a shepherd, and he talks about it sometimes." Solomon had to walk fast to keep up with her as she started toward the cliffs, the sheep following single-file behind her.

"If the sheep didn't have a shepherd," Shulamit explained, "they would soon be lost or die of starvation. They're so helpless. They don't know how to find green grass or still water. They can't drink from a bubbly stream; it has to be still."

Just as the path began its ascent, there was a sudden stir among the maidens. One of them ran up and whispered something to Shulamit, who stopped and looked around. It was evident, just as the girl had said, that all the shepherdesses were afraid.

"What are they afraid of?" Solomon asked.

"There's much superstition here in the valley. As I told you, they call this the Mountain of Blood, and many people are afraid even to walk up here."

"Are *you* afraid?"

"No, those of us who believe in Yahweh, the living God, aren't afraid. It's only those who believe in earth gods such as Baal or Hadad who are afraid."

"I don't understand."

"It's quite simple; some of the worshipers of Baal believe that Saul lost the battle and was killed because Baal didn't wish the forces of the living God to take over this land, and now they believe the ground is cursed."

"I see," Solomon said thoughtfully.

"I'll take you myself. I've told them to stay down here with the sheep until we come back."

Solomon and Shulamit followed a path that led in and around the rocks, sometimes going up rather abruptly and at other times leveling out along a ridge. They talked very little as they climbed, and stopped only once while Solomon looked out across the valley. He wanted to see just where the Philistines had been camped.

"The Philistines were camped in our village of Shunem," Shulamit told him. "My grandfather and father were among those who had harassed and plundered the caravans until the Philistines came up to stop them. It was my other grandfather, the father of my mother, who sent a messenger for Saul asking for help. He believed the Philistines could be driven out of our valley completely."

"With the Philistines camping in your village, where did your family go?"

"The men went to fight with Saul, and the women and children fled to neighboring villages."

They mounted the last steep ascent and came out onto a gentle hillside. The grass was parched and brown, and here and there rocks protruded in great gnarled masses. Solomon began to pace back and forth, looking up at the dark bulk of Gilboa's range, which lay behind the spur where they were standing. "Saul was foolish to bring his men down out of the mountains. The Philistines had chariots and swords, while Saul's army was a brave but motley bunch of slingers and stone-throwers with only a few spears and battle-axes."

"Do you think Saul lost because he had fewer men and the Philistines had chariots?" Shulamit was sitting on a boulder with her feet drawn up under her skirt.

"No, I don't. Do you remember the story of Gideon? He fought a battle in this same place against the Midianites and won. Yahweh actually made him narrow his army down—told him he had too many men. He ended up with an army of 300 men to fight an army that was far larger than the Philistine army Saul and his men fought."

While Solomon studied every aspect of the terrain, Shulamit pulled out a shepherd's flute and began to play some of the haunting harvest melodies that were her favorites. Up and down the lilting notes darted, but Solomon was so preoccupied that he didn't even notice. "Endor is in that direction?" he asked. "How far is it across the valley to the witch's cave?"

"About ten miles. You must cross the valley and climb Mount Moreh, and then it's a good ways down the other side."

"Is the witch still there?" Solomon asked.

"No, she disappeared soon after Saul lost the battle, but you can see the cave. It's often used for secret rites and rituals."

"I'd like to see the cave," said Solomon. "I'm convinced that Saul lost the battle because he went to see the witch. Without her prediction that both he and his sons would die in battle the next day, he probably wouldn't have killed himself after he was wounded."

"My mother always said that the witch was Saul's downfall too, but my grandfather said that he lost because his sword hadn't been anointed with holy oil," said Shulamit.

"Those things were only part of his problem," countered Solomon. "He was very tired, remember. It must have been almost sunrise before he arrived back at Gilboa. And with the witch's prediction, he was defeated before the battle even started."

"The villagers know only that the king of Israel lost both the battle and his life. They think the mountain is cursed, and they're afraid of it."

"I don't believe the mountain is cursed. When there's rain, it must be beautiful up here."

"Yes, there are bright red anemones and poppies. The shepherds always say that the poppies grow where blood has been spilled."

For the first time since reaching the top, he turned and looked at her. Her hazel eyes, flecked with light and framed with long lashes, were serious as she studied his face, and he was aware of some new and irresistible force that drew him to her.

He breathed deeply of the clean mountain air. The strange stirring lessened, and he was relieved. Impulsively he sat down beside her on the warm rock. Startled, she dropped her flute and stooped to retrieve it.

"Do you play?" she asked to cover her embarrassment.

"I do sometimes, but most of the time I just make up the words."

"If I play one of the folk tunes, can you make words to it?"

"Play it and I'll try."

Shulamit raised the flute to her lips, and a light, breezy tune filled the air. At first Solomon simply hummed; then, with the tune well in mind, he began to add a word here and there until he had a whole new song: "My beloved said to me, 'Rise up and come away, for lo, the winter is past, the rain is over and gone; flowers appear on the earth, the time of the singing of birds is come, and the voice of the turtle dove is heard in the land.'"

Shulamit was delighted. She clasped his arm and exclaimed, "I loved it! It was beautiful—just perfect."

Solomon drew back in surprise. As long as he could remember, no one had ever dared touch him in such a familiar fashion. For a moment, affronted, he completely forgot that he was dressed in the attire of a humble shepherd. Then, seeing the humor of the situation, he threw back his head and laughed.

Shulamit jumped up, embarrassed. Her eyes grew large and worried, but when he laughed she relaxed and joined him.

"If I play again, will you sing another song?" She perched herself again on the rock, and Solomon moved closer. He found himself enjoying the way her hair brushed his arm and the earthy odors of mint and rue that clung to her garments.

Now every movement she made was enhanced by his imagination. The way she pursed her lips to play the flute, the jingle of the small silver bells on her ankle bracelet as she tapped her foot in time to the music, and the flirtatious twinkle in her eyes so completely captivated him that he forgot to sing. In every way, she was the little shepherdess of his dreams.

By the time she had finished the merry tune and turned breathless and eager to see his reaction, he was actually speculating on the possibility of taking her back to Jerusalem as his bride. With the silver bangles and beaded choker of amber replaced with gold, she would rival any woman at court, including his own mother.

The difficulty would be his mother. Could he possibly persuade her to let him marry this lovely northern girl? His father had married Ahinoam from this same valley, to have stronger ties with the northern tribes. Such reasoning should appeal to his mother. He had never wanted to marry a princess anyway.

"Would you like to play my flute?" she offered. Their hands touched as he reached for the flute, and on sudden reckless impulse he held her hand. He was surprised at the solidness and the warmth of it.

She pulled away quickly but looked at him without embarrassment. "My hands are rough from milking goats and tending plants. I wish they were beautiful."

"You *are* beautiful, and your hands are a very nice part of you." His eyes were soft with wonder, revealing more of his feelings than did the words that he spoke.

She broke the tension with a bell-like laugh. "You must not have seen many beautiful women, then. Actually I'm just a simple lily of the valley."

"Lily of the valley? What do you mean?"

"Down there in the valley and on these lower slopes grow anemones, hyacinths, and crocuses. They're the only lilies the valley will ever see; the big white lilies grow only high up on Mount Hermon."

"I've never seen big lilies, but I've heard that they grow in the midst of thorn bushes," Solomon said.

"You're right. The goats love to eat the green shoots as they come up in the spring, so the only ones that last long enough to bloom are ones growing in patches of thorns. The shepherds always say, 'Look for the thorn bushes and you will find the big, white lilies.'"

"If you had been in that room with all the other maidens yesterday, I would surely have judged you to be a lily among the thorns." His eyes met hers for a brief moment and crinkled into a smile.

She blushed and then smiled, tossing her hair back and holding it there with her hand. He handed her the flute, unplayed, and for a moment their eyes again met and held. It was Solomon who broke the spell. "We'll have to hurry back. We've been away too long already."

He stood up and reached for her hand, helping her to her feet. It was the first time in his life that he had done such a thing for someone else, and he found that he liked it. He laughed when he saw how pleased she was, but he was again unsettled when he noticed how tenderly she looked at him.

"I want to go to the cave of the witch of Endor tomorrow. Could you go with me? Where will you be tomorrow?"

"I'm sure I'll be herding the sheep again."

"Can I ask at the gate where you've gone?"

"No, no, you mustn't do that. Just follow the trail of the sheep as you did today."

Without another word they turned and hurried down the mountain, only to find the sheep in wild confusion and the young shepherdesses weeping with fright as they thought that both Shulamit and the young man had been carried off by evil spirits.

Shulamit immediately took command, and the small procession headed back across the valley, arriving at the gate so late that they caused quite a stir. In the commotion Solomon was able to slip away to the large room where he had left his clothes and change without being noticed. He made his appearance in his mother's private reception room just as she was asking for him. To his great relief he found that she had spent the day resting; she hadn't even missed him.

"I have told our host that at the Feast of the New Moon, I'll choose a maiden from the village to warm the king's bed. I have a plan, a secret test that will help me single out the right girl."

"You have a test? What kind of test?"

"I'm not telling anyone, not even you. But I don't know why I didn't think of it sooner." She smiled happily and held out a tray of dates to Solomon.

He took one of the dates and frowned. He would be glad to settle this matter of a young maiden for his father, but for some reason he felt uncomfortable with his mother's approach. He had a strange sense of foreboding.

*　*　*

Bessim spent the next day in the large reception room, making plans for the Feast of the New Moon. "We'll show them," he said, "that we here in the north can provide as great a feast as anything they might have in the south."

His sons nodded enthusiastic agreement as they filed out of the room. Baalim, however, remained, waiting until their footsteps could no longer be heard before he spoke. "My father, one of the shepherds reported that Prince Adonijah came to the pool of Harod today and talked with our sister and the other shepherdesses."

"I saw the little vixen just before bedtime, and she said nothing of this," Bessim was wary and thoughtful. "It's obvious that she isn't safe even with the sheep."

"Perhaps if tomorrow you sent her into the vineyards with the old women—?" Baalim couldn't hide the gleam of triumph in his eyes, and Bessim realized that his son was enjoying the plight of his favorite daughter.

"You're right. Tomorrow I'll send her to the vineyards. However, I've decided that it won't hurt for her to attend the Feast of the New Moon. By then the queen will no doubt have decided which maiden she will choose for the king."

Late that night Bessim sent word by Sama that Shulamit was to spend the next day working in the vineyard instead of herding sheep.

Shulamit was already in bed and asleep, so Ramat took the message. She noticed with revulsion the smug look of satisfaction on Sama's face as she bragged, "I'm sure the queen intends to choose me."

*　*　*

Sama had always been a frustration to Ramat. Her mother, one of Ramat's serving maids, never failed to boast that Bessim was the father of her child. It always hurt Ramat when Bessim took some new woman to his bed, but it was almost unbearable that he expected her to accept the children he fathered as though they were a credit to his virility.

Sama had caused her more suffering than any of the others. Perhaps it was because Bessim, upon occasion, seemed to favor her. And now, once again, the knife had been twisted in Ramat's heart. Sama had deliberately flaunted the fact that Bessim had given her Shulamit's lovely linen robe—with embroidery that she herself had worked—to wear to the festivities. "The queen has taken a special interest in me," Sama taunted, turning to leave. "Perhaps it's because I'm Bessim's daughter?"

Ramat didn't want the queen to choose Shulamit, but at the same time it seemed unfair that the loveliest girl in Shunem should be made to tend sheep and dress vines when everyone else was celebrating with the queen.

She rose and felt her way in the darkness along the wall past Shulamit's door to her own room. She paused for a moment and looked out across the valley toward Gilboa, noticing bright specks of light glowing in the darkness. People were offering sacrifices on the High Places again. They were frightened each month when the moon totally disappeared and darkness filled the night sky. They thought only their sacrifices would make it reappear.

It wasn't generally known who these people were, but Ramat knew that Bessim and some of his sons went often to these hidden groves. Some instinct told her that it wasn't so much interest in the mysteries that drew them as the drunkenness and perverted sexual rituals that were part of their ceremonies.

"I wouldn't put it past them," she thought, "to buy charms and incantations to help accomplish their own ends." She remembered the time she had found the tightly knotted cloth reeking with the odor of pig fat hanging from a cord around Bessim's neck. It was to give him sons, he had explained.

She wished that there were ways of guaranteeing that Yahweh would make her dreams for Shulamit come true, but Yahweh made no such promises. She didn't know why she clung to her faith in Him. The earth gods seemed to be much more easily influenced. Still, it was Yahweh she had turned to in her need, and she would just have to wait and see if He had heard and would answer.

6

*L*ate in the afternoon, after riding hard and fast, Adonijah reached his country house at Shafat. Here he changed mules and swiftly disguised himself as a scribe so that he wouldn't be recognized and could move about more freely. Though he made good time from Shafat, it was well after sunset before he rode through the Fountain Gate into Jerusalem.

As he urged his mule up the narrow, winding streets, he was again reminded of the drought. Even at this hour there were people roaming the streets, their faces fearful, haunted. Women with dry, lifeless voices called to him from the shadowed doorways, asking that he have mercy on their children. Old women groaned and held out fragile hands. He passed the baker's hovel and noticed that it was securely boarded up, while the vegetable stalls stood open and dark.

He was going to the house of Eon, a wealthy merchant whose ostentatious house rose on the corner opposite the palace. He hesitated until he was sure that he hadn't been recognized by any of the people standing nearby, then he knocked.

He waited a moment and knocked again. He heard a quick, light step followed by the sound of wood rubbing on wood before a small window opened in the door. There was a whispered command and the door opened. To his surprise he saw Yasmit, the young girl he had first noticed at Solomon's birthday celebration. She was holding a lamp that cast vibrant shadows on her face and glinted from the gold headband that circled her forehead.

Adonijah was speechless as she bowed gracefully and then rose to look at him boldly, as if daring him to question her right to be there. At the same moment he saw Eon coming to greet him.

"She's my wife," Eon said, chuckling at Adonijah's obvious confusion.

"Your wife?"

"Yasmit likes to wear gold like a queen and have bread to eat, and her father wants wheat seed for his fields. She was what we merchants would call a bargain!" Eon laughed, and his high, cracked voice choked with the effort.

Yasmit tilted her chin and flashed a knowing look at Adonijah before leaving the room. Her sultry perfume lingered while the sound of her ankle bracelets became faint and indistinct.

Slowly Adonijah looked around at the changes that had taken place in Eon's courtyard. The opulent look he had always admired was gone. Instead, large clay jars stood bunched together, and big squares of pressed, dried dates and figs wrapped around with dry leaves were stacked in random piles.

Eon noticed Adonijah's reaction and shrugged. "These are hard times. It's dangerous to look wealthy—and besides, the true wealth these days lies with those who've been able to hoard seed to sell once the drought is past."

"It's that bad, then?"

Eon studied Adonijah's face before answering. "Worse than the likes of you can even imagine. People are selling their children into slavery for a little barley and some oil. Even your father has taken to fasting and prayer. It makes a good show."

"Has it done him much good?" Adonijah asked.

"If by 'good' you mean rain—no, there's been no rain, but there *has* been a great deal of repentance and confession. Even old Asa Ben-Jude, who cheated a widow out of some land years ago, confessed and with his own hands publicly replaced the markers. It's been quite interesting to see the evil deeds that have been covered for years—evil deeds confessed to now by seemingly good and honest men."

"It's rather frightening. I'm surprised that I've not been asked to confess my sins. I have a few that would probably shock the good people of Jerusalem."

"You're not starving yet, Adonijah. Your time will come—or at least that's what they say."

"But my father?"

"He's suffered most of all. The people are like little children all looking to him to find a solution." Eon shrugged and then turned, motioning Adonijah to follow him up the steps to the roof. "We mustn't let the servants hear us," he cautioned.

Adonijah had visited Eon at this same time of year when the vines that rose up over the trellis and door to Eon's retreat had been bursting with young leaves, but now they hung in limp brown ropes.

A servant removed Adonijah's dusty sandals and washed his feet. "You must understand," Eon said, "that even in my house we no longer waste water washing feet. Of course, for you it's different."

Adonijah looked around the familiar room. Here, there was no change. He sank down onto a fine linen mat and breathed deeply of the rare incense being burned in a censer above his head. "You mentioned that my father was fasting and praying."

"I went to the throne room every day of his fast," Eon said, pouring wine into finely polished brass goblets, "and was there when he finally came out of seclusion. He looked terrible: ashes, sackcloth—his eyes deep hollows and the rags hanging from his shoulders." Eon paused, and his face became dark and clouded.

"Yes, and then?"

"He called his counselors together and announced that God had shown him one more wrong that hadn't been set right."

"And what was that?"

"Saul's unfair treatment of the Gibeonites."

Adonijah leaned forward and stared in bewilderment. "The Gibeonites! How ridiculous."

Eon shook his head. "Not as ridiculous as you might think. Saul did wrong to take their city when Joshua had promised that they'd be spared."

"What does Joshua have to do with this? That promise was made long ago, when the Israelites were first coming into the land."

"Saul would have agreed with you, especially since the Gibeonites held a prized position right in the middle of the territory allotted for his tribe."

Adonijah set down his goblet and leaned back among the cushions. "I've never liked the idea of the tabernacle being at Gibeon where the Benjamites could control it and benefit from trade during the feast days, but I'm surprised that my father sees this as a *sin*. After all, the grove and the High Place of the Gibeonites were destroyed before the tabernacle was placed there.

"But Joshua—"

"One would think the God of Israel would want the High Place of Ashtaroth and Baal destroyed and would consider it quite a triumph to have his tabernacle raised over the very spot where those pagan gods had reigned for hundreds of years."

Eon leaned toward Adonijah and spoke softly. "It's a strange matter. Some say this famine is the revenge of the old earth gods for taking their High Place and grove away from them. Of course, we never know, do we?"

"It sounds as though the same men who said the rains wouldn't come unless the king's interest in his harem revived are now suggesting this."

Eon nodded and reached to refill Adonijah's wine goblet.

"So now," Adonijah asked, "what are they proposing? Is the tabernacle to be torn down and the land given back to the Gibeonites?"

"No, nothing like that. The king called the elders of the Gibeonites together and asked them how this evil against them could be righted. They insisted that they would accept no solution but revenge."

"Revenge? But Saul is dead."

"They've asked that the sons and grandsons of Saul be turned over to them—the sons of Rizpah, Saul's concubine, and Saul's grandsons that his daughter Michal raised."

Adonijah leaned forward, his eyes gleaming. "What does my father say to this?"

"He's refused to turn them over to the Gibeonites, of course. He's afraid they'd kill them. His refusal has almost caused a riot, though. The people want the famine to end, and if this is a solution, they're ready to demand it."

Slowly Adonijah twirled the goblet in his long, jeweled fingers. "Do you realize what it would mean to me, Eon, to have those ill-bred bastards of Saul's out of my way? They could cause me trouble when I make my move for the throne. This may be just the chance I've been waiting for."

Eon shook his head. "Your father won't turn them over to the Gibeonites."

"He must, Eon. He *must* turn them over. You can't imagine how often I've feared they would poison my wine or have me knifed in the back just to get me out of their way. We know they want the throne; they haven't stopped plotting since the day they arrived."

"It will be hard to convince your father. He fears Michal. She is, after all, one of his wives. You should have seen him when she confronted him."

"Michal confronted him?"

"Yes, and in the throne room. She was dressed in sackcloth and rags and said the most terrible things."

"What terrible things?"

"Threats, curses. They finally had to take her away forcibly."

"Don't worry, Eon. I'll find a way to convince him. You did right to call me home. This is my chance, and I'll not botch it."

"There's something else to think of, my prince," Eon was now standing, and Adonijah was startled at how worried he looked. "If any harm comes to the sons of Saul, the Benjamites will never forgive your father or you. They have long memories."

"Who says harm will come to those bastards? I'll swear to my father that nothing will happen to them. I'll make my father see that this is the only way."

"And if they're killed?"

"It won't be my fault or my father's. How could we possibly know what the Gibeonites would do with them?"

"But you *know* they'll kill them."

Adonijah got to his feet and walked to the door, waiting only for the servant to bring his shoes. "Don't worry about it," he said, pressing Eon's hand. "When I'm king, I'll reward you for looking after my interests so well." With that he turned and hurried down the steps.

In the front courtyard, as he paused to catch his breath, he heard somewhere above him the tinkle of sliding bracelets. He glanced up just in time to see something light and web-like flutter to the ground—apparently a woman's sheer mantle. Then he caught a glimpse of Yasmit leaning out of the window, her hand still resting on the gray stones of the casement.

For one brief moment she looked directly at him. Then she slammed the shutters closed so that only fractured bits of light shone through and music, high and light, filtered down to him.

"I'll have to visit Eon more often," Adonijah muttered as he headed for the palace gate.

* * *

The throne room was empty except for a knot of waiting men whose dark, angular features marked them as Gibeonites. Adonijah hurried past them up the steps to his father's private rooms. He paused as he heard the strident, angry voice of Joab, the commander of the troops.

"It's not that I've ever liked the upstart sons and grandsons of old King Saul," he told David. "They've always been plotting to regain the throne. But if you turn them over to the Gibeonites, they'll surely be killed. Then the Benjamites will seek revenge. You know how hot-headed their men are; they might even split off from the kingdom and encourage the rest of the northern tribes to leave with them."

David was obviously disturbed. "Joab, you've always been clever at predicting disaster. I have no intention of letting these young men be executed. However, the Lord very clearly showed me that until we right the treachery of Saul against the Gibeonites, our hands aren't clean. I have to do *something*."

"What will you do? You can't give the land back to the Gibeonites without offending Abiathar, the high priest. He's been so satisfied there. Joshua's agreement that the Gibeonites be drawers of water and hewers of wood has made that location ideal."

"That was my original thought. I wanted to move the tabernacle to Jerusalem, but the Gibeonites wouldn't accept that. They'll agree only if I give them Saul's sons and grandsons."

Joab's face was red; his voice became harsh and threatening. "Just for once, just this *once*," he thundered, "do what seems reasonable. If you side with the Gibeonites against the Benjamites, a large portion of the men in my army will go home."

"You sound as if you think I'm siding with the Gibeonites against my own people."

"If you give them the sons of Saul, that's exactly how it will look, and I want no part of it." Joab turned away abruptly and without the usual formalities rushed out to the courtyard, where he could be heard shouting for his shield-bearer.

Adonijah cleared his throat to warn David of his presence and then walked confidently into the room. "My father?" he said, kissing him on both cheeks, "I bring you greetings from Jezreel—from your wife Bathsheba and my brother Solomon."

"They're well, then?"

"Yes, my lord, they're well. News of the trouble with the Gibeonites reached me, and I came home to see if I could serve you in some way?"

"So even in the north you had heard of the trouble?" David asked with alarm.

"Such news travels fast."

David was haggard and worn from the long hours of fasting, but he had bathed and was wearing his sword and buckler again. He looped his fingers around the hilt of his sword and squared his shoulders. "It isn't easy to be king," he said. "One must be constantly dealing with both God and man. One wrong decision can bring down pain and misery on a whole country."

"You believe that taking the land from the Gibeonites has caused this famine?"

"No, no, not that alone. You can't imagine the sins that have been confessed and the wrongs that have been righted. God couldn't bless us as we were. The wrong done the Gibeonites is just the final sin that must be set right before God can intervene on our behalf."

"God sent the famine?"

"Probably not. The famine came about through natural causes, but as long as we harbored so much evil and wrong, God couldn't help us. We had cut ourselves off from Him."

"And now—when you settle this problem with the Gibeonites, the famine will end?" David seemed not to notice Adonijah's slight sneer of condescension.

"I had thought," David said, "that it would be a simple thing to move the tabernacle, but they won't settle so easily. They want me to give them the sons and grandsons of Saul at the Feast of the New Moon tomorrow night. This is difficult."

"Why, my father? If the Lord has said it?"

"The Lord didn't say anything about the family of Saul. He simply told me it was this wrong that must be set right. It's the Gibeonites themselves who have demanded this."

"Well, why not give them over?" Adonijah stood casually looking down at his fingernails.

"Why not?" David flung out his arms in frustration and began pacing back and forth. "Don't you *see*? The Gibeonites mean to take their revenge. They mean to *kill* them all. 'Give us the sons and grandsons of Saul, they insist, 'that we might hang them.'"

"I doubt that they would go *so* far." Adonijah put his hands on his hips and smiled in his most disarming manner.

"You don't think the Gibeonites mean to kill them?"

"Of course not. Why should they? What would they gain?"

David was heartened but unconvinced by Adonijah's cool appraisal of the situation. "To turn them over would solve everything," he admitted, "but—"

"You'll see," promised Adonijah. "They obviously just want to teach them a lesson."

"But Michal?"

"Never mind Michal. It must be done quickly, before Michal has had time to hear of it."

"How are you so sure the Gibeonites don't intend to kill the young men?" David was still cautious.

"Why would they? They're neighbors. They wouldn't want to make enemies of them."

David nodded and his face relaxed. "Come, then—let's go talk to the Gibeonites and settle this matter right away."

Quickly, and with little ceremony, the Gibeonites were given permission to take the young men at the next day's Feast of the New Moon.

"However, you're not to touch Mephibosheth," David warned. "He's the crippled son of my friend Jonathan, and I'll not have any unpleasantness come to him."

During the conversation with the Gibeonites, Adonijah had noticed Joab's growing frustration. "He's almost ready to band himself with those who want a new and younger king," Adonijah thought. "He's hot-tempered and strong-willed, and I want him on my side."

After the Gibeonites left, Adonijah excused himself, saying that he planned to start the long ride back to Shunem that very night. He knew the Gibeonites well, and there wasn't a doubt in his mind that they intended to kill the young men. When this happened, he didn't want to be around to remind people that it had been at his suggestion that the king made his final decision.

Joab, however, lingered to talk to David. His chin jutted forward and he held his hands behind his back as he had always done when trying to control his temper. "My lord," he said doggedly, following David from the throne room, "the Gibeonites are sure to kill the young men, and that will be far more disturbing than the unrest caused by the famine."

"Joab, those men were calm and logical. I'm sure they don't intend to harm the young men."

"You'll see. As soon as the news spreads that the Gibeonites have the young men, all the roads to the north will be full of angry Benjamites looking to avenge their kinsmen."

David was suddenly alarmed. "Bathsheba and Solomon will be returning to Jerusalem after the New-Moon festival. If there's trouble with the Benjamites ... "

"There's *sure* to be trouble," Joab blustered.

"We must send someone to Shunem to warn them, then. They'll be coming right through Benjamite territory."

"It would be better to avoid angering the Benjamites."

"I can't change what I've done. I'm convinced that the Gibeonites are reasonable people. Anyway, it's now in God's hands."

Joab knew that it was useless to say more. He bowed and then walked angrily past the guardroom to his own chambers above the North Gate.

David, meanwhile, summoned one of the guards. "Send to the house of Nathan the prophet," he ordered, "and tell him that I must see my son Nathan immediately." Nathan had always been a son David could depend on, and now, in this emergency, he was the only one who could be trusted.

* * *

When Adonijah left the throne room, he decided to go to the court of the queens to see his mother. He was devoted to her and managed to cater to all her demands, though he had to confess that she was often difficult.

He found her lying on her bed while a serving girl fanned away the flies. Haggith opened her eyes and stared at him. She had grown thin, and he noticed that she was nervously fingering the woven coverlet.

"Mother?" he said, reaching out to hold her cold hands in both of his. "Mother?" he said, "It won't be long now."

She began to cry. "But it's already been too long. That woman even has her own house across the valley. Her sons are always with the king. I know what's going on. I hear the women talking."

"Don't worry so much about Bathsheba. When I'm king, you'll have her house, her jewels, everything. I promise you."

"The house, the jewels! That's not what I want!"

"What *do* you want, Mother? Whatever you want, it will be yours when I'm king."

"Ah, when you're king, it'll be wonderful. We'll have her head on a skewer and her sons' heads on the gate for all to see." Her voice was cracked and husky, but her eyes were bright behind the lashless eyelids. "That's all I'm living for, to see her put out and disgraced."

"Mother?" he said with a grin, "your jealousy is always fresh. I never find it frail or starving."

"Just seeing her keeps venom in my veins."

He laughed again. "I have to go. I'm leaving for Shunem tonight."

"That's where Bathsheba's gone to find the king a bride." She laughed a high, mirthless laugh. "She'll see what it's like. She'll see."

"Mother, I have to go. My men are waiting."

"Go, go, go. Everyone has to go." She started to cry again.

"I'll not come again if you cry," Adonijah said, backing away.

"If you had had the disappointment I've had, you'd cry too." She wiped her tears and glared at him. He reached for her hand and raised it to his forehead in respect, then strode to the door. For just a moment he stopped.

"Your time is coming," he said. "You'll have your wish."

He didn't wait for her reply but hurried out to his waiting men.

* * *

It was late when Nathan arrived, but David was sitting up in bed waiting for him. "My son," David said, reaching out to tousle his son's fine dark hair. He loved this boy in a special way and was always mentioning his accomplishments. When Nathan had learned to read the Torah by following the pointer as it moved over the vellum and singling out the words made of square and curving lines, David's pride knew no bounds. "He's a son I'll never have to be ashamed of!" he would exclaim. "Which is more than I can say for most of my sons."

David marveled that though his son lived with Nathan the prophet and studied to be a prophet himself, he always seemed to be enjoying life more than was considered proper for someone in his role. Though he was dressed in a coarse, seamless robe and wore simple sandals made of rough goatskin, he still looked every bit the prince that he was.

"Nathan, you're going to have to go on an important errand for me," David said. "Your mother and Solomon must be warned not to return by the ridge road that leads through the land of Benjamin."

"Is there trouble with the Benjamites?"

"Not yet, but I'm sure there will be. Tribal feeling runs deep, and they'll be angry that I've given in to the Gibeonites' request."

"Ah, so you've finally decided. Well, don't worry. I'll manage everything."

"You're always studying. Has Nathan also taught you to ride and handle difficult situations?"

"Nathan may be my teacher, but I'm *your* son."

"Well said, well said!" David was pleased as always at the boy's answers. He gave him his blessing and then watched him stride out through the curtained doorway. "He's only seventeen," he thought, "and already he talks like a prophet but walks like one of my best fighting men. He'll bring them all home safely, no matter what fool thing the Benjamites may plan."

He thought for a moment of the two sons of Saul and then the grandsons that his own wife Michal had raised. He knew that it was Michal's secret hope and burning desire that one of these young men take the throne whenever the chance might present itself.

They were selfish, unruly young men who were capable of causing real trouble—and *had* caused it on more occasions than he wanted to remember. It wouldn't hurt for them to be held for a few days by the Gibeonites. It was inconceivable that any real harm would come to them. With that consoling thought, he went to bed.

He turned over and tried to sleep, but the picture of Michal, angry and vindictive, kept disturbing hm. She would blame him for everything that happened. She would have the whole tribe of Benjamin down on him with threats and accusations until the young men were safely back.

He thought for a few moments about Bathsheba and Solomon. Michal had always hated Bathsheba, and she would love to use this as an excuse to urge her tribesmen to harass Bathsheba and perhaps harm Solomon.

David turned to prayer for their safety and was asleep before he had finished the praise with which he always closed.

* * *

There was nothing unusual about the next night, nothing that alarmed anyone. The rising of the new moon was trumpeted from a tower on Olivet and then by the king's heralds on the wall above the East Gate. Almost immediately those who regularly gathered at the king's table and those who had come to celebrate the feast began to assemble in the courtyard of the palace.

The floor of the throne room was strewn with palm branches brought from En-gedi and torches flared and sputtered, but tables that in years past had groaned with plenty now offered only meager fare. There was neither bread nor barley cakes; the raisins were like small, hard stones, and the olives were bitter. Only the quail, which had been caught in nets down in the lowlands, was bountiful and tasty.

David's friends, heads of tribes, Mighty Men of David's army, and relatives all filed in and took their accustomed places. There were always new people—even foreign traders and some mercenaries—so no one noticed when a few men from Gibeon sat down with them to eat the feast. They were dark-eyed and bearded and had an intense look that should have alerted their fellow feasters of the danger to come.

The feast ended and the guests filed past the raised dais to bid the king "goodnight and a good month." Guests and host alike were leisurely and relaxed.

Outside, however, beyond the dark shadows of the wall, there was the sound of scuffling, then a cry, and finally cursing. Notified ahead of time that the Gibeonites would leave with prisoners, the palace guards stood at attention in their places. The guests, reassured by their demeanor, paused only a moment before going on to their homes. Meanwhile, the Gibeonites who had caused the commotion hurried the sons and grandsons of Saul off into the darkness, out the North Gate, and down the road to Gibeon.

Only a young serving boy saw what really happened. He ran at full speed out the Valley Gate and down the winding path that led to the houses on the western ridge. He hurried up a dark walkway and pounded frantically on a low wooden door almost hidden by an imposing stone lintel.

This house, known as the house of the ten concubines, was the house of the concubines David had banished after Absalom's revolt. It was also the house of Michal, old King Saul's daughter, the wife whom David had rejected because of her insolent attitude.

Michal was in charge of the household, and the concubines served as her willing servants. It was a position she complained of often but in actuality enjoyed.

Now it was late. There had been no celebration within this house, and it took some minutes to rouse anyone. There was first a dim light, then the sound of a latch being pushed loose, and finally a young girl holding a lighted lamp appeared.

Quickly the boy told all that he had seen, and in a great fright the girl went to summon Michal, who appeared looking disheveled and annoyed. Her eyes were dark and darting, like those of a wild bird of prey; her hair, loose and wispy, waved in snakelike strands about her face, and her mouth was twisted and bitter.

As she listened to the story, she paced wildly back and forth, clenching and unclenching her hands and cursing under her breath that she was a woman. "Here, boy, take my mule and ride to Gibeah, to the house of my uncle. See that he hears all you have to say. He'll gather the men of Benjamin, and if it's not too late . . . now go, go boy, and if you succeed, I'll give you this ring." She pulled a great, flashing ruby from her finger and held it for a moment where he could see it clearly. Putting it back on her finger, she ordered, "Go as fast as you can, or it will be too late."

She leaned out of the door and watched him ride down the dark lane. Her eyes were dry. She had long ago wept all the tears she ever intended to weep. Now she found release in throwing curses, dark and vile, out into the air to poison it and kill those she hated.

"It's David who has done this. He's done this to destroy me, to get at Saul and his house. He knows that I raised those boys to be kings, and he'll do anything in his power to defeat me and my plans. Oh, Baal Hadad," she cried, "god of the thunder, lightning, and rain. Strike him; defeat his evil purpose; bring him down!"

7

*J*ust at daybreak Ramat went to wake Shulamit. "Come, my sweet. Wake up. It's a lovely day," she said, opening the shutters to let in the first rays of the sun. Shulamit stirred, then sat up and yawned. Glancing out the window, she was alarmed. "The shepherds have already gone," she cried.

* * *

It was still so early that the sun hadn't driven the mist from the valley when they arrived at the stone watchtower. Here Shulamit and her mother stopped, letting the rest of the workers go on without them. The tower, built of stones picked up from the fields, stood off to one side of the sprawling vineyard on the lower slopes of Mount Moreh.

On the ground level there was a small domed room from which steps wound up to a roofless room at the top, bounded by a parapet. Around the base of the tower circled a small courtyard that boasted an ancient apricot tree.

"We'll both be glad of some good pomegranate wine in the middle of the day," Shulamit said, hanging the wineskin on a peg in the lower room. She pulled off her sandals and hung them on another peg.

"Be careful that you don't cut your feet on the sharp stones," her mother warned. Shulamit didn't answer but proceeded to pull up the sleeves of her dress, knotting them at the back so that she would be free to work.

She took down the hoe from a rack behind the door and went out into the bright sunlight. Silently she joined the other women, who were digging wide trenches around the base of each vine in preparation for the water that would be brought later.

Most of the workers sang as they wielded their hoes, but Shulamit was still too preoccupied with her own thoughts to join them. She couldn't help wondering what was happening to the young man. What would he think when he didn't find her? As her frustration mounted, she wielded the hoe with increasing vigor. She was surprised at how very much she cared.

By noon she was ready to stop. Her arms ached and she was hot and flushed with small riverlets of sweat making her hair kink and curl around her face. She walked toward the watchtower, thinking only of the cool wine waiting and the warm bread that her mother would be baking.

She looked up at the sound of voices. Her mother wasn't alone; someone else sat silhouetted against the sun on the low parapet.

The voice was familiar, but it took her a minute to realize that it belonged to the young man himself. Somehow he must have found her!

She felt a wild, leaping joy as she hurried into the small room. There she washed her hands and feet and rinsed off her face in the cool water she dipped from a large clay jar. Quickly she untied her sleeves, put on her sandals, and wound a jaunty turban around her head, careful to let the ends fall to one side of her face and down her back as was the fashion.

As she hurried out the door she stooped to pick up a cluster of wild thyme and pushed it into the fold of the turban just above her cheek. She had no idea how she looked, but she was so happy she didn't really care. She bounded up the stairs and came to an embarrassed stop when she saw the young man turn toward her, his eyes igniting with delight and recognition.

After the usual greetings were exchanged, Ramat took Shulamit aside and whispered, "He wants to go to the cave of Endor."

"It would be difficult to tell him how to get there, but I could take him easily."

"But your father—he would never approve."

"If he were here we could ask him, but since he isn't—"

"He's interested only in finding the cave. I suppose it would do no harm, and I could work for you in the vineyard." Thus, in such a simple way, it was decided that Shulamit would guide Solomon over Mount Moreh to the cave.

Hurriedly they ate the simple meal of freshly baked bread and lentil soup and then set out on the same path that old King Saul must have taken on the fateful night before the battle.

At first Shulamit was shy. On the way to Gilboa she had treated him with casual indifference, but now everything was changed; she wanted to please him. She couldn't account for the change, but it had something to do with his smile and the way he listened so intently when she talked.

"One of your brothers told me where I could find you," Solomon said after several minutes of silence.

"I couldn't get a message to you," Shulamit apologized.

"I understand." Again there was silence as the two walked single file up into the pine forest. Once on the far side of the hill, they began to look for someone who could tell them the way to the cave. When they finally found a young goatherd who knew the way, he backed off from them in terrible fright and refused to give them directions.

"It looks as though the cave is still a place of mystery and fear," Solomon concluded.

"He's afraid to tell. But then it's always been forbidden to visit a witch in Israel," Shulamit said.

They spent some time going back and forth along the winding paths that branched off the main path, but they couldn't find the cave. "I don't really need to find the cave," Solomon said finally. "I already know much of what I wanted to learn. Just coming this far on the night before the battle would have tired Saul. He couldn't have been at his best the next day."

"What did you hope to find?" Shulamit asked.

For a moment Solomon stood very still. When he finally answered, it was as though he were talking to himself. "I understand about God, but I've never understood about witches and the power they seem to have. If God is so good and he made the world, then who made the witches and evil? And which has the greater power?"

"Here in the north there are many who fear evil spirits and make sacrifices to them," Shulamit said.

"Yes, and in the south such practices are a great sin—but in the south we have drought, while here, where people are secretly worshiping Baal, the Kishon is still flowing and there's wheat for your grindstones and for seed."

"My mother says that there are both good and evil in the world, but it's the good that will finally win."

"That's strange. My father would say that too. He's never put it just that way, but that's what he believes."

With that Solomon stopped looking for the cave and suggested they start back. As they crested the hill, they noticed the vultures circling above them. The sky had gradually darkened and now a wind sprang up, "It looks like rain," Solomon said, laughing excitedly.

Shulamit stopped and studied the sky. "I hope it's really going to rain this time," she said. "Come, there's a cave near here where we can stay until the worst of the storm blows over." She motioned for him to follow as she left the path and pushed through some underbrush until they stood looking down into the opening of a cave.

It was the sort of cave that shepherds take shelter in at night—low-roofed but with a wide entrance partially overgrown with tall grass and thistles. Shulamit waved aside a spider web, pushed back the grass, and dropped down into the cave just as the thunder rolled ominously and the first drops of rain began to fall thick and fast.

It was obvious that she was familiar with the cave as she sank down on a rocky shelf on one side of the entrance and motioned for Solomon to sit beside her. "There," she said, pointing toward the entrance. "If you look through the branches of that tree, you can barely see Gilboa."

"I'm not interested in Gilboa anymore," Solomon said, picking up a dry stick and aimlessly drawing patterns in the dirt. "I've learned all I want to know. Now there are other questions."

"Questions? What sort of questions?"

"Well, for instance, do you think a northern girl would be happy in the south?"

Shulamit drew her feet up under her skirt and clasped her knees with her hands. "Why wouldn't *anyone* be happy in the south? My mother says that Jerusalem is the most beautiful city in the world."

"Jerusalem and all the other cities of Judah, Benjamin, and Ephraim are crowded and dark, sometimes even cold. Life is hard on our rocky hillsides. Famine has always been a close neighbor. We don't play at religion as you do here; there, it's our very life."

Shulamit marveled at his honesty. "Our valley is usually rich and prosperous, but there's a darkness here too. The fear of evil spirits and pagan gods has almost destroyed all the happiness."

Solomon shrugged. "Even the pagan gods and evil spirits don't like to live in the harshness of Judea. But you haven't answered my question."

"What question?"

"I asked if you would be happy in the south."

"How should I know? I've never been in the south. I've never even been as far as Megiddo. Why do you ask?" she said, glancing at him in time to catch the slow, enchanting smile that had already won her heart.

"Here, let me show you Judea," he said, using his stick to draw on the dirt floor. "See? These are the mountains. Now to the east there's nothing but the

Jordan River and the Dead Sea; to the south there's desert; to the west there are the Philistines, and to the north there are more mountains. Do you think you could be happy in such a place?"

Shulamit reached for the stick and drew a figure with a round head, two arms, and a long fringed robe with two feet barely, showing at the bottom. "There," she said. "That's the way any woman sees the country she lives in."

"I don't understand."

"A woman's world is made up of people, and whether the mountains are bare or the valleys rich, her world is beautiful if she sees love in her husband's eyes." Solomon looked at her with undisguised delight, and Shulamit felt her whole being melting and yielding to the love she saw in his eyes.

"I want you to come back to Jerusalem with me, to be my own little shepherdess and live with me in my barren watchtower. Will you come?" His eyes were eager and his voice persuasive.

"It's not proper for me to answer. You must speak with my father."

"You do have a father, then?"

"A very real father. You know him."

"I know him?"

"When you come to the celebration tonight, you'll meet him."

"Then I'll ask him, but first you must tell me whether you yourself would choose to come with me."

"I can't answer that. It's not our custom!"

"Look at me, then. Let me read the answer in your eyes." He pulled her to her feet and tipped her head up so that he could see her eyes clearly in the dim light. For a long moment they stood looking at each other while the rain, with its fluid screen and gentle drumming, shut them in to their own, private world.

Shulamit was overwhelmed by Solomon's nearness. His steady gaze hypnotized her, and the strong fragrance of spikenard made her senses reel. She couldn't look away, nor could she lower her eyes (as a good daughter of Rachel was taught). She saw his eyes go from her forehead to her lips, linger there for a provocative moment, and then return to her eyes. A lifetime passed in moments; she realized that she wanted to be his completely—to belong to him, and him only.

For a brief moment he looked as though he were about to kiss her. She could see that he had forgotten all about Gilboa and the problems of Judea; his total attention was centered on her. He didn't need to speak, for she could read all that he felt in his eyes. Now she was seeing someone quite different from the boy who had fallen into the thorn bush or the student who had pondered the acts of Saul. Some instinct told her that this was as new for him as it was for her.

He broke the silence first. "Here, I have something I want you to wear." He lifted a tightly braided cord from around his neck and gently fitted it over her head. At the end of the cord was a small pouch of softest doeskin that gave off a delicate fragrance. "The flowers were gathered from En-Gedi and dried. Their perfume will remind you of me," he said. Then, as if embarrassed by his own sentimentality, his tone became businesslike. "Tomorrow I'll go speak to your father."

She lifted the small pouch and smelled the rare fragrance. "My father is difficult," she said.

"Fathers are *always* difficult." He pulled her to him and kissed her, at first fondly and then with such passion it must have surprised him for he drew back and held her for a moment at arms' length. "There's one problem—a small problem, but I have no right to hold you or claim you until it's settled."

"You're already promised to someone else?" Fear was in her voice, and the light had gone out of her eyes.

"No, not really."

"It must all be done very properly. My father is particular. He'll question everything."

"Never fear. I'll be able to manage. You'll see."

The rain stopped as quickly as it had begun, and reluctantly they realized that they must leave. Back on the path they marveled at the newly rain-washed beauty of the forest. Water still dripped from the trees, and the air was fresh and fragrant with the lovely odor of pines. Walking over soft beds of pine needles, they watched the sun glint and sparkle on the raindrops strung like silver beads along the cobwebs in the grass. It was a magic, enchanted world shared only by the two of them.

As they came to the edge of the pine forest, they stopped for one last time to stand with hands entwined gazing into each other's eyes. Suddenly, high above them in the tallest pine, a nightingale began to sing. The song was sharp and clear on the fresh mountain air, and they felt as though the little unseen singer had put wings to their love.

The song ended and there was a sudden flutter and rustling of leaves as

75

the bird flew up through the branches and out into the open sky. Shulamit reluctantly turned and led the way down the path and across the field to where her mother was waiting for them at the watchtower.

* * *

Back at Bessim's fortress, Solomon went directly to his mother's rooms, where he found Jessica anointing Bathsheba's hair and preparing her makeup for the festivities of the evening.

"Mother, I must speak with you alone," he said, motioning for Jessica to leave them.

"This must be something very serious," Bathsheba said, winking at Jessica and examining her damp hair in a mirror.

"It is serious. I mean, *I'm* serious. I've found her, the girl I want to marry."

"You've *what?*" Bathsheba dropped the brass mirror in her lap and looked at him with amusement.

Solomon was annoyed that she seemed to be taking his news so lightly. "Mother, I've met the most wonderful girl. She's beautiful and gentle and intelligent.

"Impossible. You *know* it's impossible. I thought we had agreed that you must marry a princess."

"If I'm destined to be king, then it should be possible without so much effort on my part."

Bathsheba rose from her cushions. "My son," she pleaded, "don't be willful in this. Once you've married someone of royal lineage, you can marry anyone else you desire."

"But why must I marry a princess? Isn't Nathan's prophecy enough?" he asked.

"I can't believe that you would take such a chance. Of course, there is Nathan's prediction, but we must do our part to make it come true."

"The princess of Rabbath-ammon worships Molech. Her people always sacrifice the first child to their god. Had you thought of that, Mother?"

Solomon was so earnest that Bathsheba began to worry. "Who is this maiden who has so captured your heart? What's her name?"

"I don't know."

"Who's her father, then?" she asked.

"I don't know that either."

Bathsheba laughed with relief. "You don't know her name, and you don't know who her father is? Where did you meet her?"

"She's a shepherdess and a vinedresser."

"A shepherdess?" Bathsheba was completely taken aback. She rushed to him and embraced him as though he had been suddenly taken with a strange illness. "I've been afraid of this. We should have married you to the princess a year ago."

"Afraid of what?" Solomon asked as he drew back and looked at her.

"The wise men say that when a young man is ready to marry, the first girl he sees will look beautiful to him." She held him at arms' length and looked at him with growing astonishment. "What happened to your fine clothes? This cloak—of homespun? And how did you get all dusty?"

"I've been out in the fields disguised as a shepherd. It was wonderful." He laughed at her discomfiture.

Bathsheba was suddenly relieved. "Wonderful! A shepherdess, indeed. You almost made me believe it."

"Mother, the shepherdess is real, and I love her and intend to marry her."

She put her hand over his mouth and smiled. "I understand. You've been playing shepherd out in the fields, but now it's time to change your clothes and come back into the real world. There's barely enough time to get ready for the festivities."

"I'll change my clothes, but that won't change my heart. You'll see tonight. You'll love her just as much as I do." He took his mother's hand and raised it to his lips, then, with a conspiratorial wink, he left the room.

* * *

Just as the dying moon inspired fear and anxiety in the people of Shunem, so the rising of the new moon brought joy and celebration. Those living in the mountains to the east of the Jordan waited until the first glowing edge of the new moon was sighted and then ordered the great fires to be lit.

At the sighting of the fires, Bessim signaled for the trumpets to be blown, the flags unfurled, and the guests assembled. The main festivities were to be held in the great outer court of Bessim's fortress so that as many people as possible could attend.

A low dais had been set up for the queen and other dignitaries, and a canopy was stretched over the ornate cushions. Wreaths of fragrant herbs hung everywhere.

The guests had squeezed into every available corner of the courtyard; unfortunate latecomers were forced to sit on the walls or climb to neighboring roofs to get a better view. They whispered among themselves that the queen had as much as promised that she would announce her choice that very night.

Suddenly from deep within the fortress a trumpet was heard, the crowd stopped pushing and shoving and grew silent and attentive. The large double doors leading from the fortress proper into the courtyard slowly opened, and some of the queen's handmaidens hurried out to rearrange the mats and smooth the cushions on the dais.

Now the trumpeters themselves appeared on either side of the door and at a signal raised their instruments and blew a piercing staccato blast. At that moment the queen appeared, smiling, leaning on Solomon's arm.

Bessim himself saw that the queen was seated comfortably before he signaled for the entertainment to begin. Jugglers, acrobats, singers, and dancers all followed one after another, eager to entertain the young prince and his mother, the queen.

Finally, when the thin sliver of the new pascal moon was directly overhead, the queen raised her hand for silence and announced that the time had come for the choosing of the maiden.

✳ ✳ ✳

From the moment he arrived at the feast, Solomon had looked everywhere for his little shepherdess. He studied each face and listened carefully to every conversation, but he didn't see her anywhere. Finally he turned to Bessim, who was sitting beside him, and asked, "Is everyone from the village here?"

"My lord," Bessim said with a wink, "they're either here or outside trying to get in."

Once again Solomon studied each face, but he saw no one he recognized. He had almost given up when, noticing a movement in the shadows behind Bessim, he saw the face of his little shepherdess. Now, however, she was totally transformed. Carefully applied kohl outlined her hazel eyes, her lips had been reddened, and silver filigree circled her forehead and cascaded down each side of her face turning her into a stranger he could hardly recognize. Even her robes were rich and luxurious, with no hint of the homespun worn by the little shepherdess.

Their eyes met—first in the puzzlement of recognition and then in mutual bewilderment.

"This is my daughter," Bessim said.

"Your daughter?" Solomon repeated.

"This lovely young girl is your daughter?" Bathsheba echoed, noticing Solomon's interest in her.

Bessim nodded and motioned for Shulamit. "Come," he said with pride. "Come, show respect to the queen and her son."

Shulamit moved out of the shadows and it was obvious her whole attention was focused on Solomon.

In a daze she knelt and lifted the queen's hem to her forehead, but her eyes kept returning to Solomon in amazement.

"So this stunning beauty is your little shepherdess," Bathsheba whispered, nudging Solomon. "She is indeed as beautiful as you described—but hardly the simple, barefoot girl you described to me."

Solomon didn't answer. He felt terribly betrayed and deceived. Why hadn't she told him who her father was? He was embarrassed to think that he had asked her to come to Jerusalem and live in his watchtower and herd sheep with him.

Why had she been out herding sheep anyway? And why had she been working in the vineyard? One thing was certain; his lovely pastoral dream was shattered. He was suddenly tired of the whole situation and was impatient to leave as soon as possible.

"She's my only daughter," Bessim confessed as she moved back into the shadows. "She's the delight of my heart, the apple of my eye."

"The very idea of disguising herself as a shepherdess and letting me think she had nothing to do but herd sheep," Solomon thought. He remembered some of the things he had said to her and felt his face burn with embarrassment. "I'm ready to leave as soon as possible. I hope I never have to see her again," he thought.

While Solomon was angrily mulling over the unexpected situation, Bathsheba had asked all the young maidens to come stand before the dais. She then whispered some instructions to Bessim.

With a smile he nodded his approval. "The queen has asked," he said, "that the young maidens each dance the Mahanaim. Mahanaim is the queen's village across the Jordan, and the dance is her favorite. Any maiden not knowing the dance will be excused."

Half of the maidens melted back into the crowd, and there was the muffled sound of sobbing. Now all eyes were focused on those maidens who were left.

Slowly, an old woman beat a steady rhythm on a drum with her long, gnarled fingers. Silence fell over the audience. The young maidens only listened at first; they seemed to be taking the rhythm into their supple bodies. Then, with a toss of the head, a raising of the arms, and a steady beating of their feet, they began to move in the stately, seductive Mahanaim dance.

Solomon was too disturbed at first to notice what was happening until he recognized the familiar beat and the long sliding side movement with the gyrating hips. He had seen his mother dance this dance many times within the harem circle and before his father on soft summer nights when they had been called to his apartments.

"Is it possible?" he wondered with growing curiosity, "that she's going to pick a maiden who, by her dancing, will be a perpetual reminder to my father of those happy nights?"

He was startled from his reverie by Bathsheba's request that Bessim stop the dance. Solomon was surprised, then shocked to see his mother stretch out her jeweled hand toward Shulamit.

"I would like to see you dance the Mahanaim," she said. "Come," she urged, "we want to see the daughter of Bessim, our most honored host, dance for our pleasure."

Shulamit shrank back with alarm and looked at her father, who stared at the queen in consternation. Then, collecting himself and realizing the inevitability of complying with the request, Bessim motioned for Shulamit to do as the queen had asked.

Someone in the crowd whispered, "I wonder if she even knows how to dance the Mahanaim." Others laughed nervously as she came out into the light and stood poised, ready to do as the queen had asked.

The old woman had slowed the beat to an almost imperceptible murmur. Now she began a low, whispering, hesitant beat that gradually grew into a strong, seductive throbbing. It spoke of wild passions barely held in check.

All eyes were on Shulamit as she moved away from the dais and gradually began to unfold like a flower opening to the sun. Solomon could see her face highlighted by the torches, and he was struck by its controlled, expressionless beauty.

Light played in bright patches on Shulamit's arms and hair. As her feet began to move in rhythm with the music, the bells on her ankle bracelets jangled pleasantly and her hips swayed and circled with all of the subtle temptation of the Mahanaim.

She looked so like a haughty goddess that Solomon couldn't imagine that this was the same girl who had milked the goats and laughingly played her flute on Gilboa. He had to admit that he had never seen even his mother dance more beautifully.

Slowly the beat quickened, and she danced with unabashed savagery. Faster and faster the drum beat out the rhythm, and Shulamit danced on—head thrown back, hair rippling unrestrainedly, hands on her hips, feet moving in the intricate patterns of the dance.

Solomon was so caught up in the rhythm and movement that he hadn't noticed his mother watching him. Actually, Bathsheba had scarcely glanced at Shulamit; her whole attention was focused on Solomon.

She knew him well enough to be aware of the fascination that lay dormant beneath his calm exterior. She missed nothing. She saw how his eyes lost their listless boredom the moment the girl appeared, noticed the pride with which he followed her every movement. Bathsheba had seen that same look often in her husband's eyes.

She made her mind up quickly. She couldn't risk all that she had worked and planned for over the years. Solomon *had* to marry someone of rank and importance or he could lose the throne to Adonijah. And someone of rank and importance wouldn't agree to be a *second* wife. No, it was clear: he must first marry someone like the princess of Rabbath-ammon, and then he would be free to marry any girl he liked.

The dance ended in a frenzy of beating drums, flying feet, arching arms, swirling hair, and gyrating hips. Then, as the music grew softer and more hesitant, with eyes lowered and hands folded Shulamit came to a kneeling position at the queen's feet.

While the astonished villagers pounded and stamped their approval, Bathsheba reached out and raised her to her feet. "My dear," Bathsheba said, "you were superb. I am honored to choose you as the king's new wife."

The villagers went wild with joy, but Solomon stood in stunned silence. Bathsheba smiled at him as though she had no idea of his anguish.

8

*S*hulamit flashed one fleeting look at Solomon and saw that he was both appalled and angry. It was obvious he wasn't pleased to discover that she was the daughter of Bessim.

Her father, however, was inscrutable. As soon as the queen had made her announcement, he grasped Shulamit's arm roughly and ordered Ramat to take her to his own room at the top of the tower.

As soon as they were alone, Shulamit turned to her mother, "Did you see? The prince's servant is actually the prince?"

"I noticed," Ramat said wryly. "This is all so strange."

"Mother, you *must* help me. You must speak to Father. I can't possibly marry the king!"

"It's an honor, Shulamit—a great honor. I think that your father was pleased."

Shulamit paced back and forth, becoming more and more upset. "Why did she choose me? She doesn't even like me. I know, I could tell."

"She *must* like you or she wouldn't have chosen you." Ramat had come to stand behind Shulamit and was gently adjusting her mantle and the silver filigree that framed her face. "I heard the queen tell your father that she wants to speak with you."

Shulamit whirled to face her mother. "Speak with me? Why? She frightens me."

Before Ramat could answer, there was boisterous laughter on the stairs. The door burst open, and Bessim strode into the room. "Well," he blustered, "my little girl has brought great honor to her old father. If we bargain carefully—"

Shulamit turned away as Ramat whispered, "She doesn't want to marry the king."

"Oh, well," he said, shrugging. "Perhaps it's better that she cry and sulk so that the queen will have to plead, be gentle, and bring more presents?" He rubbed his hands together in eager anticipation.

"I love someone else, Father. I can't possibly marry the king." Shulamit turned and looked at her father with wide, pleading eyes.

Bessim's face instantly darkened. His whole demeanor changed. In one swift movement he grasped her hair in his fist and glared at her. "You're talking like an ill-bred peasant. Don't you know such words make it look as though I haven't sheltered you, as though I've permitted you to run about the countryside, meeting young men and letting them have their way with you? Do you understand?"

Shulamit had never seen her father in such a fit of anger. "Yes—yes, I understand, but—"

Bessim let go of her hair but paid no attention to the tears welling in her eyes. "Now we must plan," he said, pacing the room. "We must have everything decided before you see the queen."

"Father, I—"

"Most important, I must be sure that when you leave my house you're really married to the king. We'll have to see what guarantees the queen will give us."

"But Father, when the queen first came, you weren't too pleased to have me chosen," Shulamit pointed out.

"That's all changed now. We will be *rich—really* rich—if we do this right." Bessim rubbed his hands together as he muttered plans and then rejected them.

There was the sound of running and a bit of shuffling outside. Then the door was flung open to reveal Nefer, Baalak, and Urim, who crowded in to hear what was being planned. Shulamit noticed that they were rather shy and subservient toward her. They looked at her as though seeing her for the first time. "Father—" Urim said. "What does this mean? Will our sister be a queen?"

"Of course, she'll be a queen. We'll have to see that this is agreed to before she leaves our house." Bessim stroked his short beard, bit his lower lip, and made another turn around the room.

"How can we do that?" Nefer asked, his eyes shifting from Bessim to Shulamit with a crafty expression.

"We'll have the queen sign an agreement," said Bessim, puffing out his chest, hooking his thumbs in his belt, and looking at all of them with smug satisfaction.

"An agreement can be lost or cancelled," said Baalak.

"Then we'll have her swear before witnesses," Bessim said confidently.

"They can be killed or bribed," said Urim.

"Well, what would you have me do?" Bessim was now in a torment.

"There's only one way to be sure," Baalak said, lowering his voice to a whisper. "Have the young prince stand in for his father and sign the marriage papers here. Then there can be no question of her position when she reaches Jerusalem."

"That's it, we'll marry her to the king right here!" Bessim agreed, sending his sons off to get a scribe.

* * *

Shulamit was in an agony of despair as her father and brothers planned her marriage. As soon as they all left the room, she flew to her mother. "You've always been able to manage him. Tell him I can't marry the king. I *can't;* I love someone else!"

Ramat held her daughter close for a moment and tried to comfort her. "This is different. Bessim has never had such an opportunity, and he's not a man to pass it up. It'll mean money, position, and influence. He'll not give that up even if it kills the rest of us."

"Mother, listen to me. You *must* listen to me." Shulamit's eyes were dark with anguish. "I love someone else. I—I've given myself to someone else."

The words struck Ramat like a whip. "O God," she cried, "not that, not *that!*" She backed off and held Shulamit at arms' length.

"Mother, Mother!" Shulamit said, pulling her close again and hugging her. "Not my body—I've never given anyone my body—but my mind and my heart belong to him."

"Thank God, thank God," her mother said over and over again as she clung to her weeping. When she was calmer, she pulled away and looked at Shulamit. "The prince's servant, that's the young man you've given yourself to." Ramat turned with sagging shoulders and covered her face. Her long hair fell forward over her shoulders as she began to weep again. "Your father will kill me if he discovers that I let you go with him across the mountain."

"Mother, don't forget the young servant has turned out to be the prince—and he loves me. I'm sure he'll think of something. He'll never let me marry his father."

"Then the servant really is the prince? I don't understand."

"I don't either, but I know they're both the same person, and that he loves me."

"Oh, my poor one," Ramat cried, turning away so that her daughter couldn't see the pity in her eyes. "You have so much to learn. Nothing is that simple."

"Wait—just wait and you'll see. He loves me; he really loves me."

Ramat began to cry again, and this time she didn't bother to cover her face or hide the tears. "My dear one," she said, "I wish I could spare you."

"Spare me?"

"I don't doubt that he loves you. But he's a prince. He won't be able to do what he wants. You must give up this fantasy and prepare yourself to marry the king."

Shulamit shook her head. "If I were the prince, I would find a way, and he's much braver and wiser than I am."

"Oh, Shulamit, you'll break my heart." Ramat was almost in tears. "You seem to have forgotten, the prince has a mother, and she wants you for the king."

"But if I tell her that I love her son and he loves me—"

"No, no, you must never tell her that. There's a rumor that the queen has made plans for the prince to marry a foreign princess. You mustn't cross her in this. She wants her son to have every qualification for the throne."

Shulamit had never seen her mother so distraught. "Don't worry, please don't worry," she pleaded. "The prince will think of something."

Just then there was the distant sound of a trumpet being blown and voices speaking hurriedly. There was no time to say more. Bessim flung open the door and marched joyfully into the room. "Well, my little treasure. It seems that the queen is just in the mood to accept anything I might demand. She's even willing to have the prince stand in for his father. Of course, the marriage can't be consummated now, but this will still be more binding than a bit of writing."

"Then the queen has agreed to everything?" Ramat asked fearfully.

"Everything. The only concession I had to make was that my daughter be ready to travel the day after the wedding."

"When must she be married?" Ramat asked almost in a whisper.

Bessim hesitated. "When the queen has agreed to everything I'm insisting on."

"My husband," Ramat pled with growing anxiety, "when is the wedding to be?"

"Tomorrow, the wedding must be tomorrow so the queen can be home by Passover."

Shulamit cried out in protest while Bessim, having said all that was needed, hurriedly turned and left the two women alone.

* * *

Bathsheba hadn't come out well in the initial bargaining with Bessim. Sensing that she was determined to have his daughter, he had taken advantage of the situation. Now she had sent for Solomon, and Bessim was to bring the girl. The ketubah would be signed, the gifts given, and then she could prepare to leave.

There was a timid knock on the door. "You may enter," Bathsheba said as she picked up and examined a lovely piece of Egyptian linen. She was trying to decide whether to put it with the things definitely going to Bessim or with the gifts that would be given only if necessary.

"My queen?" The serving girl bowed low and kissed the hem of Bathsheba's garment. "Your servant Jessica has sent word that the young prince cannot be found, and . . ."

Bathsheba impatiently pulled the hem of her robe out of the girl's hands and threw the piece of linen back on the pile of goods definitely going to Bessim. "Where can he be?" Her voice was no longer controlled and even. "He was there with all of us in the courtyard. We can't wait for him much longer."

The young maid backed from the room just as Jessica appeared. "Jessica, there's no time to plan or talk. I'll have to see them without my son," Bathsheba said, fingering the huge piece of amber she wore on a string around her neck.

"If you'll excuse my suggestion," Jessica said, "Prince Adonijah has arrived and asked to speak to you. Perhaps—"

"But you still can't find Solomon?"

"It didn't seem right to alert everyone."

"No, no, you're right. Bring Adonijah. He may be useful for the moment, but I won't let my son escape so easily. I'll still see that he stands in for his father. I don't want him dreaming of ways to take the girl for himself."

As if by some mysterious signal, everything began to happen at once.

First it was announced that Bessim, with some of his sons, was waiting in the receiving room. Then a scribe appeared to check the wording of the agreement. Finally Adonijah, almost breathless from being hurried up the back stairs, appeared. "I bring greetings from the king," he said, bowing low before Bathsheba.

"And he's well?"

"Quite well. I was told that you need some service?"

"I've chosen the girl," said Bathsheba, "and we're ready to draw up the agreements and give the gifts. Perhaps you'll be even better at bargaining than my son. I'm sure our host will want to press for every advantage."

"Of course, he will." Adonijah had heard as he entered the gates that it was Bessim's daughter who had been chosen by the queen. When it was laughingly explained that she had been chosen in spite of her father's attempt to disguise her as a shepherdess, Adonijah understood everything and was delighted. He could just imagine Solomon's frustration.

Bathsheba let Adonijah lead her to the dais, where she had spent so much time during the last couple of days. She was acutely aware that although Bessim and his sons were present, there was no sign of the girl. "He's going to be difficult," she thought with annoyance.

She took her time getting arranged before she signaled for Bessim to come forward.

Bessim bowed. "Your Majesty, my daughter is overwhelmed with the honor and is still being prepared by her maidens. Perhaps we could proceed with other matters?"

Bathsheba saw immediately that he wasn't going to bring the girl until he had extracted every benefit possible. "By other matters, you mean the gifts?"

"No, no," he protested. "I'm not a greedy man. There are no gifts than can requite me for the loss of my daughter."

"Of course. I understand, but it's getting late." She nodded to the steward, who opened the doors to the queen's apartment and led out the serving men. They came one by one, bringing gifts and laid them before Bessim and his sons. There were fine linens from Egypt, ointments and perfumes prepared in Arabia, jeweled slippers, and carefully worked rings and bracelets.

Out of the corner of her eye the queen noticed that through the whole procedure Bessim remained unimpressed, and she wondered just what he was going to demand.

"Your Majesty," Bessim said as he carefully clasped his hands behind his back, "you have provided well for my daughter, but for those who have cared for her and raised her—" He looked down and waited, while Bathsheba drummed impatiently on the cushion beside her.

"There's gold," she said, pointing to the open chests spread out before his sons. "Divide the gold between you and your daughter." She had expected Bessim to yield, but he stood his ground, feigning a humility she knew was false. It was evident that he wanted something more.

"Your Majesty, I have gold and spices and cloth from the caravans that pass by on their way to Damascus, but there's one thing you can give me and my daughter that I would treasure."

"I have no intention of giving more than the girl is worth," Bathsheba warned. "What is it you want?"

Bessim glanced sideways at the queen while his sons leaned forward eagerly. "Land—it is land I want. There's a vineyard owned by the king's family at Baal-hamon. I've heard that it's rented out and that 1,000 pieces of silver are paid yearly by each of the renters. I want only a small parcel, one man's portion for myself and one for my daughter."

Bathsheba frowned when the vineyard was mentioned. She knew it well. It belonged to Solomon and not the king. It would be a bitter blow to her son to lose the girl he wanted and a portion of his inheritance from his great-grandfather Ahithophel at the same time. "What a crafty man this Bessim is," she whispered to Adonijah. "He senses that I want his daughter for some special reason, and he's going to make the most of it."

"He's used to bargaining with traders. I would suggest you give him what he asks for."

"But the vineyard belongs to Solomon."

The queen didn't notice that Adonijah's eyes gleamed dangerously as he answered. "If Solomon were here, I'm sure that he would be glad to give it for the king's benefit."

Bathsheba wasn't ready to give in so easily. She remembered that there was an old custom called "right of examination." She remembered how it had been dreaded in her village. The girl, completely naked, was made to parade back and forth at the ritual bath until she was either accepted or rejected by her potential mother-in-law.

With a toss of her head, she turned to Bessim. "I'm giving you certain goods in exchange for certain goods. I will be at the local mikvah tomorrow to see what I would be buying with my son's vineyard." To her delight she saw Bessim flinch and draw back in confusion. She had obviously won an advantage over him for the moment.

Without another word, Bessim left with his sons, and Adonijah went with them. As Jessica closed the door, Bathsheba sank down among the mats and cushions on the dais. "Imagine, Jessica, he wants a vineyard for his daughter."

Jessica smiled. "Perhaps she's worth a vineyard."

"The vineyard's not mine to give. It belongs to Solomon."

Jessica didn't have time to answer; once again there was the sound of footsteps on the stairs. "Perhaps it's Solomon," she said hopefully.

Bathsheba leaned forward, ready to scold her straying son, but to her astonishment and delight she saw young Nathan standing in the dim light of the doorway. He was tired and dusty. It was obvious that he had ridden hard and was exhausted.

"Mother?" he said as he sank down beside her on the low dais. "I must talk to you alone."

"Now?"

"It's important." he urged.

"Then come with me to my rooms." Quickly she dismissed the serving women, and Jessica took the lamp down from its niche and led the way into the next room.

*　*　*

Ramat and some of the servants had finished winding and rewinding Shulamit's headpiece, trying on various combinations of jewelry, and choosing the most becoming robe when Bessim arrived. "Shulamit isn't to see the queen after all," he said.

He dismissed the servants and turned to Ramat. "Solomon has disappeared, and now the queen is demanding the age-old right of the mother-in-law to inspect the bride."

"Then you've asked for something that she's reluctant to give." Ramat knew well the ways of those bargaining for a bride.

"I've asked her for a portion of their vineyard at Baal-hamon. She says it belongs to Solomon, but she didn't actually refuse. It's only right that we should benefit. I'm losing a good worker, and they're gaining one who will produce sons for their name, not mine."

"And so—?"

"The queen's no fool." Bessim stroked his chin and grinned. "She's a good bargainer. I just wish I knew why she wants this so badly. Well, let her come to the mikvah, I say. She can only be impressed by what she sees." Bessim didn't wait for a reply but turned and quickly left the room.

Ramat was obviously shaken, but Shulamit seemed encouraged. "Don't worry, Mother," she said. "You'll see, the prince loves me. He'll think of some way to rescue me."

Ramat turned away. "Love is nothing, when pitted against strength and power. The prince wasn't even there with his mother. Bessim says that he's disappeared."

"I *know* he'll think of something, some plan." Shulamit's face was radiant with hope.

"My dear, you hurt me when you talk like that. He's a prince. He can't go against tradition and defy his whole family. Tomorrow you must go to the mikvah and accept the stares and indignities of the queen. I can hardly endure the thought."

"If I have to go, I'll go." Shulamit began to unwind the headpiece and remove the jewelry.

"You must promise that you'll do nothing to disgrace your father."

Shulamit laughed as she ran her fingers through her hair. "You're afraid that I'll try to look as repulsive as possible. You forget, I want her to like me. I want her to agree to let me marry her son."

"Please."

"Don't worry," Shulamit said reassuringly as she took her sandals off, wrapped them in her mantle, and handed the bundle to her astonished mother.

"Where are you going?" Ramat asked.

"My father said the prince had disappeared, and I think I know where he is. If I can find him, there'll be nothing to worry about." She hurried out to the steps and down to the slitted window that opened onto the walled garden.

Tucking up her gown, she wriggled into the narrow opening, then paused to enjoy the scene spread out before her. The new crescent moon was riding high, and there was a soft trickling sound of water running in the irrigation ditches. The pigeons were restless and murmuring to each other in the clay houses attached to the lower wall of the fortress. The odor of damp earth mingled with the rank, musty smells that were a part of the fortress welled up around her.

Behind her, in the house, she could hear a baby crying, and then a shrill tirade from one of her brother's wives. The wives never liked it when there was music and entertainment for the men and they were left to spend their evening alone.

She saw a lighted lamp move past one of the openings in the fortress and then reappear in the crumbling wing where she and her mother lived. She smiled, knowing that it was her mother going to bed—hopefully to sleep.

Once her eyes were used to the darkness, she could see the garden quite clearly and could make out a lone figure seated on the curb of the spring. Her heart bounded: it must be the prince!

Cautiously she edged the rest of the way through the opening and grasped the rough branch as she had done so many times before. Soon she was standing beside the spring. "So your real name is Solomon," she said softly as she sat down beside him.

"How did you know I was here?"

"I just knew where you would go if you were unhappy."

"You knew that I was unhappy?" he asked.

"That's quite obvious. Did you know that everyone is looking for you?"

"Why didn't you tell me you were Bessim's daughter and not a real shepherdess?" He turned and looked at her, his eyes dark with hurt and accusation.

"Why didn't you tell me you were a prince?" She noticed that he was startled by her question.

"All my life I had wanted to meet a real shepherdess, and there you were—just the way I had imagined."

"Oh, but I am a shepherdess. I also happen to be Bessim's daughter. But you—I thought that you were one of the servants. I was so brash with you. If I had known you were the prince—"

"You would have been cold and polite and distant. That's the way everyone treats me. I wouldn't have liked that at all." He picked up a stone and dropped it over the curb into the spring. They both watched it hit the water and then looking up, their eyes met and held.

"I may have been pretending that I was a servant, but I wasn't pretending when I told you that I wanted you to come back to Jerusalem with me." Solomon's voice was suddenly husky with feeling.

"And I suppose you were angry when I proceeded to spoil everything with my dance."

"Angry and frustrated."

"If two people love each other, there should be a way," she said softly.

"Actually, I've been thinking of ways. I've thought of everything, even the most impossible of possibilities."

"Please tell me."

"I've imagined that I could put you in front of me on my mule and we could ride into Lebanon and live in a cedar tree."

"Have you ever been to Lebanon?" she asked, amused.

"No."

"Perhaps it would be better, then, if you took me to the top of Mount Hermon, where we could live in a cave!" she teased.

"Where lions have their dens and panthers prowl."

"Is there no way then?"

"Before tonight I would have given up everything for you," he said, staring at the water. "But now—"

"You don't trust me, then?"

He paused. "In a palace it's not wise to trust anyone. I find it hard to trust."

There was a long silence, and when she finally spoke it was in a voice so soft she could hardly be heard. "But I love you. The *real* you. I don't know the prince, but the prince's servant I love with all my heart."

Solomon stood up, then hesitated. "You must understand; all my life there have been people who've told me that they love me, yet I don't really know what love is."

He glanced around at the garden. "Before tonight you were like this garden to me. A garden that was secret, hidden away from the rest of the world, with many rich and strange plants. A garden watered by a mysterious spring of living water that never stopped, even in drought. A garden I would never tire of and no one would take away. Now everything is changed."

Shulamit stood up. "I'm sorry," she said, "so very sorry." She reached out to him, but he drew back. "Neither of us can change anything," she said, "unless we both want it badly enough."

Solomon seemed momentarily touched by her sincerity. "I've learned that nothing lasts forever. Even hate and jealousy fade with time, and love is far more delicate than these."

"I couldn't live if I believed that love was so changeable," she said wistfully.

Solomon frowned and folded his arms as though resisting an impulse to reach out and hold her. "In my eighteen years I've come to understand many things. I trust no one completely, and above all I've learned to take the bad with the good. I gather the bitter myrrh with my fragrant spices, eat the honeycomb with the honey, and drink wine with my milk."

"Then tomorrow after the ceremony, it will be goodbye?"

"Yes."

There was a short pause. "Don't you find me attractive anymore?"

He had been looking down at the ground and idly kicking small stones around the spring. At her words he looked up and studied her face. "I find you not just attractive but beautiful." His eyes were warm and intimate. "I'm completely undone by one glance from your lovely eyes, even a single bead from your necklace is beautiful because you've worn it." He reached out and touched the large bead in the center of her necklace. "I've never felt this way before, but I'm sure that given enough time I'll recover."

Deliberately Shulamit unfastened the hempen cord that held her beads and carefully removed the bead he had touched. "Here," she said, holding it out to him, "keep this so that when you're in Jerusalem you won't forget me."

Reluctantly Solomon reached out and let her place the bead in his hand. For a moment he stood watching its colors change in the moonlight as he turned it first one way and then the other. "It won't be easy to forget you. For a while everything I see will remind me of you."

"Then you *do* love me?" Shulamit's voice was vibrant with relief.

"You must understand," he said, backing away, "that I don't even know the meaning of love. I'm charmed and fascinated by you, but this is something I can control at will."

"Then it's goodbye." She studied his face for any sign of relenting. There was none. She drew herself up proudly. "If you're right and love is so frail, then it will die, but if *I'm* right—well, we'll see."

For a moment his rigid composure seemed to melt; his eyes grew soft and gentle. "There's no hope for love between us. You will be married to my father, the king, and once you've been taken in to him, no other man can ever touch you."

"I know it all seems hopeless," she agreed. "We may never meet again or even talk again, but none of this dismays me if only you love me."

Solomon turned to her with a bitter laugh and caught her arms in his jeweled hands. "After tomorrow I'll be returning to Jerusalem, and I can assure you that whichever way I go—through Megiddo or Tirzah—I'll be seeing you at every turn. When I see Carmel's lofty crest, I'll see again your head held high and proud in the dance last night. At Tirzah it will be the soft slope of your nose and the angle of your chin I see. The young lambs as they graze or come up from the washing in pairs will remind me of your teeth, white and perfectly mated, with not one missing. Even the odor of pines will bring back the scent of your garments, the scent of Lebanon. So you see, I won't forget you soon, but I'll not dwell on it either. You must be like a sister to me."

Each word had caught like a bramble in Shulamit's heart. "Then let me be like a sister," she said, "but as long as I wear this sachet of dried flowers from En-gedi, I'll not give up hope." She took the fragrant pouch he'd given her at the cave and held it in her hand.

His hand closed over hers. "Wear it and remember what might have been."

For a moment he seemed to drink in all that he had come to love: her softly curving mouth, her luminous hazel eyes, the proud lift of her chin. He let his fingers run through her hair until they were held prisoner in the soft tangle of curls. "The king, my father, will be held captive in your tresses. You need fear nothing; he's both gentle and kind."

"I'm not afraid."

Once more his eyes were drawn to hers, and for a moment they held. "Goodbye, my little mountain shepherdess." The words were said with great tenderness as though it were more difficult than he had thought. He tilted her chin and she could feel him struggling to suppress the wild desire to kiss her. Deliberately he turned away, and minutes later she could hear him brushing hurriedly past the grapevines and pulling down the limb of the carob tree so that he could climb through the window. She thought she saw him pause for one brief moment and look back before he disappeared into the darkness of the fortress.

It seemed an eternity before the dripping of the water in the irrigation ditch and the cooing of the doves broke through to her consciousness. The moon, a slim sliver of light, now hung just above the eastern wall, giving the garden deep shadows with sparkling accents where it lightly touched the damp leaves.

The fortress was silent and completely dark. She was reluctant to go in. Out here, in the darkness, it seemed easier to cope with her pain. Here she was alone with her own thoughts and memories—and something else, something quite elusive, but something that she had always thought of as the presence of Yahweh, God.

Yahweh, if He wanted to, could change the most difficult circumstances and make them count for some good. She forced herself to remember the story of Passover. Just thirteen more days and they would be killing a lamb and thanking God for his deliverance of their people from slavery in Egypt. The smallest child could recount the whole story. For such a God it shouldn't be too difficult to arrange circumstances so that she could marry the man she loved instead of a king she had never even seen.

"O great God of the universe," she prayed, her hands upraised and her face tilted so that she could see the huppah of stars stretched over the court-yard, "teach me your will. Give me strength so that I won't lose faith even though I see all my hopes destroyed."

She stood for a few moments waiting for a sign, an answer. When there was none, she turned and walked toward the vine-covered door that led in through the sheepcote and up to her rooms.

The prayer was right. She had a feeling that she had prayed a prayer that Yahweh would find pleasing, and in that thought she found some comfort.

* * *

When Solomon climbed out of the garden, he went directly to his mother's rooms. To his surprise he found her talking to his brother Nathan.

"Nathan!" he shouted, as he brother turned, eyes shining, to embrace him. Though they didn't look alike and seemed to be diametrically opposite each other, still they were the best of friends. "They complement each other," people said who knew them well. "Solomon is like his great-grandfather Ahithophel, and Nathan is like his father, David—but perhaps with less penchant for battle." It was almost as though the two younger brothers, Shimea and Shobab, didn't even exist, since no one ever compared them in just this way.

"Come sit down," Bathsheba ordered her sons rather impatiently, since it was getting late. She had decided to say nothing for the time being about Solomon's absence, so she launched right into the news. "Nathan has come to tell us that the famine has grown worse in Judea and that your father, the king, has given the sons of Saul and his grandsons over to the Gibeonites. In some way this is supposed to stop the famine."

"Mother is trying to tell a long story all in one sentence so she can go to bed," said Nathan. With a quick glance at his mother, he proceeded to explain to Solomon all that had happened.

Solomon followed every word with intense interest. When Nathan had finished, Solomon spoke quietly. "The Gibeonites will kill them. Did my father know this?"

"At first he refused to hand them over, but Adonijah convinced him that it was the only thing to do."

"Adonijah convinced him?" Solomon's voice was harsh.

"Yes. It seems he made a special trip just to consult with him. He said the Gibeonites would never kill the young men because they had to live so closely as neighbors."

"It's his doing again. He wants them out of the way so that he'll have a direct line to the throne. He'll get at anyone who dares stand in his way. He's dangerous." Solomon was now pacing back and forth while Nathan sat crosslegged on the cushions beside their mother.

"Solomon, my son," Bathsheba pleaded. "Nathan has just come. Let's not discuss unpleasant issues."

"Father sent me to advise you not to return home through Taanach and down the ridge to the Benjamite territory. The Benjamites will be seeking revenge for whatever has happened. We must go around by way of Gibeon," said Nathan.

"I should have been home helping my father instead of dawdling at these women's parties," said Solomon. "We can't leave soon enough to suit me. I'd suggest early tomorrow morning."

"Solomon, you've forgotten the wedding tomorrow." Bathsheba rose and with a few impatient strokes straightened her robes. "After spending all this time searching, I'm not going home without the girl."

"It's been nothing but a lot of foolishness," Solomon said with disgust. "We all know why those old men wanted a young girl brought to our father."

"At least this way I'm getting to pick her." Bathsheba's tone was sharp. She was running out of patience with the whole subject.

"You can pick her and take her to Jerusalem, but I want nothing to do with the wedding or the agreement with her father. Nathan and I will ride on ahead."

"Solomon, listen to me." Bathsheba's voice had softened. "Her father is driving a hard bargain. First, he wanted some sort of binding ceremony here before we leave, and now he wants something more—something that belongs to you."

"To me?"

"He wants two sections of your vineyard at Baal-hamon—one section for himself and one for his daughter."

"My vineyard! That's impossible. How does he dare suggest such a thing? She's not *my* bride. I don't understand."

"I've told him that I won't make any decisions until I've examined the bride. She's not worth the vineyard. Tomorrow I'll go to the mikvah and make it so unpleasant for his daughter that he'll be begging me to take her on any terms. I'll demand that a check be made to see that she's a virgin. Any fault or flaw—"

"No, *no!*" Solomon said with such feeling that both Bathsheba and Nathan looked at him with astonishment. "You will *not* put her down and degrade her. She's worth many vineyards. Take it, pay her father what he asks, but let me go back to Jerusalem with Nathan."

A look of real compassion and tenderness swept over Bathsheba's face. She put out her hand and grasped his arm. "My son, I understand more than you know, but I can change nothing. I'll give the vineyard and I'll deal gently with the maiden, but you *must* stand in for your father tomorrow evening. You have only to sit with her and sign the final agreement with her father."

"Mother!" Solomon's face was twisted in anguish as he sank down into the cushions in utter dejection.

"Nathan, take care of your brother," Bathsheba ordered rather abruptly. "He's had a difficult time, but he'll recover."

"I don't understand." Nathan stood looking from his mother to his brother in complete confusion.

"He'll tell you, I'm sure. Don't think too harshly of me in this thing. None of us can have the world just as we want it." She started to leave but on impulse turned back. "This one thing I can do: I can give you permission to ride with him back to Jerusalem after the ceremony. We'll have our retainers to protect us, and Adonijah will be an adequate guide."

She glanced once more at her oldest son and noted that he still sat with his head turned away so that she wouldn't see the hurt. She quickly left the room without waiting for a response.

9

The mikvah in Shunem was on the northern side of the village. A small spring kept the rock-hewn basin filled to the upper steps most of the year. Caper plants grew out of the crumbling stone wall that surrounded the area, and an ancient pool reflected from its dull surface an old carob tree.

Usually the women of Shunem came to the mikvah only at dusk. However, in preparation for the wedding, everyone—mothers, cousins, aunts, friends—crowded in through the Zig Zag gate, laughing and joking and ready to celebrate.

Friends of the bride sang with high-pitched, shrill voices the ancient wedding songs. Babies clung to their mothers, and old ladies sat and told of horrible happenings and humorous foibles. They whispered of brides who had been found unsuitable and remembered occasions when a future mother-in-law had demanded her right to examine the bride as Bathsheba was doing now.

Mothers who just a few hours ago had wept because their daughters had not been chosen were now openly boasting of their good fortune. Everyone secretly feared for Shulamit. "How can she face a queen?" they whispered. "It's too much for such a young girl."

Word spread quickly that Shulamit was on her way and the queen would be arriving soon. Excitement and trepidation charged the air. The women whispered or giggled nervously as they glanced toward the Zig Zag gate.

In a daze Shulamit walked through the gate and settled herself on the stone bench beside the pool where she was to be anointed and perfumed. She looked around the familiar little courtyard with growing nostalgia. It was quite a charming place.

At one time, when the village was Canaanite, the empty niche behind the bench had held the statue of a goddess. In those days the spring had bubbled out directly into the pool. Now it flowed first into the deep, circular mikvah chamber hewn out of the rock by the early Hebrew settlers. "The water for the mikvah must be flowing from a spring or from rain water," the priests had declared.

"How happy I would be," she thought, "if only I were going to meet the prince as my bridegroom." Quickly she dismissed the thought. She mustn't let herself break down in any way. She must somehow survive this day, and then she would think about Jerusalem.

Several village women scrubbed Shulamit until her teeth chattered. She clutched the stone bench lest she be pushed into the pool. Oil was rubbed into her hands and feet while her mother combed and dressed her hair, winding the long tresses with ropes of small dried wildflowers. The women sang as they worked, taking turns at making up verses to go with a simple wedding melody. "Your lips are made of honey—yes, honey and cream are under your tongue."

The words they sang were like those she had heard and sung herself at numerous weddings. The verses always grew more and more daring, until some of the women would shout, "Shame, shame!"

"His left hand will be under your head, and his right hand will embrace you. He will be like a young deer grazing upon the mountain of spices."

The song went no further, for at that moment there was the distant sound of a trumpet signaling that the queen was arriving.

"My lady, we'll need this seat for the queen," one of the chambermaids said as she chose the stone bench that Shulamit was sitting on.

Once again the trumpets sounded, and Bathsheba appeared in the archway. Shulamit noticed everything about her: the thin gold circlet in her hair, the golden ornaments that dripped from her neck and sparkled on her arms and fingers, and most of all her self-confident and regal bearing. "Where's the young maiden I chose last night?" Bathsheba asked, making her way to the bench.

"I'm here, Your Majesty," Shulamit said, coming forward to kneel before the queen.

"You kneel very prettily, but if you're to be a queen, you must rise and let me see what queenly qualities you possess."

Slowly Shulamit rose and found herself looking into the steady, direct gaze of a woman who had a mature beauty that was unnerving.

"Walk back and forth before me here, and let me see if you walk as well as you dance."

Clutching her robe around her, Shulamit walked with as much dignity as she could summon.

"Your hands—let me see your hands."

Shulamit stretched out her hands before the queen and blushed with embarrassment that her nails were broken and her long, slender fingers were calloused from working in the vineyard.

"Take off the robe," the queen ordered. Now her eyes were like flint and her voice harsh.

There was a gasp of sympathy from the women and then silence as Shulamit slowly grasped the robe in one hand and let it slide from her shoulders. For a moment she stood flushed with embarrassment. Then, with a defiant toss of her head, she again walked back and forth—now dressed only in the sparkling gold jewelry she had been given by the queen.

"You're dark," the queen said, as though searching for some flaw to criticize.

Shulamit hesitated only a moment and then pushed back her rich black hair and smiled wistfully. "I'm tanned but beautiful, my mother tells me."

"What else does your mother tell you?" The queen was obviously taken aback by Shulamit's self-confidence.

"She says that I'm tanned and beautiful as the dark tents of Kedar."

For the first time Bathsheba struggled to stifle a smile. She regained her composure by taking a sip from a silver goblet she was handed. "In Jerusalem it isn't the fashion for ladies of the court to be so tanned."

"My brothers sent me out to tend the vineyards. It's their fault my own 'vineyards' have been neglected." Shulamit looked at the queen with straightforward honesty, and it was the queen who found it necessary to turn away. "Your father has bargained as though he were offering a peacock," she said, "and in truth he has brought me a brown quail."

"Your Majesty," Shulamit replied modestly, "a bird without feathers is not too different from any other bird. If I'm to wear the feathers of a peacock, perhaps I'll look like a peacock."

"You may put your robe back on. If your father and I can come to some agreement, we'll have the ceremony today and be ready to leave early tomorrow morning."

The queen stood up, looked around at all of them, then without another word walked out the gate with her ladies hurrying behind her. For a moment there was silence. Then again the trumpets were blown, and the village women could imagine the queen riding in her palanquin and her ladies following on donkeys through the narrow lanes to Bessim's fortress.

Since there was to be no immediate consummation of the marriage, the cleansing ritual in the mikvah wasn't necessary, so Ramat hurried to finish the final preparation. First, she outlined Shulamit's dark eyes with an ivory piece dipped in powdered lapis lazuli. Then, taking out her shell palette, she blended various powders and skillfully applied them to her eyelids. Finally she untied a knot in her mantle and put into Shulamit's hand an assortment of small seeds. "Chew these," she said. "They'll make your breath sweet."

Now several young maidens stood holding the elaborate clothes that the queen had left for Shulamit to wear. One stood with linen breeches decorated with embroidery and bangles, another with a heavy, ornate robe, and the third with a mantle trimmed with bright jewels and gold thread.

Shulamit took one look at the clothes and insisted, "I'm not in Jerusalem yet, and I can't abide these clothes." She rummaged in her mother's basket and drew out the clothes that she had worn to the mikvah. They were her best, and she felt comfortable in them.

The women gasped in disbelief. They had all wished for such clothes as the queen had left and couldn't imagine why Shulamit wasn't excited about her good fortune.

"I'm ready," she said finally. The women noticed that she was no longer a laughing, carefree young girl. She had matured almost overnight into a woman.

* * *

Solomon had finally persuaded his mother to move the time of the wedding up to early afternoon so that he and Nathan could be in Megiddo by nightfall. He arrived in the courtyard for the ceremony, dressed to leave as soon as his part in the ritual was completed. He was sullen and feeling at odds with everyone. Nevertheless, his training as a prince made it possible for him to seem charming and quite debonair at the ceremony.

Bessim led Solomon to the chair of honor under a colorful canopy and then, ignoring all rules of decorum, sat down in the seat beside him, declaring that before the bride arrived he wanted to have a few words with him.

"My lord," Bessim said, "there are many advantages that can come to both of us through this union of our families. My sons and I are a terror to our enemies, but we're loyal to our friends."

"And—?" Solomon was now curious.

"We can help you control the trade route that passes along the foothills of the coast from Aphek through the pass at Megiddo and then to Hazor and on to Damascus."

At mention of the trade route, Solomon's eyes grew alive with interest. He knew that it had been his father's wish, as well as Saul's before him, to control the sea route to Damascus. All the riches from Egypt passed this way, and tribute from these caravans could make a country rich beyond imagination. "And what will you ask from us?" Solomon replied, assuming a tone of cool detachment.

Bessim couldn't help chuckling. He liked this young man and the way he anticipated the next question. "With a strong army and chariots you could take the city of Gezer, and our people would be in control of the entire coastal route."

"You don't know what you're asking." Solomon said. "Gezer is walled, with a tunnel down to its water system. It can hold out for a long siege. My father's armies have never been strong enough to take it."

Bessim dropped the subject of Gezer only to launch out in another direction. "Your father is planning to build a temple in Jerusalem." His tone of voice was casual but his look was intense. Solomon knew that somehow this was an important question to Bessim.

"He's collecting the materials, but he won't build it," Solomon said. "If the prophecies are right, I am to build it."

"There will be much trouble when it's built if everyone is expected to go up to Jerusalem to worship."

"Why do you say that?" Solomon was now alert and listening attentively.

"Why not build it here in this lovely valley? It's right on the trade route to Damascus. Furthermore, the king will need trees from Lebanon. It would be much closer to bring them here." Bessim noticed that Solomon was still not convinced. "If you persist in placing the temple in those barren mountains away from the trade routes, who will ever want to go there? It will be a terrible waste. I can assure you that the northern tribes won't want to travel up into the mountains when there's nothing to draw them but a place of worship."

"Jerusalem may be difficult for pilgrims to reach," Solomon conceded, "but it's also almost inaccessible to armies. And don't forget Jerusalem lies directly between the King's Highway and the Way of the Sea, our two important trade routes."

Bessim looked with new respect at the young prince. "If you become the next king, what will you do?"

"You mean, what will I do that will be of help to you?"

Bessim laughed. "Of course, of course! That's always one's first thought."

At this moment there was the blast of a trumpet and the jangling of tambourines, and the queen and her ladies appeared. As Bathsheba settled into the chair Bessim had vacated, she breathed a sigh of relief. "Let's make this as short as possible," she whispered.

"I couldn't agree with you more," Solomon said, signaling for the ceremony to begin.

Solomon watched with growing apprehension as two scribes hurried into the room with their reed pens, ink pots, dusting sand, beeswax, and glue. Laying their materials out neatly on low tables before the dais, they sat down cross-legged on covered mats.

There was the usual reading and questioning of the ketubbah, but Solomon paid little attention to it. He was relieved to finally press his own seal, which he wore around his neck, into the hot beeswax on the parchment and end the official matter.

Bessim was ecstatic. "My daughter," he shouted to his friends, "is to become a queen of Israel, mother of princes, reconciler of north and south." As he shouted, he waved the agreement over his head in triumph. His face was flushed, and his hair curled in wet ringlets about his sweaty face. Impulsively Bessim knelt before Bathsheba, raised the hem of her robe, and kissed it. Then, clasping Solomon's feet, he bent his head to the ground and wept. "Today I'm a proud and happy man!"

"My friend," Solomon said impatiently, "our time is limited. We must proceed with the ceremony."

"Yes, yes," said Bessim as he struggled to his feet and beckoned Nefer to get Shulamit.

Solomon watched all of this with increasing interest. He could see that Bessim was a rough, sensuous man and the seven sons were ruffians who feared neither God nor man. He couldn't imagine how Ramat had survived all these years as his second wife, or how she had managed to raise such a lovely, unspoiled young girl as Shulamit.

He remembered Shulamit's saying that it was the brothers who insisted she work in the vineyards and herd the sheep. Once again the very thought of her stabbed him like the sharp thrust of a sword. He didn't want to see her again in front of all these people, see her dressed in bridal array with the traditional chalk-white makeup, carmine mouth, and darkly lined eyes.

For the first time, the full realization of what was about to happen crashed down upon him. Perspiration broke out on his forehead, and he found himself nervously drumming on the gaily patterned armrest. He knew that he couldn't endure seeing his little shepherdess transformed into the ordinary bride, nor could he abide the thought that by this very ceremony she would be lost to him forever.

He glanced at his mother and saw that she was eagerly watching for the bride. "She knows everything," he thought, "and she doesn't even care that it's my vineyard that has been given for the bride price or that Shulamit is someone special and unique to me. Any one of the other girls she has seen could have been taken to my father."

For a brief moment he felt bitterness and anger toward his mother. "In the past she has always chosen the best for me," he thought. "She's baked me raisin cakes in the middle of the night because I was hungry. She's seen that I've had the finest clothes and the strongest mules and studied with the best teachers. But now there's one thing that I really want, and she's deliberately plotted so that it will never be mine."

He could see the dancers approaching. Their piping voices and the happy jingling of their tambourines grated on his nerves. He shifted in his seat and glanced back at his mother. Their eyes met, and to his surprise she quickly turned away, as though she couldn't bear to see the expression on his face.

He straightened his shoulders and stared straight ahead at the whirling dancers and the gaily decorated palanquin that was being carried through the gate. "Perhaps when I see her in the outrageous trappings of a bride, she'll no longer be my little shepherdess, and I'll be cured of this strange obsession," he thought.

The dancers whirled in a veritable fever of pounding feet and twining arms, jangling bells, and shaking tambourines. The piercing sound of steady drumming numbed the senses. Solomon watched all of this as though it were a nightmare, and when the palanquin was finally brought to rest at the foot of the steps, he felt such revulsion that he could hardly remain in his place.

Bessim hurried forward, his sons around him, to push back the ornate curtains and help his daughter alight. First, a slim foot laced in brown doeskin appeared, then a figure veiled from head to toe in the sheerest of Egyptian linen emerged. Solomon breathed a sigh of relief. This lovely creature gliding toward him wasn't at all like his lovely little shepherdess.

Bessim took her hand and led her up the few steps to where Solomon and his mother stood; then both knelt. Gently Bathsheba stooped and removed the veil.

Solomon gasped, and Bathsheba was obviously astonished. The guests were equally surprised. Shulamit hadn't worn the costly garments given her by the queen. Instead, she was dressed in the soft, thistle-gray homespun of the local women. She stood before them with a lovely little cap of tightly woven wildflowers on her head, her hair blowing in rippling curls down her back. Her face was flushed and natural, with only her eyes outlined in the most subtle kohl.

Shulamit stood with her head bent, her eyes lowered in the respectful stance of the traditional bride, so Solomon was able to drink in every aspect of her natural beauty. For a moment he forgot the significance of the occasion and simply enjoyed seeing not a bride for his father but his own little shepherdess—only more beautiful and desirable than he had ever seen her before.

As in a dream, he took her hand as his mother indicated. He could feel its warmth and its firmness, and he remembered nostalgically how she had held his hand the first time he met her in the walled garden.

Only once, before she pulled her hand away, did she look up, and then it was not with reproach or cold disdain but with glowing, radiant love.

Solomon was inundated by waves of what was for him a strange new emotion. He tried to repress it, frustrated that he wasn't able to control his own feelings.

He glanced around and spotted Nathan standing nearby and motioned to him. "This will be over shortly," he whispered, "and then we can be on our way." He was determined to leave as quickly as possible, hoping that once out of Shunem he would be himself again.

Later in the ceremony, he again had to stand with Shulamit. The crowd in the courtyard went wild: shouting, beating drums, and rattling tambourines. The noise was so deafening that it seemed for a moment as if they were alone, shut off from the others by their own silence. As a symbol of the union that was to exist between Shulamit and the king, Bessim handed her a goblet of wine that was to be shared between them. Shulamit sipped from the goblet and then handed it to Solomon. Softly, so that no one else could hear over the commotion, she said, "Your love is better than wine."

Solomon acted as though he had heard nothing, but his blood raced and pounded in his veins and he drank slowly, looking down at the goblet. As he handed it back to her, their hands met around the stem and their eyes sought each other. He spoke impulsively, "As one of the white lilies that grow among the thorns, so are you, my love, among all other women."

As soon as the ceremony was finished, Bessim saw to it that Shulamit was quickly ushered to the palanquin and carried from the courtyard. Solomon stood without moving, following it with his eyes until it disappeared in the long afternoon shadows beyond the arched gateway. Then he turned to find Nathan and say goodbye to his mother.

By nightfall, God willing, he would be back in Megiddo and then on his way to Jerusalem. By the time he got home he would have shaken this madness and be himself again—or so he hoped.

As he left the courtyard, he even refused to mull over the disagreeable development that was to give Adonijah the privilege of leading the caravan with his mother and Shulamit back to Jerusalem. "It's all over now," he muttered. "She's now properly married to my father, and neither I nor Adonijah can think of her as anything but a sister."

*F*or the trip back to Jerusalem Solomon and Nathan had decided to disguise themselves as merchants. It would be safer that way. They would dress in plain clothes and ride mules, in the hope that they wouldn't attract attention.

Just as they were ready to leave, Bessim appeared in the now-deserted courtyard. "You must wait and all ride together," he insisted. "My daughter will need protection on the road."

"She'll be safe with Adonijah and the rest of the queen's entourage," Solomon said, thumping his riding prod against his leg impatiently.

"The queen said that she would be going back by an indirect route." It was obvious that Bessim didn't approve of their plans, but neither Solomon nor Nathan wanted to explain about the trouble they expected from the Benjamites. They looked at each other and then back at Bessim. Finally Solomon spoke. "The main roads should be safe at this time of year."

"On the contrary," Bessim objected. "The roads are alive with bandits now that the drought has become so severe. Let them go by way of the ridge road, where there are Israelite villages and friends."

Solomon could see that Bessim wouldn't accept anything but a proper explanation. "There's trouble brewing—trouble between the king and the princes of Benjamin."

"How do you intend to go, then?" Bessim hooked his thumbs in his wide belt and stood with his feet apart as he challenged them.

Solomon leaned down and drew on the hard-packed dirt of the courtyard with his riding prod. "See? Here is the pass at Megiddo. From there we'll follow the well-traveled caravan route that hugs the foothills until we come to Aphek, here. At Aphek we'll turn east and ride to Gezer at the head of the Ajalon Valley, which extends up to Gibeon and on to Jerusalem."

"Then the plan is for the two of you to ride ahead? Of course, you'll have to stay in the local inns while they'll tent out on the hillside." Bessim rubbed his chin and paced back and forth while the princes waited. "Let me send my own sons and some of my servants with your mother's caravan at least as far as Aphek. No one will dare attack when it's noised abroad that I've given them my protection."

Solomon was relieved. "I'll consider this a personal favor, and it won't go unrewarded."

Without further delay they mounted the waiting mules and rode single file with their small band of men through the narrow, cactus-bordered lanes of Shunem and out the large gate.

When they branched off onto the road leading to Megiddo, Solomon noticed some small potted marks left by the sheep in the powdery soil on their way to Harod's Pool. Despite all his resolve, he was struck with a powerful yearning to turn back and plead with his mother to change her mind. He pulled his mule over to the side of the road and waited until he had regained a bit of his composure.

*　*　*

They spent the first night at Megiddo, and early the next morning they were up and on their way to Aphek. The sun was shining, and Solomon was determined to put all that had happened at Shunem behind him.

The road hugged the foothills, avoiding the marshy waste that lay between the hills and the sea. A sandstone ridge prevented the water that coursed down from the mountains in the rainy season from flowing into the Great Sea, so it lay trapped and useless for anything but the nesting of birds in the tall reeds and the nurturing of a dense growth of oak trees. The reeds were prized for basket-making, the birds for food, and the oaks for fuel, but the land itself was considered useless and uncrossable. "It's easy to see why the men of Israel have never taken to the sea," Nathan said, pointing to the swamp.

It was frustrating to contrast the overabundant wetness of the marshland on the right-hand side of the road with the terrain on the left: dry, parched grass, vineyards with their new leaves already shriveled and dead, almond trees with withered brown blossoms, dusty olive trees with no new leaves and no sign of fruit.

The gloom of the surroundings unsettled Solomon in his resolve to forget the disappointment he had suffered. In fact, the further he traveled from Shunem, the more he was reminded of everything that had happened there.

Suddenly he stopped and listened. There it was again: clear and crisp on the morning air, the notes of a shepherd's flute. He looked up along the ridge to find the source, half-expecting to see his little shepherdess.

He felt for one awful moment that he couldn't bear the disappointment, and then he realized that Nathan had stopped and was waiting for him. Solomon was tempted to tell him of the strange emotion that had claimed his entire attention in Shunem and that even now gave him no peace. Just as quickly he decided against it. Nathan was happily married and had a young son he adored. It would be hard for him to understand the nature of such torment.

Solomon dug his heel into the mule's side, urging it on, steeling his heart against the sound of the flute and the memories it brought.

In this way they rode past Aphek and turned east toward Gezer, where they intended to spend the second night. Gezer was a powerful walled city still held by the Canaanites, and both Solomon and Nathan had forebodings about stopping there.

To their surprise they weren't even questioned at the gate. It was just before sunset, and the entire city seemed to be preparing for a special sacrifice to the god and goddess of fertility. The booths were closed, and most of the people had crowded out into the streets; others were clustered in doorways, and some leaned out the windows, as though waiting for something or someone. "Let's join them and see what happens," Solomon said as he dismounted.

"Your curiosity will get you into trouble some day," Nathan warned as he reluctantly dismounted and crowded in among the bystanders with Solomon.

"Did you notice," Solomon whispered, "that their fields are as poor and burned as our own, but they aren't starving? They can buy grain from Egypt with revenue they've taken from the caravans."

Though it wasn't yet dark, Solomon saw an advancing procession, preceded by lighted torches and clouds of incense. Priests dressed in elaborate attire led the group as they emerged from an arched lane and moved across the open square. Temple priestesses wearing only jeweled girdles and diaphanous skirts that revealed swaying hips, slim legs, and bare feet came next.

One of them stepped out of line and looked into Solomon's eyes with a bold invitation. "You are welcome. Just follow the procession," she whispered.

Solomon was strangely stirred by her hypnotic look, but Nathan was impatient. "I've seen enough," he said. "Let's go and find a place to spend the night."

"No, let's follow them and see what happens," Solomon urged as the last of the procession turned a corner and was lost to sight.

"It's an abomination. We have no need to see such things," Nathan objected.

Solomon smiled. "Don't be so serious. Of course it's an abomination, but who in all of Israel knows what that really means. Here," Solomon said, turning and handing the bridle of his mule to one of the young men. "I'm going to go and see what this is all about."

Quickly Nathan grabbed his arm. "If you're determined to go, I'll have to go with you. I can't let you go into that foul pit alone."

"Foul pit?" Solomon laughed. "You must be exaggerating!"

Nathan turned to the rest of the men. "Go find a place where we can spend the night. We'll be back later."

✳ ✳ ✳

The two of them hurried up and around the corner, pushing through the crowds of people all going in the same direction. There was an air of excitement and festivity, with an undercurrent of something very much akin to fear.

Up ahead the singing rose with increased intensity. The tambourines jangled in a cacophony of sound, until suddenly they were silenced by the shrieking, wailing, strident call of the ram's horn. As the sound filled the narrow lanes, the people began to run. Solomon and Nathan followed the crowd to the open square where the procession had ended before some large phallic-shaped stones held upright by bases sunk into the ground. One larger stone had a roughly hewn altar at its base. It was before this altar that the priests and people gathered.

Solomon edged his way through the crowd until he could see what was happening at the altar. For some minutes he had been aware of a muffled cry, and he had expected to see the sacrifice of a lamb, but as the priest moved back, his raised knife still dripping blood, Solomon witnessed a horrible sight: a newborn babe lay on the altar, obviously dead, while the crowd clapped, sang, and shouted their approval.

Solomon stood transfixed with horror as the priest handed the limp form to a young man who placed it in a jar and quite casually covered it with a lid. Then both he and the young maiden beside him moved forward to kiss the large upright stone, making way for another young couple to move up to the altar with another small form.

When the shofar was again blown, Solomon knew without looking what was taking place on that altar. His blood ran cold and his heart throbbed with the horror of it all.

"Have you had enough?" Nathan asked.

"How ghastly! I wouldn't have believed it."

"Take a good look," Nathan insisted, "so that you won't be deceived in the future by beautiful dancing girls and elaborate processions. Those tall pillars represent the male gods of fertility, and nothing is too good to be sacrificed to them."

"But the children," Solomon asked. "Why the children?"

"We don't really know because it is a well-kept secret. Some who understand their customs have said that the firstborn child is to be sacrificed to the gods because it may very well belong to the gods."

"Why the firstborn?"

"Do you see the maidens dressed in white that followed the procession?"

"Yes."

"It's said that they're virgins who come to worship at the temple before their marriage. No man wants to marry an infertile wife, so if she doesn't conceive during her stay in the temple of the gods, she doesn't marry but stays here as a priestess. If she *does* conceive, it's logical, or so they say, for the child to be returned to the gods."

Solomon couldn't hide his aversion to the whole scene. It had changed from a pleasant lark to a frightening experience. He was ready to leave when the same priestess singled him out again. "I see that you're strangers here. Come, I'll show you the Speaking Place, where the priests receive answers from the gods."

"The Speaking Place?" Solomon had regained some of his composure and was again curious.

"Yes, it's our holiest place. The Hebrews have what they call the Holy of Holies in their tabernacle, but there's no voice that speaks from it. Only *we* have the voice. Only *our* god speaks."

"That's impossible," Solomon said. "No god speaks and answers people in a regular voice like a man."

"Come and see," she invited, smiling.

"I'm going," Solomon said. "There has to be some trick."

"Not necessarily," Nathan said, "I've heard that some of the priests of Baal can make a stone talk by calling up the demon of the stone."

Solomon turned to the girl. "My brother and I will come, though we don't believe that your god really talks."

Without another word the girl pushed back some bushes, revealing a door that opened into a cave and steps that led down into the dark and shadowed depths below.

Nathan drew back, but Solomon was more eager than ever.

The cave was large and dark; the lamp revealed nothing but an altar in the middle of the room. The priestess pointed to a small round hole in the far wall and said, "Ask the god any question, and he will answer you quite plainly."

"We're forbidden to ask anything of Baal," Nathan said quickly.

"Then I'll ask for you," the young priestess said, smiling slyly at Solomon. She bowed low before the opening and began to chant so softly that they could hardly hear her. "Tell me, O Baal, what does this young man fear?"

There was an eerie silence; then strange winds seemed to blow through the cave, and finally there was a ringing in their ears as a voice projected itself through the opening and ricocheted off the solid rock walls. "Death—he fears death," it said.

Solomon staggered back as though he had been hit. He rubbed his hands over his eyes, and Nathan had to take him firmly by the arm and insist that they leave immediately.

* * *

When they were out of the cave and hurrying away from the High Place, Solomon turned to Nathan and asked, "How could they have faked such a thing? We could see it was solid rock, with no opening other than that small hole."

"I don't know. I only know that God has forbidden us, as sons of Abraham, to get involved in these things."

"It can't hurt to investigate and ask questions," Solomon insisted. The two young men went back to the inn and sat for a long time on the rooftop, arguing under the stars about what they had seen. Nathan advocated total avoidance of such rites and practices. "It's not of God," he said repeatedly, "so it must be of Satan and his demons—and that means it's dangerous."

Solomon didn't disagree, but he couldn't see the harm in learning all that he could of just what was happening, and how.

It was late when the two finally went inside. They said goodnight and both went immediately to bed, but Solomon found that his sleep was troubled by weird voices and fearsome apparitions.

* * *

Shulamit didn't have long to grieve or to ponder the strange circumstances she found herself in. It took most of the night to gather her belongings and prepare for the trip to Jerusalem.

She was relieved when Bessim decided that her mother should go with her. Life would be so different in Jerusalem. She couldn't imagine a life that didn't involve some kind of work. What would one do without sheep to tend and green growing things to nourish?

Just as the sun rose she heard the sound of hurried footsteps, and then her door swung open. "Shulamit," her mother cried, "you haven't been down to see your father."

"I'm going, Mother," she said, slowly and lovingly fingering the worn boards of the door before closing it.

Her father was already down in the courtyard seeing that everything was packed and ready. He drew her to him and kissed her on both cheeks as though she were one of his sons. Then, embarrassed, he called for the queen's steward to bring Shulamit's camel. She had noticed her brothers standing together, looking at her with obvious envy for what seemed to them her unbelievable good fortune.

With one agile movement she stepped up into the howdah. The curtains were closed, leaving her encased in a soft cocoon of brilliantly decorated pillows and curtains.

With a grunt and a groan, the camel swayed forward onto his feet. The whole nest of pillows shifted dangerously, and for a moment Shulamit forgot all else but the dreadful lurching and swaying.

Once well upon the road, however, she parted the curtains to look back on Shunem. It looked like a toy village, and the crowd of people who had followed them out of the village looked no bigger than ants. How strange it seemed to single out her father and see how small he looked. He had been so important to her. The village was all she had ever known, and now it was getting smaller and smaller. She knew that soon she wouldn't be able to see it at all.

Gradually she watched the world recede until she could barely make out the guardtower and vineyard at the base of Mount Moreh, and the path that led up into the pine forest. How fast everything had changed. It was just a few days since she had gone with Solomon to find the cave of the witch of Endor and they had found each other instead.

She quickly closed the curtains and settled back among the cushions. She had tried to forget him, to put him out of her mind, but always she saw the vision of his smile, felt the touch of his hand, heard the sound of his voice as he told her he loved her. "I'll not give up yet," she thought. "In Jerusalem, anything is possible."

That evening, when the caravan came to a stop in the foothills some miles from Aphek, Shulamit found to her surprise that the tents were already pitched and the evening meal was being prepared. A servant told her that fresh garments, soothing lotions, and a fine array of Egyptian cosmetics awaited her in the queen's tent. She wondered if she would see the queen or have to talk to her. What would she say?

Somewhat fearfully she sought out the queen's tent. An older woman with kind eyes appeared in the soft glow of a clay lamp. "I'm Jessica," she said. "You'll find the queen waiting to share her evening meal with you as soon as you're ready."

Jessica led her to a portion of the queen's tent that seemed to have been partitioned off just for her. There were chests full of jewelry and of fine robes with mantles of every texture and color. Standing in the shadows were the serving women waiting to transform her into a lovely creature that would be comfortable dining with the queen.

"You don't have much time," Jessica warned as she let the tent flap fall into place behind her.

The minute Jessica was gone, the maidens all began to talk at once. "Shall she wear white, or is the queen wearing white?" one of the women asked as she pulled gowns from the chest and draped them over the cushions.

"Does the queen want us to lace her hair with jewels, or should she wear a simple mantle?" asked another. Shulamit was amazed that they all seemed to see her as some new object that was to be dressed and groomed for the queen's pleasure.

* * *

"I'm sure that the ride has been hard for you," the queen said, breaking off a piece of bread and dipping it in the rich, warm sauce.

"Not really, Your Highness," Shulamit answered as she tore off a piece of bread. She ate hesitantly, fearful lest she do something wrong.

"Come, come—you'll starve. We're not being formal tonight; it's just the two of us, and we can do as we please. Later Adonijah will come sit with us to while away the long evening and make plans for tomorrow."

For the first time since they met, Shulamit saw the queen as a natural, charming person. She liked the way Bathsheba folded her sleeves back and reached for the dried dates just as her own mother might have done—only with the queen there were bracelets jangling and rings flashing and the faint, lovely odor of jasmine that perpetually and rather mysteriously filled the room around her.

* * *

The long meal was finished, and the servants hurried to remove the trays and mats in preparation for Adonijah's visit. When he arrived, it was easy to see why the queen had so eagerly awaited his coming. From the moment he lifted the tent flap and entered, he looked at the queen with obvious admiration.

He came forward and bowed, exchanging the usual niceties. Only then did he seem to notice that Shulamit was present. "What a treat the king has in store for him," he said, looking her over calculatingly. "It isn't every wife who would bring her husband such a tempting morsel."

"I find it silly for any woman to waste her time being jealous of other women." Bathsheba smiled as she gathered up choice pieces of dried fruit and placed them before him.

"You'll never know jealousy, my queen. You're one of those charming people who are above such things," Adonijah said.

Bathsheba was obviously pleased and flattered. She patted a pillow beside her, and Adonijah sat down. "Since you weren't at the parties, you haven't met Adonijah," Bathsheba said, looking from one to the other. "He's the son of one of David's other wives. You'll meet her; her name is Haggith."

"Shulamit and I *have* met," Adonijah said, winking at her intimately before turning his attention back to Bathsheba. "How fortunate my father is to have such a wife. If I had ever been loved by one woman as you have loved my father—"

116

"You *do* seem to have the worst luck, but then you're always taking chances, doing foolish things that break your father's heart."

Adonijah stiffened. "My father has never really loved me."

"Now, now," Bathsheba admonished. "He's always said that he spoils you, and I think he's right."

"I suppose he *has* spoiled me in a way, but that doesn't mean he loves me." He looked down at the fruit Bathsheba had selected for him and picked the plumpest fig.

"What more do you want him to do? How could he prove his love?" she asked.

"That's easy," he said, holding the fig ready to eat between his thumb and fingers. "If he loved me, he would take me into his confidence, brag about my intelligence, and forgive me when I make mistakes." Once again his eyes lingered on Shulamit until it made her feel uncomfortable.

"He's always forgiving you for some mistake. You'll have to admit that," Bathsheba said.

"He *says* he does, but I doubt it."

"Come now, we mustn't be so gloomy in front of the new bride. She'll get a bad impression of her new husband. Really, Adonijah, you have to admit that he's the most lovable and loving person imaginable."

"I'm sorry." Adonijah bent forward so he could speak directly to Shulamit. "I'm afraid that going home has brought up a lot of unpleasant memories for me." Again his eyes had that disturbingly intimate look.

Before she had time to respond, Bathsheba had summoned Jessica. "This has been a long day for the new bride, and there will be a tiring ride again tomorrow. She must get to bed early."

Shulamit rose and bowed low before Bathsheba, but as she took the queen's hand and raised it to her lips she had a glimpse of Adonijah. He had a cold, calculating smile on his face, but more puzzling was his hungry, lustful, speculative look. It frightened her. She bowed hastily to Adonijah and then hurried after Jessica through the curtain that separated her section of the tent from the queen's.

✳ ✳ ✳

Shulamit found her mother squatting by the glowing coals that still burned in a hole dug in the sandy floor of the tent. Several maidens wrapped

117

in goat-hair blankets were sleeping around the mat that was obviously to be her bed. Shulamit wrapped a long, seamless wool piece around her shoulders and went to sit beside her mother, spreading out her hands over the coals to get them warm. "The queen doesn't seem to mind that I'm going to be her husband's bride. Isn't that strange?" Shulamit whispered.

"It *is* strange, but perhaps since he has so many wives, she's resigned to the situation," Ramat reasoned.

Again there was silence as they listened to the soft murmur of voices from the other side of the curtain. Shulamit added several pieces of charcoal, and they waited to see if they would catch fire. Finally she leaned over and whispered, "The queen thinks it's all settled, but she's wrong. I have other plans."

"Oh, Shulamit, please don't be foolish. You're married to the king now; you must remember this."

Shulamit stood up and stretched, then smiled as she helped her mother to her feet. "Don't worry, Mother," she whispered. "I have your faith and Father's spunk. I'll find a way."

*T*he next morning Solomon and Nathan rode out of Gezer and headed up the Ajalon Valley in complete silence. To Solomon it seemed there was a gloom that hung over everything. It was caused not only by his disagreement with Nathan but by the realization that the vineyard of Baal-hamon was just a short ride up the valley. There was no way around it; he would have to notify the caretakers that two of the sections were to be given to Bessim.

The vineyard had suddenly come to represent all the frustration and heartbreak he had suffered in losing Shulamit. Of course she wouldn't get the share Bessim was claiming for her; the whole thing would go to that greedy, grasping father of hers.

Solomon shifted uneasily in his saddle and gripped the reins, urging the mule to trot briskly. He wanted to get this business over with as soon as possible.

It still stung him to think that it had been his own mother who had done this to him. How could she have picked Shulamit for his father when she knew how he felt about her? How could she not have realized that the throne meant nothing to him without love?

Turning at a bend in the road, Solomon caught the first glimpse of his vineyard. It stood out lush and green, in the midst of the parched and lifeless slopes that rose on each side of the valley around it. His great-grandfather Ahithophel had been given this land by King David for bravery in fighting the Philistines, and he had held it by fending off all contenders until it was recognized by everyone as his. "How disgusting," he thought, "that I, his great-grandson, should lose it without unsheathing my sword."

Seeing his caretaker coming out to meet him, he squared his shoulders and went to give him the news. If he hurried they could be back on the road to Gibeon before noon.

* * *

The visit to the vineyard turned out to be even more difficult than Solomon had imagined. The caretaker had been pleased to show him that because of underground springs, his vines hadn't suffered from the drought. He was able to see for himself that there were small new leaves pushing out on the stems, and the tiny green nubs that would later develop into grapes were plentiful. It was obvious that this valley, hidden away in the foothills, was worth all the effort that his great-grandfather had exerted to gain and hold it. Again he felt the hot flush of anger as he remembered the ignoble way in which he had been forced to give up a part of it to Bessim.

Impulsively he drew out the bead that Shulamit had given him and rolled it between his thumb and fingers. It surprised him to realize how much he prized the gift. He unfastened the cord that held his signet stone and added the bead. He didn't want to take a chance on losing it; it was all he had to remember her by.

As he tied the cord back around his neck and felt the coolness of the bead on his chest, he realized that it would have been worth the entire vineyard and more if Shulamit could have been his.

When his business with the caretaker was finally completed, Solomon signaled his men to mount. They could still make Gibeon by dusk if they hurried. He tapped his mule with his prod and relaxed as the animal surefootedly led out along the trail.

* * *

Back on the main road Solomon became more and more conscious of the devastating effects of the drought. Every field he passed had nothing but a few stunted spears of barley. In a good year the crop wouldn't have been considered worth harvesting. He wondered if it wouldn't be a sacrilege to offer such meager sheaves on God's altar at the upcoming Feast of Firstfruits.

If there was no rain by Passover, the tension would be unbearable. The wheat seed wouldn't sprout, and there would be no harvest to celebrate fifty days hence on Shavuot, the day on which they celebrated the giving of the Law of Sinai and the harvesting of the wheat. It came exactly fifty days after Passover. "It's a frightening thing to be king," Solomon muttered to himself as he thought of his father and the constant crowds outside the palace, weeping and begging him to do something.

Solomon made a clicking sound and tapped his mule's flank, urging him out onto a ledge that overlooked the city of Gibeon. Nathan pulled up short beside him and was the first to speak. "That's strange," he said. "There doesn't seem to be anyone out in the fields or on the walls."

"The gates are open, but I don't see the guards," added Solomon. "I don't like the looks of it."

"We have nothing to fear from the Gibeonites, but if we met the Benjamites after dark it would go hard with us. They're just over that hill."

Nathan nodded. "It's all Saul's fault. He seems to have just marched in and taken the city, torn down their High Place, and then erected the Tabernacle on the same site. Of course the Gibeonites have wanted revenge. I've even heard that the Gibeonites claim Saul tried to exterminate them."

"I don't doubt that he did. You can see that Gibeon lies right in the middle of his territory, and the land is the best in this area—far better than Saul's barren hill."

Ever since Solomon could remember, the tabernacle had stood near the great Pool of Gibeon just inside the southern wall of the city. This was where they had come to celebrate the feast days and where they had brought their sacrifice and peace offerings.

Most of the worshipers had all but forgotten that at one time the Canaanites had celebrated the rites of spring here with lusty abandon and wild orgies that sometimes ended in human sacrifice. The great pool, now used to furnish water for the tabernacle, had once yielded water for the priests of Baal. Even the groves where Israel's tribesmen gathered for the communal meal following a sacrifice were once dedicated to Astarte.

Now Solomon wondered if that had been the reason his father had so wanted to build a new temple in Jerusalem. Although the Lord had forbidden him to build it, there had been no objection to his building a shelter for the Ark of the Covenant. The ark had been lost for twenty years, and David had been the one to finally bring it home.

There had been no thought of returning the ark to the tabernacle at Gibeon. Instead, David built a shelter for it by the Gihon Spring just outside Jerusalem's walls and ordered a small altar built for the morning and evening sacrifice. Many people had been drawn to worship at the spring. They enjoyed the singers, tambourines, flutes, and even trumpets, all bringing to life the songs that David was continually writing.

Nathan broke the silence. "Something has just occurred to me—something really frightening."

"What do you mean?" Solomon asked.

"Is it possible that the Gibeonites would sacrifice Saul's sons and grandsons on the old altar to appease the earth gods and stop the famine?"

Solomon looked at him with wide, startled eyes. "The Gibeonites are capable of doing anything for revenge, and perhaps the famine has hit them as hard as it hit us." Without another word they rode back to where their men waited and then headed down the road that led to the gates of Gibeon.

* * *

It was late when they rode up to the main gate of the city. They were amazed to see that there were no men standing in groups discussing the business of the day. No merchants bustled in and out. Furthermore, the seats of honor just inside the gate were all empty.

An old blind woman sat on a straw mat under an awning and urged them to let her tell their fortunes. Two women passed with empty water jars on their heads, and a young boy led some sheep through the deserted square.

"Where is everyone?" Solomon asked.

"I don't know, but there's something sinister in the atmosphere. I don't like the feeling in this place." Nathan dismounted and handed his mule's bridle to one of the serving men, then waited for Solomon to join him. "What do you think we should do?"

"We'll go to the tabernacle and ask the priests," Solomon decided. "They'll know what's happening."

The streets were as empty as the square had been. Here and there emaciated children begged for bread; old women huddled in corners with their faces turned to the wall in hopeless dejection. It was obvious that the famine was as bad here as it was in the cities of Judah.

Gradually they became aware of a fear and sense of doom in the air. The shutters on the windows were closed, and the doors were barred. It was as though the people were preparing for battle or for an invasion. Nathan was right; there was something foreboding about the silence. Something worse than famine had left its blight.

With a sudden whir of wings, a succession of dark shadows moved over the path in front of them. "Look Nathan; vultures." The large, ugly creatures had lighted on a wall just in front of them and sat eyeing them, their mouths open and eyes glinting.

Both Solomon and Nathan felt a strong impulse to leave as fast as possible. There was death in the air. Solomon flung a stone at the hated birds and watched them rise and circle over their heads and then fly off in a southeasterly direction, toward the High Place.

"With this drought even scavengers must have a hard time finding food." Nathan forced his voice to sound matter-of-fact.

"Let's hurry and finish our business. I want to get out of here." Solomon strode ahead up the lane. Neither one spoke until they reached a turn that would lead them out at the section near the grove where the tabernacle stood.

"What can be happening?" Nathan said, pointing toward the opening at the end of the lane. Crowds of people stood watching something with a deadly fascination. Men were in the trees, standing on the walls, and even looking down from the rooftops of the houses that bordered the grove; high overhead circled large birds of prey.

They stopped and listened. At first there were no sounds except for the crying of a child in one of the courtyards and the banging of a loose shutter in a sudden gust of wind. "Shh, quiet," Nathan warned. "I heard something."

They stood with every muscle tense, listening for the strange, haunting sound both of them had heard. When they didn't hear it again, they relaxed and moved slowly forward. Suddenly Solomon clutched Nathan's arm. "There it is again!" he said.

This time there was no mistaking the sound. It was hardly human, and yet it was a sound they had both heard often in the court of the queens—a sound that had the power to churn their blood and make their hair stand on end, even now that they were grown. "The lament for the dead—it's the lament for the dead," Nathan whispered, his voice hoarse with dread.

As in a nightmare they went forward, knowing that they couldn't spare themselves from the sight that awaited them. Suddenly through the lifeless, drought-stricken branches of the trees they saw the bloody, beaten body of a young man impaled on a spear whose shaft was firmly wedged in the ground. His clothes, which were half-torn from his naked legs and arms, hung in shreds. His hands and feet moved in aimless circles as the wind whipped and tore through the grove.

As though on a whim the wind changed, and the terrible odor of rotting flesh stung their nostrils and gagged them; still they couldn't turn away. Instead, they covered their noses with the edge of their headpiece and pressed forward to where they could see more clearly.

Solomon gasped and clutched Nathan as he saw that it wasn't just one young man but many. To their utter dismay they recognized them as the sons and grandsons of Saul. The two sons of Saul were hanging in the very center. Their faces were matted with blood, and their robes that had been carefully embroidered by their mother were now torn and caked with mud and flapped about their lifeless bodies in shreds. It would have been impossible to recognize which was the elder if not for the great ring with the signet of Saul still on his finger.

Their eyes took in every detail of the horrible sight; they spared themselves nothing. Solomon's hands shook as he wiped the sweat from his brow, and Nathan's knees threatened to fold under him.

There was a movement of circling shadows and, with a great whir of wings, a huge vulture dropped through the fetid air and landed with talons outspread on the dark curls of the eldest son's head. At the same instant they heard a low, animal like rasping sound that seemed to come from the very depths of the earth, and an old woman covered in ashes and wielding a worn mantle rose up out of the rock itself.

The mantle snapped and tore at the hideous bird until, with an angry cry, he shot up above their heads to join his fellows circling the open space and the great rock. Mingling with the cry of the bird was the wild, uncontrolled keening of the old woman.

She stood before them with head back, hair blowing unheeded in the wind, and watched the birds until they settled on the ramparts of the wall. Solomon saw her frail hands struggle to pull the pieces of the torn robes about the eldest son's bare legs, then grasp his limp, unfeeling hand and hold it tenderly against her cheek.

In all this time she never looked at anyone, but the eerie keening rose and fell, mingling with the blowing wind and slowly dying only when she sank again, exhausted, to the ground.

Solomon, followed by Nathan, pushed toward an opening in the crowd. He had seen more than he could endure; now he just wanted to get away from the terrible sight. All happy memories of feasting in the grove and playing on the great rock were gone. He wondered if he could ever come to the tabernacle without remembering the horror of what had taken place here.

Only later, when they were back in the large open market before the gate, did Solomon speak. "It was Rizpah," he said, looking straight ahead and swallowing hard.

"It was so quiet. The people didn't say anything; they just stood there. I think they were ashamed. Rizpah made them ashamed," Nathan said.

"Of course they were ashamed. Imagine a frail little woman doing a thing like that."

Solomon made a quick decision. "Come on. We're not staying here tonight." It would be dark before they reached the valley below Gibeon, and quite late before they reached home, but now they could think of nothing more important than being back within the safety of Jerusalem's high walls.

As Solomon urged his mule along the narrow mountain path, the terrible scene kept reappearing over and over again in his mind. He could see the young men hanging there, and smell again the putrid odor of decaying flesh. Far more horrible was the thought of Rizpah, alone and unprotected, braving the men of Gibeon, wild animals, and fierce birds in order to shield the dead bodies of her sons.

Pitiful beyond all else was the most tender way she had held her son's limp and mangled hand against her cheek. Solomon could scarcely endure it. There was heaviness in his chest that wouldn't go away, and his eyes bore into the darkness of the road ahead of him wide and troubled.

They moved out of the pine forest and for the first time saw the crescent moon above the evening star. It seemed impossible that the night could be so beautiful after such a day.

"Nathan," Solomon said softly as his brother rode up to join him. "Nathan, it seems to me that of all the loves a man might find in the world, he'll never find a greater love than that of his mother."

"You're thinking of Rizpah."

Solomon saw Nathan's face soften in the moonlight, and he had to strain to hear the words he spoke. "I never saw a braver sight or so much love expended on such worthless fellows."

There seemed nothing more to say, and the two of them waited in silence for their men to catch up. Everyone was tired and hungry, but no one regretted not staying in Gibeon. They would have to go the long way around, and it would be almost sunrise when they reached Jerusalem. There would be no sleep for the young princes that night. David would want to hear everything before they could retire.

With a sharp command, Solomon led the men out onto the main path, hoping that they would meet none of the Benjamites before they saw the great North Gate of Jerusalem.

* * *

David had already heard the news. Michal had come herself, then the chief leaders of the tribe of Benjamin, and finally the priests from the tabernacle. They cared nothing for the revenge that the Gibeonites felt they deserved, and nothing for the word of the Lord that had come to David in regard to the famine. All they could talk of was the cruelty of the Gibeonites and their own anger that David had given the young men into their hands.

Michal had been wild and incoherent, blaming first David and then his God for what had happened. The priests had pointed out that the Gibeonites weren't only getting revenge on Saul and his house but were also appeasing the old earth gods by carrying out the human sacrifice that was part of their pagan rites.

"Worst of all," one priest said, "the Gibeonites have done this on the sacred rock before the Tabernacle. How can we celebrate Passover with the sons and grandsons of Saul hanging at the very door of our tabernacle?"

"It was their intention to embarrass us," a second priest countered.

Finally David whirled to face them, shouting, "I delivered the word of the Lord as I received it. What the Gibeonites have done is on their heads, not mine."

The encounter had ended with further angry words and bitter resentment. David was drained and exhausted, but more than that he was alarmed for the safety of Bathsheba and his sons. He knew the whole tribe of Benjamin blamed him for what had happened and would be looking for ways to avenge the young men's death.

"Let David suffer as we have suffered. Then he will understand," one of them had been heard to say.

What better revenge could they wreak than to take his beloved Bathsheba and his two favorite sons? It was common knowledge that the queen's caravan would be returning in time for Passover. They could easily arrange to capture it and hold them for ransom—or worse yet, have them killed in the same manner that Saul's sons were killed.

* * *

When Solomon and Nathan rode through the North Gate and into the courtyard, they found David with his arms outstretched in welcome. He didn't let them observe the usual formality of kissing his hand but held them close and kept repeating, "Thank God, thank God, you're safe."

"Yes, we're safe and glad to be home," Solomon said, straightening his cloak and adjusting his short sword.

"And your mother—where is your mother?" David peered into the darkness behind them, his face lined and anxious.

"She's coming tomorrow with Adonijah."

"By way of Gibeon?" His voice was tense and husky.

"Yes."

Relief flooded over him. "Ah, then she'll be safe. The Benjamites have threatened such terrible things. I don't know but what it would have been easier to face God and the starving people of Jerusalem than to have to face Michal and her tribesmen. There's a different rumor every hour. Now they say that they intend to kill us all and level the palace to the ground. I knew they'd be angry, but I had no idea it would be this bad."

Nathan and Solomon looked at each other, and then Solomon spoke, his voice low, fighting for control. "Father, it was awful. We saw it. The Gibeonites hung Saul's sons and grandsons in the grove before the tabernacle."

Nathan continued: "All the men of Gibeon were there watching Rizpah beat off the birds and wild dogs. The odor was stifling, and blood was everywhere." Nathan's voice trailed off and he couldn't go on, but his face registered the horror he felt.

"Rizpah? Rizpah was there?" David was obviously stunned.

"We could hardly recognize her," Solomon volunteered. "She was like a crazy woman; her hair covered with ashes and her clothes streaked with blood. I can't tell you how awful it was." His brow was furrowed and his eyes bloodshot; the horror of what he had seen was stamped on his face in such a way that David needed no more details.

The king ran his fingers through his hair. "The priests are right, then. How can we go up to the tabernacle at Gibeon for Passover after this?" With a look of terrible anguish he turned from them and paced the room, impatiently kicking aside his leg armor and waking his armor-bearer and servants.

"It's obvious that's just what the Gibeonites intend," Solomon said. "They want to make it so distasteful to worship in Gibeon that the tabernacle will have to be moved."

"Moving the tabernacle now would solve nothing," David said. "It's the enmity between my family and Saul's that must somehow be healed."

"Father," Solomon interrupted, "things have gone too far. It's impossible—" Solomon couldn't imagine his father even trying to breach such a chasm.

David put his arms lovingly around his sons' shoulders. "You must go to bed. You're both exhausted. Leave this problem with me. The Lord will show me a way. There's always a solution if one is willing to sacrifice one's pride, and at my age pride seems a very small and foolish thing. Good night. You're good sons." With that he led them out and again bade them good night.

* * *

Solomon tossed and turned, unable to sleep. He looked around the familiar room; the pale moonlight pouring through the latticed windows made the vivid colors of the carpets and cushions come alive. Everything was just the way it had been when he left, but now he himself was somehow different.

The trip to Shunem had changed everything. He fingered the bead given him by Shulamit. Only if his father didn't consummate the marriage could she truly belong to the next king. There was little chance of that happening; the old counselors would see to that. A little detail like that wouldn't bother Adonijah, of course. "He'd like nothing better than to gain the throne, and Shulamit besides." He dismissed the thought immediately. It was too devastating to even imagine.

He turned over again, and now his mind lingered on the sight of the princes impaled in Gibeon. "If Adonijah had his way, that's just where he would put me. He is that ruthless and that ambitious." The thought was unsettling enough to make it difficult for him to sleep until the sky was beginning to brighten and a rooster crowed. He finally slept a troubled sleep that left him fatigued and moody the next day.

12

*T*he slim slice of crescent moon hung low over the cypress trees as
the caravan carrying the queen and her entourage wound its way
up the last steep ascent and came to a stop near a clump of mulberry trees.
The retainers had already pitched camp for the night. Shulamit opened
the curtains of her howdah and saw the dark bulk of the queen's great
tent outlined against the fading mauve of the sky and the bright, crackling
fires. The fragrant odor of bread and lentil soup wafted over to her, and
she knew there would be something warm and delicious waiting for them.

She had been told that there was a village nearby, but there was no sign of
wall, turret, or mud-brick courtyard. She saw only the deepening blue-black
sky, with ash-gray trees and jagged rocks outlined against its softness. The
place had an air of singular beauty.

She closed her curtains and leaned back among the cushions. She could
still hear everything going on around her. Suddenly, quite close by, a sharp
command was given and her camel lunged forward to kneel. The curtains
swung crazily back and forth as she held tightly to the saddle-rods so she
wouldn't be thrown out.

For a moment there was silence as she waited for someone to help her
dismount. Then clear and distinct on the evening air, she heard voices. The
speaker seemed to be out of breath from running but fortunately the tone of
his voice was that of relief and not alarm. "The Benjamites had planned to
attack the queen's caravan," he gasped, "but they were intercepted by David's
Mighty Men—no danger now."

She couldn't determine who the messenger was talking to as the man's
voice was lower and more controlled than that of the messenger. He seemed
to ask some questions and give instructions. Then there was the sound of running, as though the messenger was off again on some other errand.

Almost immediately her curtains were flung back by a hand that was
white and soft and bore on the first finger a large ruby ring. She was relieved
to see a smiling Adonijah. So it was he who had been talking to the messenger.

She took his outstretched hand and let him help her from the howdah. She searched his face for any hint of alarm or for a reason as to why he would be helping her when there were so many servants available, but there was nothing unusual about his manner. He continued to smile in a most relaxed sort of way.

Apart from making her uncomfortable by letting his eyes linger where her ropes of beads stopped and the soft folds of her dress clung to her breasts, he was most attentive and flattering. She could find no fault in what he said, and she warmed to the thoughtful way he anticipated her every need.

He left her at the entrance to the great tent. She thought it a bit strange that he still had said nothing about the danger that the messenger claimed they had just escaped. Instead he bowed, as was the custom, and raised her hand to his forehead before disappearing with a smile into the darkness.

* * *

Later that evening Shulamit had a leisurely dinner with the queen. When there was still no mention of an attempt to attack the caravan, she began to think that she had imagined the whole conversation.

As she was leaving, the queen smiled and said, "Tomorrow night at this time we'll be in Jerusalem."

Shulamit promptly forgot everything else. Back in her own section of the tent, the words haunted her. All the time her maids were combing her hair, smoothing out her flaxen sheets, and helping her into bed, she was worrying. "Surely," she thought, "I won't be ushered in to the king without some preparation."

She lifted the braided cord and for a moment cradled the small pouch of fragrant dried flowers in her hand. It brought back so many memories of the prince. "He loves me," she thought. "I'll not give him up easily. As long as he isn't married to someone else and I haven't been taken in to the king, there's still hope."

She lay in the soft darkness watching the incense burner sway with the slow movement of the tent pole until she drifted off to sleep. She didn't even wake up when her mother came from one of the neighboring tents and drew the heavy fox-skin robe over her because the night had turned suddenly cold.

* * *

It was late. The coals in the brazier were no longer glowing when Shulamit woke with a strange feeling of foreboding. She listened. At first she heard nothing but the creaking of the tent poles as they bent under the weight of the heavy goatskin covering.

Then she noticed light seeping in from under the curtain that divided her side of the tent from the queen's. She sat up; something was wrong. Voices could be heard whispering with an urgency that carried on the cool night air even though the exact words were lost.

Quite abruptly the tent's partition was flung aside, and Shulamit saw the worried face of the queen with someone in the shadows behind her. "Shulamit!" The queen's voice was low and controlled, but with just a slight edge of fear. "Adonijah has just received word that the nephews of Michal and the sons of Rizpah have been executed by the Gibeonites with the king's permission and that the Benjamites are seeking revenge. They're already on the way here to capture us."

Adonijah stepped forward into the light and took command of the situation. "It will be too dangerous for all of us to travel together."

The queen looked surprised and concerned. "But of course you must ride with me," she said.

Adonijah shook his head. "Undoubtedly I'm in the most danger as I'm next in line for the throne. You would be much safer with a few specially picked retainers."

"And Shulamit?" the queen asked testily.

"They would know nothing about her. She can ride with me and my men." He said it all so matter-of-factly that it sounded perfectly logical.

During this exchange Shulamit had grown more and more disturbed. "I must send for my mother right away," she said, looking from Bathsheba to Adonijah.

Adonijah was instantly wary. "No one must be told—not even your mother. Believe me, she'll be quite safe," he said. There was the faint sound of movement outside the tent, then whispered commands, and Adonijah disappeared into the darkness.

"What shall I wear? What shall I take?" Shulamit looked in bewilderment at all of the chests and woven baskets filled with her belongings.

"Nothing," the queen said. "There's no time. You'll need your warmest clothes. Now hurry. Adonijah will be back to get you at any moment." With that the queen dropped the tent flap. Her low, musical voice could be heard for a moment, giving commands; then there was silence.

Shulamit flung the fox-skin robe back and got up. With teeth chattering, she pulled on her badger-skin sandals and wrapped a warm woolen cloak around her. She stood still and listened. There were more voices, and then the sound of light footsteps on gravel. She lifted the tent flap just in time to see the queen, on an ordinary gray mule, ride out with several retainers. The campfires had died down, and the night seemed peaceful and quiet. The moon had set, but the stars were unusually bright. It was cold. She shivered and wished she were safe at home in Shunem.

"I hope you don't mind riding a mule," Adonijah loomed up beside her with no warning.

"I often rode a mule at home," she said.

As they rode out of the camp, she thought of the message she had heard before dismounting from the howdah. Why were they fleeing in such haste if the messenger was right and the Benjamites had been stopped by David's men? She decided to ask Adonijah about it at the first opportunity.

As they rode along, Adonijah said nothing, but at times he looked back to make sure she was following him. If she was too far behind, he waited for her to catch up. They rode in this way until the trail they followed had led up several steep cliffs and down into a deep valley. There they came to a small village that lay half-hidden among dusty, old olive trees.

Adonijah stopped beside a rather imposing doorway recessed in a vine-covered wall. He pulled a hempen rope that hung from a small opening in the door; there was the hollow sound of wood hitting wood, and then silence. He cursed and pulled the rope again, this time with more vigor. Slowly the door opened and a very old man stood blinking and squinting in the pale moonlight. Then, recognizing Adonijah, he threw himself down on the ground, kissing the mule's hooves and then Adonijah's feet. The prince pulled him to his feet and ordered him to hurry and prepare them something warm to drink.

"Come," Adonijah said as he turned to help Shulamit down from the mule. "We'll stop here for a rest before going on to Jerusalem."

Shulamit followed him into what seemed to be the reception room of a large country house. Someone had already lit a small clay lamp in one of the wall niches, and she could dimly see that the room was lavishly furnished with carpets and cushions, a silver brazier, several brass incense burners, and a large chest delicately carved and inlaid with ivory.

"Where are we? What is this place?" Shulamit asked.

"This is my country house. I visit here when I'm tired of life in the city and at court." Adonijah was about to sink down onto one of the cushions when the door opened and two young women entered. One carried a wine jug and the other some golden goblets. When they saw Shulamit, their faces clouded.

Shulamit took one of the goblets, but when she held it out for the wine to be poured, she was almost certain the young girl deliberately tried to spill some of it on her gown. She quickly stepped aside and it splashed onto the cushions, making an ugly red stain.

Adonijah, scolding all the while, reached out and took the wine glass handed him. "You can't even pour a glass of wine. How do you expect I'll take you to Jerusalem? You'd be an embarrassment to me."

Now several small children came into the room, rubbing their eyes and yawning. Adonijah caught them up in his arms and said something personal to each in turn, asking them questions that they answered with only a shy nod.

Shulamit was charmed at this domestic side of Adonijah. She was just going to make a comment when, to her surprise, his whole demeanor changed. He put the children down and hurried them back into the great hall of the house. He quickly closed and securely bolted the door before turning around to face her.

"Now," he said, "you have seen two of my younger wives and their children. They live here. They keep my house and manage things in general, but they're simple village women who wouldn't fit into my life in Jerusalem."

"I could see that they weren't pleased with me." Shulamit stood, awkwardly twirling the goblet in her hands.

Adonijah laughed. "They're jealous ones. They thought you were a new bride I'd brought home. It won't hurt them to wonder. They're saucy creatures who need the whip of jealousy to keep them in line." He sat down and motioned for Shulamit to come sit beside him.

It would have been unthinkable to refuse, so Shulamit sank down on the mat a full cushion away from him. "Why have you brought me here?" she asked, cutting across the niceties with her usual candor.

For a moment Adonijah was taken aback. Then he leaned forward and spoke earnestly. "You're so intuitive. Of course I've brought you here for a very special reason."

"So it's true that there was no danger? The Benjamites were already stopped by David's troops, and you've deliberately deceived the queen."

It was obvious that she had caught him off guard, but he smiled his confusion away. "You're making it sound so awful. I don't know how you could know all this, but yes, yes—I was desperate. I had to see you alone."

"Why alone?" Her eyes snapped dangerously as she pulled farther away from him.

"You must understand . . ." he pleaded. "It was my only chance."

"Only chance?"

"My only chance to tell you that I'm hopelessly, madly in love with you. When my father dies, I'll be the next king. Important people are backing me. I lack only one thing: a woman to be my wife and queen."

"But you obviously have wives and children."

"These women? They're only humble country girls who could never be part of my life at court. I need *you*."

"But I'm already married to the king."

"Yes, yes, I know. But, as king, I'll inherit the wives of my father's harem when he dies. I can't take for myself any that have actually lain with him, however, and that's why I had to see you, had to formulate a plan."

"A plan?"

"It isn't easy, but it's possible. You have only to tell my father that there's someone at home in Shunem whom you love, and he'll not touch you."

"But you don't understand," Shulamit objected. "There *is* someone I love. I've even pledged myself to him." She sat up very straight and looked at him with troubled eyes.

Adonijah stroked his short beard and grimaced. "Solomon?"

"How could you possibly have guessed?"

"You've pledged yourself to him, you say?" A mocking half-smile played around his lips. "How can you have pledged yourself when you're the same as married to the king?"

"I've done nothing wrong. I only told him that I love him and gave him a token of my love."

"What did you give?" His eyes had turned a cold, hard green, and his mouth was rigid.

Shulamit touched the beads around her neck before she spoke. "You wouldn't think it a very great thing, but when given with one's whole heart, the token means everything."

"Come," he urged, "tell me, what have you given him?"

"It's nothing of any real value, I assure you."

"Let me guess. Perhaps a ring?"

"No, no. I didn't own a ring. This is something I've worn since I was a child."

"A comb from your hair?" he ventured.

"No, nothing so large. It's a small thing, of little significance in itself." As she spoke, she quite unconsciously fingered the beads around her neck.

Adonijah noticed and laughed, pointing at the necklace. "Your beads— you gave him one of your beads."

Shulamit drew back. "How did you know?"

"It's simple. If you care about someone as much as I care about you, you observe—and you know things about her. Please, may I see the beads? They look like something called amber," he said, stretching out his hand.

Shulamit untied the cord they were strung on and handed them to him. "They're really of no great value."

"No, no, I think you're mistaken. I don't know a great deal about such things, but I have a friend who collects precious stones. He can give me some idea of their value." With that he slipped the beads into the wide belt of his tunic and stood up. "We must be on our way," he said. "The queen will be there before us, and they'll worry."

The guards were already back on their mules and waiting for Adonijah as he rode through the gate. He signaled for them to start and then drew up beside Shulamit. "Remember what I have said. You don't love me now, but in the future you will. It's already written in the stars that you'll be mine."

He didn't wait for an answer but rode out along the path at a fast pace, leaving the guards behind to escort Shulamit.

* * *

Solomon was awakened by one of his younger brothers shaking him rather roughly. "Our mother has just ridden in the North Gate, and our father wants you to come down with him to greet her."

It was a great relief to see that Bathsheba had arrived safely. Solomon was overjoyed, and he had seldom seen his father so happy. David ignored the servants and went himself to help her down from her mule. He held her cold hands in his larger warm ones as he took in every aspect of her face. With one impatient gesture he dismissed the servants and led her back to his own chamber.

"Your feet are cold," he said as he seated her on a low bench and pulled off her light slippers to massage her feet.

"My lord," she said, rubbing her hands together to warm them, "it was so frightening. Only Adonijah's quick thinking rescued us from the Benjamites."

"What nonsense is this?" David laughed. "My Mighty Men drove the only organized band of Benjamites back and locked them in Saul's fortress. I even sent word to Adonijah so you wouldn't worry. Where is Adonijah?"

"He suggested that we divide into two companies so we wouldn't attract attention. He should be coming soon with your new bride."

"New bride?" David's countenance clouded. "So you *did* pick someone after all?"

Bathsheba reached out and tenderly toyed with his beard. "I made sure she could dance the Mahanaim so she would remind you of me."

David captured her hand in his and laughed as he stood up. "There will be no time for new brides for quite some time. The people are almost rioting in the streets, as you must have heard, and the Benjamites are all aflame because of what happened to Saul's sons and grandsons."

Solomon had heard enough. He realized that Adonijah had tricked his mother on purpose so he could be alone with Shulamit. He raised the curtain and slipped out, going quickly to the guard station on the wall to await his brother's arrival.

* * *

By the time Adonijah and Shulamit finally came riding up to the North Gate, the moon was low in the west. Noticing that the two were engaged in conversation, Solomon felt choking hatred for Adonijah and frustration with Shulamit for being so impressed with him.

He found that in spite of his anger, he could not tear himself away but stood and watched as Adonijah helped her off the mule and led her through the second gate into the court of the queens. "No doubt he'll linger as long as possible," he muttered, heading down the uneven steps beside the tower.

He found himself hurrying toward the Throne Room. He had to know how long Adonijah stayed, and when he left. He hated this feeling of urgency and anger over a girl who couldn't possibly mean anything to him. "She's to be my father's wife," he whispered, forcing himself to face the facts. "She's nothing to me now."

In the throne room he paced back and forth, not caring that he might wake the guards and various members of David's Mighty Men who slept there. It seemed an eternity before the curtain to the court of the queens was pushed aside and Adonijah stepped out and headed for his own rooms.

Solomon noticed his smug look of satisfaction and was determined to confront him, to accuse him of lying to get his way. For a few moments Solomon stood flexing his muscles and adjusting his jeweled belt. Then, with quick, sure strides, he walked down the long hall to Adonijah's rooms.

When Adonijah saw Solomon, his face registered surprise and then froze into a smirk. "Why, might I ask, am I being so honored at this unseemly hour?"

Solomon leaned back against the doorframe, arms folded, apparently relaxed. When he spoke, his voice was quiet and controlled, displaying none of the emotion he was fighting to hold in check. "You told the queen there was to be an attack by the Benjamites when you knew they had already been defeated by the king's men. Do you admit this?"

For a fleeting second Adonijah's eyes betrayed his guilt and then narrowed as his left hand worked slowly and deliberately to straighten the fold in his sleeve. "Yes, yes, I deceived her," he said, looking at Solomon boldly.

Solomon was surprised that Adonijah had admitted his deceit, but he had no intention of letting the admission pass. He needed to make the most of his advantage. "Why would you do such a thing?" he asked.

Adonijah took the silver goblet of wine his servant handed him and laughed. "I simply wanted some time alone with a lovely young maiden." His eyes glinted with triumph over the upturned goblet as he observed Solomon's frustration.

Solomon was annoyed at himself for allowing the wild flood of anger to surface. When he finally responded, his words were clipped and his eyes flashed. "It will do you no good to try to win her. She belongs to the king, and if it's a dalliance you have in mind, you should be aware that there's someone else she loves."

"There is? That's very interesting," Adonijah countered with the smug assurance of one who knows a secret.

"Yes, very interesting. She even gave this person a token of her love." It was obvious that Solomon expected Adonijah to wilt under the revelation.

Instead, Adonijah laughed almost hysterically as he reached into his belt and drew something out. With deliberation he grasped the end of a cord so that Shulamit's beads swayed in the air. Slowly he advanced toward Solomon, swinging the beads in front of his face.

"I believe the token you're referring to was a bead. Am I right? Well, only one short hour at my house in the village and all that was forgotten. See? She gave me the whole string to remember her by."

As the lamplight caught the yellow glow of the beads, Solomon grabbed them from him. "I don't believe a word you've said." His voice was amazingly steady as he turned on his heel and started from the room.

Adonijah sprang after him to spit out his last bit of news. "You can't ignore the facts. I have the beads. I've also lain with her, and she's mine."

The words cut through Solomon like a knife. Everything fit into place so perfectly. The two of them riding up late, then the beads. After all, how could he have gotten the beads if she hadn't given them to him?

Solomon bolted down the hall. Hot anger flooded through him in an uncontrollable surge. He felt physically ill, his eyeballs burned, his head felt ready to burst, and his stomach cramped. It was obvious to him that Shulamit had betrayed the love she had pledged to him.

He looked at the hated beads in his hand and decided to take them to his mother. She could give them back to Shulamit. Then he thought better of it. He wanted to be sure she got the beads and realized that he knew of her treachery. He stuffed them into his belt. It was almost time for the feast of Passover. "I'll return them to her myself at the feast," Solomon muttered as he entered his own rooms.

13

*T*he rounding moon rose over the sleeping city and for a moment shone in through the open shutters of David's room. Satiated with love, he had fallen asleep in Bethsheba's lap and was unaware that she studied his face in the moonlight, lovingly touching the wisps of gray in his hair and beard. Her thoughts had been first of him and their love and then had turned to her favorite son, Solomon.

"He's in love with that girl," she thought as her hand paused in midair. She again pictured Solomon's eyes as he watched Shulamit dance on the night of the competition. "I must see that he's gone from here for a while."

She looked down at the king, his head resting peacefully in her lap. She was sure that this young, inexperienced girl couldn't take him from her. They had been through too much together; their love was too strong. But Solomon! The girl could get him easily, and it would mean the ruin of all her own ambitions for him.

Gently she bent down and whispered, "My lord, we have something that must be decided soon."

"What's that?" David asked as he opened his eyes and turned so he could catch her face in his hands and kiss her.

"Something exciting—something that would help my lord accomplish the desire of his heart."

"The desire of my heart?" David smiled, thinking how like her grandfather Ahithophel she was at times.

"Yes, my lord. I know that more than anything else in the world, you wish to have a temple built on Mount Moriah."

He sat up and grew suddenly serious. "Now it is urgent," he said. "We'll no longer be able to worship freely at the tabernacle in Gibeon. This slaughter has desecrated the entire area."

"So this temple is to be grander than the temples of the Canaanites or the Philistines?"

"Yes. For the one true God it must be grander than any temple ever built by man."

"Then, my lord, send my son Solomon to Egypt. He must see their temples and their manner of building so that he will know what it means to build the most beautiful temple in the world." She could tell by the quick way he turned his head and looked at her that he was excited by her suggestion.

"Of course! That's exactly what must be done. We're still a nation of sheepherders and vine growers. What do we know of building great temples?" The moment of love was gone from his mind. He rose and lit one of the lamps, then fumbled among the papers that had fallen at the foot of his great bed.

Bathsheba knew that David was unaware both of her kiss and of her departure, but she didn't care. She had planted an idea that would blossom into exactly the thing she wanted for her son.

* * *

When Bathsheba had gone, David blew out the flickering flame of the lamp and lay back on his bed. He slept poorly, troubled by restless dreams of the famine. The faces of his people rose up out of the darkness, and their eyes pleaded with him to rescue them from the living death that had trapped them. One after the other he saw them pass, shriveled and misshapen. There was no laughter, no joy.

He awoke with a start and got out of bed, groping his way over to the small window through which he could look out at the predawn sky. There wasn't a cloud in sight, and the moon hung clear and bright above the palm tree. It would be round and full by Passover.

The thought of Passover and the problem of celebrating it at Gibeon stung him afresh. "O Lord," he pleaded, "how can we celebrate Passover when your name is profaned among the heathen and the place where your holy tabernacle stands has become loathsome?"

Exhausted, he rested his elbows on the base of the small window and cradled his head in his hands. His shoulders slumped, and he felt a numbness come over him. Three years of famine were too much, and now to have his country divided further by the treachery of the Gibeonites was unthinkable. He felt pinioned between his people and his God. No mortal should have to bear so much responsibility and pain.

"O Lord, my Lord," he prayed over and over, too distraught to form into words all of his anguish.

* * *

Slowly David felt the struggle within him cease. He raised his head and let the calm pour over him with its healing freshness. He became aware of the moonlight bathing the frames of the window and glinting from the jewels on his fingers. The very air was still with a vibrant expectancy. It was then, as had happened so often before, that he heard the voice of God coming from some remote corner of his soul. He knew that it was God because the thought was not his thought, and the answer was something alien to his thinking.

"Bring back the bones of Saul and of Jonathan from the place in Jabesh-gilead where they are buried. Take down the bodies of the grandsons and sons of Saul that hang before the tabernacle and bring them all to Zelah. Bury them there in the sepulcher of Kish, Saul's father. The hurt will be healed, and I will hear your entreaty for the land."

David didn't know how long he stood in this state of intense awareness, nor did he know how it was that he could be so sure this was the answer that he sought. But clearly the time to act had come.

With a great shout he woke his armor-bearer and called the young guards who slept outside his door. "Go wake all my Mighty Men and have them here, ready to ride, by sunrise," he ordered.

* * *

David's battle wound was bothering him again, but he ignored it, as he insisted on mounting with his men. "The tribe of Benjamin has suffered a great hurt," he said. "If there is to be healing, Saul and Jonathan must be brought home from Jabesh-gilead as heroes and buried in the family tomb."

At the same time he ordered his men to gather up the broken bodies of Saul's grandsons and sons that hung before the tabernacle in Gibeon. Finally he sent one of his own white mules for Rizpah, that she might come to Zelah and be comforted in seeing that her sons were buried with honor.

News spread quickly as the king and his men, returning with the bodies, passed through one village after another. Men, women, and children gathered at the roadside and leaned from windows and rooftops to see the procession as it wound its way back from the fords of the Jordan to Tirzah, then down the ridge to Shechem, past the ruins of Shiloh, on to Rimmon, and finally to the caves at Zelah. Here the men of Benjamin reluctantly joined with the men of Judah.

With great weeping and wailing, they carried the bodies of Saul's sons and grandsons into the cave and laid them to rest.

When they came to place the body of Jonathan in the tomb, David moved out from among his men and came to stand before the shroud, obviously lost in memories of the past. With one hand he reached up and drew his cloak from his shoulders and slowly spread it over his friend's bier. Then, to everyone's amazement, he unfastened his jeweled belt and finally his favorite short sword and laid them both on the cloak. "See," they whispered, "he remembers how Jonathan gave him his cloak and girdle and sword when they first met."

The tribesmen fingered the soft cloth of the cloak and touched the sword and girdle. They were made of finer material than any of them had ever seen, and they were sure that the king couldn't replace them. One of the men started to give them back to David, but David motioned for them to be left just as they were. "Jonathan was a great and a good man," he said, "and would have been king of Israel if he had lived."

Though he was still smarting from hurt and disillusionment, Solomon had gone to Jabesh-gilead with his father. He hadn't been prepared for the fear he felt when they first encountered the men of Benjamin. Their faces had been dark and their eyes red-rimmed and hostile. Now everything had changed. The Benjamites had been impressed and deeply moved by David's generosity.

David sat down on one of the jagged rocks and called for his scribes to bring his harp. As he started to sing, his voice was choked with emotion and they had to strain to hear the words. It was, as Solomon had thought, the lament for Jonathan. "He doesn't forget, no matter what happens," he marveled, forcing down the lump in his throat.

As the last notes died on the air, Solomon noticed something strange was happening. First, there was a slight breeze that gently stirred the tall grass; then clouds, dark and threatening, rolled in from the west, blotting out the sun.

The breeze grew stronger until it whipped up small eddies of dust along the road, bent the branches of the fig trees that grew wild on the hillside, and tossed the birds across the sky.

Suddenly a drop of water fell on a young boy's outstretched hand, and then another splashed on a stone, and still another ran down the face of an old man. No one spoke. They stood clumped together with upturned faces, watching the quickly changing sky. Now faster and faster the great, splashing drops began to fall.

"Rain! It's raining!" someone shouted as the rain began to fall in great, pelting gusts. The shout was taken up by others until the mountains rang with their glad cries.

Solomon was one of the first to mount his mule and struggle against the strong thrusts of wind now shrieking and whistling around the jagged rocks and over the scrub pines. Through the slanting rain he saw men dancing for joy, shouting and laughing to feel rain pounding on their upturned faces.

He caught a brief glimpse of his father standing with hands raised, his robes whipping around him and tears mingling with the rain to stream down his face, while the men of Benjamin pushed forward to embrace him or knelt to kiss the hem of his robe.

Solomon found shelter under a small tree and shielded his eyes to get a better view. Everything was a blur of moving shadows, nothing distinct. Then again he caught a glimpse of his father surrounded by his Mighty Men, all laughing and hugging the Benjamites two or three at a time as the rain fell around them in great spouting torrents.

Dripping wet, David led the joyful band through the palace gates and on into the throne room, where there was a fire burning in a brazier and his wives and small children were gathered to welcome him home.

"We've spent the day searching out all the leaven from the rooms of the palace," one of the smaller sons exclaimed, "but we waited for you to come before we looked in the throne room."

David picked up the small boy. He had almost forgotten that it was the beginning of the Feast of Unleavened Bread. "The tapers, where are the tapers?" David asked. "We can't search for the leaven without more light."

Servants came running with coals to light the children's tapers. Then David started around the room with them, searching the dark corners and under the stairs for any stray piece of bread that might have been hidden there. There must be no bread made from the flour and leaven of the past left by sundown.

Solomon stood in the shadows where he could observe everything but not be seen. He had noticed right away that Shulamit and Adonijah were missing. He tried to reason with himself, but his emotions were still not under control. Once again he felt a sharp hurt, as though he had been stabbed. It amazed him that with all his resolve he could still feel such pain.

Now his father was speaking again. "Do you know why we do this?" he asked, looking down at the children's upturned faces.

"To get ready for Passover," one child answered.

"So we will be rid of the bad leaven," a small boy said.

"And why must we be rid of the leaven?" David asked.

"Because leaven is like sin, and we can't celebrate Passover in a house filled with sin." It was obvious that the boy had been studying with the priests.

David nodded his approval and then turned to the tribesmen and officials who had come back with him to the palace. "Do you understand now? The wrong done the Gibeonites was like the last piece of leaven that had to be removed before God could heal our land and send us rain. It wasn't the whole sin, but it was like the last piece of old bread that lies hidden and forgotten in a dark corner until we go searching for it with a lighted taper."

Solomon edged closer so he wouldn't miss a word. "Some of you have thought that the God of Israel is weaker than the gods of our neighbors. You have thought that He could save our fathers from the mighty Pharaoh but couldn't give us rain. Now you see that you were wrong.

The people seemed to be drinking in the peaceful scene. The torchlight and tapers gave a soft glow to the room, and the warm fire in the brazier snapped and crackled as a new armful of dried thorns was thrown into the huge brass bowl.

Suddenly, as though from a great distance, came a wild, penetrating wail. It was a woman's voice, high and fierce, advancing out of the darkness of the long hall and getting louder as it came toward the throne room.

The listeners froze, awestruck as the cry echoed through the women's court, bouncing off the walls and charging the air with its vibrations. The loud crash of some large object being overturned was followed by a thud, then the shattering explosion of clay jars breaking against stone pavement.

With one violent rip, the curtain leading from the women's quarters was pulled down. In the doorway stood a woman, ranting and frenzied, hair matted with ashes, dress torn, eyes blazing in their dark sockets.

She came toward them, crouching like some wild beast, and then reached up with a bony hand and pulled a torch loose from the wall. As she turned and faced them, they saw that it was Saul's daughter and David's first wife, Michal.

144

The torchlight etched the cruel wrinkles and deep circles under her eyes; it heightened the gray of her stiffened hair and the rigidity of her bitter mouth. "My lord." She spat out the words as she came to stand before David.

"Michal!" David whispered, staring at her in disbelief.

"My lord," she repeated, her voice rasping and husky, "you have collected your filthy leaven and have rid Israel of every threat to your throne. You've even buried your dead in the tombs of Kish, and it has rained and rained—but not because of what you did, nor is it from your God."

"She blasphemes!" one of the men exclaimed in horror.

"You really thought it was your God?" She laughed hysterically. "You thought it was your God who sent the rain, but you're wrong. It was Baal. He saw the sacrifice of my sister's lovely boys on his altar, and even he was forced to weep. He wept; Baal wept!"

"Enough—we've heard enough. She talks against our God and our king," someone shouted from the shadows, and others began to murmur against her.

"Come, Abigail. She needs your help," David said to one of his wives. He moved toward Michal himself, but she sprang back and spat at his feet.

"I need no help. I have the dark gods of Baal and Hadad to defend me." Slowly she began to back away. Her eyes, darting from one person to another, were bold and threatening. "I'm leaving now, but you won't be rid of me. This thing that you have done will divide Israel forever. It will *never* be forgotten." With one swift motion she turned and flung the torch into its holder; then, with head held high, she walked through the door to the court of the queens and disappeared into the darkness.

David didn't move or speak. Gradually his men came, one by one, to kiss his hand or the hem of his robe and murmur their goodbyes. His eyes were tired and his expression was bleak and troubled.

Solomon felt helpless. He couldn't bear to see his father so dejected. The humiliation of having one of his wives appear in such a temper on a holy feast day was bad enough, but that she should say the rain had come at Baal's command was unforgivable. Then to fling at him the accusation that there would still be enmity between Judah and the Benjamites could not be overlooked. It was an unthinkable affront.

David looked around the room at the sad, upturned faces of his family and friends and then, without a word or change of expression, turned and walked to his room. In the few moments Michal had taken to deliver her stinging attack, the king had aged visibly. Even his walk had slowed and his shoulders drooped.

Solomon followed him. "My father," he said hesitantly, "I'm so sorry."

"You needn't be." David's voice was muffled, but when he turned and looked at Solomon he seemed to have regained some of his composure. "Israel has seen God's own miracle today. The Benjamites are restored, and the famine is over."

"But what of Michal's blasphemy? She said it was the Gibeonites' sacrifice of the princes to Baal that brought the rain."

"She was angry. It's not what she believes in her heart."

"But it's confusing."

David turned from the window and looked with astonishment at Solomon. "Confusing? What's confusing? It all seems quite obvious to me: Yahweh, the God of Israel, honored our repentance and sent the rain."

"But to the Canaanites it would have been the sacrifice of Saul's sons and grandsons that brought the rain. How do we know that we're right and they're wrong? There are so many of them."

"Truth isn't determined by how many or how few believe a thing. Truth is determined by what we actually experience," said David.

"In Gezer I went to a cave where a person can ask questions. Out of the very wall of the cave their god will answer. They say that our God dwells in the dark of the Holy of Holies and is silent."

"You went to the sacred cave in Gezer?"

"Yes, although Nathan tried to discourage me," Solomon admitted.

David paced back and forth. Finally he stopped in the middle of the room and looked at Solomon. "Don't be deceived, my son, by such tricks. I've been told that there's a secret entrance to a room behind the cave and that a priest goes in to answer the questions as though their god were speaking. We, the seed of Abraham, are the only people who haven't invented a God to our own liking; instead we worship a God who from time to time has revealed Himself to us."

"I don't understand."

"Tomorrow is Passover. That's something that actually took place in our world. El Shaddai, the almighty God, delivered our people from slavery. We didn't imagine him to be El Shaddai; we experienced His might and His power in our behalf and then we named Him El Shaddai. The feast reminds us of what our God has actually done for us. This is how He speaks and has spoken."

Solomon was surprised. "Then our God doesn't dwell in the tabernacle at Gibeon?"

"He meets us there and we go there to sacrifice, but our God is much bigger than that. When I fought the giant, I fought in the name of Jehovah-Sabaoth, the God of Hosts. When God made promises to Abraham, it was in the name of Adonai-Jehovah, the Lord God. And when He created the world, we knew him as Elo-him, the creator God. Our God has many names because we have experienced Him in many ways."

"It seems to me to be an insult to worship such a great God in a tabernacle covered with goatskin."

"I have the materials for something finer, but our people aren't builders," said David. "We have the pattern given us by Moses, but we need the skill to work with stone, wood, and metal. How would you like to go and visit the country most proficient in building temples?"

"I've always wanted to visit your friend Hiram in Phoenicia."

"No, my son," David said. "It isn't to Phoenicia you are to go. Even the Phoenicians don't know enough to build the great temple I have in mind. You will go to Egypt. I've already sent a messenger to the Pharaoh, telling him of your coming."

"Egypt!" Solomon was excited. He had always wanted to go to Egypt.

"Egypt is weak and needing allies. They're glad to meet with ambassadors from even small countries."

"When will I leave? How long will I stay?" Solomon could hardly contain his excitement. The dull hurt of the last few weeks was suddenly lightened as he thought of this welcome escape.

"You should leave soon after Passover. You won't be able to return in fifty days for Shavuot, but you should be home for Rosh Hashanah on the first day of Tishri—or at least by the Day of Atonement on the tenth."

"Can Nathan go with me?"

David hesitated but finally agreed. "I suppose it would be helpful to have him along. He must be told quickly."

Solomon left his father's rooms in a mood of high adventure. Even finding Shulamit's beads still in his belt didn't dim his enthusiasm. He was determined to find a way to give the beads back to her so that he could be free of the torment he had endured. "Surely," he reasoned, "by the time I get back from Egypt it won't matter to me what Shulamit does or says."

14

$\mathcal{T}$he court of the queens had a charm all its own. The large courtyard around which the rooms and apartments were grouped had
a weathered look that made it seem warm and inviting. Attached to the
courtyard was a garden of fruits with a gate called the Valley Gate that
opened onto a path leading down to the Tyropoeon Valley. The women
rarely visited this garden, as it was also accessible from the king's rooms
and contained the cages in which the king and his sons kept their collection of lions, panthers, and various wild birds.

Other than the Valley Gate, there were only three gates leading out of the
court. There was a main gate; a latticed, curtained doorway that led down some
steps into an area behind the throne in the throne room; and the Postern Gate,
a very small gate that opened into the lower city. It was through this last gate
that some of the young women of Jerusalem came each day to act as companions and ladies-in-waiting for the wives and concubines of David and his sons.

A few steps up from the courtyard was a large reception room where
feasts and celebrations were held. Opening from this room was the king's
grand bedchamber. It was to this room that Shulamit would be taken when it
was decided that the marriage should be consummated.

At the far end of the large courtyard was a small, private section reserved
for new wives. Here the new bride learned the ways of the palace and was prepared for her meeting with the king. Old Tikva was in complete charge here.
"You're not to mingle with the other wives or leave your own courtyard until
the time of purification is over," she warned Shulamit on her first day in the
court of the queens.

Having made this statement, she firmly closed the heavy door and reached
through the hole to latch it behind her. Shulamit looked around the room and
saw that, though it was plain and unpretentious, it was comfortable. There
were colored mats, straw-filled cushions, and a clay brazier in which a bright
fire burned. Someone had placed a basket of thorns beside the brazier for fuel.

She had just started out to her own small courtyard when she heard distant laughter and then the sound of running feet. Suddenly there was a room-ful of curious young women clustered around her. "We're the young maidens from Jerusalem who are to prepare you for your marriage to the king," one of them explained.

The young maidens had heard that she was from the north, and they were curious about her. When they discovered during the regular massage how tan she was from the sun, and that her hands were dry and her feet calloused, they all gathered around and admonished her. "You foolish girl," they scolded. "You've let the sun darken your skin until you resemble a brown fig."

"It's not I who has done this," Shulamit said, sitting up and pulling the wrap around her. "My brothers were jealous of me and sent me out to work in the vineyard."

"The vineyard? You worked in a vineyard?" they chorused.

"Yes. I worked in a vineyard; I herded goats and sheep; I often baked bread over an outdoor oven." Shulamit laughed, her eyes twinkling with de-light at their confusion.

"But don't you want to be beautiful?" one of them asked.

"Don't you want to be loved?" asked another.

"Of course I want to be beautiful. And as for love, I'm already in love." Shulamit lay back on the marble slab and waited for the brisk rubbing to continue.

"In love? You're in love?" They gasped.

"Are you in love with the king?" another one asked.

"No."

"Does the king know that you're already in love with someone else?"

"No, but Solomon knows." Shulamit opened one eye in time to see their astonishment.

"Solomon!"

"Solomon is the one I love, and he loves me—but that's where it ends. Nothing can be done about it. I know it's unusual."

"It's not unusual that you should love the prince but that he should love you."

"Yes, he loves me, but since I'm already married to the king . . ." Tears gathered in her eyes. Awkwardly she brushed them away and tried to smile.

"You really know the prince?" asked one of the other girls, staring at Shulamit with undisguised envy.

"Oh, yes," Shulamit said, blushing with the joy of remembering. "My beloved is tan and handsome. His head is beautiful like a golden statue, and his hair is dark and wavy. When you run your fingers through it, it's like the finest silk."

"You ran your fingers through his hair?"

"Well, yes," she said, pausing to study the questioner before hurrying on to tell more. "His arms are strong and firm, like warm gold."

"He didn't *kiss* you, did he?" The tall girl again voiced the question all of them wanted to ask.

"Yes. Yes, he did kiss me."

"He kissed you? Solomon actually *kissed* you?" The maidens looked at one another and then back at Shulamit.

"What's it like to be kissed by Solomon?" the tall maid asked with growing respect.

"Oh, it's wonderful. Even his lips are perfumed," she smiled, showing the dimples in her cheeks.

"Perfumed? His lips are perfumed?" they chorused.

"His lips have the faint odor of lilies, and his breath is like myrrh. I'm sure that if you gathered 10,000 princes, there would be no one as handsome as Solomon."

There was a long silence as they stood studying Shulamit. Finally one of the bolder maids spoke. "We've all loved Solomon, but it was useless; he never noticed any of us. But if he *had,* and if he had kissed one of us—"

The order of the day would have been totally disrupted if old Tikva hadn't come in at this moment and vented her disapproval. As the maidens hurried to do her bidding, she commented to Shulamit, "If you had been going to marry Solomon, they would have hated you, but now that you're in such a hopeless situation, they'll do anything to help you."

This proved to be true. Each one of the maidens began to think of ways in which Shulamit could escape her marriage to the king and be free to pursue her romance with Solomon.

They all agreed that she must be brought out of hiding so the prince would at least see her. When they mentioned this to Shulamit, they were surprised to find that she didn't agree. "No, no," she said. "It isn't good to force love. There's a time for everything. My mother says that if it's God's will, it will work out."

The maidens felt sorry for Shulamit. They saw that she wasn't used to the ways of the court and its ambitious people. It would be impossible for there to be a happy outcome to her love, and if she was depending on the God of Israel to perform a miracle, it was indeed hopeless.

* * *

As it finally happened, Bathsheba herself arranged for Shulamit's first outing. She had decided to let Shulamit attend the Passover Seder with Sarah, Nathan's young wife. There had been so much contention and division caused by Michal's outburst that a show of loyalty to the king was important.

"Brides who haven't been brought in to the king are usually not allowed outside their rooms," Sarah explained when she came to get Shulamit.

Shulamit liked this quiet, friendly young girl right away. "You're expecting a child?" Shulamit asked as she followed her up the steps to the second floor above the courtyard.

They stood for a few moments, drinking in the magic atmosphere of the full pascal moon until, loud and clear on the night air, they heard the trumpets being blown at the North Gate and then an answering blast from somewhere inside the palace. "We must hurry," Sarah said. "The king and the princes are just arriving from the tabernacle."

They pushed their way into the crowded reception room. It was almost unbearably stuffy. The odors of pungent perfumes mingled with that of the incense that burned in great brass bowls hung by chains from the ceiling. Wall torches gave off sputtering darts of light that now and then served to brighten some child's face or accent a woman's delicate profile.

Women were sitting on mats of fine linen and leaning on brightly colored armrests, while their children and grandchildren crowded around them. For a moment the conversation stopped; all turned to look at Shulamit with a mixture of curiosity and hostility.

"Move, move." Old Tikva had sized up the situation and was making room for them to sit with the concubines.

* * *

No sooner was Shulamit seated than the serving women began to carry in the food and set it down on reed mats that covered the open space down the center of the room. The food was much the same as would be eaten in the simplest home in Jerusalem: bitter herbs, matzah, wine, and roast lamb—the same food that had been eaten by the Israelites on their last night as slaves in Egypt.

Once again the distant sound of a trumpet echoed and reechoed through the palace. All eyes turned to the open door as David entered the room. There was a rough maleness about him, in spite of his fine clothes and perfumed elegance. He was handsome in a rugged, battle-scarred sense, and Shulamit found that she was strangely attracted to him.

But then she gasped in surprise and felt a tingling thrill of joy as Solomon moved forward to stand beside his mother. He stood so straight, chin slightly tilted, watching his father with pride.

Sarah pointed to her husband, Nathan, who stood holding their son, Mattatha, by the hand. "See," she whispered, "the king has chosen Mattatha to answer the pascal questions."

When the questions were finished, Mattatha went back to sit with his father, and for the first time Shulamit noticed an older woman sitting near the king. She wore an elaborate crown and ordered the servants around as if there were no one else in the room.

"Who is that woman?" Shulamit asked Sarah.

"Oh, that's Haggith," Sarah said. "She's actually the queen, though David ignores her and gives all his attention to Bathsheba. There have been some terrible scenes between those two women. David never takes sides. He just backs off and lets them fight it out as best they can."

"How awful. She seems to be angry about something."

"I'm sure she is angry. Bathsheba and her sons arrived with David, and it was my son—Bathsheba's grandson—who answered the Seder questions."

Shulamit found little that was appealing about Haggith. It was evident that, like Adonijah, she was selfish and resentful.

The thought of Adonijah reminded her again of the unpleasant conversation she had had with him at his house. Suddenly a new thought intruded on the pleasant celebration. "What if I'm able to persuade the king to put off the consummation of the marriage, and Adonijah gains the throne? Will he not be able to claim me as his bride?"

Panic rose within her. It was unthinkable that she should be the wife of David, but absolutely impossible if Adonijah should have his way. There was a sudden hush, and Shulamit saw that the king had risen and was motioning for Solomon and Nathan to rise.

"I've asked Solomon and Nathan to go to Egypt for me, and they've agreed," David announced. "They're packed and ready to leave early tomorrow, and they'll return in time for the Festival of Sukkot in the fall."

He proceeded to describe where they would go and the purpose of their visit, but Shulamit heard nothing. All she could think of was how far away Egypt must be and that by the time he came back, if everything went as planned, she would be married to the king.

The speech was finally over and everyone stood. Shulamit noticed that Solomon kept looking around the room as though he were expecting to see someone. For a moment she thought he had recognized her, but when David and the young princes all left the room he went with them, and the rest of the wives and concubines followed. Sarah had gone early, so Shulamit was left to return to her rooms alone. She stood at the head of the stairs and listened as their voices floated back up to her and then grew fainter as they walked out into the courtyard.

She had reached the dark landing before she heard the sound of someone running across the courtyard below. She stopped and listened. The runner had turned in at the doorway and was coming up the steps two at a time. It was almost too dark to see even her hand in front of her face, but when she smelled the familiar odor of spikenard, she knew that it must be Solomon.

"My love?" she whispered hesitantly as a shadowy form loomed up before her.

It was indeed Solomon—but an angry, vindictive Solomon who held something out toward her. "Why? Why did you give these to Adonijah?" he demanded. "Why have you done this to me?" She felt something thrust into her hand, and as quickly as he had come he was gone, going down the stairs and across the courtyard.

It was too dark to see what he had given her, so she was completely bewildered by the hostility in his voice. It was painful to have been so close to him and to have expected such a different response, only to have the meeting end disastrously.

She brushed past the two serving girls who were waiting in her room and knelt down beside the small earthen lamp. To her utter astonishment she saw that it was her own beads he had given her. How had Solomon gotten them away from Adonijah? What did he mean by what he had said? Somehow he must have discovered that Adonijah had the beads and concluded that she had given them to him.

She paced back and forth in her small room, ignoring the serving girls as they came to lay out her sleeping mats. Over and over again she weighed all the facts. Solomon would be leaving in the morning and would be gone at least six months. He would go believing that she had given him only one of her beads in pledge of her love but had given Adonijah the whole remaining string. She saw it all clearly now. It was another one of Adonijah's tricks.

The serving maids were already asleep on the floor in the outer room by the door when she finally lay down on her mat and tried to sleep herself. Still she kept hearing the cruel words: "Why have you done this to me?"

She turned over and tried again to sleep, but it was impossible. She had to *do* something. She had to find a way to explain.

Shivering, she got out of bed and reached for her warm woolen robe. Cautiously she stepped over the two sleeping girls and walked out into the courtyard.

She remembered hearing that Nathan and Solomon would spend most of the night at the homes of relatives and friends saying goodbye. At this time of night there would be only a few lighted houses, and it shouldn't be impossible to find the one in which the princes were being entertained.

Quickly she made up her mind. There could be no greater punishment than to know that Solomon had ridden off angry and disillusioned. She *had* to find a way of seeing him.

✳ ✳ ✳

The Postern Gate didn't even grate on its hinges, and within moments she found herself outside in the lane. She stopped to breathe deeply of the fresh, moist air, enjoying the familiar odor of wet earth and damp stones before quickly moving down the shadowy side of the lane near the wall.

As she came out at a crossing, she noticed several houses where a dim light crept around the tightly closed shutters, but they were humble houses and she decided that the princes wouldn't be found there. Further down the lane she was startled when an old woman flung open a shutter and leaned far out to look down at her. Shulamit pulled her robe more closely about her as she heard the woman hiss, "Whore!" then close the shutters with a bang.

She turned a corner and almost bumped into a night watchman. Quickly she pulled her mantle across her face and tried to hurry past, but he held her in his firm grasp. "What are you doing out on the streets like this?" he growled.

"I'm looking for one of the princes. I have a message that must be given him tonight."

"A likely story," the watchman said, eyeing her more closely.

"It's true. I must see Solomon. He's leaving in the morning, and I have a message that must be delivered." She reached deep into the lining of her mantle and produced a small gold piece. "Can you tell me where the young princes have gone?"

"Come," the man said as he dropped the piece into his pouch. "I'll not be responsible for taking you there, but I can show you the place." He led the way down one lane and through another side street, stopping finally before an ornate wooden door that stood open to reveal a dimly lighted interior that throbbed with music and laughter.

The watchman pulled a cord that sent a wooden clapper banging and brought an old man to the door. "Asa," the watchman said, "Go fetch the young prince Solomon. One of his sisters is waiting to see him."

The watchman left, and the old man hobbled off toward the main room. Shulamit hugged her mantle more closely around her. She knew Solomon would probably be angry that she had come, but she had to see him before he left and tell him the truth.

"My sister?" She recognized Solomon's voice. Then, without further warning he came walking through the door and stopped in stunned amazement when he saw who it was.

"Yes, your sister," Shulamit said for the benefit of the old man, but her eyes were dark and questioning. Solomon turned from her angrily and would have gone back inside had she not reached out and grabbed his arm. "Come. You must come. It's important," she pleaded.

"I must see my friends. It's impossible now. Why have you come?" He was genuinely angry, and yet she couldn't let him go.

"Please come—for just a short time. You're leaving, and you mustn't go without an explanation." She clung to him tenaciously.

"Where would you have me go? There's no place we can go together." She could tell that at last he was relenting, though his voice was still cold and his words clipped.

"To my mother's house," she urged. Reluctantly Solomon agreed to go with her up the street toward the houses on the wall near the Water Gate.

Several of the king's guesthouses nestled in the corner of the wall, and Solomon knew which house had been given to her mother. A serving girl opened the door, and within moments Ramat was coming toward them with an eager smile and outstretched arms.

"The prince can't stay. I've taken him from a celebration," Shulamit said as Ramat led them into the main room. Seeing that they wanted to talk, she left them seated on the colorful mats while she went to the roof.

"How did you get these?" Shulamit asked, as she held out the offending beads.

"I got them from Adonijah," Solomon said, letting his feelings show in the tone of his voice and the flash of indignation in his eyes.

"What did Adonijah tell you? How did he say he happened to have them?"

"He said you gave them to him as a token of your love."

"And you believed him?"

"Of course I believed him. It's not possible for a man to unclasp a woman's beads without her consent." He was looking directly at her, his eyes hard and accusing.

"Are you in the habit of believing everything Adonijah tells you?" she challenged.

"No, of course not. But there was evidence."

"Well, it's all very simple. Adonijah tricked me into giving him the beads. He said that he thought they were valuable and he wanted to show them to one of his friends. I had no idea he would use them in this way." Shulamit's eyes were pleading, and her voice was soft and convincing.

"Both you and Adonijah were missing from the Feast of Unleavened Bread. I thought—" His eyes searched her face for some bit of encouragement.

"I don't know where Adonijah was or is, but I've been a virtual prisoner in the special apartment reserved for the king's new wives. There are fifteen young maidens from the city and several servants who watch over me from morning till night. Even my own mother hasn't been able to see me."

"Then how—?"

"How did I get away tonight? It's Passover: the maidens went home, and my serving girls were exhausted. Even the guard at the Postern Gate must have been home celebrating."

"You came by yourself? No one knows you're here?"

"I couldn't let you go to Egypt thinking I'd given my beads to Adonijah."

Solomon searched her face for any hint of duplicity as he broached the last subject. "There's still another matter." he said. "Adonijah not only told me that you had given him the beads, but he also told me that you had given yourself to him at his villa."

Shulamit uttered a cry of indignation. "How could he do such a thing? And how could you believe such a thing?" She burst into tears, covering her face with her skirt.

Solomon was overwhelmed with the enormity of Adonijah's lies and the hurt he had caused, but he was delighted to see that Shulamit felt as he did about his brother. Without knowing just how it came about, he was holding her in his arms and comforting her. "I should have known better. I should have recognized it as one of his tricks."

He was suddenly acutely aware of all the things that were at work to separate them—not the least being the trip he was about to make to Egypt. It would be months before he would even see her again. "I shall think of you every day while I'm gone." he said.

"I'm so afraid, so terribly afraid. You'll be gone for such a long time. Who can tell what will happen to both of us?" She felt the joy of having his arms tighten around her as he pulled her to her feet.

He didn't answer but instead silenced her questions with an eager, hungry kiss. He drew back and studied her face. "I always think of you as my own bride," he said. "That day in your father's courtyard I didn't feel that I was standing in for my father but rather that I was marrying you, with all that means to us here in Israel."

"If I can't be your bride, I wish I were your sister. Then I could kiss you openly in public and no one would despise me."

Solomon's eyes were bright with love, and his voice had grown tender. "How very sweet your love is, my little sister and bride." He took her hand in his and stooped to kiss her again. "Your lips are like sweet nectar. Even your robes smell of pine and lavender—the very smell of the mountains of Lebanon."

Shulamit laughed. "The soft hands and sweet lips are due to the hard work of the maidens of Jerusalem. Only the woodsy mountain smell is my own. I've packed my garments in dried flowers and needles from my valley at home."

He bent and kissed her again, this time pulling her to him roughly and kissing her with a hungry insistence that asked for more. She felt his hands move eagerly down her spine and then stop. He drew back and held her at arms' length. "Our time is up. I have to go." He said the words as though he were fighting to maintain control.

"You may never come back to me. We may never be together just like this again," Shulamit said sadly.

For a moment he hesitated, and then he drew her to him and held her close. "My mother and father defied the rules and grasped love, not counting the cost. Their love was very special and unique, but many people were hurt, many disillusioned. It even almost destroyed their love for each other. I'm determined not to make the same mistake."

Slowly he released her so that he could look again in her eyes. "You're like the walled garden in Shunem. Everything I would ever want is in that garden, but I mustn't climb the wall and steal its fruit."

Shulamit grew serious as she contemplated what he was trying to tell her. Then her eyes danced with mischief as she pulled his face down for one last kiss. "I'll pray every day that the north wind will come and blow upon my garden and scatter the fragrance abroad so that you won't forget me."

"How I would love to stay and explore all the delights of the garden," he said, "but it isn't yet mine."

"Then every day and every night I'll pray, 'O Jehovah, ruler of the universe, let my beloved, and only my beloved, come to his garden and eat its choicest fruits.'" Although her eyes were laughing through the tears, her voice had a catch in it that belied her lighthearted words.

He raised her hand and kissed the palm, then very gently folded her fingers over it. "There, keep my kiss until I come again to claim you as my bride." With that he turned, lifted the curtain of the door and left.

She stood in the middle of the room, listening to his retreating footsteps and holding tightly closed the hand he had kissed. She was overwhelmed with such a sense of foreboding that she longed to run after him and bring him back. There was still time to change things, but in a few months it might be too late. As his footsteps grew fainter, her whole world seemed to be disappearing with him into the darkness of the night.

Her mother came and walked with her as far as the Postern Gate. To her relief she found the gate still open and was able to slip in unnoticed. In her own chamber, however, she found her maidens shaken and fearful, huddling together as they tried to decide what to do. "Where have you been?" they chorused.

"I've visited the house of my mother," she answered as they removed her soaked sandals and damp cloak.

"You saw *only* your mother?" one of them asked, rubbing Shulamit's cold feet.

"My mother and the prince."

"The prince!" They were excited and shocked.

"I had time only to say goodbye to him."

"Did he kiss you?" they whispered, pressing close to catch every word.

"Yes, he kissed me." Shulamit started braiding her own long, dark hair, but one of the maidens reached out to do it for her.

"And—?"

"We said goodbye."

"Nothing more?"

"What did you expect?" she said, looking from one to the other.

"If you had lain with him, they would have been forced to give you to him as his bride," said the tall maid with her usual bluntness.

Shulamit swung around, pulling the half-finished braid out of the girl's hand. "It isn't good to force love before its time."

Nothing more was said, but most of the maidens, when they discussed it the next day, agreed that she was not likely to have another chance.

* * *

It was early morning when Solomon and Nathan came to bid their father goodbye before joining the caravan that would take them to Egypt.

"My son," David said with his hand on Nathan's shoulder, "Egypt isn't what she once was, but she's still a land of beauty and wisdom. There's much we can learn from her. You must observe the crafts, the building materials, and the methods, and techniques of building.

"You, my son Solomon, must grasp the essence of beauty," he said, putting his other hand on Solomon's shoulder. "The time will go quickly. You have only until Tishri, the seventh month, when I'll expect you back."

He kissed them and gave them his blessing, then stood proudly watching them ride away.

* * *

It was inevitable that the news of Shulamit's adventure should reach Tikva and eventually Bathsheba. "She's still young," Tikva explained in telling Bathsheba. "I would suggest that she be brought to the king as soon as possible."

Bathsheba had dismissed her maids and was alone with Tikva, looking over several pieces of jewelry that had been left for her inspection. When Tikva told the whole story of Shulamit's meeting with Solomon, Bathsheba sprang up and paced the room with a sure, deliberate movement that was meant to hide her anger.

"I can't understand why he's so attracted to her. It's as if she has somehow cast a spell over him."

"You will have nothing to fear once she's been taken in to the king," Tikva reminded her.

"Ohhhhhh," Bathsheba sputtered as she stooped to fling the jewelry back into the sandalwood box and slammed down the lid. "How can I be sure that this creature won't charm the king in the same way?"

"My lady, there have been many concubines and wives, yet he has always returned to you." Tikva bent and retrieved the sandalwood box so she wouldn't have to look at the hurt and bewilderment in Bathsheba's face.

"Of course he has returned to me. I was the only one who didn't try to bind him with tears and promises, but I'm not so sure that I can hold him against this little schemer."

Tikva laughed. "You must excuse me, my lady. Shulamit is just a simple country girl. She can't compare with you for charm and wit. You have *nothing* to fear. Let her go in to the king and get it over with. She'll soon be back in the harem, waiting with all the rest of the concubines and wives."

"But my son—I must find a way of tearing every memory of her from his heart or she'll ruin him." Bathsheba leaned against the wall, exhausted.

"My lady—forgive me for giving you advice?"

"Tikva, you know I welcome good advice. What are you thinking?"

"See that the prince is married as soon as possible. When he returns from Egypt, have all the plans made so he can't have them changed."

Bathsheba adjusted her circlet crown as she studied old Tikva's face. She walked to the door and hesitated. "Say nothing of this to anyone. I'll manage everything." With that she was gone, leaving old Tikva to wonder just what she was going to do.

* * *

That night as she lay in the curve of David's arm, she said casually, "It's time for our oldest son to take a wife."

"You mean Solomon?"

"Yes."

"Has he mentioned anyone he specially favors?" David asked.

"No, there's no one, but we must make the choice for his own good."

David turned slightly, facing her so he could see the moonlight touching the silver streaks in her hair and making her look almost young again. "If only we could find another Bathsheba, how happy he would be."

Bathsheba stiffened. "Solomon must marry a princess, or he won't be able to hold the throne."

"A princess? You must have someone in mind. An Egyptian?"

"No. Her name is Naamah, a princess of Rabbath-ammon and grand-daughter of Nahash."

"A worshiper of the idol Moloch, no doubt?"

"But my lord," said Bathsheba, rising up on one elbow so that she could see him better, "she's just a young girl, and she'll be alone here. It won't be long until she'll be doing as we tell her."

"It's been my experience that most women aren't so easy to lead."

"It would be to our advantage to have a strong link with Rabbath-ammon, if we're to control the King's Highway."

David smiled. "What a diplomat you are. You must have been thinking of this for months."

"You'll talk to our son?"

David pulled her down to him and kissed her words away. "I'll tell him as soon as he comes back, but we must start negotiations with the Ammonites now. This will take time."

Bathsheba smiled in the darkness as she gently traced the outline of his face and then bent and kissed him, lest he see the extent of her pleasure.

15

To Solomon and Nathan, who had spent their lives in a rugged, mountainous region, Bubastis, the home of Egypt's new ruling dynasty was a great surprise. The delta land was flat and verdant, with canals and waterways running like blue threads through its variegated tapestry. It was astonishing to the princes to learn that these people never needed to depend on the rain. The yearly inundation of the land by the Nile, and the constant supply of water to irrigate, freed them most of the time from the fear of drought and famine.

As one of the young Egyptian princes explained, "When we see the Dog Star Sirius on the southern horizon at daybreak, we know the Nile is ready to rise. We need no other water."

Flowers grew everywhere, giving the air a constant fragrance—but one that changed with every hour of the day. Lotus and chrysanthemum, mandrake and roses spilled in great profusion over walkways and climbed the ancient stone trellises. At night there was the pleasant mingling of all these various odors, with the heady addition of jasmine and tuberose.

The sounds were also delightfully varied. In the morning Solomon and Nathan awoke to the cooing of pigeons mingled with the creaking of waterwheels and the slow splashing of oars as some unknown boat made its way down to Memphis. At night they were lulled to sleep by the muffled sound of high, sweet voices mixed with the tinkling bells of the sistrum being shaken in a distant courtyard. Now and then they heard the piercingly sweet notes of a nightingale.

Life was relaxed and leisurely for the young princes. They had been given rooms in one of the many guesthouses in Pharaoh's garden and were treated with the respect due their position. The Egyptians hadn't forgotten that the Hebrews had been their slaves, and it was difficult for them to get over some preconceived ideas they held about them. One of the Egyptian princes admitted that he had thought of them as barbaric goat herders who were fanatically religious.

The Egyptians, curious about life in Israel, were full of questions. They were surprised to learn that the Israelites enjoyed many feast days that were celebrated with dancing and singing, and even kept one day out of seven as a day of rest. In Egypt the new day began with sunrise in the morning, and they all laughed to find that in Jerusalem and all of Israel the new day was counted from sunset the night before.

They were also amazed to find that their former slaves were almost as concerned about cleanliness as they were themselves. "We always wash before eating and bathe on the Sabbath before prayers," Nathan told one of the princes.

Most of all, the young Egyptian princes found it hard to believe that the Israelites worshiped only one God. They couldn't imagine how one God could be everyplace, taking care of all the people at once. It was much better, they argued, to have gods that were in charge of only one village or one aspect of life.

"Our village is protected and cared for by the god Bastet, the cat goddess, and her son the lion god, Mihos. Before you travel on to Memphis, you must see our lovely city and the temple of Bastet," the young prince Shoshenq said.

The princes traveled up and down the Nile, viewing with growing amazement the wonders of Egypt. The huge manmade mountains they called pyramids astounded them, and the strange half-man, half-lion called the Sphinx puzzled them. The temples were more than impressive, but it was the gods of Egypt that seemed most peculiar. Thoth with the head of an ibis, Horus with the head of a hawk, and Anubis with the head of a jackal were all honored and respected deities.

* * *

The time passed quickly. Nathan went to every building site possible and asked questions. He examined materials and even talked to the workers until he understood each stage, from the initial design to the finished temple or palace.

Solomon, on the other hand, spent his time in seeming leisure and dalliance—yet all the time he was aware of everything that happened around him. He noted each nuance of manner or custom; every delicacy served him was remembered; the odors that floated from the sails of the barges or were circulated by the ostrich fans were tabulated.

Solomon observed the freshness of the pillared rooms open to the outside and the frescoes of flowers and animals painted on the walls. He loved the gardens, with peacocks walking on green grass while white swans floated by in the lotus ponds. Most of all, he was enchanted by the idea of moving swiftly and effortlessly on the water in boats and barges.

All these impressions were gathered and evaluated, with the hope that somehow they could be adapted to life back in Israel.

In spite of all the lavish entertainment and exciting trips, Solomon found that he wasn't able to forget Shulamit for long. As time went on he received news from Jerusalem, but no one mentioned her. He carefully scanned the parchments brought by messengers for news of his father, but there was nothing but greetings and advice.

He was afraid to let his mind dwell on the possibility that she was already in his father's bed or hidden away in David's harem with the other forgotten wives.

Relaxing by the lotus pool in the garden outside his rooms, he was surprised to find himself counting the days until they would be leaving Egypt. At home in Jerusalem they would have just finished counting the omer: the fifty days from Passover to Shavuot. He could imagine the whole celebration, and he was desperately homesick. It would be three more months until the feast of Sukkot.

They *must* be home for Sukkot. This was the feast when all Israel gathered in the final harvest of the year, the harvest of fruit and olives. It was a magical time, when young maidens would be singing and treading the grapes in the vats, old women would be squeezing the juice from the ripe pomegranates, and young boys would be chasing each other up the low fig trees to get the first ripe fruit.

Solomon had always looked forward to the seventh month, but now he looked forward to it with mixed feelings. If Shulamit was lost to him forever, there would be no happy homecoming or joyful festival. He began to wonder if the whole trip to Egypt hadn't been a terrible mistake.

* * *

Back in Jerusalem the days had gone slowly for Shulamit. Each one seemed the same. Always there was the arrival of old Tikva and then the young maidens, who began to organize her day.

Under their constant attention she was slowly changing. Her hair was now glossy black, and her hands were soft and the nails long. When she looked in the round brass hand mirror, she was surprised to see that her face had taken on the aspect of a beautiful woman she could hardly recognize.

She thought about Solomon all the time. She could almost imagine his slow, amused smile or hear his voice exclaiming over the new whiteness of her hands or the dusting of lapis lazuli on her eyelids. "Your hands, my love," he would say, "are white like the lilies, and your eyes are fringed in blue like the Nile at night."

At times she mentioned him to the maidens who attended her, and they always gave her the same advice. They had seen many young brides and concubines taken to the king's bed or in to one of the princes and then discarded. "Take love when you find it, and don't wait," they advised.

She was sitting out in the small courtyard thinking of these things as the maidens combed her hair and argued over the headpiece she would wear, when suddenly there was a disturbance in the outer room. A man's voice could be heard speaking softly but firmly, obviously demanding something.

Shulamit was frightened. Even the women of the harem were forbidden to visit her, and it was unthinkable that a man should be in the outer room talking to her maidens.

She stood up as he appeared in the shadows of the door. "How beautiful the king's new bride has become!" It was Adonijah. His words were complimentary, but his eyes were possessive and lustful.

Adonijah moved out into the sunlight. "I haven't risked a good tongue-lashing by old Tikva just to see you with all these fluttering pigeons," he complained. "Tell them to go." His voice was petulant, like that of a spoiled child.

Shulamit grabbed the arm of the youngest maid and pulled her over to her side as the rest fled from the courtyard. "It's not the custom for young maidens to be alone with men," she said.

Adonijah threw back his head and laughed. "I've no intention of taking you now. I don't want to spoil the game."

"I don't understand." Shulamit backed away from him but held firmly to the serving girl's arm.

"First, you must let this poor girl go." He reached toward the maid, but Shulamit put her arm around her and backed away.

"All right," he sulked, "let the girl stay. I've simply come to tell you news that will be common knowledge by tomorrow."

"What news could possibly be of any concern to me?" she said, turning from him.

"Your marriage to the king is to be consummated. Is that not news?" His voice had a note of triumph in it, and his eyes were now cold and calculating.

As he had anticipated, Shulamit let go of the girl and whirled to face him. "How do you know this?"

"I've seen Bathsheba," he said, "and she assures me that this is true." He was obviously enjoying every minute of her discomfort.

"Why are *you* the one to break this news to me?" Shulamit asked.

Without answering, he took the young maid by the arm and led her to the door. "I don't want your maidens spreading what I have to say all over Jerusalem."

He waited until the girl's footsteps could be heard crossing the threshold of the outer door. Then he grabbed Shulamit and swung her around into his arms. "Now, my lovely, you're where you belong."

Shulamit began to struggle and push, turning her face so that he couldn't kiss her. "You've lied to me again. You always lie. You lied to Solomon about the beads, and I despise you.

"You're a little wildcat, and I love wildcats," he said, releasing her with a push that flung her back against the wall. "Listen to me. I'm going to be the next king. As I told you before, I'll inherit all my father's wives. If you play the game right, you can be queen."

Shulamit glared at him as she straightened her gown and ran her hands through her hair. "I'll *never* be your queen."

At her words his eyes flashed. "Solomon won't get the crown, but you can still be queen—my queen."

"I need no advice from you."

He shrugged. "I'm tired of women who grovel. I'll enjoy seeing you compete for my attention when I'm king," he said with a self-satisfied smile. "I can wait."

"Then you'll have a long wait," she said. "I'll *never* marry you." As she backed away, she saw his cool, practiced facade begin to crumble. The crumbling was more frightening than his swaggering bravado.

"Come, tell me now," he said angrily, "am I not just as handsome as all of David's other sons? Don't I smile and say the same meaningless pleasantries?

Am I not dressed by the same weavers? Don't I use the same fragrances? Why, then, should you not choose to love me?"

Shulamit recognized that he was speaking to her from some hidden depth that lay beneath the petty jealousies and tricks of what he had called "the game." Suddenly she wanted to say something that would explain her feelings in terms that didn't shout so loudly of rejection. "You're jealous of Solomon," she said, "and that's wrong."

"My father has always favored him, his mother fights like a tiger for him, and the women swoon when he passes. Why shouldn't I be jealous?"

"My mother says that love comes to us because someone else has the ability to love, not because we're so lovable ourselves. She also says that if we're worthy of love, it will come to us." Shulamit saw his face harden back into its manipulative mask, and again she wanted to be free of him. "For myself, I would suggest that love isn't something one demands of others."

Adonijah understood very little of what she said, but he had regained his composure. He straightened his short sword and smoothed the fringe on his cloak. At the door he turned and looked at her once more, smiling his old, self-assured smile. "I just wanted to remind you that if you're clever, you can yet be queen of Israel."

With that he turned on his heel and was gone as quickly as he had come. Shulamit sank down on the cool stones at the edge of her small, herb garden and faced the fact that her marriage to David was something she would soon have to deal with.

*I*t was an old superstition that no marriages should take place or be consummated during the counting of the omer, during the fifty days from Passover to Shavuot. For this reason it had been decided that Shulamit should not be taken in to the king until after the firstfruits celebration. The counting was, for most, a happy time of anticipation, especially now that the drought was over and the crops healthy. However, for Shulamit each day's counting only brought her closer to the fulfillment of a marriage she didn't want and dashed all her hopes of ever being Solomon's bride.

Gradually, as the days passed, the atmosphere in her small courtyard changed. The sound of the flute and drums was no longer heard; the shuffling and jingle of dancing jeweled feet had stopped. The young maidens were too busy to think of anything but the last rounds of baths, pine rubs, and henna dips for the prospective bride.

"Give up this foolish idea of loving Solomon," the young maidens urged. "You'll be one of David's queens. Isn't that enough?"

Shulamit wanted to shout at them, "No, it *isn't* enough." How could they think her marriage would make her happy when it would mean giving up Solomon forever?

The feast, with its celebration of the wheat harvest and the giving of the Law at Mount Sinai, passed. The day when Shulamit was to be taken to the king finally arrived.

Early in the morning, old Tikva took her out to the great courtyard at the center of the women's apartments and showed her where she would sit beside the king under the great wedding huppah. "When the feasting is over, the king will lead you up those steps to his own special chamber behind the reception room," she said. The steps were the same ones leading to the room where the Passover had been celebrated and where she had met Solomon in the darkness on the landing.

"There's the room." Tikva was pointing to some latticed windows that looked down on the courtyard.

Shulamit shivered. There seemed to be no possible way of escape. By the time Solomon returned for the Sukkot celebration in the fall, she would be forever doomed to a life without him. Most painful of all, she would continue to live right here in the harem of the king, where every day she would see the wives Solomon married and the children they bore him.

Back in her own courtyard, surrounded again by the fluttering excitement of her maidens, she had little time to think. She sat on a large cushion on a raised dais and let them do as they pleased. They had wrought such a change that she could hardly recognize even her own hands, which had been painted with miniature black flowers in fine, featherlike lines.

Shulamit felt uncomfortable in the heavily embroidered robes. It was as though her trim, well-groomed body, sleek with the fragrant oil, was encased in a shroud. Looking down at her toes peeping out from beneath the thick embroidery, she was surprised to see how fragile they looked laced with golden straps and sparkling with jeweled toe rings.

One of the maidens brought a bronze mirror, so she could see the wonderful transformation. Shulamit studied the face as though it didn't belong to her. "Every inch of me has been changed," she thought. "I'm no longer the simple shepherd girl. I wonder if Solomon will still love me."

Old Tikva took the mirror from her gently. "The king is a good and great man. His wives all envy you," she said with a touch of reproof.

At the mention of David's other wives, Shulamit felt a new and sudden alarm. Of course they would be looking at her with envious, critical eyes, and she couldn't hope to find one friend among them.

When she was ready, her mother came to spend the last few minutes with her. "You mustn't despair," she said as she saw how unhappy her daughter was.

"Solomon doesn't know. I can't even say goodbye to him." Her lovely eyes were large and troubled.

Her mother said no more but placed her hands on her head and, in a calm, sweet voice, gave her blessing. "May the God of Sarah and Rebekah be with you, and may you remember always God's words to Sarah: 'Is anything too hard for the Lord?'"

Shulamit heard her mother's words, but they seemed empty expressions.

She wanted to cry out, "Yes, Mother—yes, some things *are* too hard for the Lord."

It was late; her maidens had already returned with their tambourines and streamers, singing the raucous wedding songs. Before she knew it, she was being lifted from the dais and edged toward the door. She had one last glimpse of her mother standing against the wall, head raised so that the sunlight caught her loving smile.

* * *

The courtyard was filled with the wives of David and the wives of his sons, concubines, and other relatives—all waiting for her arrival. From under her veil she looked around the courtyard and recognized only one woman, and that was Haggith. She was sitting apart from the others with several of her serving women. She looked especially out of sorts and disagreeable. Bathsheba wasn't among them, and Shulamit wondered briefly where she was and why she hadn't come.

The maidens led her to David, who waited on cushions at the far end of the room. Rising to take her hand, he invited her to join him. He was unusually jovial and solicitous of her welfare, breaking off the choicest portions of the honey cakes for her and even holding his own golden cup for her to sip the king's special wine.

Gradually Shulamit began to relax. Just before she was led away to the king's upper chamber for the night, she grew brave enough to look at him. To her surprise she saw that, despite his fine robes, ornate rings, and circlet crown, he was just a man like other men—only with more charm and magnetism. "Perhaps," she thought, "I may be able to reason with him. He's a good man, and kind."

As the last dancers were whirling and dipping before them, an idea began to take shape in her mind. It was so simple that she wondered if it would work. "Please, Tikva," she whispered while David was talking to one of his small grandsons, "get my flute and take it to the bridal chamber. Place it in the window niche where I can find it easily," she instructed.

She saw Tikva move through the crush of women and children out into the darkness at the back of the courtyard.

* * *

Shulamit, moving as if in a dream, hardly knew how she reached the richly decorated room that was David's private apartment above the court of the women. She was vaguely aware that David was relaxed and completely in control of the situation. He quickly dismissed the servants and came to where she was standing. Very gently he lifted her thin veil, leaving only the cap of rosebuds.

For a long moment he stood looking at her with evident approval. "I don't know why they have to spoil something that's already perfect with all this paint," he said. "You're so caked with their lotions and powders you can't even smile." His jeweled forefinger lightly traced the gentle curve of her chin.

"If there were some water—"

"Of course, there's water. That's just the thing. Stay right here. They have you so weighted down with those robes you can hardly move." She watched him go to a small room off to one side, then heard the splash of water being poured from a jar.

"Do you do this with all your brides?" she asked as he gently wiped her face with the wet cloth.

He laughed. "No, I've never done it before, but I've wanted to. There," he said, backing off to get a better look. "You look like a normal human being, and you're much more beautiful. I sometimes think they make women up like that just to scare the men. Well, I'm too old to be scared anymore."

Again he laughed, leading her to the brightly colored mats that were covered with luxurious furs and banked with cushions. She tried to sit down, but the heavy embroidery was too cumbersome. "I've sent for some cakes and wine and a few guinea fowl," he said. "They always forget to feed the bride and groom any *real* food at these things." As he talked, he opened a chest and pulled out various colorful linen robes. He handed her one. "Do you think this would fit?" he asked.

She held it up and saw that it was actually a man's short tunic. He helped her unlace the ornate robe she wore and didn't seem to mind that she turned her back to him so that he wouldn't see her bare breasts as she lifted the tunic and put it on. She smiled shyly as she looked down at the tunic with the harem pants protruding beneath it. She didn't look very glamorous, but she was comfortable.

The meal that the servants brought was a superb feast carefully arranged on silver and gold platters. David ate heartily, as though relieved to have the ceremony over and be able at last to relax. He talked to her and urged her to eat, but she could scarcely touch a bite. She was still wondering how she could tell him about Solomon.

"My lord," she said, as the last servant disappeared through the door with the empty tray. "I have one wish that I hope you'll grant me on my wedding night!"

It was the custom that every bride could ask for one gift on the wedding night, and David braced himself as though expecting some unpleasant surprise. "And what could my northern beauty want?"

"It's a simple thing. I wish to hear you play your harp just for me." She could see that David was both surprised and pleased. He hesitated only a moment, then he called for one of his servants and asked him to bring his harp.

He slowly drew his fingers across the strings, then plucked each one. He bent down and listened while he tightened one of the strings. "What sort of song do you want to hear?" he asked her.

"A song of the outdoors, springtime, and blooming things!"

"Ah, you really *were* a little shepherdess, then?" He turned and looked at her, his eyes shining with interest. "I'll sing you the songs I sang as a boy out herding my sheep. They're simple tunes. We'll see if they're the same ones you sing in the north."

He began to sing some of his favorites. Most of them Shulamit recognized as songs that were also sung by shepherds in Shunem, and she sang along with him.

"It's late," he said finally, leaning his harp against the wall. He reached for the small oil lamp and pinched out the flame, leaving only the light from the brazier and the soft glow from a hanging alabaster globe.

He moved toward her to take her in his arms, and Shulamit braced herself for her last ploy. "My lord," she whispered, "let me play a few songs on my shepherd's flute for you." When he didn't answer, she reached for the flute and began to play the lovely, plaintive songs she had learned out on the hillside with her sheep. Before she had finished the second song, his breathing became deep and even, and she knew that he was asleep.

Shulamit didn't sleep, but lay awake planning what she would do. She had escaped now only because David was tired, but in the morning it could be a very different matter. She would have to tell him the truth. But how? At all costs she mustn't reject or anger him.

* * *

The first rays of the sun filtered through the shutters, and still she hadn't slept. She could hear the early-morning cooing of the doves in their clay nests under the eaves and the crowing of a cock in some distant courtyard. Very carefully she slipped from the bed and stood on the cold stone floor, shivering. There would be just a short time now until he would awaken; she had to think fast.

Quickly she pulled a large fur throw from the bed and wrapped herself in it so that her teeth didn't chatter so. Then, seeing the chest in the corner, she went and sat crosslegged on the top. Slowly she raised her flute and mimicked the warbling notes of the weaver bird.

He didn't move but lay just as she had left him. She set the flute aside and began to whistle the tender, sweet notes of the nightingale. She saw him slowly turn over on his back and stretch; then, as though remembering the night before, he sat up abruptly and looked at the empty place beside him. Then he looked over to her corner, where the sound of the nightingale was still vibrating on the air.

"Nightingales don't sing in the morning," he said.

"This nightingale can sing at any time," Shulamit said, laughing.

"Then you aren't angry?" He was obviously remembering the night before.

"Is one ever angry when a prayer is answered?"

"No, of course not. But I don't understand."

"It wouldn't be right to marry the king without being able to give him the complete love and devotion he deserved," she said.

Pondering her statement, he didn't answer right away. "Then—there's someone else?"

"Yes, my lord."

"Perhaps a handsome, young northern shepherd?"

"Yes, my lord. At least when I met him he was dressed like a shepherd, and acted like one, but he wasn't from the north."

"Not from the north?"

"No, my lord."

"Could he possibly have been from Jerusalem?"

"Yes, my lord."

"Do I know this fellow who passed himself off as a shepherd? Could he possibly be one of my men?"

173

"Yes, my lord." She could see that his mind was actively sorting through all of the men who had gone north with Bathsheba.

"Could it be one of my sons? Adonijah would never have been mistaken for a shepherd, but Solomon would love the romance of just such a situation. Could it have been my own son Solomon?"

"Yes, my lord." She answered in such a soft whisper that he had to lean forward to hear her.

He waited for a long moment, and his brows drew down as he thought of the words to ask what he *must* ask. "Then my son has already bedded you and is trying to make a fool of me?"

"Oh no, my lord!" she said, springing from the chest and kneeling beside him on the floor. "He said he wouldn't commit the sin of his father, and so he wouldn't have me."

"He said that, did he? That he wouldn't commit the sin of his father? He really told you that?" David was out of bed, buckling on his short sword and fastening his greaves. "I wouldn't have known that any of my sons had the wisdom to learn from someone else's mistakes."

"He's very wise—and honest and completely lovable."

"So you love this son of mine?"

"Oh, yes, with all my heart." Shulamit's shining face and enthusiasm demonstrated more than words just how very much she did love Solomon.

"And last night you planned to escape so that you could save yourself for my son. What makes you think that Adonijah may not come to the throne after me? Then you would be *his* bride. Have you thought of that?"

"Yes, my lord."

"And you were willing to take that chance?"

"Yes, my lord. It's in God's hands."

A tender look crossed David's face, as he came to stand before her. He looked down at her bowed head with its wild tendrils of hair curling naturally, and with one jeweled finger he lifted her chin so that he could look in her eyes. "You're a very brave girl. You've risked much for this love of yours, and I hope that someday you'll be rewarded. Solomon will, of course, have married other women before that time, but if, as I have planned, he does become king, you will be his wife. I'll tell the counselors today that I didn't consummate the marriage. That much I can do for you." He stood fingering the fringe on his cloak and thinking for a moment, then turned and walked from the room.

Shulamit hugged the great fur to her and walked to the window to open the shutter. She looked down into the courtyard that was just coming to life and realized that she would now be one of those women. She would have to face their questions and their scorn. She would be known as a bride whom the king had rejected. Their mockery would be as fierce as their jealousy had been.

A cool breeze banged one of the shutters closed and frightened the pigeons from their nests. She saw them rise up in a cloud just as they did at her father's house in Shunem. "They're like pure white prayers rising up to the throne of God," she thought.

* * *

By the time Shulamit joined them for the noon meal, David's other wives and the young maidens who had attended her for the last months had all heard that the marriage hadn't been consummated. The mixture of curiosity and pity on their faces was harder to bear than their earlier hostility.

Abigail, who was in charge when Bathsheba wasn't present, was suddenly kind to her. Haggith ignored her. If she was no longer competition and had no influence, she wasn't interested in her. Maacah, the mother of Absalom and Tamar, hugged her and wept, while the rest of the concubines viewed her in utter silence with wide, kohl-rimmed eyes.

Only Sarah, Nathan's young wife, was able to express her sympathy and then take up their friendship as though nothing had happened. Sarah had come with Mattatha to stay in the court of the queens while Nathan was in Egypt, and Shulamit had noticed that the little boy was the delight of his grandmother, Bathsheba. Whenever she came into the courtyard, he dropped whatever he was doing and ran, arms outstretched, to be hugged and kissed.

Bathsheba wasn't with the other wives very often. Though she had the best rooms and her own spacious courtyard, she preferred to spend most of her time in the house David had given her across the valley, or at her grandfather's old home in Giloh.

It was Sarah who told Shulamit of Bathsheba's strange reaction to the news that the marriage hadn't been consummated. "She seemed disappointed," Sarah said, with puzzlement evident in her voice.

* * *

Shulamit was barely settled in her new rooms when she heard a light tapping on the shutters of her window and saw a familiar jeweled hand reach through the hole in the door and unlatch it. It was, as she had suspected, Adonijah. He stooped to enter and stood for a moment without speaking, looking down at her, his eager, hungry eyes blazing with excitement. "I've heard the news from the king himself," he said finally. "You managed very well, and now my sweet, you will be mine—perhaps, if I have my way, even before my father dies." He reached and took her hand, not noticing that she shrank from him.

"I didn't do it for *you*," she said, pulling away from him. "It was for Solomon. I'll have him or no one."

Adonijah's laugh was both triumphant and cynical. "Then you'll most likely have no one. The arrangements are being made for Solomon to marry the princess of Rabbath-ammon."

She suspected that it was another trick, and so she challenged him. "Solomon isn't even back from Egypt. Who told you this?"

"The queen. She's made all the plans."

"But the king hasn't agreed. He won't agree until Solomon returns."

"And there you're wrong, my pretty little vixen. They've asked me to leave immediately to make the arrangements. They plan to have the wedding as soon as possible after Solomon's return from Egypt." He stood with one hand on his short sword and the other on his hip. He looked as though he had just won some great prize and was still reveling in it.

Shulamit jumped up and turned her back to him so that he couldn't see her tears. "Perhaps the princess will refuse."

"Never. Her people are now practically our vassals, and they want desperately to make a treaty with us. The princess will be part of the agreement."

She swung around and challenged him again. "But she's a worshiper of idols, and that's forbidden. Solomon won't agree."

"He'll agree because it's for Israel. He'll do anything to make his country strong."

"When Solomon comes back, you'll see. He'll not agree to marry her."

"You poor, innocent girl," Adonijah said, trying to embrace her as she struggled to free herself. "Now you're dealing with ambitious princes and kings, not romantic poets."

"Solomon is different. You'll see." She had pulled free of him and was backing off, smoothing down her gown.

Adonijah threw back his head and laughed. "That mother of his will convince him that it's his duty, and he'll marry her. Solomon will lose everything he really wants. How bitter he'll be." For a moment Adonijah's face was twisted in a grimace of anticipation. He rubbed his hands together and gloated. Then, with a sardonic laugh, he turned, ducked his head as he went through the door, and was gone.

Shulamit closed the door and bolted it and then stood with her back against it, thinking. If they were really sending Adonijah to Rabbath-ammon, the decision must have already been made that Solomon must marry the princess. For a moment she felt utterly despondent and hopeless. Then, brushing back her hair with one hand, she struggled to regain her composure. "He'll *never* agree. I know he won't. He'll think of something."

She sank down among the cushions and reviewed all that Adonijah had said. It could be just another one of his tricks, but she doubted it. It had the ominous ring of truth, and she was worried.

* * *

As the news spread through the court of the queens that the marriage of Shulamit had not been consummated, all of the maidens gathered to ask questions and to console her. To their surprise they found that she wasn't angry with David, nor did she have some titillating story to tell. She seemed to have accepted the situation without ill feelings; however, they all agreed there was a new sadness in her demeanor.

That same evening Shulamit's mother came to see her, and Shulamit dismissed the maidens so she could talk to her alone. Shulamit briefly told her all that had happened in David's room, and then she burst into tears as she told of Adonijah's visit.

"My dear," her mother responded, "don't be surprised if Solomon *does* marry the princess."

"No, no—he won't do that. I couldn't bear it." Shulamit paced the floor of her little room in an agony of hurt.

"My darling," her mother comforted her, "you may yet belong to him when his father dies. It isn't as though Solomon were a poor man and couldn't afford a second wife."

"I know all of that, Mother," she cried, "but something would be gone, spoiled, ruined. I couldn't endure it, and besides, if Adonijah gets the throne,

177

he'll be the one to inherit his father's wives."

Ramat patted her hand. "I know, but you must learn to accept what comes in life and make the best of it. This world isn't perfect."

"I'm not asking for perfection in everything—only that my love for Solomon and his love for me not be spoiled."

"Unfortunately, we don't own and control other people unless they're our slaves, and slaves aren't known to love their owners."

"Then what am I to do?" Shulamit sank down on one of the mats and hid her face in her hands.

"You're free to do only one thing, my daughter: you're free to love. No one can stop you from loving."

"But what of his love for me?"

"That's something he must give freely. You can't demand it. That's one of the laws of love."

"What you're saying is too hard." Tears spilled from Shulamit's eyes.

Her mother knelt down beside her and tried to comfort her. "I have to go, but remember what I've said. It's the only way to have peace. You're free to love—and that's all."

As they said goodbye and Shulamit watched her mother go toward the Postern Gate, it occurred to her that Ramat's advice had come out of her own experience. It must have been the lesson she had learned in the long years of living with Bessim and enduring his penchant for beautiful young girls. "Is there then no way," she thought, "to love without enduring such pain?"

She thought again of Adonijah's visit. He had been so sure; he had made such careful plans. It was obvious that he wanted her only because he was competing with Solomon. She wondered if there was anything powerful enough or strong enough to stop him. Her mother would say that the situation was in God's hands and she must pray.

She did pray, but nothing changed. Everything seemed only to get worse.

*U*ndoubtedly the whole scandal of Shulamit's rejection by the king would have been discussed for weeks if something far more serious hadn't suddenly demanded the city's complete attention.

It was first rumored and then proven that the Philistines were again arming for battle. They had heard of the large wheat crop just harvested up on the ridge and planned to come up and raid the newly bulging storage bins. It was one of their favorite ploys: to defeat the enemy in battle and then cripple them by taking their food supply.

One of the Israelite spies who sat daily in the markets of Gath reported that a giant named Saph had said, "We mustn't let Israel get strong again, now that the famine is over."

When it came time for the troops to march out to meet the enemy, Shulamit joined the rest of the women in chanting and singing, in shaking of tambourines and beating of drums. Their high-pitched voices rose over the Shofar's wailing, and their drums thudded louder than the pounding bare feet of the men as they marched out the great North Gate.

For Shulamit it was an inspiring sight: the army of Israel, with David in a chariot leading his Mighty Men; the captains leading their foot soldiers, all with phylacteries bound on their left arms with black cord, the leather boxes holding the sacred words of Moses as protection against the arrows of the uncircumcised Philistines.

The women stood on the wall and watched until the last baggage cart disappeared over the ridge to the west and the voices of their men could no longer be heard floating back on the crisp morning air. They were anxious and fearful. The army wasn't as large as it had been before the famine, and David was no longer the strong, muscular man he had been during earlier battles.

Two days passed with word coming back only sporadically of battles fought and barely won. The men were fighting against both the Philistine confederation and the giants they had armed and trained. The third day there was no news at all. No breathless runners appeared with reports from the field, and no wounded men came straggling home. Women and children, old men and servants huddled in small, apprehensive groups and spoke in hushed voices, trying vainly to reassure each other.

Finally, at nightfall on the fourth day, a young runner stumbled through the North Gate, completely exhausted. When he caught his breath enough to speak, he told them the fearful news: "The Philistines have been driven back, but David, the light of Israel, was almost snuffed out."

* * *

Long before the army of Israel came in sight in the Valley of Rephaim, the people gathered on the walls to welcome them. When at last David was sighted, still riding in his chariot, a great tidal wave of emotion swept through the mob. They pushed and shoved in a frenzy to get down from the wall so they could run out to greet him.

Everyone seemed to realize that this would be the last time any of them would ever see David returning home victorious from an encounter with the Philistines. Their eyes grew moist and their voices choked with feeling as they rushed to surround his chariot.

A hush hung suspended in the evening air as they noticed that David leaned heavily on his armor-bearer. It hurt them even more to see with what effort he held his head erect and raised his hand in greeting.

"Abishai," he called, and they were aware that his jaw was firm and his voice strong, even though his eyes registered pain.

The young man came forward, and David ordered him to bring the head of the giant Saph. They all watched in horrified silence while one of the captains drove a nail through the giant's tangled mass of hair, pinioning the huge head to the post beside the gate.

"But for this young man's bravery," David said, pointing to Abishai, "it would have been my head that hung on the gates of Gath tonight."

For a long moment they stood mesmerized by the terrible sight. Then with one accord some of the captains lifted David from the chariot and bore him into the city. The people pushed and shoved again as they tried to get close to him. Everyone wanted to say a word of encouragement, or just to kiss his hand or his robe in gratitude.

Shulamit had witnessed David's return with deep compassion. She wished she dared offer to nurse him back to health. She decided it would be bold and out of place. He had so many friends eager to sit with him and wait on him that he didn't need anyone else.

As it turned out, it was the king himself who called for Shulamit. It was a hot day, and as Shulamit entered the king's rooms, she saw David sitting up in the midst of his great bed with a clutter of parchments and swatches of material spilling out over the linen covering. She was amazed at how pale and ill he looked. "My lord?" she said, bowing to the ground beside the bed while his counselors, Mighty Men, and attendants looked at her with new appreciation.

"Ah, the little nightingale," he said, smiling wanly. "It was my counselors who first recommended that I have someone to warm my feet." He turned to look around the room, and many of the men guiltily turned their heads, not wanting to meet his eyes. "Now it's not only my feet that are chilled, but my whole body."

"My lord, I know very well how to massage your feet so that they'll be warm again"

David smiled weakly. "No, it isn't that. I want to hear you play the flute again. The songs of the shepherd are the songs I want to hear."

"My flute is back in the court of the queens," she apologized.

"Never mind. I have my old flute. I made it myself. See if it won't play as well as your northern reed." He rummaged around under the bed and brought out a well-turned flute.

In just such a simple way it became a regular occurrence for the king to call for Shulamit. At first she only played for him, but gradually she gave him the herbal medicines her mother made, massaged his cold feet, and rubbed his aching back with oil of eucalyptus.

When Bathsheba realized that Shulamit was being called so often by the king, she was angry. She had hoped that the king would consummate the marriage and then forget about her. Now she was constantly confronted by this girl she had taken such a dislike to. However, the king was definitely not well, and Bathsheba didn't want to make him worse by insisting that Shulamit leave. She decided that she would have to wait until the appropriate time, and then it would be an easy matter to get rid of Shulamit.

* * *

So it was that several months later, as the people were preparing for the fruit harvest and the Feast of Trumpets that would herald in the seventh month, Shulamit was in the king's chambers when news came that Solomon and his company were approaching Hebron. Such wild jubilation prevailed that no one noticed that Shulamit had dropped an armful of the king's choicest parchments.

She was in a fever of excitement, hoping to be allowed to stay until Solomon arrived. Just to be in the same room with him would be happiness enough. To look in his eyes and revel in the familiar warmth of recognition would be more than she had hoped for.

Now with Adonijah's news that she might lose him in a marriage to the princess of Rabbath-ammon, these small blessings became doubly precious. She couldn't imagine how he could have held her hand without her becoming speechless with joy, or kissed her without her fainting.

The king was feeling better, so it was agreed that he would ride down to the Fountain Gate to welcome his sons. It wasn't until later that night that he returned with Solomon to his bedchamber.

* * *

There was a hint of chill in the high-ceilinged room, so Shulamit, sitting on a cushion, was feeding thorns into the glowing coals of the brazier. Suddenly she heard the king's laughter and then Solomon's low, vibrant answer to some question. She jumped up and waited eagerly in the shadows near the great chest that held the king's formal clothes.

The king came into the room with Nathan at his side and flung his crown upon the bed so vigorously that it rolled off onto the floor. One of the servants hurried to retrieve it, and at that moment Shulamit saw Solomon as he appeared in the doorway. His face was bright with excitement, as he looked around the room in delight at being home again.

When he drew back with a sharp movement, Shulamit knew he had seen her. For the first time she realized that he would have to be told of the wedding night and its outcome. She trembled at the thought that he might not understand.

"This is Shulamit," David said as he noticed Solomon looking at her.

"Yes, yes. I know Shulamit very well. She's one of Jezreel Valley's rarest lilies."

"You must understand, my son, that while you were gone, it was decided that my marriage to her should be consummated." Solomon's face clouded, and he turned and walked toward the window, obviously deeply shaken.

"My son," David said, quickly following him and placing a hand on his shoulder, "the maiden wouldn't have me—said she loved some shepherd lad she had met in Jezreel—so I released her."

Solomon swung around sharply and faced his father. It was obvious that he didn't understand what his father was trying to tell him. "I released her," David repeated, "without consummating the marriage."

Slowly Solomon's frown melted into an eager smile. "Then it's possible?"

"Yes, my son. At some future date when I'm no longer here, if you're king after me, she will be yours. However, in the meantime we've started proceedings for your marriage to the princess of Rabbath-ammon."

"You've already decided?"

"Yes. Right now Adonijah is in Rabbath-ammon making the initial arrangements." David stood with his back to Solomon while the young armorbearer unfastened his short sword and unclasped his belt, so he didn't see the look of loathing on his son's face.

"Why Adonijah? Why this hurry?"

David didn't seem to notice the angry intonation of his son's voice. He simply shrugged and threw up his hands in a gesture of resignation. "You are to go to your mother. She'll explain everything. I would imagine she's getting impatient." Greatly agitated, Solomon turned and left the room.

Shulamit didn't leave until the king was in his bed. She brought him a honeyed drink mixed with herbs, straightened the cushions behind him, and gently removed his harp and some of the manuscripts from the bed. When she saw the king's eyes close, she quietly slipped from the room and headed for the court of the queens.

She knew the way perfectly, so she didn't carry a lamp. First, she went to the antechamber. From there stairs led up to the reception room above the court of the queens. Here she paused, as there was a light in the bedchamber and she knew Bathsheba must be there.

She tiptoed quietly across the cold stones of the floor and started down the steps to the courtyard below. The stairs were so dark and uneven that she had to lightly touch the stones along the wall to steady herself. When she became aware of someone ahead of her, standing in the deep shadows of the landing, she paused. Out of the darkness came the distinct sound of a dove cooing.

"Oh, my dove," she whispered joyfully, as she skipped lightly down to the landing and threw herself into Solomon's arms.

"How did you know it was me?" he asked, when he finally drew back and tried to see her.

"My darling," she said, almost laughing with joy, "I know your voice even when it's disguised as a dove."

Again they marveled at the love they felt for each other. "All the time I was in Egypt I thought of you," he said. "Everything reminded me of you—even the mare harnessed to Pharaoh's chariot."

Shulamit stifled a laugh. "The mare—?"

"You don't understand. If you had only seen her: head high, with jeweled trappings and prancing feet, preening herself in all her glory before the balcony on which we stood. The pharaoh explained that when he rode out with his mare, it threw the stallions in the enemy's army into complete disarray."

"But the mare—?" Again she had to stifle a laugh, but then almost at once she became serious. "Can they make you marry the princess?" she asked, a flicker of alarm in her voice.

"Don't worry." He held her close and kissed her hungrily. "I'll think of something."

"I must go. They'll miss me," she said. Then impulsively she reached up and cupped his face in her hands. "Be careful, my darling," she said. "When I was working out in the vineyards, we used to say that it was the little foxes that spoiled the vines. The plans of Adonijah and your mother could very well be those little foxes?"

Solomon chuckled. *"They're* not the little foxes. *We're* the only ones who can destroy this vine. Believe in me. Trust me."

"Oh, I will. I will," she promised, holding him close. Suddenly voices were heard in the upper reception room. "I must go," she whispered, and then without another word hurried down the steps and out into the courtyard.

She could hear him going back up the steps toward his mother's room. Once again she felt cold fear envelop her as she realized the forces that were pitted against their love. "Please, please, dear God," she whispered, "don't let him marry the princess of Rabbath-ammon." She drew out the fragrant pouch of dried flowers that he had given her in Shunem and pressed her lips against its smooth folds.

* * *

184

The month of Tishri was brought in with the Feast of Trumpets. This was the beginning of the civil new year, just as Passover was the beginning of the religious new year. The trumpets were all of gold, and the priests blowing them were dressed in garments rendered a dazzling white by the fuller's magic.

David sat on his throne in his finest robes, and on this day the high priest, Abiathar, always came to greet him and pledge his allegiance. Ever since the priests had been killed at Nob by King Saul and Abiathar escaped to join David in the caves of Adullam, they had been close friends. Only in recent years had there developed a conflict between them, and it was serious enough to prompt the prediction that Abiathar would soon no longer be considered David's friend.

The conflict had arisen over the Ark of the Covenant. After it was found by David's men, Abiathar expected it to be returned to its place in the tabernacle at Gibeon. Instead, David had ordered a shrine prepared for it down by the Gihon Spring and was even now composing a whole new service of song and praise—using Zadok as the priest.

After Abiathar had publicly pledged his allegiance, as was the custom on the New Year, he asked to see David privately. Solomon and Nathan, with several other princes, joined David as he came down from the throne and walked with Abiathar back into his own rooms.

Shulamit had just brought a silver bowl of golden apricots to place by the king's bed when the room filled with people.

"How beautiful: apples of gold in vessels of silver." Shulamit swung around and saw that Solomon had come in and was standing in the doorway behind her.

"How fine the robes of the high priest," she responded. "Is it true that the twelve signet stones he wears on the ephod bear the names of each tribe engraved on them?" she whispered.

"Every stone is different. They're a constant reminder that their names are engraved on his heart as they are engraved on the stones. He can't for a moment forget one single tribe."

Shulamit was deeply moved and seeing that everyone was busy talking, she grew bold enough to speak. "Engrave me on the signet of your heart," she said, giving Solomon a serious, searching look, "and I'll not ask for anything more."

Solomon saw that she wasn't joking. "My love," he declared, touching his phylactery, "not only are you engraved on my heart, but you are also like the seal I wear on my arm."

There was no time to say anything more, but it was as though the most solemn of pledges had been exchanged.

The high priest, obviously upset, walked to the door. "I'll not come again unless you call me," he said.

In that brief instant he turned, and Shulamit had a full view of the ephod. It seemed one of the loveliest garments she had ever seen. Each stone was the same size but all were different, and on each was engraved the name of one of the tribes. There was surely no greater symbol of love than this, and Solomon had promised to engrave her name in the same way on his heart and, more than that, to bind her name on his arm as permanent as the wearing of his phylacteries.

* * *

Everyone in the palace fasted on Yom Kippur, the Day of Atonement, but only the men rode up to Gibeon. There they watched as two goats were brought out into the courtyard—one to be sacrificed for the sins of the people, and the other to be sent out into the wilderness to Azazel. It was a time of repentance and restoration, a time of forgetting the hurts and grudges of the past year, a time essential if the joyful Feast of Sukkot that followed was to be the celebration of thanksgiving and praise it was meant to be.

This year, for the celebration of Sukkot, David's family all rode down to Bethlehem for a reunion in the large stone house built by Boaz so long ago. Jesse and David's mother were no longer there to welcome them, and Bathsheba had excused herself, but all of David's other wives, his brothers and their wives and children had come down to celebrate the feast. Even David's two half-sisters, Zeruiah and Abigail, daughters of old Nahash, were there with their families.

A large booth of palm fronds was built on the rooftop, just as it had been built the first year that Boaz lived in the house. In the evening the family gathered to eat together and celebrate under the light of the full moon and brilliant stars.

Solomon and Nathan were sitting with their father in a rare moment of relaxed conversation. "My father," Solomon said, "have you ever wondered why God let his chosen people become slaves in Egypt?"

"Of course, I've wondered. It's a question often discussed but never answered." His smile betrayed the amusement he felt at Solomon's earnest questioning.

Solomon didn't see the smile and so continued, warming to his subject. "Egypt is a land of wealth, with an old and proven culture. Rough herdsmen like Joseph and his brethren could never have become kings and princes and men of learning without their association with people like the Egyptians. What school could they attend that would teach them all they needed to learn? Who would tutor them? Only a slave learns such things. He hates the bondage and the lack of freedom, of course, but it's the only way a superior culture can be passed on to those less fortunate."

"I don't understand," David said. "What are you trying to say? That God was *good* in letting us be slaves of the Egyptians? You forget that our father Abraham was an honored citizen of the great civilization of Ur."

Solomon smiled. He knew that he had riled his father. "Don't we find out in the end of every matter that God has been good to us? We learned much as slaves that we couldn't have learned any other way. What Egyptian would agree to take any one of us into his home and carefully teach us the minutest details of Egyptian culture without our somehow benefiting him?"

"It's so strange, my son, how you're always seeing the other side of things. Perhaps you have inherited your penchant for questioning from your great-grandfather Ahithophel. Never forget: it led him to disaster."

The discussion was brought to an abrupt close as a great commotion broke out in the women's quarters of the old family home. The men froze as they listened. Nathan stood up, his face white and his eyes wide and questioning. Sarah had been in pain from the moment they had arrived, and it had been necessary to call in the old village midwife. "Something must have gone wrong," he said as he hurried toward the women's quarters.

* * *

The celebration, which had started so joyfully with the women riding in garlanded carts, ended in the burial of both Sarah and an infant daughter. Nathan was wild with grief. He clung to Sarah's cold, ravished body and would not let her be wrapped in the winding clothes. Finally Solomon and his two younger brothers, Shimea and Shobab, took him back to the inner rooms that had belonged to Boaz and tried to comfort him.

Nathan called for his son, Mattatha, and when they brought the little boy he held him close and wept bitter tears. "You're all that's left of Sarah," he said, rocking back and forth in his agony.

After they had all followed the body to the tombs of David and had seen the great rock rolled back in place over the grave, Nathan said, "When I go back to Jerusalem, I will have only two loves: one will be my son, and the other the work that God has given me in building the temple with Solomon."

Shulamit had been with Sarah at the very last—had seen the baby, so small and so blue, struggle for breath and then lie still and cold. She had tightened her hold on Sarah's hand and been surprised when she felt the hand relax. Within the flicker of an eyelash her friend was gone, and Shulamit found herself overwhelmed with grief.

* * *

That evening, when the somber group came straggling back to the palace, they found that Adonijah had returned from Rabbath-ammon. His smile was oiled with satisfaction and his gestures were deliberate and cunning. "Hanun, the king, has agreed to give his daughter to Solomon if you'll sign this agreement," he told David. He drew out from his cloak a parchment sealed with red wax and bearing the emblem of the kings of Rabbath-ammon.

"What does he want?" David asked as he leaned his arm on the window casing.

"Not much for what he's willing to give. For instance, he'll help protect the King's Highway if he can be given half the revenue."

"That clever fellow is obviously thinking that he'll use us and collect most of the benefit. What else does he want?"

"He mentioned that he'd like to have his crown back. It was especially designed."

"His *crown?*" David shouted. "He's asking to take back his kingdom as though he were no longer a vassal of mine. He's lucky I let him stay and call himself a king. He can keep his daughter; she's probably a worshiper of idols anyway and would try to bring her disgusting practices here."

"No, Father, she's just a young girl. She wouldn't have that much influence." Adonijah concealed the fact that he had assured the Ammonite king there was no need to specify in writing that she could come with her idols and her priests. "My father would take that for granted," he had assured him.

David slumped down onto the side of his bed. "I haven't been well since my encounter with the Philistines and the giant, Saph. I wish to see Solomon married before I die, and these things take time, so we must set about the matter with all diligence. However, I'll not agree to all he wants. I'm sure he doesn't expect it. I hope the girl's at least pretty."

Adonijah hesitated. "She's interesting," he said.

"Then you must go tell Bathsheba. She is in Giloh. Perhaps the terms won't suit her after all."

Adonijah turned and left the room, walking lightheartedly down the corridor. He had just what he wanted. After he saw Bathsheba and set the wedding plans in motion, he intended to meet with his friends at the house of Eon. Both Joab, David's nephew and army general, and Abiathar, the high priest, had now agreed to side with him in his revolt and crown him secretly.

Adonijah smiled as he thought of the cunning involved in his carefully laid plans. "The king is old and now, with his battle wound, won't be able to rule much longer," he had told them. "Side with me, and I'll put you in charge of everything when I come into power."

The takeover would happen so fast that no one would have time to oppose it. At one blow he would have both the crown and Shulamit for his wife. "She'll forget Solomon once she's queen," he reasoned. "In fact," he confided to one of his lesser followers, "when she finds out that Solomon is going to marry the princess of Rabbath-ammon, she'll have nothing more to do with him."

He rode out the gate and turned onto the road that led to Bathsheba's home in Giloh. He hummed a teasing little ditty. He was sure of success. Of course if Solomon or his brothers caused him too much trouble, he would quietly do away with them. Quietly, very quietly. No one would know. That was what a king had to do.

*B*athsheba hadn't gone with the family to Bethlehem. She had excused herself, saying that she was too tired. Actually, she hadn't made her decision until she heard that Shulamit planned to go. Though Bathsheba wouldn't admit it even to herself, she had begun to feel supplanted, displaced by this "mere snippet" of a girl who had somehow stolen her son's heart and made herself indispensable to the king.

Now, as Jessica announced that Adonijah was asking to see her, she felt strangely encouraged. "I've been expecting you," she said as she patted a place beside her on one of the low mats. "How did you find the princess of Rabbath-ammon?"

"She's attractive in her own way," he said rather cautiously as he sat down. "She has dark hair and brown eyes. She's well proportioned, even seductive."

"Does she smile? Is she pleasant?"

"I would imagine she *could* smile if things pleased her."

"Was she eager to marry my son?"

"No, no, she wasn't eager until her father said he would insist that she be the first wife and also the next queen of Israel."

"And of course you agreed?"

"Yes, I agreed. To agree doesn't change anything in the future."

Bathsheba beamed. "You've served me well, and I'll see that you're rewarded."

"Then may I ask a favor sometime?"

"If it doesn't conflict with my own plans."

Adonijah smiled at her and nodded. "I know better than to come against your plans." He stood up and moved toward the door. "We understand each other perfectly."

She let him kiss her outstretched hand and then watched as he hurried from the room.

The lamp in the wall niche flickered, making large shadows on the ceiling. There was a quietness about the room that usually came at this time of the evening. She stood and moved to where she could look out the latticed window down into the moon-drenched courtyard. "Solomon is so wise in most things." she thought. "How can he be so blind and lacking in ambition as to even have considered marrying the girl from Shunem?"

She leaned her head against the cool stones and found her thoughts going round and round the problem. "Even his trip to Egypt hasn't put her out of his mind. I hope that this marriage to a young, dark-haired, seductive woman will wipe all thoughts of the Shunemmite from his mind."

* * *

All during the dry season, before the early rains of winter, communication between the king of Rabbath-ammon and Israel's King David went back and forth, with Hanun trying to get the greatest advantage possible. The negotiations became so cumbersome and complicated that Solomon began to hope that his marriage to the princess would never come about.

In the meantime life in Jerusalem had settled into a predictable pattern. Every morning Solomon would go to the throne room to observe his father's methods of handling the business and even private family disputes of the tribesmen. In the afternoons, when David retired with Solomon to his own rooms, Nathan and Adonijah would often join them to discuss the plans for the great temple.

"See, my sons," David said one day, stepping out onto the small balcony that opened from his room, "see that woman looking out of her window? Now watch: she's seen someone."

The woman shut the window and within minutes was out on the street, waiting heavily veiled at the street corner. "I happen to know that her husband is gone," David said. "Now watch, and learn wisdom."

Adonijah noticed right away that it was Yasmit and lingered in the deep shadow of the doorway to hear what his father would say.

As a young man approached her, the woman lifted her veil. Laughing brazenly, she pulled him into the shadow of the gateway and kissed him; then, linking her arm in his, they went into her house.

David's eyes rested on Adonijah as he said, "Remember, it is wisdom to drink water from your own cisterns. There's a wise old saying that expresses the same thought: don't let your fountains nourish another man's vineyard."

Adonijah wondered if his father could have seen him going into the house when Eon wasn't home. He was so confused that he couldn't look his father in the eye. Muttering something about an appointment, he hastily turned and left the room.

During these times Shulamit was often in the king's rooms. Solomon loved to watch as she stirred the coals in the brazier so that the light flared up and illuminated her lovely features with its soft glow. Or he enjoyed the lively tunes she played on her flute. She was so vital and alive, always interested in things.

Though he saw her often, he couldn't speak to her openly because of Adonijah, who was always within hearing distance and kept an eye on them. Gradually they developed a pleasant, cryptic banter that had meaning only to themselves.

"I heard that my beloved went down to his gardens to gather spices," Shulamit would say, after hearing that Solomon had gone on an outing with one of the prominent families of Jerusalem who had marriageable daughters.

"Only to pasture my flock," he would reply, hoping she would know that he had taken some of his friends with him.

"Yes, to pasture the flock and to gather lilies." Both of them knew that lilies were other young ladies.

Solomon, aggrieved at the hurt in her tone, would quickly reply, "My beloved can be sure that I am hers and she is mine."

He would be relieved to see her eyes twinkle as she replied, "Ah, it's only the flock that feeds among the lilies?"

Since early summer Shulamit had had permission to take the women of the harem on short excursions to the Garden of Nuts within the Kidron Valley and to the family's olive groves at Bethlehem. David was pleased to hear that his wives were kept occupied. He had even suggested that since he could no longer spare the time for rides into the country, some of his sons would be glad to escort them. Certainly Adonijah was always eager and available. In fact, it was almost impossible to plan anything without his interference.

* * *

Adonijah's perpetual presence annoyed Shulamit, and she was determined to find a way around the problem. One day, after hearing from her maidens that Solomon was riding down to the springs below Bethlehem, she approached him as he rose from receiving his father's blessing. "Where are you herding your sheep tomorrow?" she asked casually, hoping that he would remember the first time he had set out to find her in Shunem.

He hesitated, then smiled in recognition. "Just follow the tracks of the flocks and take your kids close to the shepherd's tents."

She turned away without answering, but she could see the puzzled look on Adonijah's face. She knew from Solomon's response that it would be all right for her to bring the women to the springs. Now if only Adonijah would not be there.

* * *

That evening, as Shulamit sat with her maidens making preparations for the next day's outing, her mother came with news that Bessim was sick and had sent for her. "I feel that I must go to him," she said sadly.

"When will you have to leave?" Shulamit left her maidens to finish packing the baskets and led her mother into her own section of the court of the queens.

"I'll have to wait for a caravan going north. I must be ready to go any day now. I have no idea how sick Bessim is."

"It's possible that he's not sick at all, but just lonesome," Shulamit ventured.

Her mother smiled. "One way or the other, I must go."

"Come, sit down. I have so much to tell you," Shulamit said, picking up the reeds she was weaving into a basket. "Tomorrow my maidens and I are riding down to the springs, and Solomon will be there with some of his friends."

"Then you're still in love with the prince? But he's as good as married to the princess of Rabbath-ammon."

"Mother!" Shulamit exclaimed, her eyes flashing and her words sharp and distinct. "He'll not marry the princess. He'll not agree. Besides, in a way I'm really married to Solomon, since my marriage to the king wasn't consummated."

"Oh, my dear child. Don't be so confused. You're married to the king, because he's the one who made a commitment to your father."

"But—" Shulamit protested as she twisted and untwisted the broken reeds.

"Can't you trust Yahweh to work it out?" her mother asked gently.

For a long moment Shulamit didn't speak. Finally, with a sigh of resignation and a tug at the reeds, she said, "No, I'm afraid to trust."

Her mother stood up. "If you take things into your own hands and go by your own rules, you can't expect Yahweh to have anything to do with it."

She stooped down and touched the soft, curling hair around her daughter's forehead. "Oh, my dear, remember what I've said. Love, once it's fully awakened, is like a fire out of control; it can burn down whole villages."

Shulamit didn't answer so her mother left, closing the door quietly behind her.

* * *

The next morning when the women gathered in the courtyard for their expedition, it was discovered that most of the queens and some of the maidens weren't going. Several of them expressed their apprehension at riding through Bethlehem, where Sarah had met such an untimely end. "It was the evil Lilith," the superstitious women whispered, "who out of jealousy for her beauty stole her and her child."

To Shulamit Lilith meant very little, but she did miss Sarah. Going back along the same road to Bethlehem brought back bittersweet memories of the last trip at the Feast of Sukkot, and of Sarah's death.

* * *

Solomon often rode out to these springs. It had always been one of his favorite places. Even as a child he had enjoyed playing in and around the gray rocks that burst out of the ground in gnarled and distorted shapes. The sound of running water and the fragrance of the cedars and firs gave the spot a unique charm.

Lately he had thought it might be possible to dig great reservoirs to catch the water and then have it piped up to Jerusalem. The new temple would need a great deal of water, and this was one of the ways he intended to go about getting what was needed.

On his arrival Solomon had ordered his men to put up a dark tent of goat's hair with bright fringes and tassels. Inside the tent he had ordered his servants to spread carpets and cushions and to lay out a meal.

By the time the women arrived, all was ready. The children, running ahead of their mothers, squealed with delight, and the young women chattered enthusiastically as they helped the older women settle themselves in the large tent. Then, to everyone's delight, Solomon singled out Shulamit and led her to the head of the low table spread with every delicacy imaginable. The women noticed how his eyes softened when he looked at her, and how she seemed to glow with a fresh, dewlike beauty.

Once in a while the women were able to catch bits of their conversation, and it seemed that he couldn't say enough in her praise. "When I first saw you today, riding with your women down out of the fir trees, I thought to myself, 'She is indeed like a lily among thorns.'"

To their amusement they heard her reply, "As an apple tree among the more common trees, so is Solomon among the king's sons."

Eventually Solomon and Shulamit were left alone. Some of the maidens drifted out into the fields, and Shulamit's mother took others to look for sweet and bitter herbs near the springs.

As Solomon moved closer to her, he could smell the rich, heady odor of jasmine, and noticed the way her hair curled against his arm. He tilted her chin so that he could look in her eyes. They were open and frank with an unmistakable yearning of love that threatened to envelop him.

He could never remember just what he said, but he knew that words of love poured out in a torrent. Wanting only to claim her as his own, he forgot all of his resolves and merely reveled in the pure joy of being with her.

Suddenly she pulled away from him and jumped to her feet. Her hair billowed and floated around her face so that she had to throw her head back and run her fingers through the curls. For a moment she seemed dazed, then she said, "It's getting late. We must start back."

She didn't look at him again, but reached for her mantle and took great pains adjusting it until it suited her. "Will you marry the princess of Rabbath-ammon as they say?" she asked.

Solomon rose and pulled her into his arms hungrily. "Must we talk of the future? Can't we love as others do, without—?"

"My lord," she said, putting one small finger over his lips. "Isn't it true that you're responsible for a vineyard at Baal-hamon?"

He laughed, wondering what she was getting at. "Yes, yes, I'm responsible for the vineyard."

"You would be considered foolish to rent it out to people who neither paid you for it nor cared for the vines."

Again he laughed. "It takes a long time to grow a vineyard like the one at Baal-hamon. I would never let it out to one who wouldn't value it and care for it as I do."

"My lord," she said gently, taking his face between her hands, "I am my own vineyard. I'm responsible for my own vines. I must neither care for someone else's vines and neglect my own nor give mine out to caretakers who cannot care for them."

Solomon grew serious. He admired her pluck. "You're right. I can't care for the vineyard, so I shouldn't steal its fruit."

She reached up and kissed him, then whispered, "I hope it won't be long before you can claim my vineyard as your own."

With that she left him and walked with a swinging stride out of the pavilion to gather up the other women and young maidens for their ride back to Jerusalem.

* * *

Later that night Solomon told his brother Nathan about the adventure at the springs. "I was surprised at the ease with which I threw over all my inhibitions and restraints. I wanted her and I would have taken her."

"I thought you had decided . . ."

"Of course I had, but the temptation of the moment was almost too great. I had this feeling that something was going to come between us, and I wanted to hold on to what we had."

"How, then, did you escape?"

Solomon paused, remembering every detail of Shulamit's face. "It was my little shepherdess. She compared herself to a vineyard and said that no one should have the vineyard unless he was able to care for it."

Nathan laughed. "I've never heard it put that way before, but she's right."

"You can't imagine how I felt—at first terribly disappointed and frustrated, but then I couldn't help admiring her. Now I'm even more obsessed with her; I can't get her out of my mind."

"As you yourself are always saying, 'There's a time for everything,' and we can pray that there will be a time for love also." Mattatha came running out to show his father the rough skin on which he had drawn some letters. Nathan caught him up in his arms, said good night, and disappeared with him into the darkness.

Solomon dismissed his serving men and sat alone, thinking of all that had happened during the day—from the first moment he saw Shulamit riding into the glade with her maidens until he watched them leave. It had been a rare experience for him. Having met someone as an equal, he had let his heart rather than his head rule for a few moments.

The palace was unusually quiet. There was no moon, and a strong, insistent breeze blew his shutters open. He rose to close them and felt a gust of rain on his face and hands. So the early rains had begun. He was glad until he realized that there would be no more trips out into the villages and fields with Shulamit. It would be too cold and wet.

He fastened the shutters and pinched out the flame of his lamp, but he didn't go to bed or to sleep for a long time.

* * *

Back in the court of the queens, the young maidens gathered around Shulamit, demanding to hear just what had happened after they left her in the tent with Solomon. "We can see," one insisted, "that your eyes are brighter, and you look as though—"

"As though what?" Shulamit said as she continued to tie together small bunches of dried flowers that she was sewing into small pouches of cloth to tuck in her clothes chest.

"As though you had surrendered to love," the girl answered, giggling and hiding her face behind her friend's shoulder.

Shulamit dropped her hands in her lap and looked around at them. "Well, you're wrong. I've told you before: one mustn't wake love before its time."

Their faces registered disappointment. "But what if he has to marry the princess of Rabbath-ammon?"

"If he has to marry her, nothing I've done or not done will change anything."

"But if you had only given yourself to him—"

Shulamit was tying one bunch of flowers with strips of straw and pulled so hard the straw broke and flowers went flying in every direction. "Well then, we'll just have to see what sort of cord it takes to bind the heart of a prince. He knows that I love him with all my heart, and I must trust that that cord is strong enough to hold him."

Later that night, as she lay in the darkness of her room and listened to the first hesitant drops of rain on her shutters, she wasn't so brave. "We won't be riding out again until spring, and by spring anything can have happened."

*I*n spite of the cold winter rains that swept down upon Jerusalem, Bathsheba herself planned one other excursion. This time the women were to visit the king's groves at En-gedi, the lovely spring of the wild goats. "It's always warm and pleasant there, and they're still harvesting some of the fruits. It's an ideal time to visit," Bathsheba told the women as she urged them all to go.

As it turned out, Bathsheba decided at the last moment not to go with them. She gave no reason, but it was whispered that she had changed her mind after a messenger from Rabbath-ammon arrived.

Bathsheba sent Solomon and the women off on their adventure, then hurried to a place behind a curtain where she could hear and see everything that went on in the throne room.

She arrived just as Adonijah was ushering the officials from Rabbath-ammon into David's presence. "My lord," he said, bowing before his father and then waiting while the visitors made a great show of prostrating themselves before David. "My lord," he began again, "the king of Rabbath-ammon has granted all of the special points you insisted on."

He signaled for the scribe to hand the parchment of agreement to the counselors. "The king is now asking only that Solomon come to Rabbath-ammon himself to sign the papers and discuss plans for the wedding."

After the men had gone, Adonijah mounted the steps to the throne and spoke privately with his father. "Prince Solomon has just ridden with the maidens down to En-gedi. It's important that he himself greet the messengers and make preparations to ride back with them as soon as possible. I would be willing to ride down to the spring and bring him back."

The king was pleased. It would be a long, cold ride, and he was delighted that Adonijah was willing to do this for his brother. "If you hurry, you may be able to make the trip down and back before sunset," he said, giving Adonijah a warm smile.

✳ ✳ ✳

Shulamit was overwhelmed by the beauty of En-gedi, a lovely oasis wedged between the bleak, treeless cliffs and the dull, gray, motionless water of the Dead Sea. It was a favorite habitat of small songbirds and of the wild goats that had given the place its name. Palm trees bordered the lush green that stretched from the top of the rift right down to the sandy shore of the Dead Sea. Here and there stood strange trees, planted from seeds brought by traders from distant lands. High up the face of the cliff, hidden in the rich foliage of vines and ferns, was a waterfall that cascaded into a mirror-like pool.

In the absence of Bathsheba, Solomon had planned the day carefully. He first took Shulamit to a spot thick with henna plants. She had wanted to see where the fragrant dried flowers had come from that he had given her to wear in the little pouch around her neck. "I'm surprised that you still wear such a common ornament," he marveled.

"I treasure this above any of my other jewelry," she said. "I always wear it."

He was deeply touched and slightly embarrassed to discover that this humble gift was so prized. "Come," he said, "I want to take you up to see the great waterfall and the lovely pool at its base." They had just started up the path when they spotted a cloud of dust moving along the road from Jericho. It was a band of men riding fast, as though they brought important news, so Solomon decided to wait and see what would develop.

As soon as he recognized Adonijah at the head of the little band, he regretted having waited. He knew instinctively that the news must be to Adonijah's liking or he wouldn't have come. "I must speak with you privately," Adonijah said, swinging off the mule and looking at Solomon with a know-ing smirk. "I've just come from the king. He wants you to return to Jerusalem immediately."

Solomon was cautious. "Is there no written message?"

With a frown Adonijah pulled a parchment from his belt. "It will tell you nothing, but there you see the signature and the king's seal."

Solomon took the parchment and broke the seal with one slow move-ment. Adonijah was right. The message was brief; Solomon was to return im-mediately to Jerusalem.

"Are you riding back with me?" Solomon asked.

"Not immediately. I have business of my own here." He looked at Shulamit and winked.

Solomon glanced at Shulamit but could read nothing in her expression.

He felt again a smoldering frustration. Adonijah's wink, his sudden appearance, and his easy manner bothered Solomon. Surely Adonijah wouldn't look so confident without *some* encouragement from Shulamit.

With a brisk command Solomon summoned several of his men, deliberately ignoring Shulamit. He didn't want to give Adonijah anything to gloat over.

As he rode off, the hot wind blew eddies of dust around him, covering him with a fine film until he was forced to shield his face with his headcloth. This didn't deter Solomon from urging his mule on faster and faster. He rode like a madman, driven by the picture of Adonijah taking Shulamit to the waterfall and enjoying her company for the rest of the day. This was the same torment he had suffered leaving Shunem, and he was determined to rid himself of it at whatever cost.

* * *

After Solomon left, Adonijah asked to speak with Shulamit alone, but she refused. He finally told her in front of everyone, "The papers are signed; the arrangements are all made. When Solomon gets to Jerusalem, he'll find that within a month he is to be on his way to Rabbath-ammon to marry the princess." Shulamit was now so used to Adonijah's plots to discredit Solomon that she resolved not to let him see how upset she was by his news. "So he's to marry the princess," she said, as calmly as possible. "No doubt this will assure him of the crown, as Bathsheba has intended."

The smile vanished from Adonijah's face. He became tense and his eyes narrowed as he pulled her aside and whispered, "He'll *never* get the throne. My plans are set. My friends have been alerted. I'll be king before my father dies—and then you'll be mine. Solomon will have *nothing*." He said the last word with such force and his eyes glinted so threateningly that Shulamit had to fight down a growing panic. She was determined to show no emotion until he was gone.

Adonijah was in no mood to linger any longer. He had plans to make and people to see. He gathered his men, mounted, and rode out the way he had come.

Shulamit managed a calm exterior until he disappeared from sight. Then, deeply disturbed, she left the camp and climbed alone up the rugged path. She stopped at a place where she could look out over the palm trees and fertile oasis across the dull expanse of the Dead Sea to the mountains of Moab. "Beyond those cliffs lies the King's Highway," she thought, "and it's for this trade route that they want Solomon to marry the princess. He won't agree. I know he won't."

*　*　*

Though Shulamit heard many rumors about Solomon in the next few days, she didn't see him; neither was she called by the king. She sat in her little apartment wondering what was happening and expecting at any moment to receive a message from her prince.

"He's soon going to Rabbath-ammon to sign the papers and maybe even marry the princess," various maidens kept reporting. No one seemed to realize that the words *Rabbath-ammon* were like poison darts to her. And when her maidens so much as mentioned love, she snapped, "I'm sick of love." She meant it too. The pain was too terrible; the agony was never-ending. After all, her worst fears seemed to be coming to pass, and Solomon hadn't even bothered to come and explain. She felt a loathing for the princess of Rabbath-ammon and anger at Bathsheba. "How can Bathsheba be so cruel and so ambitious that she's ready to sacrifice everything, even her son's happiness, for the crown?" she fumed.

But then, at times she wondered if this marriage wasn't just what Solomon himself wanted. After all no one was forcing him. It was his own decision; he had chosen to go to Rabbath-ammon.

To make it even more difficult, a caravan had arrived with one of Bessim's sons to take her mother back to Shunem. Shulamit knew that her mother had to go. "Nothing else could persuade me to leave you at this time," her mother said, "but I can't stay when Bessim needs me so badly."

Reluctantly Shulamit helped her close up the little house in the hope that she would be able to return soon. Then she waved bravely as her mother rode off down the cobbled street toward the South Gate, where she would join the caravan that was take her home.

*　*　*

The day before Solomon was to leave for Rabbath-ammon passed as a nightmare to Shulamit. There were celebrations and banquets, but she attended none of them. To her annoyance, her maidens returned describing everything.

"He's more handsome than ever," one of them said. "There's no prince, even in Egypt, as handsome and fine as Solomon."

When they realized that she hadn't gone to the celebration with the rest of the wives, they began to ask questions. "What's happened? Are you no longer in love? Why didn't you go?"

"You know very well what's happened," she said, irritation evident in her voice. She had been playing a game with one of the younger maids, and they noticed that she was moving her pieces recklessly. "My beloved is going to the City of Waters, where he will no doubt feed on rare spices and dark lilies. Everything has been decided."

Suddenly the maidens were all solicitous. They noticed with what care she had dressed, and how often she glanced up expectantly, only to be disappointed. Each one tried to think of something to say to comfort Shulamit. "He's so busy getting ready that he has no time," they said. "At least you're married to the king."

"I had no proper wedding huppah. The only banner over me has been Solomon's love, and now even that's gone." The sun was setting, and still there had been no word from him. He was actually going to Rabbath-ammon without trying to explain things to her or say how sorry he was that everything had worked out so disastrously.

When it grew late and Solomon still hadn't come, the maidens came to help Shulamit get ready for bed. They were silent, not knowing what to say. As they helped her into bed, she turned her back to them, and they knew she didn't want them. She slept fitfully. Toward dawn she dreamed that she was running endlessly to reach some destination that was always further on. Through it all she seemed to hear a soft but steady knocking. Startled, she sat up and listened. "Come, open the door. I must see you." The voice was muffled and indistinct.

"Who is it?" she asked, thinking the voice must be part of her dream.

"Please, my darling, open quickly. Morning is almost here; my hair is wet with dew. They'll be calling for me at any moment." The voice she had most loved to hear now twisted in her like a knife. How could he come so late? It was *too* late. There was no time for explanations. He had perhaps even planned it that way.

"I've taken off my robes and can't put them on again." She knew that her words would hurt him, but she couldn't bear the pain of seeing him when he had come only to tell her that he was leaving after all.

"My darling, I *must* see you. Don't let me go without hearing your sweet voice telling me that you love me."

"I've washed my feet. I don't want to get them soiled." Her words were sharp and harsh. Why should he have waited until now to tell her that he was going to Rabbath-ammon as his mother wanted him to? She imagined now that he had acquiesced without protest.

To her surprise he knocked again. Then, in the dim light of the lamp, she saw a flash of red and realized that it was from one of the rings he wore. He had put his hand in through the hole in the door and was going to unbolt it himself.

All her anger melted. He hadn't forgotten her. Something beyond his control had happened, and he hadn't been *able* to come sooner. Perhaps even yet they could flee together through the night and escape this terrible thing that was about to separate them.

She jumped up and grabbed the vial of fragrant myrrh, splashing it carelessly on her hands. He mustn't go without one last embrace, one last kiss.

Suddenly, faint on the early morning air, she heard the trumpeted notes of the salute to the princes of Judah. The latch was abruptly silent, the hand withdrawn, and she could hear his footsteps hurrying from the court. The echo sounded hollow and remote. She opened the door, knowing that he was already gone—gone with only her cruel words for company on the long ride to Rabbath-ammon.

Shulamit slipped into a robe and snatched up her veil, fastening it about her face as she ran. The Postern Gate was open. She paused and heard the echo of his footsteps running through the mist and tried to follow him but a few abrupt turns, and she was lost in the maze of winding streets that twisted in and out among the tall stone houses. Now there was no sound but the soft, hurried padding of her slippers on the cobblestones echoing eerily in the encircling fog.

She stopped and listened, but she could hear nothing. She knew that she was lost and had no idea what direction to go. Then, faint and indistinct, she heard again the trumpet's call. "He must be riding out of the city through the South Gate," she thought as she leaned against a wooden door and brushed the hair from her eyes.

Anguish and despair swept over her in waves. She couldn't imagine how she was still alive and suffering so. Her knees grew suddenly weak, and she had to feel her way from door to door in the oppressive silence of the predawn blackness.

She came to an open space and realized that she was standing just yards from the door of her mother's small, empty house. The door opened easily, and she rushed over to the steps leading up to the city wall. She *must* get one last glimpse of his company riding out toward Jericho.

At the top of the steps her gown caught on a hyssop plant whose roots still clung to a crack in the wall. She pulled it loose, ignoring the tearing sound, and hurried up to the top.

The wall was broad, with a waist-high parapet, but from where she stood she could see nothing. She realized that he would have to pass along the Kidron Valley beneath the Water Gate. Perhaps she could see him from there.

She ran along the wall until she came to the guardhouse at the Water Gate, where the steps wound down to the courtyard below. Once again she leaned over the parapet. Glancing up to the dark bulk of Mount Olivet across the Kidron Valley, she saw lights. It was too late! Within a short time even the torches of his company would have passed over the brow of the hill.

In a state of total frustration, she turned to retrace her steps. Suddenly she heard a snarl and a grunt close by; then there was the flash of torches uncovered. In the harsh light she saw that she was surrounded by some of the tough mercenaries that guarded the wall at night. "Oho," one of them said, grasping her arm and swinging her around to face him, "She's a real beauty."

"Let me go," she demanded, trying frantically to free herself.

"No nice girl would be out at this hour. I'd say you're asking for anything you get." A face, red and ugly, was revealed by the torchlight as she was pushed back against the rough stones of the parapet.

"I'm one of the king's wives!" She pulled herself free but left her mantle in the hands of the red-faced man.

"A likely story," a third man said as he loomed out of the darkness and grabbed her around the waist while a fourth man hit her across the mouth.

"You'll pay dearly when the king finds out." She was now flailing with her arms and kicking as best she could. In response, the guards were raining blows down on her with angry curses.

"You're no wife of our king. You're just a whore out looking for a man," the first man said, running a leather whip through his fingers threateningly and then snapping it on the ground so that it bruised her feet.

In desperation she shouted, "Look at my clothes. Aren't they the garments of a queen?" Just as suddenly as they had attacked her, they loosed her and fell back, looking with horror at the lovely embroidered robe that was now in shreds.

Shulamit didn't wait for their reaction but turned and fled. As she ran, she heard one of them gasp, "It *was* one of the king's women."

She was faint, sore, and out of breath when she reached the steps that led down to her mother's empty house. She stopped for a moment to catch her breath and glanced out across the valley toward where she had seen the lights. They were still there, moving slowly up the crest of Olivet, and she had to turn away; she couldn't bear the sight. "O Yahweh," she sobbed, "could any battle wound hurt worse than this?"

Slowly she felt her way down the stairs and limped back up the lane that led to the Postern Gate into the palace proper.

Back at her own door she paused and ran her hand over the latch that his hand had touched such a short time ago. Regret flooded over her as she thought of the angry words she had spoken. He was gone. In Rabbath-ammon he would remember only that she hadn't been willing even to slip on her robe or dirty her feet to see him.

One of her maidens awoke and hurried to help her out of her torn robe. Shulamit said nothing when the girl put ointment on her bruises, but when she brought a bowl of water to wash her feet she burst into tears and couldn't be comforted.

20

I've taken off my robes and can't put them on again. I've bathed my feet and don't want to soil them!" The words burned in his brain as if a hot iron had etched them there. All the way to the South Gate where the little band of his friends were waiting with his mule, the hurting words echoed and reechoed around him.

Without a word to his men he mounted, and before the signal was given he tapped his mule sharply, making it charge off into the blackness beyond the gate. Everything around him seemed blurred by the cruel words churning in his mind. Had she misunderstood his preoccupation with preparations for the journey? But these were matters of business and not of the heart. A man never mixed the two; she should know that.

At the crest of Olivet he motioned for the caravan to halt. He needed time to think and sort out and control these emotions that were so new to him. He couldn't enjoy a moment of the ride in such a turmoil. Without a word of explanation to his men he left them and rode out alone to the edge of the cliff, where he could take a last look at the city. He wasn't surprised to see that, though the sky was brightening in the east, Jerusalem was still shrouded in darkness.

Suddenly his eyes were drawn to several small bursts of light that flashed from the top of the wall at the point where steps led down to the Gihon Spring. For a moment he thought he heard shouting and then laughter, coarse and profane; then once again it was still. "She's probably sleeping," he thought bitterly.

He dismounted and breathed deeply, waiting for the tight bands that bound his chest to loosen. The air was damp. All signs of the recent drought had vanished. Birds stirred in the low thorn bushes, giving small waking sounds that were answered by other birds hidden in the dark foliage of an olive tree.

Twigs snapped under his feet, and the loose gravel made a crunching sound that seemed louder than normal. He stood at the cliff edge, grieving wordlessly. The sky behind him pinkened, but Jerusalem, on the distant slope of Mount Moriah, still looked like a black crown cushioned on mist.

Solomon struggled to find meaning in Shulamit's rejection. There must be some explanation! One name kept flashing before him, demanding attention. Adonijah! It was almost certain that Adonijah, with his insistence that he was to be the next king, had something to do with her change of heart. Perhaps she had believed him; perhaps, in a moment of ambitious clarity, she had given him her love.

He paced back and forth in the cold, flexing his fingers and watching his breath form small clouds. There were plenty of strange instances to ponder: the strand of beads, her ride into Jerusalem alone with Adonijah, the prince's boast that he had lain with her. She had never really explained all those things.

Finally he remembered the way Adonijah had suddenly appeared at En-gedi—almost as though it had all been carefully planned. The look Adonijah had given her on his arrival there had been meaningful. Was there some secret between them? Would he have acted that way if she hadn't encouraged him?

He kicked a stone viciously and listened to it bounce down the cliff from one jutting rock to the next. "I'll have no more to do with love," he promised himself. "It's too costly and too painful."

With what seemed a sudden push, the sun was up above the distant mountains, flooding the valleys and splattering the rocks on the rounded dome of Moriah with yellow gold. Solomon shook off his gloomy thoughts, reminded of a time years ago when he had passed this same spot with his mother. She had clapped her hands in happiness at the sight. "You, my son," she had said, turning to him with her eyes shining, "will build the temple of the living God on that ugly, bare rock."

That had been the first time he had envisioned the temple, with its golden doors reflecting the morning sun and its creamy stones turned red as rubies in the intense light. A jeweled footstool for Jehovah was how he had pictured it. All the priests and Levites would be dressed in dazzling white, making sacrifices at a great altar, while the people would be filled with joy and singing praises as the smoke from the sacrifice ascended with their prayers.

It was the prophet Nathan, before Solomon was born, who first prophesied that he would build the temple. His father had believed it, but his mother had lived it. She had built all her hopes on that one prophecy. It had been the dream she cherished in her heart, crooned to him in lullabies; she had argued its rightness, planned incessantly for its fulfillment until it was etched upon his mind like the scribe's writing in soft clay.

Now, as part of that dream, she had made plans for him to marry the princess of Rabbath-ammon. It was politically expedient; without one battle being fought or one soldier killed, they would have a treaty much stronger than David had ever managed with all his military victories.

Solomon remounted and turned to retrace his steps along the path. "My mother's right. To marry Bessim's daughter would give me only the strength of his seven sons, while to marry the princess of Rabbath-ammon would secure for me the King's Highway. To do this would be exhibiting real wisdom," he thought. Not the wisdom his brother Nathan talked about, but the wisdom that made a man successful as a king. "If a man has wisdom, everything else will automatically come to him," Solomon concluded.

* * *

They spent the night in Jericho, which was pleasantly warm. They had left Jerusalem wrapped in wool robes, and in Jericho they had to change into the lightest of linen. Solomon's men had prepared everything; when he arrived there was nothing to do but wash, say his evening prayers, and sit down to a dinner of roast lamb.

Later that evening Solomon talked to one of his Ammonite guides. "Tell me about your city," he encouraged as he settled back among the cushions in his tent. "I know that it was founded by our kinsman, Lot, after he fled from Sodom and had children by his own daughters. Wasn't it his youngest daughter who gave birth to Ben-Ammi, the father of the Ammonites?"

"You're right, my lord." The officer smiled at Solomon's hesitation in mentioning the scandal. "It was the older daughter who gave birth to Moab, the father of the Moabites. We've always had close ties with Moab. They're indeed our distant kinsmen."

"I've been told that giants dwelt on the far side of the Jordan and that these grandsons of Lot had to build great walls around their cities until they could overcome them and drive them out. Is that true?" Solomon asked.

The young man nodded. "You can still see the massebahs and menhirs that were probably erected by the giants to honor their dead, or as part of their ritual sacrifice. There's also a great iron bedstead that was taken from King Og of Bashan when we conquered him. We call the giants the Zamzummim."

"Your people worship the great idol Moloch?"

At mention of Moloch the man looked frightened. He hesitated and backed off, shaking his head. "I don't want to say anything about him. He isn't a god who takes lightly to having his name published about." It was obvious that the man didn't want to talk anymore, so Solomon dismissed him.

Before he went to bed, he wondered briefly about the princess. Adonijah had said that she was attractive, but from other, more reliable sources he had learned that she was seductive and provocative but definitely not attractive. "It doesn't matter," he thought. "I'm through with love. It's too painful. I'll marry only for gain."

* * *

The palace of Rabbath-ammon was built on the highest point of the walled city. On dark days its walls of gray stone seemed to melt into the clouds that floated just above them. "Rabbath-ammon has its head in the clouds and its feet in the water" was a favorite saying.

Indeed, at the base of the city were underground springs that came alive in the rainy season, giving the city the name "City of Waters." The springs fed into the Jabbok, which wound through the valleys and finally spilled out into the Jordan. The people of Rabbath-ammon weren't tillers of the soil, for it was rocky and poor; they were shepherds, vinedressers, and tradesmen who prided themselves on either revenue or pillage from the King's Highway.

* * *

On this particular day, when the whole city was waiting for the prince from Israel to arrive, Naamah, the king's daughter, had gone out to be alone on the stone terrace that opened from her rooms.

She favored this view of the mountains around the city. Great storks swooped down and perched for a moment on the stone ledge; eagles and hawks appeared suddenly and hung motionless in the blue sky, then disappeared. Her favorites, though, were the black crows. These birds, which never left, were greedy, rapacious creatures that pleased her sense of daring competition. They drove the smaller birds from the ledge and fought with hard, beady eyes for the bits of meat she fed them.

She had her own falcon as well, which afforded her many a vicarious thrill as she loosed it from the height of the terrace and watched it swoop down and grasp some small bird in its beak.

Naamah was a strange girl with an abnormal interest in the occult. For her own amusement she kept a snake in a woven basket by her bed. When she learned that the women who attended her were frightened by snakes, she was even more determined to keep it.

She had only to bring the snake out of its basket and let it slither across her arm and up around her neck for the women to run screaming from her rooms. "It isn't natural for a girl to take so to snakes," her father, Hanun, said, laughing nervously as he made her a priestess in the temple of Moloch.

She had done well as a priestess. She had quickly learned the idiosyncrasies of the god who stood huge and ugly, with metal arms outstretched over an ever-burning fire in his lap. His awesome power and strength thrilled her, and she yearned to be his favorite. He was a demanding and ruthless god. No one was ever sure of his favor. Newborn babies kept him appeased and at bay so that he wouldn't break out and destroy the people with plagues, pestilence, or famine. Poor men with too many mouths to feed and rich men who wanted special favors all came with young children to be sacrificed. At times he accepted a calf or a lamb, but only an infant guaranteed his absolute favor.

Naamah first heard by accident that she was to be married to one of the princes of Israel. She heard her mother say to one of the older priestesses, "My daughter isn't beautiful. We must have her schooled in all the arts of seduction if she's to compete successfully with Solomon's other wives."

"Or gain any control," the priestess had added.

Naamah liked to be in control of any situation, and the prospect of being a stranger in a strange country didn't appeal to her. When it was suggested that she spend extra time with the older priestess, she readily agreed. She had been an apt pupil and had learned elements of both seduction and witchcraft. Now she felt capable of handling any situation.

Only one problem remained, and she had settled that herself. She had feared that Moloch, when she left him, would lash out and wreak his vengeance upon her. "You must promise him something; give him something valuable," the old priestess advised her.

Naamah agreed, and on the appointed day she had gone with her handmaidens down the rock steps and through the silent groves of bay trees and ancient flagstone terraces to the dark grotto of the god.

211

She left her handmaidens with their gifts at the opening and followed the old priestess down the smooth, cool steps into the very presence of the great iron god.

There was the sound of water dripping at one side of the cave, and the eternal fire burned in the belly of the great idol with a low, echoing roar. There were more steps and then she saw him, the god Moloch, sitting huge and immovable, his red-hot metal arms reaching out over the flames. The light from the fire flickered in weird patterns on the wall of the cave, and Moloch's eyes, made of large emeralds, seemed to glow with their own special light.

One after the other, the lambs the women had brought were placed on the hungry arms, and then incense. The sickening smell of burning hair and flesh mingled with the fragrance of the incense and then it was gone, lost in a whirl of flame and blue smoke.

Naamah felt the monster's hot breath on her face and arms and in that moment experienced a strange phenomenon: it seemed that the eyes of Moloch came alive for a brief second and focused on her. She was terrified. Flinging herself prostrate onto the warm stones of the cave, she swore with a binding oath that Moloch should have her first child.

* * *

From the terrace Naamah saw the prince and his entourage arrive in the lower courtyard. He was reclining in a beautifully wrought palanquin carried by four of his men. She watched until he stepped out and greeted the officials. In that brief moment she noticed every detail of his bearing and was impressed. "If I had to choose between the two princes of Judah whom I've seen, I would much prefer this one," she said to her maidens.

That he wasn't married she had known, but that he had never lain with a woman she found out from one of her servants who had traveled to Jerusalem. She felt a thrill of almost evil anticipation as she thought of how easy it would be to teach him the joy of lust. She would lead him gently into the labyrinth with protestations that she was frightened and shy. All the while, though, she would be enticing him with the subtle artistry learned from the temple prostitutes.

She found that most of the Hebrews knew nothing of the orgies on the High Places. They spoke of love more often than lust, and their God didn't encourage promiscuity. She had been told that on the Sabbath, for as long as could be remembered, they had bathed and worshiped and then gone home to eat and enjoy their marital rites. It was said that they were a lusty people when once aroused but that their God had set up boundaries and limits. Instead of encouraging sexual perversion and license, as the fertility gods did, the God of Israel set down rules and encouraged a balance.

What this obedience to their God meant, Naamah could just imagine. She knew that they could have more than one wife, but there seemed to be no place in their philosophy for prostitutes or temple priestesses, male or female. She had been told that there were strict rules against a man's lying with another man or using an animal. Knowing this much, she concluded that most Hebrews were innocent of the darker side of sex.

*　*　*

As it turned out, after a month of feasting and discussing the wedding terms, Hanun backed off from the final signing of the marriage contract. He did so in his typical manner, by asking for changes that were so impossible that neither David nor Solomon could agree. "I must have my crown back, and also first choice of the revenue from the King's Highway. In return I'll give the king of Israel permission to defend the highway and will pay what I feel the service is worth."

Hanun had at first been so eager to make a deal that these demands came as a surprise to Solomon and his men. "I would guess," one of the advisers said, "that the wily, old king wants to wait and see which one of Israel's princes actually becomes king before he signs the agreement giving his daughter as pledge."

"You mean he's afraid that Adonijah may become king after he's given the princess to me?" Solomon jumped up and paced back and forth as he considered every angle in the situation.

"Exactly," the adviser nodded.

"If we leave with no agreement, he could join with Moab and the Edomites in a strong confederation that would prevent our having *any* control of the trade route."

"We would have to fight many battles to regain our advantage," the adviser agreed.

"When I'm king I plan to launch some ships in the Red Sea at Ezion-geber. Once we've learned the secrets of the winds and the water currents, we can take over all the business that's now done by camel caravans. But all this depends on my control of the King's Highway." Solomon hadn't intended to divulge his plans in this way, but he was alarmed by the turn of events.

He continued to pace, deep in thought, while his men waited anxiously. "Perhaps," he said finally, looking around at all of them with a smile, "we can still come to some favorable agreement."

"But how, my lord?" The men were eager to hear of any solution.

"Ben-Ezra," Solomon said enthusiastically, "draw up another treaty. It will say that the princess will be given to the new king of Israel as soon as he has mounted the throne of his father and is wearing his crown."

"How brilliant! Why didn't we think of this sooner?" The counselors, encouraged and eager, gathered around the scribe to work out the exact wording of the new treaty.

* * *

The next day, with all due ceremony, the revised treaty was presented to Hanun. He was sitting on his gold and ebony throne, his feet resting on a carved stone that had been heated to keep his feet warm. Though the throne room wasn't as large as David's, it was far more lavishly furnished. Huge stands of brass smoked continually with fragrant incense, swords, and shields covered the entire wall behind the throne, and Hanun's wise men and counselors sat cross-legged on mats interwoven with gold thread and leaned back against cushions filled with goose down rather than the straw that was used in Israel.

As Hanun studied the new treaty with his counselors, Solomon and his men retreated a proper distance and waited. Solomon quickly assessed the opulent appointments of the room and determined once again that the King's Highway was worth any sacrifice. Even marriage to the unsmiling, plain princess wouldn't be too great a price to pay.

"Just one more thing we would insist on," Hanun's chief counselor whispered as he pointed to the part of the agreement that referred to the princess. "The princess must be the new king of Israel's queen, and her son must be the next king of Israel."

Solomon asked for the agreement and stood studying it for some minutes. "God willing, there will be no son by this woman," he thought as he handed the parchment back to the scribes. "If the king of Rabbath-ammon, the vassal of my father, keeps his part of the bargain," he said, "we will agree that the princess will be queen of Israel and any son born will be the next king."

There followed the usual formalities of rereading the documents, dropping red beeswax at the end of each, and pressing both Solomon's signet and Hanun's in the hardening wax.

At last it was over. At some future date—most likely after Passover the following year—the princess would be brought to Jerusalem to become the new queen. Solomon winced at the thought that this dour, unresponsive young girl should be the queen of Israel, but he knew that Hanun was too proud to accept any other position for his daughter. It was that or nothing, and Solomon wanted that trade route. "I'll decide what to do about the princess later," he thought. He handed the sealed scroll to his adviser and went into the great hall, where a royal feast had been laid.

* * *

In Jerusalem that same night Adonijah, with a small band of armed men, found his way to the house of Joab, the commander of David's army. The door to the courtyard was open, and Joab himself met the prince with a nod of approval and a firm handclasp. The room they then entered was filled with men of importance, and they all bowed before Adonijah as though he were already their king.

The time was short—they didn't want to take any chance of being discovered—so each man spoke quickly. They all had grievances with the king, and they all looked to Adonijah for help, though they weren't yet ready for open rebellion.

"The king isn't well, and Solomon plans to take the crown as soon as his father dies." Abiathar, the high priest from Gibeon, spoke softly, rolling his eyes in obvious disapproval.

"We all agree that Solomon is too young and inexperienced," Joab retorted.

"He's Bathsheba's son. That should be enough to end his hopes of gaining the crown," said one of the lesser priests.

"Ah, but don't forget the prophecy of Nathan; he said that Solomon was to build the temple," an old man, who had been one of David's counselors, interjected.

"He can build the temple," Adonijah said, "but let someone who's experienced rule."

215

They tentatively planned to gather, at an appointed time, at En-rogel. There they would crown Adonijah before the king or any of Solomon's followers knew what was happening. Then they would lead him back to the palace with fanfare and excitement, as though everything had been done with the king's approval.

The meeting came to an end and they all left, going in different directions so as not to arouse suspicion.

Adonijah left with only his armor-bearer and a few other men. As he neared the great open space in front of the palace gate, he glanced up at the dark windows of Eon's house. The merchant hadn't been at the meeting, and Adonijah was puzzled.

"My lord." The voice was soft and enticing, and Adonijah recognized it immediately. He stopped and studied the house for a moment; then, seeing that the gate was partially open, he walked over to investigate.

"My lord." This time the voice seemed to come from someplace behind the gate. As Adonijah hesitated, a jeweled hand reached out of the darkness and grasped his wrist, pulling him into the courtyard. It was Yasmit.

"Eon wasn't present tonight at the meeting," Adonijah said.

"My husband has gone on a trip and will be gone for several days." She ran her fingers up his arm and entwined both hands around his neck.

"Are you sure?"

"Of course. Why else would he take such a large purse with him?"

"You were waiting for me, then?" he said.

"Perhaps. Come, my bed is perfumed with spices, and the sheets are lined with roses."

Adonijah asked no more questions. He went in after her and didn't leave until the moon was down and the roosters were crowing from the rooftops of the city.

21

*S*olomon was gone for more than a month, and during this time there were harsh winds and freezing rains in Jerusalem. Shulamit hardly noticed the weather as she busied herself in a flurry of activities. The bitter cold made David's bones ache, and she spent most of her time ministering to his needs. When she had a few hours to herself, she worked feverishly at weaving baskets or making strips of embroidery to be stitched on the new spring garments. All the time her mind was constantly brooding over the outcome of Solomon's mission to Rabbath-ammon. "He loves me," she said to herself over and over again. "So he'll find some way to avoid marrying the princess." When doubts arose, as they often did, she quickly stifled them and plunged into some new activity with renewed vigor.

The other wives and her own maidens noticed how pale and thin she had grown, and though they suspected that the changes were due to Solomon's absence, no one dared speak of it openly.

One day when the sun had come out and warmed the courtyard and the women were all sitting around a woven mat sorting dried figs, they heard the loud thud of a walking stick beating on the inner door to the women's quarters. They motioned to each other to be silent as they all listened.

They heard Tikva unbolt the door, then a voice speaking in a low, confidential tone, and finally the slow, labored shuffling of Tikva coming back into the courtyard. The women waited curiously to see what was wanted or who would be called. "Shulamit—where's Shulamit?" Tikva sounded impatient "She's wanted in the receiving room right away!"

Shulamit entered the receiving room hesitantly. The shutters weren't open, so the room had a closed-in, stuffy odor that mingled with the fragrant odor of spikenard. For a brief moment she thought it might be Solomon.

"My dear, where are your queenly clothes?" She recognized Adonijah's voice and tried to draw back, but he had clasped her firmly around the waist and bent down to kiss her. She turned her head quickly and flung one arm across her face. He backed off but still held her in a firm grip. "It's no use to push me away, my little wildcat," he said. "It only makes me want you all the more."

"It isn't right—my lord," she said, pushing against him in an effort to get away.

"So you're still waiting for young Solomon?" She could see his mocking eyes in the dim light. "Don't be surprised if he comes back with the wedding papers all signed and sealed."

"You're a trickster, and I'll not believe a word you say."

He threw his head back and laughed. "You'll find that this is no trick. He's signed an agreement to marry her even though she worships idols." Again he laughed uproariously. "But he'll not get the throne."

With one hard shove Shulamit pushed him from her and stood trembling with anger. "I'll never believe anything you tell me. You're always twisting things to your own advantage."

"Not this time. His mother will tell you herself. The messenger came with the news just a short time ago."

He walked to the door and stood with the full light flooding in upon him. "Yes, despite all your prayers and hopes, the ambitious fellow has agreed to marry the princess—and that leaves you free for me."

"Impossible!" she retorted, backing away into the shadows.

Smiling, he leaned toward her and whispered, "There are plans afoot that will make me king before two moons have waxed and waned."

Shulamit was now genuinely startled. This was no idle threat. He was just crafty enough to manage some such maneuver. She watched him reach into his wide sash and pull out a tightly rolled scroll. With one flick of his wrist he let it unroll before her astonished eyes. "See? Here are the names of the men pledged to me. They're ready to fight if necessary."

He paused to let her take in the full import of his revelation and then quickly rolled the scroll back into its case and stuffed it in his sash. "I must go now." He patted the bulge it made in his sash. "I don't ask love, you know. That would actually spoil it all."

"And since you don't wish for love—?"

Adonijah had already turned to leave, but at her question he stopped, and his handsome face took on a contemplative aspect. "Ah, my dear. It will be more pleasure than I can imagine to possess you—and to have snatched you right out of the arms of my brother!" The last words were drawn out with relish. Then, once again patting the bulge in his sash, he turned and walked out the open door.

Shulamit went directly to her rooms, not wanting to let anyone see her drawn face and quivering lips. She was sure that she couldn't control her voice, and the tears came to her eyes unbidden.

She dismissed her little maidens with a nod and stood just inside her door, wilted and spent with the anguish that continued to sweep over her. Without lighting her lamp or removing her robes, she sank down onto her mat and buried her head in her hands. Voices rose and fell on the far side of the door. Laughter answered a terse statement. She wanted to sleep, to forget everything, to be left alone for just a short time without the constant, choking ache.

* * *

"Shulamit! Shulamit!" It was Tikva calling in her familiar wavering voice. She was fumbling with the lock, and Shulamit could hear her labored breathing. There was an urgency in the old woman's voice that made Shulamit answer quickly and hurry to unbolt the door. "The queen has called for you. Her servant Jessica is here to take you across the valley to her house."

"What does the queen want?"

"I don't know. I was simply told to get you dressed in your best clothes quickly. You must hurry."

Shulamit let Tikva help her dress. She was too nervous and jittery to protest, her mind flying in all directions and drawing various conclusions.

* * *

As she rode out the Valley Gate on a donkey behind Jessica, Shulamit struggled to compose herself. The queen wasn't one to waste time, and Shulamit knew that there was some reason she wanted to see her. She couldn't imagine what that reason was, however. Now that Bathsheba had won and Solomon was going to marry the princess, why would she concern herself with a simple village girl from Shunem?

They stopped before Bathsheba's large stone house hidden in a clump of pine trees on the western ridge. Jessica helped her dismount and led the way into the house and up a wide, circling stone staircase that ended on the second floor. "Go, she's expecting you. I'll wait here," Jessica said, holding the clay lamp high to light the way.

Shulamit removed her shoes, as was the custom, and entered Bathsheba's room. A cloud of billowing incense greeted her. "My dear, you've come more quickly than I had imagined possible."

Shulamit bowed low, kissing the hem of the queen's garment as was expected of her. When she raised her eyes, she saw the queen quite clearly, no longer obscured by the incense. Curiosity was evident in the queen's long, lingering gaze. She leaned over and patted a cushion opposite her. "Here, sit where I can see you better," she urged. The queen reached for a woven mat that held some raisin cakes. "These were made with my own hands," she said.

Shulamit took one, expecting to find it hard and dry like the cakes served in the court of the queens, but to her surprise it was moist and delicately flavored. She flashed a quick look of approval, and the queen dropped her eyes lest she appear too pleased. "You must be wondering why I've called you here."

"I felt honored," Shulamit said cautiously.

"You must know that I've been deeply disappointed in you." Again the queen didn't look at her but fingered the tassel on one of the pillows as she waited for her to reply.

"Disappointed? I thought you would be pleased that the marriage to your husband wasn't consummated."

"Perhaps I would have been pleased if it had been my lord's choice not to consummate the marriage, but I've heard from those I trust that he went off to the marriage bed early and with great eagerness." The last words were said in the same sweet voice, with an emphasis that conveyed her true feelings.

"The king—" Shulamit started to explain.

"No, it wasn't the king. *You* somehow convinced him, and that means that you must hold some strange power over him that's greater than his own desires."

"I have no strange power, I assure you," Shulamit said.

"I've also heard that the king now calls for you to be his 'little serving maid'—to minister to his needs and play your flute. This is a most ominous power that you hold." The queen's eyes flashed dangerously.

"He's like a father to me. I used to play my flute and wait upon my father as I now do the king."

"And my son—what magic have you worked upon my son?" The queen's face had grown red with anger fermenting just below the surface.

"I have no hold on your son—though once he loved me, and I've loved

220

him in return." Shulamit said with quiet resignation. She looked down at her hands to hide the emotion that welled up within her at the mention of Solomon.

"Ah, you do admit it then?" Bathsheba's voice was no longer soft but was now tinged with anger.

"Yes," Shulamit said, raising her troubled eyes to meet the queen's harsh gaze. "I'm not ashamed to say that I love the prince."

"Oh, no!" Bathsheba's hands flew to her breast, and she turned away. When she spoke again, it was with a forced formality. "Surely you've heard that he's to marry the princess of Rabbath-ammon?"

"Yes, I've heard."

"And you still insist that you love him, though you're married to the king?"

"I never chose to love him, nor can I choose to stop loving him. It isn't so simple."

There was a long pause as Bathsheba tried to regain her composure by smoothing out the cushions and restacking them in the corner to her left. It was obvious that she wasn't used to having her view challenged or to being answered so frankly.

"No, you can't help loving him, I suppose, but you *can* agree that you won't seek him out or encourage him in any way. It's necessary that he marry the princess if he's to be king.

"I want him to be king, if that's what he wants."

"Of course, he wants it. He's always wanted it. Even when he was a little boy he—" She caught herself being too friendly and paused to look at Shulamit in a calculating way, as though trying to determine how convinced she was.

"There are those who are plotting against him."

The queen was cautious. "There's no one plotting. Everyone loves my son. They all love my son and want him to be king."

"Not everyone loves him, and those who don't *are* plotting." Shulamit hadn't yet determined whether to tell the queen about Adonijah. The warning had been blurted out before she had time to make any such decision.

"Who—who's plotting?" Bathsheba leaned toward Shulamit, her voice insistent and demanding.

"One of the other princes."

"Adonijah, you mean." Bathsheba looked relieved. "Adonijah is all talk. He'll never make a move. He's too lazy, too content, and too interested in women." She had obviously dismissed the subject and was ready to call Jessica.

"But I saw a scroll. The names of all his supporters were written on it."

"What names?"

"I didn't read the names, but I saw the scroll. He intends to revolt and take the throne."

"So *he's* confided in you too, not just the king and Solomon, but now the elder prince is telling you his plans. How proud and vain you must be to have these men all sharing secrets with you!" Bathsheba's voice was tipped with venom, and Shulamit sensed both frustration and anger behind her sharp words.

"I want to help you," Shulamit pleaded.

"Help me? You think it's helping me for you to be the constant companion of my husband and the distraction of my son?"

"I've done nothing wrong."

"You may *think* you've done nothing wrong, but it seems to me that you've caused more trouble than anyone else I've ever known. And now you're trying to cause dissension by accusing Adonijah of this horrible crime." Bathsheba had jumped up, agitated, and was walking around the room, straightening a cushion, closing a shutter, and finally picking up the tray of raisin cakes. Then she motioned for Shulamit to stand. "When the princess of Rabbath-ammon comes, I'll expect you to give her all the honor due her position and forget that you've ever known my son."

Shulamit was horrified at the pent-up feeling behind this lovely woman's words. Seeing herself through Bathsheba's eyes, she was a troublemaker and a fool. She realized that she was neither wanted or needed. Their earlier purpose for bringing her to Jerusalem had been fulfilled, and she had become an embarrassment to them.

* * *

Riding back down the path through the dripping olive trees, Shulamit had only one thought: "How can I rid myself of my love for Solomon? It clings to me like a leech; there's no escape from it. I'm worse off than a prisoner. Even if I should leave and return home to Shunem, the pain would go with me. There it would be even more acute, because I couldn't see him."

When she reached the Postern Gate, she found one of her little serving maidens waiting for her. She tried to excuse herself and walked hurriedly across the courtyard to her rooms, but the maiden followed. At the door she whispered, "I've heard that the prince will come tomorrow. Aren't you happy?"

The girl had meant to please her, but the words stung Shulamit like the lash of a whip. She struggled to regain control. "I'm through with love," she said, looking past the girl into the deserted courtyard. Then, for a brief moment before she shut the door, she saw both surprise and pity on the girl's face, and she couldn't bear it.

Quickly she latched the door and then stood touching the bolt as she remembered the last words she had heard him say: "Don't let me go without hearing your sweet voice telling me that you love me."

She bitterly regretted having let him go without some word of love, even though she knew that wouldn't have changed anything. He was a prince, not a common man who could choose what he wanted. What had she expected of him, anyway?

She sank down on her mat and lay her head back on the cushions, pulling the fur covering around her to keep out the chill. "I suppose I wanted him to refuse the princess as I refused the king. Words are easy; only actions tell who really loves."

*O*nce the news reached Jerusalem that Solomon had been able to draw up a friendly agreement with the king of Rabbath-ammon, wild excitement reigned. To gain such an advantage without a major battle was astonishing. Even the poorest merchant could imagine the wealth that might be his through Israel's control of this major trade route.

A small reception had been planned to celebrate Solomon's return, but soon everything was expanded. Shields from the Tower of David were taken down and polished; officers and foot soldiers alike were in a frenzy of activity, repairing their gear and mending their uniforms so that they could march in an honor guard. Finally it was decided that the young maidens should weave garlands and dance in the open courtyard before the palace.

Shulamit had just warmed two large stones to put at David's feet when a messenger arrived with the news that Solomon and his men had been sighted coming up the far side of Olivet. Immediately everything else was forgotten. David's men flung open chests and brought out his various crowns and pieces of armor to decide what he should wear for this happy occasion.

Picking up a large, ornate crown from the hands of a young page, David chuckled. "I suppose I should wear this. I'll never forget the day my men brought it to me. We had just captured the city of Rabbath-ammon."

"It would indeed be fitting, my lord," one of his counselors said. "It's too heavy and too large. It must have been made for one of the old giants."

"My lord, you're not well." Shulamit was alarmed to see the king out of bed.

"We'll not worry about aches and pains today. I must see my son and hear the good news with my own ears." Shulamit backed into the shadows and was preparing to leave when she heard a familiar voice.

"My father!" The voice was sharp and petulant. Everyone turned to view Adonijah, who stood clutching the draperies of the door in his clenched fist. "Why should the whole city be turned upside down just because my brother is returning from Rabbath-ammon?"

David was surprised by the outburst, but he recovered quickly. "It does seem that things have gotten a bit out of hand, but you must admit that the news is good."

"When I returned just a few weeks ago, there was no such celebration."

Shulamit didn't wait to hear David's answer. She only wanted to escape before Adonijah noticed her. Glancing back over her shoulder, she saw him drop the curtain and rush forward to grasp the crown of Rabbath-ammon in his eager hands.

* * *

Long before she reached the latticed door that led into the court of the queens, she could hear the sound of sistrums being shaken, high, excited laughter, and a cacophony of voices. She hesitated, not wanting to face the happy, questioning faces and the wild celebrating.

Summoning all the courage she possessed, she opened the door and stepped into the courtyard. Instantly the noise and laughter stopped; maidens and queens, small children and servants turned to look at her. There was a long moment of awkward silence, and then her own maidens clustered around her. One of the brasher young women asked the question they all wanted answered: "Do you still love the prince now that he's made arrangements for a marriage with the princess of Rabbath-ammon?"

Shulamit turned from them, biting her lip to keep back the tears, but they wouldn't make way for her to pass. Their eyes all focused on her, hemmed her in, demanding to know just how she felt.

"I'm sick of love," she whispered as she averted her eyes so they couldn't see the pain. Once again she tried to push her way through them, but they would not move to let her pass. Finally, with all the pent-up anger she had felt for so long, she turned and faced them. "Go, go to the festivities. You'll see how his mother intends to use this marriage to gain the crown for him!"

The maidens were speechless. They had never seen Shulamit angry, and it surprised them. Quietly they made way for her to pass. She could feel their pitying eyes following her to the door of her rooms; she managed to look calm and reserved until she was alone. Then she flung herself down on her mat in utter despair.

She knew they would discuss all that she had said, and the way she had said it, until every last morsel of meaning was squeezed out of it. They would see as plainly as she had that Solomon's ambition was greater than his love.

She got up and walked out into her own courtyard. She could hear the maiden's voices as they prepared to leave for the festivities. She could picture them gathering up the garlands of olive leaves and purple thistle and crowding in wild excitement through the latticed doors. Then they were gone and it was quiet. "Oh great God of the universe," she whispered, "do you care that such tragedies take place in the court of David's wives?"

* * *

Solomon greeted his friends, laughed with Nathan, and admired the progress of his favorite little nephew. He spent most of his time, however, hoping to catch a glimpse of Shulamit. When he finally concluded that she wasn't present, he was very disappointed. Later, when he determined that Adonijah was also missing, he became disturbed. Though he refused to sink into the abyss of speculation that had consumed him on other occasions, still his mind wouldn't let the question go. "Is it possible," he thought with growing agitation, "that in the end Adonijah will get the one prize I want more than anything else?"

Now he began to see how his own actions must look to Shulamit. She wouldn't understand that his interest in the princess was only political. It was even possible, he realized, that she would think he actually loved the princess.

He silently upbraided himself for being a stupid, ambitious fellow— while all the time he was having to smile and even joke with his friends.

"I must see Shulamit," he confided to Nathan later in the evening.

Nathan frowned. "I thought this trip to Rabbath-ammon would have changed all that."

Solomon threw him a quick look of disbelief. "The princess isn't someone I would *choose* to marry."

"I had heard that she wasn't beautiful, but—"

"You're right, but that isn't the worst of it. There's a hardness about her, and she seems to have a desire to manipulate everyone to her own ends."

"She'll cause little harm from the court of the queens."

"Yes, if only she'll be content to stay there."

Nathan laughed. "From what I've observed of the other women, they'll manage to control her. They don't like to see one woman getting all the advantages."

For the first time since his return Solomon laughed heartily. "I'm sure it will be quite a shock for her. Now, can you help me? I must talk to Shulamit alone."

Nathan hesitated. "Be patient," he said. "If you gain the throne, she'll be yours."

"You don't understand. It's possible for her to be mine legally, while her heart has been given to someone else. I must settle this matter of Adonijah. It may be that she actually loves him as he keeps telling me."

"I've heard enough to know that she doesn't love Adonijah. She probably fears him."

"I still must see her. We didn't part in a pleasant way."

Nathan was thoughtful for a moment. "You'll be staying at our mother's house on the western ridge?"

"Yes."

"Then, it's simple. Send Jessica to bring Shulamit to the house. It will be away from the prying eyes of the court and still not private enough to cause tongues to wag should it be discovered."

"But our mother—?"

"She spends most of her time at the house in Giloh. She knows you'll want to entertain friends."

"I have a feeling she would be happy with anyone but Shulamit." Solomon put his arm around his brother and hugged him. "Thank you for always understanding. I'll see her, and then perhaps I can be at peace with myself."

* * *

The festivities were over and things had settled back into their usual routine before Solomon could arrange to see Shulamit. Just as Nathan had suggested, Jessica rode over to the palace and waited while old Tikva went to get her.

Tikva rattled the latch and called in her rasping voice, "Shu-la-meet."

Shulamit was sitting with a few of her maidens, taking advantage of the first warm rays of the spring sun. She had been weaving on a small loom and teaching the maidens some of the country songs of the north. They had their sistrums and tambourines, which they shook in time to the sad, haunting tunes. At first they didn't hear Tikva.

"Shu-la-meet," she was no longer just rattling the lock but was pounding on the door.

"I'm coming. I'm coming." Shulamit set down the small loom and ran to the door.

"One of the queen's servants has come with a mule to take you to the queen's house across the ridge."

The maidens crowding behind her overheard the message and were excited. They dropped their instruments and ran to the large chest under the window and began to pull out the various things they thought Shulamit should wear.

Remembering the elegance of the queen on her last visit and not wanting to look like a poor shepherdess from the north, she let her friends dress her in one of her new robes of fine Egyptian linen. Then impulsively, they borrowed additional finery from some of the other wives, until she stood before them a vision of loveliness.

Her hair was loose and flowing but covered with a soft mantle held in place by gold ornaments that interlaced over her forehead. Her neck was roped with gold spangles that gleamed and sparkled in the soft lamplight. Though she had grown pale and thinner in the past months, her eyes still flashed with interest, and at times her cheeks dimpled in a wistful smile.

* * *

Shulamit dismounted in the same darkened courtyard and was ushered up the same wide steps. An old woman, bent almost double with age, motioned for her to enter at a doorway halfway up the stairs, then disappeared behind some tapestries.

The room she entered wasn't nearly as large as the one the queen had entertained her in. It was more lavishly hung, however, and was carpeted with beautifully woven designs in dark red and purple. The fragrance of spikenard mingled with more subtle odors she couldn't identify. Several hanging lamps gave off a faint, flickering glow. Large mats were arranged against the wall, and cushions of every variety were piled comfortably across the back and into the corners.

Shulamit forgot her fears for the moment. She was so enchanted by the room that she didn't hear footsteps behind her, and Solomon was able to stand and observe her face before she sensed his presence and turned to look at him.

"My lord!" she gasped.

"Shulamit, my darling," he said, covering the distance in two quick steps and drawing her into his arms. His kiss was harsh and hungry.

"My lord," she said again, catching her breath, "this is unseemly."

"Unseemly! Is it unseemly because you've already given yourself to my brother Adonijah?" Solomon's words were clipped and brittle. His eyes, no longer tender, were cold, piercing javelins.

"I've given myself to no one—not to the king, nor to Adonijah. It is *you* who has spoiled our love." Her eyes were dark and accusing, and her hands were clenched into fists as she glared at him.

"I—have spoiled our love? I've only done my duty as a prince of Israel, while you—"

"Only your *duty*! I've heard that you've been rejoicing over the agreement you signed to marry the princess of Rabbath-ammon." Her eyes flashed and her mantle fell back, exposing her waving hair and the soft tendrils around her face.

"Never. I never rejoiced over the marriage, only the treaty, and it was you who hadn't the time to put on your robe or dirty your feet to kiss me good-bye." Solomon's voice was no longer cold and angry, but reproachful.

"I was angry, yes—and jealous. I wanted no more torture." She turned her back to hide the tears that welled up at the memory of his leaving.

He was suddenly moved by her frailty. He could tell by her words and manner that she hadn't encouraged Adonijah, and he knew that she had risked much for his sake on the night of her marriage to his father. He noticed the soft curls and the way her small bare feet peeped out from under the flowing robes.

He could no longer speak harshly to her. He wanted desperately to gather her up in his arms and escape from the palace—to flee to some remote place where they could lead their own lives without the complications of the court.

"You're beautiful even when you're angry," he said impulsively. She stiffened, her back still to him, setting herself to resist him. "You're as beautiful, my love, as Tirzah—as lovely as Jerusalem. Must you be angry when we have so little time together?"

"I am angry," she said, whirling around to face him. She impatiently brushed two bright tears from her eyes. "I went to great trouble to save myself for you, but you, you—"

"My love, my love," he pleaded, "don't look at me like that. I can't endure such condemnation. Your eyes cut me like sharp knives."

"And your actions have cut like swords. You're merciless and cruel." Again she turned from him and dabbed at the tears that rolled down her cheeks.

Solomon grew silent as he waited, hoping that her anger was spent. Cautiously he reached out and touched her hair. "This lovely hair is like a flock of goats on the slopes of Gilead. When I saw them there near Rabbath-ammon, I thought of you and wished that I could return home to you and only you."

He moved so that he could see her better. "Let me see you smile just once. Those lips that are like soft crimson ribbons are bewitching when you smile; your teeth peep out like little lambs, and not one of them is missing." Still she didn't turn around, though he gently ran his hand through her hair and let the curls wrap around his fingers. She moved away and pulled her mantle back up over her head.

"Am I to see nothing of your lovely face at all?" Solomon coaxed. "Nothing but your temples, like smooth pieces of pomegranate, almost hidden by this veil?"

"I'm through with love," she said.

He grasped her arms and drew her back against him so that he could whisper in her ear, and she didn't resist him. "Nay, my little shepherdess," he chided, using the rough speech of the shepherds, "you're not through with love already when ye've had so little of it."

Still she didn't pull away, and he quickly took advantage of the moment to turn her around so that he could look in her eyes. She wouldn't return his gaze but looked out past him to the far corner of the room.

"My love," he said seriously, all joking now gone, "in the court of the queens there are queens and concubines, and virgins without number, and none of them is equal to you in beauty or loveliness. There's no one else like you. You're special—the only child of your mother."

"I don't belong here," she said, pushing against him to free herself of his arms and his searching gaze.

"Of course you belong here. I hear that your maidens have nicknamed you 'Happy.' Even the queens and concubines call you 'Happy' and praise you."

She twisted from him and stood proud and tall, her chin raised and her head averted so that he couldn't see the emotion playing on her face.

"Who's this?" he teased. "I don't think I know this woman. She looks fresh as the dawn, lovely and remote as the moon, and warm as the sun; but when she's piqued, she's as terrible as an army with banners."

"I'm *not* as terrible as an army with banners. Is it strange to you that I don't know how to manage with a lover who goes down to pasture his flock in strange gardens and gathers lilies there?"

Solomon shrugged. "It's the nature of men. Your father had many wives, and my father had both wives and concubines, but there's always a favorite, and to me *you* are that favorite."

When she answered, her voice was so low that he had to bend down to hear her. "You said that you wouldn't take a woman as your father took your mother?"

"And indeed I won't. He saw what he wanted and took it. I've seen nothing I want but you, and yet I'll not take you until it can be with honor and integrity."

"But the princess—"

"That's a matter of treaties and agreements, and I wish it didn't have to be. It's not my choice; it's what I must do for Israel."

"I don't like it. There's something wrong about it."

Solomon stiffened. "Believe me, I don't like it either, but a prince can't do just what he likes."

He saw her steely resolve soften and reached out to fold her in his arms. For a moment she clung to him, and he kissed her.

He felt her fingers twining in his hair and her young, rounded breasts pressed against his chest. Swiftly he picked her up in his arms and, pushing all thought of principle from his mind, carried her to his inner room and put her down on the red-fox-skin covering of his couch.

"How delightful you are in every way," he said as he sat down beside her. His eyes moved from the length of her lashes, the pink of her cheeks, and the dimple in her chin to the jingling bits of gold that dripped from chains around her neck.

"You, my love, aren't a lily at all, but a wonderful, tall palm tree whose breasts are its clusters of dates." He nuzzled her ear and drank in the warm fragrance of her perfume. "More than anything I want to climb the palm and claim its branches." He ran his hand up the slim smoothness of her leg.

"No, no." She stiffened and pulled away from him. "I'm not your palm tree. I'm a walled garden, a fountain closed. It's dangerous to wake love before its time." She jumped from the couch and, holding her mantle in her hand, ran toward the door. There he stopped her.

"I'm sorry," he said, "I didn't intend this."

"I must go." With one strong push she freed herself and ran out the door, forgetting her slippers.

Solomon picked up the slippers almost reverently and held them, small and delicate, in his hands. The jeweled thongs were braided with gold, and the leather soles were decorated with lovely cutwork. "This is undoubtedly all I can have of her," he muttered, "unless I can win the crown and take her honorably."

* * *

Back in her room again, holding her cold feet close to the brazier, Shulamit thought about all that had happened. She threw some sweet-smelling herbs on the hot coals and wiggled her toes to bring some life back into them.

"I almost stayed," she said as the enormity of it swept over her. "I'll have to leave Jerusalem. I can't stay here much longer." She thought of Adonijah's vengeance, Bathsheba's anger, and the thousand threads of complexity that she was entangled in. She wrapped her arms around her knees and sat looking into the dying coals of the brazier. It was easy to say that she had to leave, but how she would go about such a difficult thing she didn't know.

23

*I*n the days that followed, Shulamit became more and more convinced that she must find some way of leaving Jerusalem. However, the more she thought about it, the more impossible it seemed. While David's wives were allowed a great deal of freedom to go on small excursions, none of them had ever returned for even a short visit to her home. It wasn't the custom.

Shulamit now faced many problems. Though she saw Solomon every day in his father's rooms, their meetings were a constant frustration to her. She was powerfully drawn to him and at the same time disillusioned to find that his ambition took precedence over everything else. It seemed that he would agree to anything as long as it advanced his cause.

She saw Adonijah almost daily also, and he frightened her. He spent much of his time at the North Gate hearing complaints. He gave the impression that since his father was getting too old to manage things, he was the one actually in charge. In this way he was building up a body of men whose support could be depended upon.

He now had a chariot, fifty footmen to run before him, and a trumpeter to announce his coming. He would be very hard to stop—yet if he weren't stopped, Shulamit knew that she would fall into his hands like a bird into a trap.

Apart from a few winks and some sly remarks, he hadn't sought her out in any special way for quite some time. However, she wasn't to be spared. Her most unpleasant encounter with Adonijah came about quite unexpectedly on the day of the Feast of the New Moon in the month of Abib, the month of Passover—almost exactly a year since her arrival in Jerusalem.

Shulamit had just picked up her loom and was mindlessly weaving when she heard the sound of footsteps hurrying across the outer court. Looking up, she saw a young girl who looked slightly familiar standing in the doorway. She seemed nervous—perhaps even hostile—but none of this was evident in her voice. "One of the maidens has been taken suddenly ill, and the queen is asking for you," she said.

Shulamit quickly gathered up some of her choice herbs in a basket and followed the messenger out the door. As she rode along, she paid little attention; the path was now quite familiar. Only when they reached the western ridge and the girl rode on past the dark house of Bathsheba was she puzzled.

The girl had avoided all questions, and there was a sullen antagonism that exhibited itself in everything she said or did. Finally they stopped before a well-built house half-hidden in the pines. Shulamit looked closely at the girl as they dismounted and found that she was older than she had thought. But there was definitely something familiar about her.

For a moment the girl stood glaring at her with tight-lipped arrogance. Then she turned and led the way up an inner stairway. She knocked on a door at the first landing. "I've done as you asked." She spat out the words with bitterness and then turned and hurried down the stairs.

Slowly the door swung open, and Shulamit looked up to see an old woman staring at her.

"The queen is supposed to have called for me," Shulamit said.

"I am the queen—the *real* queen." The woman drew herself up proudly, and Shulamit saw that indeed she wore a gold circlet in her tangled hair. Her clothes, though worn and stained, were heavy with embroidery.

"The queen?" Shulamit was puzzled. "The real queen?"

"I am Haggith, the real queen of Israel. When my son is king, I'll be given my rightful place again." She made a great show of readjusting the gold circlet to her liking.

"You sent for me?" Shulamit was still puzzled.

"Who did you think had sent for you in the name of the queen? I hope it wasn't that whore the king favors. Unlucky woman, her time is almost over." She turned and started to leave.

"Where is the young woman who's sick?" Shulamit called after her.

"There is none," a familiar male voice answered. Shulamit stood frozen with fright and disgust as the curtains parted and Adonijah appeared.

He was dressed in rich, jeweled garments and wore a prince's circlet on his head. He was smiling, his handsome mouth twisted into a sardonic grimace. "Don't look so worried, my love. If my brother Solomon can call you to his rooms, surely I can do the same."

"But—" Shulamit started to object.

"Don't worry. I'll not touch you. That can wait until after Passover."

"Passover!" Shulamit was startled. Passover was just two weeks away.

"By Passover, or soon afterwards, I will have secured the throne—and you'll be mine." He reached out and encircled her waist with his long, jeweled fingers.

"That's impossible." Shulamit tried to fight down her panic.

"Not impossible at all. Come and see the room I'm preparing for you. Right now this is my secret meeting place, but soon the whole house will be yours." Adonijah held the curtain back and motioned for her to enter.

Shulamit stood in the doorway, looking into the room that for all its lavish appointments seemed more like a storehouse than a home. Large wooden chests, bolted and strapped with leather, were piled on top of each other in a random fashion; candlesticks, alabaster lamps, jeweled idols, pottery storage jars, and piles of rare materials were scattered everywhere.

"As the oldest son of my father, I'll inherit everything of real value." He walked across the room and flung open one of the chests, pulling out a handful of the glittering jewelry for Shulamit to see.

Slowly he let the jewelry drop from his hands and fall back into the chest. "This will all belong to the woman who controls my heart," he said with a smile and a knowing wink. Shulamit saw his smiling face loom over her and felt his arms crushing her to his chest.

"My lord," she said, trying to pull away and summoning all the cold dignity possible, "love isn't something you buy."

"When I hold Jerusalem and all of Israel in my hand, you'll not dismiss my gift so lightly." His eyes flashed dangerously.

With a strong push Shulamit freed herself. "When do you intend to do all this?" she asked as she adjusted her mantle and gave a defiant lift to her chin.

"Soon, very soon." He was clearly annoyed by her resistance but regained his composure and spoke with deliberate coolness. "The plans have all been made. I'll take advantage of the king's preoccupation with Passover. Abiathar, the high priest, will anoint me, and Joab has pledged the army to defend me if necessary. Then there are the tribesmen who will be here for Passover. And your own brothers, they'll be here for my anointing."

"My brothers?"

"I've gained their support by sharing with them my plans to make you queen." Adonijah was obviously enjoying her discomfort.

"And the king?"

"I'll have mercy on my father, of course. However, my brother Solomon and his mother may have to be sacrificed for the good of Israel."

"You're being foolish. Don't you realize that I'll go right back and warn them?"

"Of course, you will," he said, gleefully rubbing his hands together. "I expect that, but they won't believe you. I know them."

"I'll tell Solomon that you intend to take the crown and have him killed."

"Yes, yes, I want you to tell them all. They won't want to hear such bad news, and it will be easy to convince them that it's false."

"Then why are you telling me?"

"Ah, you have no idea of the pleasure one gets from planning something so preposterous that no one believes it—and then carrying it out. You'll be the only person who can understand and appreciate the skill with which it will have all been accomplished."

"You're evil—really evil. Even though you're one of David's sons, you're still evil." With a look of revulsion she backed away from him toward the door, but he followed her.

"I'm not evil," he said, laughing as though it were a joke, "just clever, as you'll see. After I'm king I'll bring you again to this room to possess you, and then you'll understand." He ran his hand up her arm and gathered her hair into his fist, holding her so that she couldn't even turn her head.

"If there's still a God in Israel who hears and answers prayers, you won't take the crown and you won't have me." She tugged to free herself. Gradually his grip loosened, and then he let her go.

"If, if," he said with a tinge of mockery. "*If* there's a God in Israel." He laughed a tight-lipped, cynical laugh as he opened the door and shouted for his wife.

For the first time Shulamit realized that the woman she had taken for a maid was one of the wives she had seen earlier at Adonijah's country house. No wonder the young woman had looked hostile. "I'll make my own way back to the palace," she said as the porter brought her mule.

Before Adonijah could answer, Shulamit was headed out the gate and riding back down the path that led into the valley and then up the hill to the Valley Gate.

✳ ✳ ✳

That was the last Shulamit had seen of him, but from that moment on, her heart had been held in a tight, choking grip of fear. She hadn't realized that her own brothers were backing Adonijah. They would undoubtedly insist on her marriage to him. Only her father would understand, and he was too sick to help her.

Adding to her fright was the realization that Adonijah really intended to get Solomon and Bathsheba out of his way, even if it meant killing them. With his jealous hatred of Solomon, he would relish the thought of both torture and death. For the first time she realized how dangerously obsessed with jealousy Adonijah had become. "His jealousy is like a terrible disease for which there is no cure," she thought.

* * *

The next evening, after the prayers before the ark at the Gihon Spring, Adonijah waited for Solomon and joined him as he mounted the long stairs to the Water Gate. Quite casually he mentioned that Solomon must have noticed that neither he nor Shulamit was at the Feast of the New Moon.

When he got no response he went on. "Actually, she wasn't at the feast because she was visiting me." He emphasized each word with an aura of mystery, hoping to produce the usual angry response.

Solomon was stunned. Pain and hurt were evident in his eyes, but he answered with a harshness that surprised Adonijah. "And you could hardly wait to tell me," he said as he turned and hurried up the steps.

The next day when Shulamit was again attending the king and Solomon arrived, she called him aside and tried to warn him about Adonijah's plot. She was surprised to find him cool and unresponsive. He said, "No doubt you learned this on your recent visit to his house." His words were like well-aimed darts.

"Yes, but you must understand." She tried to explain, but he wouldn't listen.

"I now see things quite clearly," he said. "I *do* understand." With a frigid reserve he moved away, refusing even to look at her.

Shulamit realized that once again Adonijah had cleverly managed to plant the seeds of dissension—seeds that were terribly hard to root out.

David noticed that something was wrong between Shulamit and Solomon one evening as he sat playing his harp and composing new words as he went along. Two of his best scribes sat cross-legged on each side of him, writing down the words as fast as he sang them. "Catching the golden nuggets as they fall from his inspired lips, lest they be lost," was how one of them described it. The tune could be improvised fresh each time it was sung, but the words must remain the same.

He put down his harp, dismissed the scribes, and motioned for Solomon and Shulamit to come over to him. "Now what's the trouble?" he asked as he looked from one to the other.

Solomon finally explained. "My brother Adonijah has been bragging to Shulamit. He told her that he had plans to seize the crown. It's only an idle threat, of course. He likes to disrupt things."

"I've never disciplined the boy in any way," David said, shaking his head sadly. "I know he's often selfish and proud, but he loves me. He'd never do anything to hurt me."

Shulamit realized with dismay that neither of them intended to take her warning seriously. Though they both knew Adonijah's weaknesses, they couldn't imagine his planning something so violent and mercenary as an overthrow. They thought it was all just talk. How could such elaborate plotting take place without their knowledge?

* * *

Shulamit asked to be dismissed and went quickly to her rooms. Shutting the door, she paced back and forth trying to think what should be done. She knew that Bathsheba wouldn't listen to her, and she had no way of talking to anyone else of any importance. It was just as Adonijah had said; no one would listen to her.

Gradually she became calmer, and once again she went over the possibilities. She *must* find someone who would listen. It would have to be someone who came regularly to the king's rooms—someone who was as concerned about Solomon as she was.

"Nathan, Solomon's brother," she thought. Nathan was often in the king's rooms. He would listen, and perhaps he would understand the danger. It wouldn't be easy to convince him, however.

Her opportunity came late that same afternoon, when Nathan brought Mattatha to see his grandfather.

David loved the little boy. He always had him run to get the harp, and the two would sit together making up songs. David would strum and sing while Mattatha clapped. "The Lord is my shepherd; I am His sheep . . ." The songs were all simple ones that a little boy could understand.

While Nathan was watching with fond fatherly pride, Shulamit asked quietly, "May I have a word with you?"

Startled, he nodded and stepped out of the hearing of the young palace guards and old tribesmen. As quickly as possible Shulamit told him of her encounter with Adonijah and his threats against the king and Solomon. "You must warn the prophet, your teacher," she urged. "He'll know what to do, and the king will listen to him."

There was no time to say more, because David was getting ready to make one of his scheduled appearances in the throne room. Shulamit hoped that Nathan had understood all that she had told him. She couldn't tell whether he had taken the message seriously or not; nevertheless, she felt relieved. "It's in God's hands now," she thought as she watched the procession forming on each side of the door.

* * *

Back in Shunem the brothers were sitting late into the night around the glowing coals of several braziers in a narrow, smoke-filled room. They all feared that Bessim wouldn't live long, and each one wanted to be present when he gave his blessing and parceled out the inheritance. They knew of many instances when a member of the family had been cheated out of his inheritance by his own brothers just because he had been away from home at the time of the father's death. They didn't intend to let this happen to them.

"While you were out in the fields today," Nefer said as he reached into a basket of nuts and began cracking them in his strong hands, "messengers came from Jerusalem. The king isn't well, and plans are being made to crown Adonijah king during Passover week. He needs our help and says that he'll reward us well."

For a moment there was silence as each man thought of all that this would mean. Finally Baalak said, "We'll have to tell him that our father is dying, and we must all stay to bury him. He'll understand."

"It would be a shame to gain the small inheritance of our father and miss the larger one the prince would give us," said Urim.

Again there was silence, broken only by the splitting sound as a nut was cracked. None of them wanted to lose the one, sure advantage of the inheritance from their father.

Finally Nefer threw the rest of the uncracked nuts back into the basket and stood up. "I'm willing to go for all of us. I'll represent our interests in Adonijah's rebellion, but first I must insist on taking a son from each one of you to hold as surety."

There was a moment of silence as the men thought through the situation. Then one by one they stood and, with a handclasp, sealed the agreement with Nefer.

* * *

As soon as Nefer and his nephews reached Jerusalem, he sent a message to Shulamit in the court of the queens, asking to see her. He knew that she had a mind of her own and could be difficult. He wanted no unforeseen problems. If Prince Adonijah wanted her as his queen, Nefer intended to see that she cooperated in every way.

Shulamit received her brother in the small reception room. She was surprised at how much older he had grown, and how serious. Even more astonishing was the respect she saw in his eyes. He was most assuredly impressed with her position.

Nefer gave her messages from her father and some newly woven material from her mother. He seemed ill at ease but remained perched on the edge of his seat twisting and untwisting the fringes on the armrest.

Suddenly he whispered, "I've come to back Prince Adonijah in his revolt. It will take place right after Passover, while the tribesmen are still here."

Shulamit was alarmed; her worst fears were coming true. She wanted to tell Nefer everything, make him see his mistake. As it happened, she didn't have time; at that moment old Tikva appeared at the door to escort Nefer back to the throne room, where he was being paged.

Shulamit stood for a moment and watched them walk across the courtyard while she struggled to regain her composure. Passover was only a few days away. No one would listen to her even if she explained all that she knew. "I must find a way to leave," she thought over and over again. "If Adonijah should succeed in his revolt, he'll demand that I become his queen, and my brothers will force me to accept."

24

As Passover approached, Adonijah spent less time with David and more time winning the people's favor. He was usually found sitting at the North Gate talking with the elders and greeting the various tribesmen who had come for the feast. Always he reminded them, "It's best to spare the king. He's not well. I can just as easily answer your questions and solve your problems."

Every waking moment was used judiciously to further his cause. He was no longer angry that Solomon spent so much time with his father. Instead, he was delighted with the arrangement.

Everything was fitting into place, and he was just priding himself on his ability to be discreet and careful. Then a most unfortunate thing happened. It not only embarrassed Adonijah but also made enemies of some of his most devoted followers.

It happened at midmorning, when everyone was busy preparing for Passover. Adonijah, who had spent the night at his country house, arrived in his chariot at the North Gate dressed in his most splendid attire. The guards above the gate blew the usual salute to the princes of Judah, and the tribesmen and wealthy merchants bowed before him as he walked to the highest seat in their midst and sat down.

He was just looking around, ready to greet everyone, when there was a spine-tingling cry from the crowded lanes below them in the city. Mingled with the cry were curses and shouting that brought everyone at the gate to their feet. Only Adonijah remained seated and apparently calm. He was more annoyed than interested until suddenly he caught a glimpse of a woman being dragged toward the gate by two large men. As they came closer and the crowds drew back to let them pass, Adonijah saw that the woman was Yasmit.

The color drained from his face as he realized that they were coming toward him. Desperately he tried to think of some way to avoid the inevitable confrontation. She began to pull away and kick the men who were holding her in a sudden, desperate effort to free herself. Then, with a surge of panic, he realized that she was coming to him for help.

"My lord, my lord," she shrieked. With one wild twist she wrenched herself free and frantically clawed her way toward him through the crowd.

He instinctively shrank back into the shadows and turned his face away, but her cries almost deafened him. He felt her long fingernails dig into the flesh of his feet.

"My lord," she begged, lifting a tear-streaked, contorted face so he couldn't help but see the terror in her eyes. "These men are going to kill me," she cried.

Adonijah was horrified. It was evident that she intended to draw him into the situation, perhaps even expose his relationship to her. He watched helplessly as the men elbowed their way to stand before him. "This woman was taken in adultery," an older man Adonijah recognized as one of David's palace guards said, grabbing Yasmit by the hair and pulling her to her feet.

"Where are your two witnesses?" Adonijah managed to ask. He knew it was difficult to find two witnesses unless there had been careful planning and a trap to catch the offender.

"We're the two witnesses," the men said as they once again grabbed Yasmit by the arms.

"This man," a well-dressed Jebusite said, pointing at one of the men, "was jealous of the attention this woman paid me."

"Woman, where is your husband?" Adonijah asked. "Why is *he* not here bringing the charges?" He had regained his composure with difficulty and now stood with judicial gravity, ready to mete out whatever justice was demanded by the crowd.

"'Woman, you call me." Yasmit spat at him and her eyes blazed. "You've shared my bed and begged for my kisses, and now you pretend not to know me!"

The men looked at Adonijah in astonishment. The crowd, which had been boisterous, now edged closer and waited in eager anticipation to hear what he would say. For a moment he reeled under the blow and then, squaring his shoulders, he ordered, "Take this woman away." His eyes were hard and unflinching. "I don't know her. Take her away."

Once again the men grabbed her and would have carried her off, but she pulled away and threw herself at Adonijah's feet. Her eyes were frantic with fear; her voice was plaintive. Wrapping her arms around his ankles in a desperate grip, she wheedled like a spoiled child. "Please, my lord, help me. Eon will be back before sunset. He would be forever grateful."

Adonijah motioned for one of his men to pull her away. "There are two witnesses, and that's all that's necessary." Adonijah spoke to the palace guards. "Take her out and do with her as the law demands."

The crowd parted, and Yasmit was dragged from their midst, wilted and beaten. Men with stones urged others in the crowd to come with them to the Valley of Hinnon where they could join in the sport of ridding Israel of corruption.

Everyone was so caught up in the drama that no one noticed as Adonijah sank down onto the bench, mopping his brow, and then called for his chariot. Neither did they notice that the Jebusite who had spoken earlier stood for a few moments watching the crowd of men hurrying the small, bright-green figure out the gate to the path that led down to the field of stoning. With a shrug he started to follow at a great distance.

✳ ✳ ✳

Late that night, as Adonijah was sitting alone and sleepless in his house on the western ridge, there came a knock on the door. One of his young servants apologized, saying, "There's a Jebusite here who insists that he must see you. He says it's important."

At first Adonijah was going to refuse, but then remembering the Jebusite at the gate that morning, he agreed to see him.

"My lord," the man said bowing low and accepting the seat Adonijah offered him.

"What brings you here at this hour?" Adonijah was gruff and impatient.

"It has to do with the woman called Yasmit."

"The woman who was sentenced and stoned today?" Adonijah fingered the hem of his sleeve and tried to look unconcerned.

"The woman who was sentenced but *not* stoned."

Adonijah's face registered surprise. "Not stoned?" he stammered.

"Ah, yes, I thought you would be interested." The Jebusite's eyes were knowing. He nodded his head sagely and stroked his beard, taking his time before he spoke again. "All of us who professed love for her would have let them have their way with her, but one little old man, flailing his arms and shouting curses, stood up to them all. He braved the stones and the ridicule and rescued her at the last moment."

"Then she's still—?" Adonijah couldn't bring himself to look at the Jebusite.

"Just barely."

"A little old man, you say, rescued her?"

"Yes."

"Eon?"

"Yes. He was coming home with his camels and donkeys laden with gold."

"He himself tried to rescue her?"

"Not just *tried*. He *did* rescue her. Perhaps she'll love him now."

"Yasmit love Eon? She's a strange one. It seems that all of his gold hasn't been able to buy what she gives to others at no cost."

There was a long silence between them, and then the Jebusite shrugged. "If the city was Jebusite, the woman would make a valuable temple priestess."

"The corruption of the Canaanites and the Jebusites is well known to us."

"It seems that only the *women* of Israel are corrupt."

"It is written that both the man and the woman taken in adultery must be stoned. In that way we rid our country of evil." Adonijah was smug and self-righteous.

"But, as we saw today, many of the men who have visited Yasmit were either holding the stones or condemning her."

Now Adonijah became nervous. "It's obvious that the woman tempted them. It was her fault."

The Jebusite leaned forward and looked straight at Adonijah. "That puzzles me. I've heard that she never left her house. They came to her."

"But nevertheless she tempted them." Adonijah, frowning, spoke with slow deliberation.

"I see. The woman must be punished because she's able to exercise some strange power over a man—and this isn't to be tolerated."

Adonijah was annoyed with the turn the conversation had taken, and even more disturbed with the outcome of the confrontation with Yasmit. Now he would lose Eon's valuable financial support as well as his ability to enlist the other merchants for his cause. He stood up, signaling to the Jebusite that the audience was ended, then watched him bow and turn to leave.

"One moment," Adonijah commanded. "You realize, of course, that the woman was lying. She tried to ruin me. I won't forget it." He lifted his jaw defiantly and clasped his hands behind his back.

The Jebusite nodded knowingly, then bowed to the floor and without another word left the room.

*　*　*

The Passover went much as usual. There had been the expected influx of people, the gathering for the sacrifice at Gibeon, and then the quiet, lamp-lighted family meal.

In the palace David had officiated at the pascal meal, but he hadn't been well enough to ride out to Gibeon. Instead, he rode down to the Gihon Spring, where the ark was enshrined in a cubical stone enclosure and draped with curtains and skins, just like the tabernacle at Gibeon. He offered sacrifices on the simple altar built of unshaped stones, and a choir of Levites chanted the lovely antiphonal songs that he had written.

It was a natural setting. Several ancient olive trees shaded the small stone shrine and the altar, grass grew between the flagstones of the courtyard, and several almond trees stood at the entrance to the cave that contained the spring. A great deal of water was needed for the sacrifices, so it had been decided that the ark should come to rest beside the spring until the temple could be built.

Zadok had gradually become the priest who officiated before the ark at the Gihon. He loved the music and the innovations made possible by the simplicity of the setting and greater informality. Abiathar, descendant of old Eli and rightful high priest, maintained the tabernacle at Gibeon, with all its Mosaic rituals still rigidly enforced.

Adonijah had observed Abiathar and David's growing estrangement and was determined to take advantage of it. On the third day after Passover, Adonijah made his move. He had gathered all of his followers at the Serpent Rock called En-rogel. There, in the presence of his supporters, Adonijah was anointed by the high priest and proclaimed the new king.

*　*　*

While all of this was taking place, Bathsheba was going about her usual morning chores of feeding the pigeons and ordering her servants to prepare the bins for storage of the newly harvested barley. Suddenly there was a violent knocking at the front gate. "There are a group of officials waiting outside," one of her handmaidens reported.

Bathsheba was annoyed to have her quiet morning so rudely interrupted. She sent Jessica to welcome them and then hurried to change from her simple outer robes to something more regal.

"My lady," Jessica came running, her eyes round with alarm and her voice trembling. "It's Nathan, the prophet. He asked if we had heard the trumpets and the beating of drums. He says to come to the roof and listen."

Bathsheba dropped her mirror and left her jewelry spilling out of its sandalwood box. Her jar of rosewater caught in her skirts and splashed out across the tiles as she ran after Jessica.

"Listen!" Nathan said as he held up one finger and leaned out over the parapet. Faint and far away at first, and then louder and louder, they could hear shouts of rejoicing, the tambourines, sistrums, and drums, and every so often the triumphant blast of the silver trumpets.

"What's happening?" Bathsheba asked, clutching Nathan's arm and making him turn so that his kindly eyes met hers.

"Can you imagine that son of Haggith is now king—and David doesn't even know it?" he blustered.

"Adonijah is king? I don't understand."

"He invited all the king's sons except Solomon, and then all of the important men—especially David's general, Joab, and the high priest Abiathar—to crown him at En-rogel. Of course he didn't invite me or Zadok or Benaiah and the house guards, or David's Mighty Men. He's been down there sacrificing sheep and oxen and celebrating under the big tents he erected for the occasion."

Bathsheba clutched his arm with such ferocity that his skin was bruised beneath the rough cloth. "You must go to the king. You must tell him this immediately. It may already be too late."

"No, it's not I who must go to the king, but you yourself. Be sure to tell him that if Adonijah is king, it won't be long before both you and your son will be killed. When you've finished, I'll come and confirm everything that you've said."

Without further discussion the two hurried down the narrow outside steps and mounted the donkeys waiting at the gate. Nathan was pale, and Bathsheba trembled so that her fingers grew stiff and rigid as she clutched the reins for support.

* * *

Shulamit heard a flurry outside the door of the king's chamber as she sat watch near his bed. The guards told someone that the king was sleeping and couldn't be disturbed. She thought that she heard a woman's voice reply with a quick, sharp command, and then the curtain was pulled back.

With a start she recognized Bathsheba, who was no longer the queenly person Shulamit had known her to be. Her undergarment and mantle were of the dark homespun material common people wore; only her cloak was of royal pattern and design. She threw her mantle back, and Shulamit noticed that her face was pale and her eyes large and frightened with none of the tasteful artistry of makeup she was noted for.

"My lady," said Shulamit, "the king isn't well."

Bathsheba didn't seem to hear her. She brushed past and bowed low beside the bed, her forehead touching the cold stones of the floor and her hands spread out before her in supplication.

David stirred and struggled to raise himself. "Bathsheba?" he said. It was obvious that he was genuinely surprised. He rubbed his hands across his eyes and then sat up, letting Shulamit pile cushions behind him for support.

"My lord," Bathsheba said, raising her head to look at the king, "you promised me that my son Solomon would sit upon the throne, but now—right now—Adonijah is being crowned by the high priest."

Shulamit was stunned. She grew cold with fright as she heard the king, still unbelieving, say, "How can that be?" He searched among the furs until he found his crown. "They obviously have no crown."

"My lord, Abiathar has the same cruse of oil that you were anointed with at Bethlehem, and now all of Israel will be waiting to see if you confirm him as your choice."

David was bewildered, unable to comprehend the situation. In spite of Shulamit's warning he hadn't thought this possible. He hadn't thought Adonijah was that ambitious.

"We have no time," urged Bathsheba. "You must act quickly. When you've gone to be with your fathers, if Adonijah is king, my son and I will be arrested and executed as criminals."

"You say he's being anointed now? Are they celebrating already?"

"Yes, my lord. We must act fast." Still David hesitated. So many times one or more of his wives had been hysterical over the treatment of one of their children. To move fast, he had learned, was to invite disaster.

Shulamit wondered if the king would remember her own warning. "I'll check into this," he said, "and if I find that Adonijah has really had himself anointed and crowned, I'll have to see what can be done about it. Don't worry, my dear. Everything will be all right."

There was again a flurry of excitement outside the king's door, and one of the guards announced, "The prophet Nathan to see the king."

Bathsheba left the room as Nathan entered and knelt before the king. "My lord," he said, "I've come to confirm all that Bathsheba has told you."

* * *

Shulamit waited to hear no more. Even if Bathsheba had her way and Solomon was quickly anointed by Zadok and crowned, it would then be a question of Abiathar's right to anoint the next king as opposed to Zadok's. Abiathar had credentials, and Zadok had none. And with Joab went the whole army of Israel, leaving Solomon with only Benaiah and the king's house guards.

As she hurried out into the courtyard, she thought quickly of what she must do. Her only hope was to get word to her father of the danger she was in. Nefer would be leaving Jerusalem early the next morning. At all costs she must manage to see him before he left.

* * *

In the scribe's small quarters Shulamit found only a young boy and a very old man. The old man seemed to be teaching the boy to write his letters on the freshly strewn sand of the floor. "Do you know the inn in Bethphage, beyond the crest of Olivet?" she asked the boy.

"Yes, my lady," he said, noticing her fine clothes and golden circlet.

"Could you take a message for me to the young camel driver from Shunem named Nefer Ben-Bessim?"

"Of course, my lady," he said, jumping up and dusting off his short tunic.

She had him repeat after her the message: "I'll be in the king's garden, the lower Garden of Nuts, early tomorrow morning when the caravan passes. I'll have a message for my father."

When he left, Shulamit turned back toward the court of the queens. Suddenly she heard a great clatter of hooves and men shouting orders in quick, gruff tones. The passage in front of the doorway quickly filled with

248

men, and Shulamit was pushed back into the shadows. "What's the cause of all this commotion?" she asked one of the guards.

"It's the young prince. The king has given him his own mule to ride, and Zadok has a cruse of oil. They're going to crown him at the Gihon."

Shulamit stood on tiptoe so she could see. There, sitting on the king's own white mule and dressed in regal splendor, was Solomon. He was no longer the lighthearted, sometimes frivolous prince, but instead a young man who in all seriousness had pitted himself against his crafty brother in a bid for the throne. He wasn't smiling; he greeted no one but sat apart and silent, jaw set, eyes steady and bold, waiting for the signal to move.

A wave of excitement passed over the waiting attendants as they raised the standards of the house of David. There was the trumpets' crisp, staccato intonation, the drums' vibrant roll and finally, the familiar cry of allegiance to David and his house.

With tears blinding her eyes, Shulamit stood and watched until the procession moved from the courtyard. The moment of high ecstasy turned to fear as she realized that this was no easy thing he had undertaken. Adonijah was already crowned by the recognized leaders of Israel. Solomon had only Nathan's prophecy, his father's promise, and his mother's hope—along with the house guards and the Mighty Men, who were still loyal to David.

Now he was committed to a course that would give him either the throne or the executioner's knife. With this commitment he had become a man—a man who would take a chance at the right time and wouldn't fear the consequences.

She had never loved him so much, yet had never felt more alienated from him. She wished she could have explained to him that she had been tricked by Adonijah into going to his house. She wished they could have straightened out all the misunderstandings. No matter what happened, until the problem of Adonijah was finally settled once and for all, it was no longer safe for her to stay in Jerusalem.

25

*S*ince early morning most of the people of Jerusalem had known that Adonijah had taken things into his own hands. Nervous and unsettled, they speculated on the meaning of this strange turn of events.

As the day progressed, they became even more bewildered. About noon they heard shouting and singing, then a stirring burst of trumpets on the eastern wall. News spread quickly that Solomon had also been crowned—but at the king's request.

Jonathan, the son of Abiathar, the high priest, brought the news to Adonijah as he was still feasting and celebrating with his men in the large, colorful tents erected beside the Serpent Stone at En-rogel.

Immediately Adonijah sent Joab out to investigate. In minutes he returned. "Listen," he shouted as he held up his hand, signaling them to be quiet. "The whole city is in an uproar."

In a panic the feasters rushed out of the tents and found that it was as he had said: people were singing and shouting, beating drums and clashing cymbals, laughing and ululating, as they poured out into the streets and hurried toward the Water Gate to be a part of the celebration.

It was obvious that Adonijah had been outwitted. Stealthily his men melted away, leaving the wine goblets overturned, the roast lamb only partially eaten, and the woven mats and linen cushions lay in great disarray. "He'll kill me!" Adonijah exclaimed, turning to Abiathar with terror-stricken eyes.

"You must come with me to the tabernacle; I'll give you sanctuary there. Not even the king would be so bold as to take a man from before the presence of his God."

Adonijah mounted his mule and fled after Abiathar, riding up the Hinnon Valley to avoid passing the Gihon Spring, where Solomon's men were still celebrating.

Some of David's men who were standing on the wall saw him fleeing. They jumped on their donkeys and followed him up the northern ridge road to Gibeon.

David's men were fearless. They brushed aside the doorkeepers of the tabernacle and charged into the central court, where they found Adonijah clinging in terror to the horns of the altar. "I won't leave," he said, "until my brother, the king, promises that he'll not kill me."

A messenger was sent to Solomon while the king's men stood with drawn swords surrounding Adonijah. When the messenger returned, he pushed through the curious bystanders and delivered the message to Adonijah personally. "Your brother, the king, has spoken. If Adonijah proves to be a worthy man," he said, "not one of his hairs shall fall to the ground, but if wickedness is found in him, he shall die."

Without another word the men put up their swords, pried Adonijah's rigid fingers from the altar's brass horns, and set him on his mule.

It was early evening as he rode through the great North Gate and into the courtyard, which was aglow with the flickering light of one hundred torches. He dismounted and walked with the dignity of a prince, though his eyes were cold and distrustful. His robes, so carefully designed for his own coronation, were now dusty and torn.

"Kneel!" The order was sharp and forceful. Adonijah looked first at the old warrior who had spoken and then around the room. Finally he looked back at his brother, who sat straight and unflinching on David's throne as though he had always been king. His robes weren't as fine as the ones Adonijah wore. He had been taken by surprise in the clothes he was wearing that morning, and the great purple robe with its fur trim looked incongruous over his everyday garb. However, the crown was sparkling and glorious in the torchlight, and it sat on his head as though it belonged there.

As Solomon looked down at Adonijah, he could almost see the plotting that was already going on behind the sullen stance. "He's thinking that the game isn't over yet. However," he thought, "it's almost impossible for him to regain his following. I have nothing to fear from him now."

"Kneel!" The order was given again, and this time the men who had brought him moved in closer, their leader resting his hand on the hilt of his short sword in a threatening way. Adonijah knelt quickly, and his face no longer registered the rebellion that had been evident when he entered.

"Go to your house," Solomon ordered. He could see that Adonijah was relieved as he got to his feet and hurried out of the room.

Solomon breathed a sigh of relief. It was a wretched business, and he didn't want this night of his coronation spoiled by having to deal with Adonijah.

The night was one such as Jerusalem would never see again. Pipers played the old songs, young maidens and children sang as they waved palm branches, women clustered in windows, shaking tambourines, and in the streets and alleyways the old men danced the hora with unbounded joy.

The king's room was filled with old warriors, garbed prophets, and curious tribesmen. David had given his son his advice and blessing and then had returned to his bed.

In a touching scene David asked that the curtains to his room be pulled back so he could see the throne as Solomon received tribute from the various tribes. "Blessed be the God of Israel, who has chosen my son to sit on my throne before I die." David had raised himself up in the bed to bow in homage to his son.

* * *

Tikva brought Shulamit the news of what was happening, describing for her the confrontation with Adonijah and Solomon's generous treatment of his brother.

* * *

"So he's to go home?" Shulamit asked.

"Yes, and I'm sure that means that he'll no longer ride up the Kidron Valley with fifty men running before him with banners. Foolish one," she said, picking up the oil lamp to leave.

"Tell the maidens that we'll be going down to the Garden of Nuts tomorrow. The young, green almonds will be just right for eating," Shulamit said, without her usual enthusiasm.

Tikva nodded and went out, leaving Shulamit sitting despondently among the cushions of her bed. "I hope that the boy found Nefer and gave him my message," she thought. "As long as Adonijah is free, I'm not safe—and neither is Solomon.

She could hear, faint and faraway, the voices laughing and singing, rejoicing over Solomon's victory. She wished that she could be there to join in the celebration, but ever since Adonijah had tricked her into visiting his house, Solomon had been cool and indifferent. "Nefer is my only hope," she again concluded.

She stood up and opened the shutters of her room, so she could look out into the deserted courtyard. The moon was full. The leaves of the fig tree rustled in the cool breeze, and she was desperately lonesome.

The Garden of Nuts, in the lower portion of the Kidron Valley where the stream bubbled over rocks and around grassy knolls, made a pleasant escape for the king's family.

At this time of year the almond tree had lost its white blooms and was covered with small, bright-green nubs that were tart and crunchy. Once in the garden with their cushions spread out under the trees, the maidens took out their spindles and embroidery strips, their hand harps and sistrums, and soon the grove was filled with song and laughter.

A short distance from the garden ran the road along which the caravans leaving Jerusalem would have to travel. Shulamit seated herself under one of the larger trees and listened for the light jingle of camel bells and the soft, padding sound made by camels' feet.

The caravans always assembled at the Fountain Gate before dawn to take advantage of the crisp morning breeze. Shulamit had just settled herself when she heard the familiar sounds of a caravan approaching. She jumped up and ran to the roadway, peering through the morning mist for the lead camel and its driver. "Is this the caravan going—?" she began.

Before she had time to finish, Nefer jumped down into the middle of the road. "Shulamit!" he exclaimed.

Quickly she drew him aside and explained her plight. She hesitated to bother him with all the details, but she did want him to tell her father of the danger she was in.

"I was with Prince Adonijah until he was taken by the king," Nefer said. "There may be difficult times ahead for everyone. Perhaps you'd better come home with me until the wheat is harvested?"

"You're suggesting I leave *now*?"

"Of course."

"But I can't get permission to leave!"

He tucked his thumbs in his sash as her father often did and looked down at her with commanding intensity. "Then don't ask them—just leave."

"Just leave without telling anyone? I can't."

"Let your maidens tell them when they return home. By that time it will be too late for anyone to come after you."

Shulamit knew that he was right, and yet she hesitated. What would Solomon think of her? She knew he would think she had deserted him.

"Well," said Nefer, "what are you going to do? I have an extra mule you could ride."

"I don't know," she said, running her fingers through her hair in confusion. "I can't decide so fast."

"It's impossible for us to wait. We must take advantage of the early-morning hours. Are you coming?"

She glanced at the maidens and hesitated. By going she would probably lose Solomon forever. He couldn't possibly understand why she would leave just as he was crowned. He would surely view her departure as a desertion just when he needed her most.

She had nothing to remember him by but the pouch of dried flowers from En-gedi that she wore around her neck. I must leave him something, something to remember me by. Impulsively she untied the hempen cord that held her beads. "Here," she said, dropping them in her serving maid's hand. "Give these to Solomon, tell him to keep these as a pledge of my love."

As she mounted the mule and covered her face to leave, the young girl ran quickly to tell the other maidens what had happened. They jumped up and hurried out to the road, where they could just see the caravan disappearing in the morning mist. "Come back! Come back!" they shouted after her.

To Shulamit the words were filled with the poignancy and sadness of all that was now lost to her. How could she endure seeing those enchanted places in Shunem where memory would forever remind her of the happy, unspoiled love they had shared?

"Oh, Shulamit, come back. Let us see you once more." One little maiden had caught up with the caravan and briefly touched Shulamit's hand before she dropped back in tears.

As they mounted to the ridge road, the mists fell back and the sky grew rosy with the rising sun high over Abu Tor. Everything looked strange and somehow misshapen. Shulamit couldn't think clearly; her mind was a tangle of conflicting emotions.

Her love for Solomon and despair at leaving him in the midst of such a terrible misunderstanding was overshadowed only by her paralyzing fright of Adonijah and what he planned to do. What would happen to Solomon, Bathsheba, and even David she didn't know, but she was certain that she could no longer help them. Adonijah, with his jealousy and hurt pride burning at white-hot intensity, was capable of anything. When David died, there would be more trouble. She knew that Adonijah hadn't given up yet.

26

I'm sure the queen would appreciate hearing this from your own lips," Jessica said as she led the little maiden with the beads up the dark stairs. Bathsheba was sitting with her women out on the roof of her house.

* * *

When Jessica whispered a few words of explanation, the queen stopped the whirling of her spindle and looked intently at the girl. "Shulamit has gone home?" Bathsheba questioned.

"Yes, my queen." The girl bowed to the floor and lifted the hem of the queen's robe to her lips.

"How is this possible?"

"One of her brothers was passing by the Garden of Nuts with his caravan, and—"

"You mean she just left? She didn't ask permission? She didn't take any of her things?" The queen's voice had risen to a pitch the serving girls had seldom heard before.

"Yes, my queen, she took nothing." The girl was so frightened that her voice could scarcely be heard.

"She left no message?"

"Only these." The girl pulled the beads from the folds of her sash and held them out to Bathsheba.

"What's this?" Bathsheba held the beads between two fingers, studying them carefully.

"They're her beads. She asked me to give them to the young king."

"To Solomon?" With an impatient snap Bathsheba tucked them into one of the deep pockets in her sleeve. "So she's still thinking of him. His little shepherdess, as he called her. Well, it's better that she goes back to her sheep. Solomon will forget her soon enough if she's not around." For a moment she sat contemplating the whole situation and then she shrugged. "Don't worry about the beads," she told the girl. "I'll see to them."

Bathsheba whispered to a servant who sat behind her. The girl fetched a length of material and handed it to the kneeling maiden. "The queen is pleased that you brought her the beads," she said. "This is a small reminder that you're to forget them now. See that you don't mention this to anyone."

By midmorning word had spread in the court of the queens, and then out into the palace, that Shulamit was gone. When it was found out that she hadn't gotten permission from the king—hadn't even bothered to go back to the palace for her clothes—many were shocked. "She's always been impulsive," they said. "She never really obeyed the rules."

Finally a group of indignant men, encouraged by Adonijah, went to David himself. "My lord," they said, "the Shunemmite maid has gone. What would you have us do?"

David questioned them closely. When he found that she had left with one of her brothers in a passing caravan, he surprised them all by laughing. "So the little nightingale is out of the cage. She loved the trees and fields too much to be happy inside these dark walls."

"But my lord," his counselors complained, "you can't let her just go like this. She must be brought back and punished."

"Punished?"

"Yes, or the other wives—"

"What do the other wives have to do with this?"

"My father—" Adonijah started to speak for the men, who were now impatient and almost angry, and then he grew silent, remembering that he wasn't in good standing with his father.

"Oh, I see. It isn't *my* wives who concern you. You're afraid it will encourage your own wives to some rebellion."

"Yes, my lord. If one can flaunt tradition—"

David was silent for a moment. He pushed his crown back on his head and seemed to be studying the crude diagram he had drawn of the temple. In one hand he held a piece of charcoal, and from time to time he touched up a corner or straightened a wall. Finally, still drawing carefully, he answered them. "No, I won't punish the little Shulamit. She has brought something of the fields and the sky back into my life, and if she can no longer live here, I understand." The words were said with such finality that Adonijah and the counselors melted away, and none of them dared mention it to him again.

* * *

Though Adonijah had told David the news of Shulamit's leaving, Solomon had ridden down to Hebron on business and heard nothing. "Leave it to me, I'll tell my brother, the king." Adonijah quietly told the distraught counselors. "I assure you he'll not take it as calmly as my father."

Just after sunset, before the city gates were closed, it was reported that Solomon was approaching from the south. Adonijah hurried down to the throne room ready to accost him.

At the sound of trumpets and marching feet, the standard bearers formed in two lines on either side of the door and stood at rigid attention. There was obviously none of the laxity that had characterized David's regime. These men had been given a sense of pride and a vision of majesty that were already changing their demeanor.

Again the trumpets blew, the standards were raised, and Solomon appeared in the doorway. His dark head was held high; his eyes were bold and fearless. His legs, laced with badger-skin thongs, were like brass pillars under the short tunic, and his strong hands held a finely tooled riding prod.

"My lord," Adonijah said as he hurried to bow before his brother, "our father is disturbed. It's best that I speak with you alone before you see him."

"You may speak." Solomon's voice had a strong timbre to it that made Adonijah hesitate to raise his head.

"It would be best if I saw you alone, my lord. It's a family matter." It was obvious that Adonijah was trying to make his voice sound meek and subservient, but there was a slight note of elation in it that he couldn't hide.

There was a pause. Solomon was reluctant to grant his request. "A family matter, you say?"

"Yes, my lord, a family matter."

"Come then," Solomon said. Without bothering to help Adonijah to his feet, he moved into the lighted area near the throne.

"I was the only one she told." Adonijah stood slightly behind Solomon's right elbow and spoke softly.

"I don't understand." Solomon was immediately wary and cautious.

"She hadn't planned it until she heard that you had been crowned king."

"Who are you talking about? What plans?" Solomon sounded calm and in control, but his hand tightened on the lapel of his short cloak.

"Why, the maid from Shunem, Shulamit; she's gone back home to Bessim and her brothers."

"You lie!" Solomon turned so fast and raised his arm in such a threatening way that Adonijah fell back and had to take a moment to regain his composure.

"This is no lie."

"But there's no reason—"

"Only that she couldn't endure the thought that, should our father die, she would belong to you instead of me."

Solomon's eyes darkened. "It's just a rumor." Solomon's voice had become harsh and tormented.

Adonijah smiled a long, slow, gloating smile. "Go see our father. He'll tell you that she's gone."

With long, quick strides Solomon walked to the steps and flung back the curtain to his father's room. With only the briefest of formalities he plunged right in. "I've just heard that Shulamit has left?"

"Yes, my son, it seems that she has left."

"How could she? Where did she go? Why did she leave?"

"It seems to have been some impulsive decision," David said without looking up. "She's like a wild nightingale. They don't sing very long in captivity."

Bolting from his father's room, Solomon walked behind the throne and down the hallway to his rooms, recently vacated by Adonijah. He hated these rooms. They had the same oppressive fragrance that always clung to Adonijah's clothes, and there was a coldness about them that wouldn't be dispelled by fires or incense. Now they were crowded with scribes and tribal leaders, just as his father's rooms had been; unlike his father, he found their presence annoying. Now, in his frustration and hurt, even his brother Nathan couldn't reason with him. It was as though his ears were closed and his heart turned to stone.

Over and over he pondered the strange turn of events, and always he came to the same conclusion: "If Adonijah isn't right, why did she go just as I was crowned king?"

Impulsively he decided to go visit his mother. There was just the slightest chance that she might know something.

He dressed simply and went to see her as her son and not as the king. He sat down beside her and listened absentmindedly as she told him of the progress she had made in carding wool for a new hanging and of the fine dye she had bought from some merchants. Finally, when he could wait no longer, he broached the subject he was burning to discuss. "Then there's no word in the court of the queens about the strange disappearance of the maid from Shunem?"

"Oh yes," Bathsheba said rather coyly, as though just remembering. "A little maid did come and report that Shulamit had left with a brother."

"There was no message, then?"

"She was always impulsive."

"It's unnatural that she should leave without saying goodbye."

"Perhaps she was in a hurry."

Solomon didn't answer but rose and strode toward the door.

"Solomon!" Bathsheba's voice had a sharpness that had always made her sons and serving maids listen. "I've sent a messenger to Shunem."

Solomon turned and looked at her with a trace of alarm. "A messenger to Shunem?"

"Yes. I've told that father of hers, and her brothers, that we're taking back the vineyard since they'll have the maiden at home."

Solomon was too confused and stunned by all that had happened to respond. The vineyard meant nothing to him compared to Shulamit. He didn't even want to discuss it. With one tormented look he turned and fled.

Bathsheba had expected *some* reaction but not this silence or this look of aching pain. A terrible fear began to gnaw within her that her love for him was to bring him only unhappiness.

* * *

Later that night Bathsheba asked Jessica to bring her the box of jewelry that had her choicest pieces in it. It was a teakwood box with an ivory carving of two lions on its cover. She opened it and dangled the beads over it for a brief moment. "This is the right place for these beads. They're the sort of thing I would expect a country girl to wear. Nothing expensive or special about them—but nevertheless Solomon is just sentimental enough to treasure them, read some hidden message in them, and risk everything for that girl." With one swift movement she dropped them in the box and slammed the lid down. Without looking at Jessica, she handed her the box to place back in the wall niche where it would be safe.

* * *

Shulamit hadn't expected a royal welcome at home, but she was totally unprepared for the almost hostile suspicion with which her brothers greeted her. They were all present when she entered her father's room in the tower. Their faces dark and inscrutable, they stood clumped together as though there were some threat leveled at them just by her presence. In contrast to their faces was the tear-stained, welcoming face of her father, who was lying propped up by large straw-filled pillows in a bed piled high with fox-skin throws.

As he reached out to her, she could see that his arms had become sinewy and his hands clawlike. "My Abishag, my little Abishag." As he clung to her and wept, she marveled that he used the old nickname as an endearment.

He held her at arms' length and squinted. Shulamit was shocked to realize that even his eyesight was fading.

"I called you Abishag," he said, and laughed a dry, rasping laugh that left him coughing and gasping for breath. "'Her father's shame,' that's what they said." His hand loosed its hold, and with one bony finger he reached up and touched the golden circlet that she still wore as a sign that she was a member of the royal family. "I never thought to see my daughter rise so high."

He beamed a toothless grin, and Shulamit found herself struggling to recognize in the ravaged face some hint of the robust man she had left the year before. She could see that it was as her brother had said; he wasn't expected to live long.

"My father!" Shulamit turned and saw that her brother Baalak had stepped out from the others. Though he addressed her father, he hadn't taken his eyes off her. "This daughter that you're so proud of has no doubt come home to heap disgrace upon your name."

"Disgrace?" Bessim was puzzled.

"My father, it's rumored that she was rejected by the king and that both the princes have had their way with her. No doubt she's come home to birth a bastard child away from the court."

The old man's hands dropped, and his eyes grew wild and bewildered. His voice took on a plaintive whine, "I used to say that we would enclose her with boards of cedar, but in Jerusalem I had no control."

"And when you saw that I had no breasts, you used to say that you would build upon my flat wall towers of silver." Shulamit was annoyed but not angry. She ran her hands over her full, rounded breasts and said, "You were right; I *was* a wall. But now my breasts are like towers, and though I wasn't enclosed with cedar boards, I haven't come home in disgrace."

"But a messenger has come from the queen demanding that we give back the vineyard, and we thought—" Baalak said.

"I *wasn't* rejected by the king, and the princes *haven't* had their way with me. I'm still a walled garden, a fountain sealed, just as I was when I went to Jerusalem."

"But the vineyard?"

"Undoubtedly since I've come home she wants the property back." Shulamit stood up and looked at all of them unflinchingly, though they muttered among themselves and their frowns deepened.

"We don't need or want the king's vineyard," Bessim said. "What's a vineyard compared to having my daughter back?" Bessim's face was transformed with joy as he looked again at Shulamit. He patted the mat next to him inviting her to sit down.

"But the vineyard produces rare grapes even in drought," Nefer said.

"And while she says she's still closed up like a private garden and no one has defiled her, we'll never get so much for her again," Urim complained.

"Why, if we can stand to part with her, we'll ask *twice* as much, since she's been chosen by the queen and lived in the palace." It was a long sentence, and Bessim broke out in a coughing fit that left him gasping for breath and leaning heavily on Shulamit. She supported his head and held the clay pot for him to spit into.

Shulamit's mother had been waiting outside the curtains. Now she entered, brandishing a fly whisk made of long, tasseled reeds. She scolded the brothers for upsetting their father and spoiling his enjoyment of his daughter, then drove them from the room.

* * *

Later that night, when Shulamit sat with her mother picking stones from the lentils they would cook for soup the next day, she said, "My father called me Abishag today, and for the first time it was as if we shared some lovely joke together."

"It was no joke when you were young to hear Siva's sons torment my only child. Bessim never saw it then. He loved me, and he thought it of no consequence that she had borne him seven sons and I none—or that the whole village made fun of me."

"And you were jealous of her and of the other women who had sons?"

"Of course. I couldn't even pray or light the Sabbath candles. God had failed me. I almost hated God." She said the last words in a whisper, and her head was averted so that Shulamit couldn't see the trembling of her lips.

"And then—?"

"And then one day I simply put it in God's hands and trusted Him. It took weeks and months before the bitterness was gone." There was silence then, except for the crackling of thorns burning in a clay firepot. "You have no baggage?" her mother said, finally getting up and brushing back her long hair from her face.

"There was no time. I had intended just to send a message, but Nefer convinced me that I should leave."

"There was some trouble, then?" Her mother squatted beside the fire so she could add a few more nettles to keep it burning.

"There's been nothing but trouble, and there will be more. When David dies, Adonijah is sure to try again for the throne. I realized how helpless I was; he could have forced me to go with him."

"It's good that you've come. I don't think Bessim has long to live. He kept calling for you and wanting to see you."

"Why didn't you send for me?"

"You're a queen, and I was told that it's impossible for one of the queens or concubines to leave the palace without the king's permission and a special arrangement."

"That's true."

"How, then, did you come?"

"I was down in the Garden of Nuts with my maidens when Nefer passed with his caravan, and he persuaded me to leave and come home with him."

Her mother poured water from a large earthen jar into a clay bowl and set it to warm over the hot fire. "You just left, without permission?"

Shulamit could tell that her mother was alarmed. She tried to calm her but succeeded only in disturbing her more. Finally she told her everything and ended by saying, "Adonijah is terribly jealous of Solomon and secretly hates Bathsheba, so if he gains power he would use any excuse to have them executed. I'm so afraid for them."

Her mother stood up slowly and brushed her hair back from her face.

"Jealousy is a terrible thing. One hardly knows what touches off the fire, but that it burns like Sheol is very evident."

"You sound as though—" Shulamit was surprised at the vehemence with which her mother spoke.

"Of course I've battled it—as a young girl wanting Bessim to myself, wanting to possess this man whom 1 loved so much. It was terrible. There were times I wanted to die, and there were times I wanted Siva and her seven sons to die. Are you surprised?"

"No, Mother, I understand. But does loving mean one is always to be tormented with this jealousy?"

"Jealousy has very little to do with love. It more often deals in the desire for possession. I wanted to possess this man I loved, while Adonijah wants to possess a position or a place that belongs to someone else—a form of coveting that's mentioned in the commandments of Moses."

"I don't understand."

"There's no time to talk now. You must eat your barley gruel and go to bed."

Shulamit was too tired to sort through all the intricacies of her situation. She accepted the gruel and relaxed in the joy of being home and free of court intrigues. She knew it wouldn't last, but for this one night she wanted more than anything to be a child again in the familiar surroundings of her home.

27

*A*t the Feast of the New Moon in the months of Iyyar, Sivan, Tammuz, and Ab, Adonijah put in a dutiful appearance at the king's table, and everyone concluded that he had finally accepted Solomon's kingship.

Secretly, however, Adonijah was holding meetings with his friends and making new plans to overthrow Solomon. "While my father is still alive, we'll quietly build support for our cause," Adonijah had told his followers. "Then, when he dies, I'll take the throne."

Adonijah had grown cautious. While in the past he had enlisted runners with banners, now he rode quite simply on a mule, with only a few men in attendance. In this way he was able to leave the city without being noticed, and by the end of Elul, five months after Solomon was anointed, he had visited most of the tribes. Shunem he had saved to visit last.

He felt an increasing urgency to move quickly, as his father was having more "bad" days. On the Day of Atonement, in the month of Tishri, David had insisted on fasting as usual but then had been too weak to ride over to the tabernacle at Gibeon for the great sacrifice. His eyes had grown misty at the sound of the shofar, and when he stood in his bare feet on the cold stones of the floor he had become faint and his sons had helped him back to bed. Seeing this, Adonijah realized that there wasn't much time.

❋ ❋ ❋

Adonijah arrived in Shunem in the early afternoon. Bessim's sons all rode out to welcome him, accompanied by trumpeters, tambourine players, and men who danced the old tribal sword dance.

There was no doubt in their minds that Adonijah would win back the throne after his father's death.

Adonijah was smooth and polished. He looked like a prince and he made promises like a prince, and that was exactly what they wanted.

Shulamit was appalled when her brothers came carrying boxes of rich treasure and piled them in her room. Admiration shone on their faces as Urim announced, "The king won't live much longer. When he dies, Solomon will be overthrown and Adonijah will be king."

". . . and you believe him?"

"He wants you for his queen." Urim was obviously impressed.

"What did you tell him?" Shulamit demanded.

"We agreed, of course," they chorused.

"He can't buy my love." She was so angry that she hardly felt the pain of Nefer's tightening grip as he grasped her arm and swung her around to face him.

"No one's talking about love." Nefer's eyes flashed dangerously, but Shulamit took no notice.

"Look in the chests," Baalak said. "I'll wager that you won't refuse then. And there are groves and fields and high positions for all of us. We'll not let you spoil everything again." He let the jewels drip through his fingers enticingly.

With a quick, swooping movement Shulamit's mother placed herself between the angry brothers and her daughter. "Come, come," she said. "Some things can neither be bought nor sold. They can only be given."

Baalak and Nefer glared at her and clenched their fists in frustration. "No woman can decide to marry or not to marry. It's her father and brothers who must choose."

"Then let her father make the choice—but take the jewels back to the prince. He can't buy her love."

With dark looks and muttered remarks the brothers carried the boxes from the room. They could be heard for the rest of the day shouting to each other in their anger and frustration.

* * *

It was during Sukkot, the Feast of the Ingathering, while Adonijah was still in Shunem, that David died. A messenger dressed in black, carrying a black standard with a crudely shaped lion sketched in gray threads, brought the news. "All the roads to Jerusalem are packed," he reported. "Brave men are openly weeping. The king's captains, Mighty Men, and counselors, all dressed in sackcloth, have crowded into the throne room, where ashes to sprinkle on their heads are being passed in great bowls."

"We must leave immediately," Adonijah told the brothers.

"Of course."

"Your sister must come with us." His expression was hard and unflinching, and the brothers were afraid.

Nefer brought the news to Shulamit and her mother. "You must be ready to ride within the hour," he said, and no amount of questioning would induce him to tell where they were going or why. He stood on the landing holding a torch, and they could see his nostrils flaring with excitement and his eyes glowing with anticipation. "Take nothing but a few dried figs or dates. We'll be riding hard without stopping."

Shulamit was instantly suspicious. "What—"

"We'll go wake Bessim," her mother said. "If there's some trick or mischief afoot, Bessim will protect us, even in his weakened condition."

*　*　*

"Wake up, Abba," Shulamit whispered a few minutes later as she bent over Bessim, the light of her lamp making his unshaven face look bloated.

He started, then turned over, and finally raised himself on one elbow. "What's this?" he demanded, blinking in the harsh light.

"Abba, my brothers are insisting that I ride with them. They are going with the prince, but they won't tell where or why. Is this some plan of yours?"

"To ride at this hour of the night? How ridiculous. Send for them. We'll soon find out what they're up to." He was more like himself, strong and forceful. He hadn't given his blessing, nor had he divided up his wealth, so his sons were still careful to seek his advice and obey his slightest command.

*　*　*

They came crowding into his bedchamber—big, strong men with a cat-like walk and faces like stone.

"Where's the prince?" Bessim asked. "Before he goes off like this with my sons I must have words with him."

Adonijah came forward to stand at the foot of Bessim's bed. "What's all this disturbance?" Bessim demanded. "Where's everyone going? And why should my daughter go with you?"

Shulamit noticed that Adonijah seemed to have been caught off guard, but he quickly recovered and stared at the old man without blinking. "My father, the king, is dead. I'm the rightful heir, and I intend to hurry back to Jerusalem and put things right."

Shulamit hadn't known that David had died. It was as though her worst fears were coming true right here in this small room. She felt overwhelmed by grief, and at the same time gripped by an almost irrational fear. She had hoped to escape by coming home, but it was evident that no place was safe.

"And my sons?" Bessim continued to ask questions quite calmly.

"They have offered to come with me. I'll reward them well."

"And my daughter?"

"I intend to make her my queen."

Bessim craned his neck and shaded his eyes so he could get a better look at Adonijah. "And if your plans misfire, what will happen to my daughter and these foolish, overgrown boys of mine?"

Adonijah stiffened and tossed his head in a proud gesture of defiance. Bessim's words had deeply offended him. "There'll be no mistake. My plans are carefully formed."

Bessim looked around at all of them and then back at Shulamit. "Take my sons; they'll not be happy here. But Shulamit is staying."

"But Father . . ." Nefer complained.

"When it's all over and Adonijah is crowned, that's time enough to send for my daughter."

"It's important that she be there to receive the crown with me." Adonijah was almost in a frenzy over the old man's stubbornness.

"When you have your crown, then we'll see. We've had enough of Jerusalem for a while." Bessim's eyes protruded and his lips formed a stubborn pout that the sons knew meant he wouldn't change his mind.

Shulamit could see that her father had won. Quietly, without another word, the brothers slipped one by one from the room. Only Nefer stayed for his father's blessing.

Adonijah, the last to go, came around the bed and took Shulamit's hand before she could hide it in her sleeve. He tried to look in her eyes, but she averted her head. "Forget Solomon. Forget you ever knew him. He has always stolen what was rightfully mine: my father's love, your love, and now the throne. I swear before God, he'll not live an hour after I'm king." With that he turned on his heel and walked with a quick, light step to the door.

In her mother's rooms Shulamit poured out her frustration and fear.

"Adonijah will do anything to ruin Solomon. He's so well organized, while Solomon is unaware that he's even plotting."

"But there's Nathan's prophecy; Solomon, not Adonijah, is to build the temple."

Shulamit was impatient in her anxiety. "What's a prophecy against someone like Adonijah?" she said.

Her mother pulled her cloak more tightly around her shoulders. The rooms were open to the sky, and now in the early fall it was warm only when the sun shone directly on them. "Come," her mother said. "Let's go to the roof where we can see them leave."

They climbed the uneven stone steps and stood at the parapet near the grape arbor, its brown, leafy vines no longer bent low with the dark-purple grapes. They could hear the trumpets and see the brothers mounting their mules. The prince was already sitting on his white mule, his short sword flashing in the sunlight.

The command was given, and all of them rode out the gate. "They're like poisoned arrows aimed right at Solomon's heart," Shulamit said.

"Now, now," her mother chided. "We've already seen one miracle today. Adonijah wasn't able to take you with him, and I believe we'll soon hear of his defeat." Without looking to see if Shulamit was following, Ramat hurried down the steps and could be heard humming cheerfully as she went about making some cheese out of the clabbered milk.

Shulamit was amazed that her mother could be so confident. It would take more than a miracle to protect Solomon from Adonijah's ambitious plotting. He had every intention of killing his brother. For a brief moment she was flooded with memories of Solomon: his slow, confident smile, his arms holding her tight while his eyes explored her face with evident delight.

She remembered all the times she had told her maidens that love must not be wakened before its time. Perhaps they had been right after all. Love was such a fragile thing. Perhaps it had to be taken when it was offered, the cup drained before it was snatched away and never returned.

She turned and listlessly walked down the stairs to join her mother in the tedious job of grinding wheat for the next day's bread.

* * *

David's death had come as a great shock to the people of Israel. When news of his death was first whispered in the streets and lanes, the Sukkot celebration came to an abrupt stop. Food was left uneaten on the low tables, lights flickered and went out in the deserted booths, children dressed in festive clothes lingered, bored, in open doorways, and someone's goat straggled down the street unattended.

People huddled around the palace gate waiting for news. They watched for some sign of life or motion from the narrow windows of David's rooms. The shutters hung open, and from time to time a light glinted on the frames and then was quickly gone. When deep groans and wild, frenzied weeping rose and fell on the night air the crowds winced, imagining David's wives and concubines venting their grief.

At sunrise there was a sudden stir and commotion in the courtyard of the palace. The terrible, shrieking notes of the shofar were blown from the wall, while drums beat their steady dirge.

Solomon led the way, followed by the other princes, as they came through the great carved door of the palace. Behind them came the captains of David's Mighty Men, who carried the elaborately wrapped body of the dead king. High above the crowd the trumpeters appeared and for the last time blew the familiar fanfare that was always played when the king approached.

Like a great dam bursting, the people began to weep and lament as they followed the procession down to the king's tomb in the center of the city. "I want to be at rest in the midst of my people," David had said when he built the tomb.

"He will be protected here from looters," the people said as they placed the shrouded form on the cold stone couch and piled their most precious treasures around it.

* * *

Solomon, as king, managed every aspect of his father's funeral with respect and composure, winning the admiration of the people.

At the end of the long day he led his mother back to David's room. She wept but didn't grieve openly as some of the other wives and concubines did. It was reported that they were shrieking, pulling their hair, throwing themselves on the floor, and keeping the servants busy bringing them soothing teas and medicinal potions.

Haggith, claiming the center of attention, clung to the posts of David's empty bed and refused to leave. "I was his queen. No one can take him from me now," she cried. "Take the whore and her bastard son away. They have no place here now. It's *my* son who is the rightful king," she ranted as Solomon and Bathsheba entered the room.

She finally had to be removed forcefully. Some of the concubines led her back to the court of the queens, where she sat in the courtyard pronouncing curses upon Bathsheba.

Solomon watched his mother for any sign of embarrassment, but he saw none—only grief too deep for tears. She had a word for each of the mourners who came to kiss her hand or lift the hem of her robe to their lips. Some of her bitterest critics, who had fought to have her punished or banished from the court, came to express their sympathy. On this day of her greatest sorrow, Bathsheba loved them all and they loved her.

* * *

Late that night Solomon and his brother Nathan escaped for a few moments from the press of people and walked out to the small garden where the king's wild animals were caged. The moon was full and bright. The mysterious, tawny beasts could be seen quite clearly through the bars.

Solomon picked a branch from the leafy grapevine and broke it into small pieces as he spoke. "I have many enemies, and soon it may come to either their death or my own. I've been thinking a great deal about death; it must be stronger than anything."

"Why would you say that?" Nathan challenged.

"Death can bring to nothing the strongest man, the mightiest king. Even a pharaoh isn't spared, nor are wild beasts or beautiful women."

"But death seems to attack only when his enemy is weak and helpless."

"Not always. Death could enter that cage and do battle with the lion, and the lion would lose. No, Nathan, death is the strongest thing in the world. It isn't water or rocks as I first thought, but death, that's the strongest of all."

"It's hard to argue with you. You have such impressive facts. Your conclusion seems wrong to me, though. Some things—plants and vines—seem to die and then come to life again in the spring."

Solomon shook his head. "No matter how many springs there are for this vine, eventually death will triumph. Some year it will fail to bud and blossom."

"As usual, you're too convincing for me." Nathan broke off a stick and threw it into the cage just to see the lion spring to the front of the cage, eyes glinting, neck ruff standing on end, and tail moving in measured beats. From his throat came the ominous rumble and then the roar that always struck terror to their hearts.

"From now on," Solomon said, "I'm no longer an irresponsible young man. I'm *king*. The Lion of Judah must sometimes roar and, if attacked, must even kill." Solomon's face was chiseled by the moonlight into sharp angles of determination. His eyes were steady and his shoulders thrown back. There seemed to be no fear in him—no fear at all.

* * *

The first test of Solomon's strength came as a result of Adonijah's cunning. The prince, now back in Jerusalem, was afraid that Solomon would call for Shulamit and make her his queen before his own revolt brought him to the throne. For this reason, he devised a scheme that would immediately secure her for himself.

"Bathsheba doesn't like Shulamit," he reasoned. "She'll be glad to help me even though I oppose her son."

He took only one of his trusted servants and rode across the valley to see Bathsheba. He was right; she was delighted to help. He could see the slow, calculated working of her mind as she planned with him just how she could best present his case to Solomon. "You must go soon," he told her, "or Solomon will ride to Shunem and claim her for himself."

* * *

Seeing with amusement the quick, frightened look she darted in his direction, Adonijah was satisfied that she wouldn't wait past the next morning to do his bidding.

When Solomon heard that his mother had come to the throne room, he went down the three steps and bowed low to show his respect, then led her to the honored seat beside him.

"I hope you won't refuse my first request," she said almost shyly.

"You know that I'll always give you what you desire." He smiled warmly at her.

She leaned close to him so that those standing around couldn't hear.

"Your brother Adonijah is feeling cheated, and it would be well to have him as a friend rather than an enemy." Her look was wary, as at the mention of Adonijah Solomon had stiffened and his eyes had grown cold.

He waited wordlessly, so she continued. "He asks only that you give him Shulamit as his wife."

Solomon jumped to his feet, toppling his throne backwards and breaking one of the ivory panels. "Have you inherited nothing of the wisdom of your grandfather?" he exclaimed, crushing a parchment that he had been reading. "He may as well ask for the throne as ask for one of David's wives. He's the older brother and has Abiathar, Joab, and an untold number of tribesmen waiting with knives pointed at my throat. Well, he's grown too bold in his plotting!"

Solomon was no longer aware of his mother or the milling officers and tribesmen. He shouted for the commander of the house guards. "Benaiah—send me Benaiah," he thundered in a voice so powerful that bystanders scarcely recognized it as coming from their king.

Benaiah, who had been at the palace gate, now hurried through the way that opened before him in the crowd and knelt before the king.

Solomon's head was thrown back, his eyes closed. The sound of something ripping and tearing broke the deadly silence of the room. Everyone was stunned to see the king had torn his fine robe from top to bottom. Then, with a great cry he shouted, "May God strike me dead if Adonijah doesn't die this very day. I swear it by the living God—the God who has given me the throne of my father, David, and this kingdom he promised me. Come, Benaiah, stand on your feet. Here's my own sword with which you will administer justice."

Benaiah grabbed the sword and left the room. No one moved; no word was spoken. Emotionally exhausted, Solomon stood frozen in a block of anguish. He made no sound, but the air was charged with the enormity of his action. He was no longer one of them. In some mysterious way he had truly become king, with all the weight of power and responsibility mixing and hardening in him before their very eyes.

Ira, one of David's Mighty Men, was the first to drop to his knees. Then quickly, one after another, they all fell to their knees and bowed their heads to the floor. For the first time, of their own free will, they recognized him as their king.

He turned to his mother and, seeing that she was about to faint, took her by the hand and helped her to her feet. Then, without a backward look, he led her from the room.

* * *

Adonijah had gathered a few of his most trusted supporters in his house on the western ridge. They were plotting the next move and waiting to hear how Bathsheba had fared in her audience with the king. They were interrupted by shouting at the gate followed by a great commotion down in the courtyard. They could hear cursing and then the sound of running as someone came up the stairs and banged at the closed door. "In the name of King Solomon, open!" They all recognized the voice as belonging to Benaiah.

Adonijah winked at his men. "Now you'll see how even the mother of your king works to bring about her son's ruin and give me the desire of my heart. How can he refuse his own mother?"

With another wink he lifted the latch and opened the door.

The sight of Benaiah with drawn sword and scowling visage erased the smile from Adonijah's face. No one breathed. The room pulsated with fear.

"For villainous treachery, the king has ordered your execution!" The words rang out in the silence of the room as Adonijah backed from the door and grasped his own short sword.

"But I'm his brother . . ." He got no further, for the sharp blade of Benaiah's sword had entered up to the hilt, and Adonijah fell to the floor in a pool of blood.

"A jealous plotter you always were, and now you've gotten your just reward," Benaiah said as he pulled his sword out and wiped it on Adonijah's fine cloak. Turning, he walked back down the steps while Adonijah's friends fled in all directions.

Out of one of the back rooms came the women, who had heard the uproar. When they saw what had happened, they turned to shield Haggith from the terrible sight, but it was too late. She pushed them aside and walked with wide, startled eyes to where the blood was running out across the floor. She pulled her ornate skirts back and stared in shocked disbelief at the crumpled form of her son.

"Adonijah," she whispered, as she walked to where she could see his face. "Adonijah," she shouted with obvious alarm bending down and shaking his shoulder, turning him so she could see that it was really her son. "Adonijah!" she screamed as she flung herself across his limp form and gathered him in her arms.

She huddled on the floor, holding his head and kissing his cheeks and wild strands of hair. "Come, come," she pleaded over and over again. "You're going to be all right."

When she finally realized that he was dead, her grief knew no bounds. All her life had been spent in grooming this son to wear the crown and put down her most hated rival, Bathsheba. By her own logical deduction, her son should have been crowned and Bathsheba's son refused. Where was Yahweh in all of this? With such careful planning, so many important people on his side, how could things have gone so wrong?"

As they carried Adonijah's body to the caves at Bethlehem for burial, Haggith lay in her bed with her face to the wall, refusing any comfort. "My life is over," she moaned. "Would that it had been I who died instead of my son."

28

*B*athsheba hardly recognized this angry young man, obsessed with traitors, as her charming son. He wasn't satisfied, it seemed, with ridding the court of his own brother Adonijah. Later that same day he ordered Benaiah to go into the sacred precinct of the tabernacle at Gibeon and slay Joab as he clung to the horns of the altar.

"Have no mercy on this man," Solomon had ordered. "He's not only a traitor to me, but in my father's reign he was guilty of slaying many innocent men."

Bathsheba had hurried to his chambers and pleaded with him. "You know," she urged, "that the horns of the altar have always been a safe retreat for anyone—even the worst criminal fleeing for his life. You're taking a great chance on angering the people."

It seemed obvious to Bathsheba that Abiathar had carefully planned this so that Solomon would be discredited either way. If he chose to let Joab go, he would be judged a weak king; if he had Joab killed, they would say he was cruel and lacking in proper respect for the tabernacle.

Not only did Solomon ignore her warning, but he went even further and banished the old high priest Abiathar to Anathoth. On the same day he ordered the priestly vestments put on Zadok and named him the new high priest. Bathsheba was frightened. She hadn't imagined his kingship beginning with such violence, nor had she thought that so suddenly she would lose all influence over him.

Back at home across the valley she locked herself in her rooms and paced the floor, expecting a riot at any moment. Instead, to her surprise, the people seemed to accept Solomon's actions as right and proper. "Justice has been meted out," they said. "Let no guilty person think that he will escape punishment."

"The people are impressed with the strength of their new king," Jessica reported. "That so soon after being crowned he should act so boldly and so fearlessly has astonished everyone."

Bathsheba was reassured—but from this time on, there was a subtle rift between Solomon and his mother. On the one hand, Bathsheba couldn't understand his harsh actions and refusal to listen to her advice. Solomon, on the other hand, resented his mother's interference.

Gradually Bathsheba came to understand some of the forces that had been at work to alienate them. She learned about the well-organized plans Adonijah had formulated to take the throne from Solomon and marry the Shunemmite maiden. She realized how completely she had fallen into Adonijah's trap, and it made her feel guilty. She also felt guilty when she saw Solomon's drawn and tired look and realized that she had deliberately hidden from him the knowledge that in her jewelry box she kept the beads that should have been given to him.

Though she was bitterly against it, she had to admit that, by rights, Shulamit now belonged to Solomon. It was entirely appropriate for Solomon to send for her and take her as his wife. Whatever misunderstandings were left between them could be smoothed over or explained away, and Solomon would be happy again.

She quickly rejected the thought. It would be too difficult, she decided, to explain to Solomon why she had deliberately kept the beads from him. And she was still convinced that the girl exercised some strange power over others. David had thought she was indispensable, Adonijah had wanted her, and it was evident that Solomon had loved her.

At once she decided to get rid of the beads and forget the whole thing. She quickly took down the sandalwood box and pulled out the beads. Should she throw them away? They weren't really valuable, though they were rather unique. She fingered them, then counted them, and finally concluded that it would be best if she had Jessica give them to one of the young maidens who came to the court of the queens.

She called for Jessica and was about to hand her the beads when she hesitated. Then with one decisive movement she dropped the beads back in the box, slammed down the lid, and handed it to Jessica. "Put this back in the wall niche," she said. "I've changed my mind."

She sat for a long time, thinking about her son. In the early summer after the Feasts of Passover and Shavuot, when the rains had stopped and the roads were more passable, Solomon would marry the princess of Rabbath-ammon. That would put an end to this whole problem. He would forget about this young girl from Shunem who had caused so much trouble. It was better that way.

* * *

The rains came in great, cold gusts and blew about the palace, leaving the air sharp and frosty. The throne room was dreary and cold despite the braziers that burned constantly and the singing and storytelling that went on until late into the night.

During the whole winter season Solomon spent very little time relaxing with his friends. He was too busy. Even Nathan, who had been made the king's chief counselor and saw him often on public business, rarely saw him in private.

Other counselors were added gradually until Solomon had new men of his own choosing from every section of the country and every tribe. All of this took time, but those watching him realized that he was working at a feverish pace that hinted at some deep unhappiness.

Worst of all, he made excuses so that he wouldn't have to see his mother. It was obvious enough that all the court was aware of it before Bathsheba finally took action to remedy the situation.

Their meeting came about a week before Passover and concerned the disposition of Haggith. Adonijah's mother was so bitter and resentful that she had become a constant reminder to everyone of her son's unfortunate death. It was feared by some that she would stir up another rebellion.

"Why won't she move to Adonijah's house across the valley?" Solomon asked his mother. They were sitting in the reception room above the court of the queens, and they could look down and see Haggith "holding court" with her ladies.

"She wants to be where she can keep track of all that's happening and where her complaints will be heard," Bathsheba said.

"She has quite a group gathered around her. Is it always like that?"

"Always. They're all city women, flattered by her attention."

"And your friends?"

"I don't sit here anymore. It's too unpleasant," Bathsheba said. "I spend most of my time in the house across the valley or at Giloh."

For the first time Solomon realized how difficult these past months had been for his mother. It was obvious that she had lost some of the control she had enjoyed while his father was alive. It made him angry to think that Haggith, who had always encouraged Adonijah's pride and rebellion, should be in a position that made his own mother uncomfortable. "Why haven't you told me this before?" he asked, taking one of his favorite raisin cakes from the woven basket she passed him.

"You've been too busy with other matters. I didn't want to disturb you."

"Disturb me!" he said. "It disturbs me far more to find that my mother hasn't been happy."

With these words the old relationship between mother and son was once again restored. Bathsheba knew that he hadn't been conscious of neglect. It was just that he had preferred to keep busy and forget his own unhappiness. In fact, as she saw how very unhappy he was, she felt even more guilty about the beads.

Later that morning she told Jessica all that had happened: how with a simple order from Solomon, Haggith would be moved out of the court of the queens to the old house of Adonijah across the valley. "Solomon was so kind," she said. "I believe all the past misunderstanding is now forgotten."

"Perhaps *some* of it is forgotten," Jessica said, "But I assure you that he hasn't forgotten the girl from Shunem."

At mention of the Shunemmite, Bathsheba sat up very straight; her mouth tightened and her eyebrows drew together in a disapproving frown. "Must that girl always come between us? Is there no rest from her?"

"No rest unless you settle it with Solomon."

"Settle it? How do you mean 'settle it'?"

"You must tell him the truth about the beads and let him decide for himself if he wants to forget her."

"Of course he *must* forget her. She's a troublemaker and a flirt."

Jessica hesitated. She had always spoken frankly to Bathsheba, and she was determined to do so now, though it was difficult. "Do you realize how much alike you are?" she said finally.

"What do you mean? We have nothing in common, as far as I can see."

"You both love plants and flowers—the earth and living things. You both dance with a sort of inborn magic, and there's something about both of you that attracts people."

"I never tried to bewitch anyone, as she seems to have done."

Jessica laughed in spite of the tension between them. "Why do you think

Haggith has hated you so? You were the king's favorite. He forgot everyone else when you were around. All of his other wives and all of his children were blotted out as he basked in your sunshine."

Bathsheba sank back into the cushions and dropped the whirling spindle. Her face grew clouded, and she didn't answer right away. Jessica was frightened. It was as though she had wounded her in some way; the queen couldn't respond lightly as she usually would.

"So that's what happened to Haggith, and now it's happening to me." She idly stroked the pile of raw wool in the basket beside her as Jessica waited, not daring to break into her thoughts. When she finally spoke it was with a heavy resignation. "I must see that Haggith isn't moved from the court of the queens. It's her only pleasure, and I've had so much. I can't deny her this."

"But isn't it dangerous? She says terrible things about you. She even invents things to say."

Bathsheba stood up. "I must go to her."

"Go to her?" Jessica was now alarmed. "What would you do? What would you say?"

Bathsheba didn't even look at Jessica as she gathered up the spindle and carding brush and handed them to her. "Put these away. I have to hurry." Bathsheba pulled her woolen robe more tightly around her and started for the door. "I never understood before," she said rather wistfully. "Maybe if I went to her and told her that I understand, it would relieve some of her pain."

Jessica wanted to stop her, but she was gone. Her footsteps could be heard going down the steps to the lower courtyard. Jessica was appalled at having set in motion this fearful encounter. Haggith had grown hard over the years. It was too late to try to heal the wound. There would only be trouble and more trouble from this approach.

She heard a scream. Running to the window, she saw that Haggith was flailing with her arms at the palace guards who were insisting that she come with them. With another scream she fainted, and the guards backed off in bewilderment.

At that moment Bathsheba swept into the courtyard, her small circlet crown sparkling and her woolen throw trailing unnoticed behind her. From the window where Jessica stood no words could be heard. It was evident, however, that Bathsheba was dismissing the guards. Then she saw her push her way in among the women and squat down so that she could talk to Haggith.

Haggith began to rouse, and again Bathsheba could be seen explaining something. When she finished no one in the courtyard moved. The women just stared at Bathsheba. Finally Haggith slowly got to her feet, then with one haughty look at Bathsheba she stalked off to her rooms. Jessica watched as the other women left without a word, and Bathsheba slowly retraced her steps. It was obvious that the attempt to reconcile with Haggith had failed.

* * *

It was a week after Passover when Bathsheba ordered Jessica to bring her the sandalwood box. "I've decided to give Solomon the beads. What will happen after that I can't even imagine."

"There were other misunderstandings beside the beads," Jessica said, "Perhaps now is the time to set them right."

"I don't know how I could have been so blind. You were right; she's very much like the girl I used to be in Lodebar. How could I have missed seeing it? I've done a terrible thing in the name of love, and now I must set it right in any way I can. Did you say there were other misunderstandings? What do you know? What else went wrong?"

Jessica had heard from some of the maidens how Shulamit had been tricked into going to Adonijah's house, and then how Adonijah had used that visit to torment both Solomon and Shulamit. "So," she concluded, after explaining it all to Bathsheba, "you see it wasn't just the fact that she left so suddenly that upset Solomon. Adonijah told him she left because she didn't want him to claim her as his bride. If he hears about the beads, he'll know that wasn't true."

"Why *did* she leave?" Bathsheba asked. "Does anyone know?"

"She knew that Adonijah wouldn't give up easily. No one would listen to her warning against him, and she was afraid he would win and claim her as his bride."

"Oh Jessica," Bathsheba cried as her hands flew to her blushing cheeks. "I'm so ashamed. She tried to warn me, and I wouldn't listen to anything against Adonijah."

* * *

Solomon hadn't been to his mother's house across the valley since their falling out, and he came now with the obvious intention of a brief visit. She had told him of her encounter with and change of heart toward Haggith, and he was genuinely curious. His mother had never been a woman to make mistakes; at least she would never admit she made them. Once she determined something was right, she seldom changed her mind about it.

The reception room was just as he remembered it, although it was evident that Bathsheba had planned something special. She brought out a clay bowl of hot coals and insisted on baking him some of his favorite cakes over the fire. He was touched by her thoughtfulness—but at the same time wondered what it could be that she wanted from him.

When he had finished the cakes and Jessica had removed the fire pot, he started to say all the thank-yous and niceties in preparation for leaving. Bathsheba stopped him, "No doubt, you wonder why I've called you," she said. "It's about the Shunemmite maiden. I want to set things right, ask your forgiveness."

Solomon stiffened. The wound was still too raw to be probed. "I'm finished with all of that," he said. "I don't want to discuss it."

"But you loved her, and she loved you."

He was surprised at how deeply these words could still hurt him, and that his mother would speak of her in those terms. "I don't want to hear about her anymore. I found her love to be false."

"You've judged her false because she left without a word just as you became king?"

"I think it's obvious that if she had loved me, she would have stayed—or at least left some word."

Bathsheba became so disturbed that she got up and walked back and forth across the room. "There are some things I must tell you," she said finally. "Part of what I have to say is a confession. I'm embarrassed and ashamed of what I've done, and I hope you'll find it in your heart to forgive me."

Solomon was astounded. He had never heard his mother talk like this before. As she told him all that Jessica had told her, he didn't move or react in any way, but when she told him of the beads, it was as though some inner barrier slowly began to crumble. He reached out and took the beads. All the time his eyes were traveling over them as though they were objects of rare beauty.

"I've heard that you're planning a trip to Meggido, and I have taken the liberty to plan on riding with you as far as the checkpoint. Then I'll go on to the pool of Harod where I'll camp. I've already sent word to Shunem that I'm coming and would like to see Shulamit again."

"What reason did you give?" Solomon asked cautiously.

"I didn't give them any reason. I simply told them that I would appreciate seeing Shulamit dance the Mahanaim."

Solomon stood up. He was frustrated and upset that his mother had taken things into her own hands in such a manner. Even knowing that he had been mistaken about Shulamit's intentions didn't heal the hurt. "I'll be glad to have you ride with me," he said, "but I'll not join you at the springs." His voice was firm and businesslike. Bathsheba knew that she couldn't change his mind.

Solomon felt nothing but confusion as he rode home with the beads safely tucked in his wide sash. He knew that Shulamit had meant them as reassurance of her love, but he still couldn't understand why she had left. Bathsheba had told him that she was afraid Adonijah would win the throne after David's death and try to claim her. "I'll not risk so much pain again," he thought. "I'll stay at Megiddo. I have a lot of work to do and don't need the added distraction." With that he settled the matter and refused to think of it anymore.

* * *

For a long time Solomon had been planning to make the Megiddo checkpoint on the trade route a prominent military base. As he and Bathsheba and his men rode out the North Gate and headed toward Aphek several days later, he tried not to think of anything but the checklist he had made of questions to ask of the captain in charge at Megiddo.

* * *

Bathsheba's message, stamped and closed with the queen's seal, was greeted in Shunem with mixed emotions. The brothers were wary; Bessim, who had gotten better, was elated, and Ramat was sure that her prayers had been answered. To everyone's surprise Shulamit was provoked. "Almost a year has passed, and I haven't heard a word from Solomon. Even now there's no message from him. It's only from his mother."

"But Bathsheba has asked for you."

"I don't trust her. I don't know why she's doing this. She's never liked me."

"People do change," Ramat interjected.

"Not Bathsheba. She's the queen, and once she makes up her mind about someone, she isn't noted for ever changing it."

"Perhaps the king is coming with her."

"The king! I don't want to see the king. I've been so hurt, so embarrassed." Ramat could see that Shulamit was serious. Something had happened in Jerusalem that really hurt her deeply.

"Can you tell me about it?" Ramat asked.

"Everything went wrong. I had such faith in him when he said that he loved me. I was *sure* that he loved me. But he went right ahead with plans to marry the princess of Rabbath-ammon. He didn't even bother to come and explain. Now it's been a whole year since I left Jerusalem, and I've not heard a word from him."

"But he did love you, and you loved him."

"Only words. I have only words to prove that he loved me—and this." Shulamit took the small pouch of dried flowers from around her neck and handed it to her mother.

Ramat held it in her hand and examined its careful workmanship, then smelled it. "The fragrance is gone," she said.

"It's been gone for quite a while."

"But of course the fragrance is gone if you haven't put in new flowers and oil."

"I really want to forget," Shulamit protested.

"Things might still work out."

"How can you say that?"

"Because it seems to me you still have a choice," Ramat said, fingering the pouch.

"I have a choice?"

"Yes. Usually we have some sort of choice. Let's say that love is like this little pouch. At first, it's all filled with love. Gradually we add a grievance here and there, until the love is crowded out and only the grievances remain."

"And so—?"

"The choice comes, whether to keep the grievances or be willing to get rid of them. The pouch is small; it can't hold both love and grievances, so one has to go." Ramat said no more but lovingly reached up and put the braided cord around Shulamit's neck.

Ramat began planning for the queen's visit with enthusiasm. She went through the box of Shulamit's things that had been sent from Jerusalem and picked out the loveliest gown and the most elegant jewelry. Bessim, even more enthusiastic, was determined that his daughter must go see Bathsheba, and she must be dressed as befitted a queen.

Shulamit decided to let them have their way. On the night that she was to be taken to the queen's encampment by the Pool of Harod, she let her mother and her friends dress her as they thought best.

* * *

Ramat could hardly contain her excitement, but Shulamit was detached, almost dispassionate, until Ramat called her aside. "Has it occurred to you that Bathsheba may have staged all this for her son? He may be coming with her. By all rights you're now his wife, and if he still loves you—as I think he does—he may be coming to take you back with him."

Shulamit was stunned. She had been disappointed so often that this possibility hadn't even occurred to her. "Mother," she said, the alarm evident in her voice, "what would I do? What would I say? He's hurt me in so many ways."

"As I've told you, you have a choice to make."

"But he's been so thoughtless," she protested.

"Perhaps he sees things differently. Maybe he doesn't understand your coming home just as he was crowned."

"I left a message."

"I've found that things aren't often as they seem."

"His mother thinks the very worst of me," said Shulamit.

"People change. If we're to be happy, we must be willing to forget the past."

There was no more time as at that moment there was a knock on the door, and Urim called through the latch hole, "The queen has sent a palanquin. You must hurry."

* * *

As Shulamit settled herself into the palanquin, Ramat whispered, "Remember you have a choice. No one else can make it for you."

The curtains closed and Shulamit was on her way. She felt the gentle rocking, heard the bearers' muffled voices and pounding bare feet. The darkness around her was fragrant with odors that reminded her of Jerusalem. Once again all the disappointments and frustrations swirled around her.

She was embarrassed to remember how sure she had been that Solomon loved her, when she'd had so little evidence. If he did love her, how could he have gone to Egypt knowing that before he returned his father would have claimed her? How had he signed the agreement to marry the princess of Rabbath-ammon? And now how could he have let a whole year go by without even trying to contact her? It was evident that he *didn't* love her.

Out of habit she fingered the little pouch of En-gedi flowers and remembered her mother's words: "You have a choice."

How easy it must seem to her mother. To choose to love was something easy to talk about but hard to do. People take advantage of a person who loves freely and without complaint. What was love anyway? Must it always be so costly? She could imagine no happy ending to this adventure. "If only it were possible to go back and start over again, so many things would be different."

* * *

As she stepped from the palanquin and entered the queen's tent, she had the strange feeling that everything was just as it had been in the past when she had come into this tent for the first time. She glanced around and saw that the queen was seated in the midst of her women; some were new, but most Shulamit recognized. There was no sign of Solomon or any of the queen's other sons. She felt relieved.

Shulamit came forward and knelt before the queen, raising the hem of her robe to her lips in respect.

To her surprise Bathsheba quickly took her by the hand. "You're a queen. There's no need for you to bow before me now. Come, sit here beside me. We have much to discuss."

"I no longer wear the gold circlet. I'm just a simple, village maiden again."

Bathsheba smiled. "Then we have much in common. I have also been a simple, village maiden."

"But that was long ago."

"The Mahanaim was our village dance, and I must admit that you dance it better than I have ever done."

"I'm honored. I'll be happy to dance for you again."

"In time we'll come to that. Now I've brought you raisin cakes from Jerusalem and flagons of wine from the vineyards of En-gedi."

Shulamit was puzzled. Bathsheba was so warm and friendly. She asked about her family, the goats she herded, and the plants she picked for medicinal purposes. Then she told stories of her own days in Lodebar until Shulamit felt comfortable and relaxed. She remembered her mother's comment that people change. She had to admit that, impossible as it seemed, the queen now appeared genuinely to like her. What had brought about such a change, Shulamit couldn't imagine.

Some hard knot of resentment and pain began to melt inside her. She felt that she couldn't speak, or she would cry. She could feel her anger dissolving, evaporating, but not without a struggle. Something wanted to cry out against the unfairness of the past. Hold on to the knot. Stiffen and strengthen the knot. Keep it hard and intact. It was only a moment the battle raged, and yet to Shulamit it seemed an eternity. Then, with a sigh, she determined to let it go. The struggle ceased; the knot loosened and was gone.

She was abruptly brought back to the reality of the present by the queen's gentle request: "Would you mind dancing the Mahanaim just as you danced it when I first came to Shunem? I've brought Jerusalem's best drummers, and musicians to play the sistrum and the flute and to sing."

Shulamit glanced up and saw that the queen was smiling at her. There was truly none of the old animosity. As the music throbbed and trilled, Shulamit smiled back at the queen. A great joy flooded through her as she responded to the familiar beat and the nostalgic twang of the sistrum.

Slowly, keeping time to the music, she rose. The music quickened and she began to walk with a slow, sliding half-step around the circle of light that fell from the lamps fastened to the tent poles.

There was an air of excitement as the old women increased the beat and Shulamit dipped and twisted, holding her mantle like a wedding huppah over her head and then letting it trail on the floor. Finally she dropped it altogether as she whirled and dipped, making the shadows vibrate on the tent walls. The night air rang with clapping and singing.

Gradually the beat slowed and Shulamit followed, every movement becoming more definite and accentuated until, as the music died, she sank to the floor in the center of a pool of light.

There were the usual immediate exclamations of approval and admiration, but as Shulamit raised her head she saw that the women were melting away into the shadows. The queen was gone, and in moments she was alone in the tent. Too dazed to comprehend what had happened, she stood bewildered and confused until she saw Solomon moving slowly toward her out of the shadows.

* * *

He was more handsome than she had remembered him, and he now walked with the confidence of a king. Her senses reeled with the familiar odor of spikenard as he reached for her hands. His eyes lingered hungrily on her hair and her lips. When he looked in her eyes he said with remorse, "I'm sorry for all the hurt you've suffered. There were so many things I didn't understand. My mother kept the beads. I've just found out about them."

"I thought you didn't care."

"Everything was so confusing."

"It wasn't your fault," she said.

"I was jealous and wary."

"You had a right to—"

He didn't let her finish the sentence. He pulled her to him and kissed her, at first hesitantly and then, as she responded, eagerly and insistently. Slowly he released her. "Your dancing took me back to that night so long ago when I saw you dance for the first time. Can we forget all that's happened and start over again?"

"I was so afraid you hadn't come."

"I hadn't planned to come, but as I sat in Meggido and thought about you, I *had* to come." He picked her up and carried her into his section of the tent and laid her down among the cushions.

"What are you thinking, my love?" she asked, noticing that he had grown thoughtful.

"I'm sorry about the vineyard. I'm sure my mother is sorry too. You're worth many vineyards."

"That's quite an exaggeration," she said, blushing.

"It's no exaggeration," he said. "See how beautiful your feet are, even in slippers! And the joints of your thighs are like the work of a clever jeweler." He was tracing the embroidered lilies around the top edge of the harem trousers, where they fit low on her hips.

She reached out and held his hand. "I want to hear more about how valuable I am, and then we'll see about the price."

"Price?" He was puzzled.

"You rent out your vineyard at Baal-hamon for a price, but my vineyard belongs to me and is not for rent or sale," she said seriously, but with a twinkle in her eyes.

Solomon, intrigued, smiled as he traced an imaginary circle around her navel. "Your vineyard is wonderfully enticing. The rounded goblet of your navel is beautiful, and your belly is like a heap of wheat belted with lilies."

"And—?" she said, urging him on.

"Your neck is like a tower of ivory, and your eyes are like the fish pools in Heshbon by the gate of Bath-rabbim." He paused, held by the look in her eyes, but she was enjoying this and wanted to hear more.

"And my nose?"

"Your nose is like the tower of Lebanon."

"How could a nose look like the tower of Lebanon?" she asked, laughing.

"I didn't say it *looked* like the tower; I said it *was* like the tower." They laughed together.

"And my head?"

"Your head is like Mount Carmel when it's covered with dark-purple foliage." She broke out in wild peals of laughter that he finally stifled with kisses.

"And—?" she said again, still wanting to hear what he would say.

"And the roof of your mouth is like the best wine," he said, seriously and with feeling. The joking and playing had stopped; he wanted to change the game to something less frivolous.

"My brothers thought that I had come home in disgrace. They said they had heard that both princes had had their way with me. I told them that I was still a walled garden and a fountain sealed, and they were surprised. What would *you* say that I am?"

"I would say that you're like a palm tree, and your breasts are lovely clusters of grapes."

"Grapes on a palm tree? How very strange."

"I didn't say that I would be logical. In fact, I've dreamed of climbing the palm and—"

Shulamit put her hand over his mouth before he could say any more, and he laughed as he pulled away. "What price must I pay for all the delights I'm to gain?" he said. "Must I give you back a portion of my vineyard, or do you intend to ask for the whole thing?"

"No, no," she said. "My vineyard is my own, and I will give it to you freely. Of course, a gift for my parents wouldn't be refused. They've spent much time and taken great care with my vineyard."

Solomon didn't answer right away, and Shulamit could see that he was deeply touched. From his years at court he knew how people took advantage of the bridegroom. He couldn't imagine someone willing to give herself freely, without price.

Shulamit sat up and began to put on her robe and arrange her mantle. "I must go now," she said, standing up.

"But I thought—"

"I know. I'm yours by every right, but this is neither the time nor the place to give you my love."

Solomon jumped to his feet and tried to pull her to him, but she gently held him back. "You would have only the dancer tonight, and I want to give you the little shepherdess you fell in love with."

"But how will you do that?" he asked.

"Come to the fortress and get me early in the morning before the shepherds leave with their flocks. We'll go out to the villages and into the fields, and there I'll give you my love."

"But—"

She put her hand over his mouth. "We're fortunate; we can forget the past and start over again."

"There's no need to forget *all* of the past. I'll always remember that you were a walled garden and a fountain sealed to everyone but me."

Reluctantly he took her to the tent door, helped her into the palanquin, and then watched her ride off into the night toward Shunem. Long after the palanquin was lost from sight in the darkness, he stood at the tent door marveling at the unexpected joy she had brought him.

* * *

Solomon told his mother all that had happened, and she was amused. "That girl reminds me more and more of myself at her age."

"You loved my father very much, didn't you."

"Not *loved*. I *love* him, and he loves me. Even death hasn't dimmed our love."

After she left, he went to bed and pondered what she had said. "Could it be," he wondered, "that love is stronger than death? Could it be possible that love is the strongest thing in the world? Water can't quench it, and death can't destroy it. How strange," he thought, "that something so invisible and so fragile can be so strong."

With that he turned over and tried to go to sleep. His crown and all the responsibilities that went with being a king were back in Jerusalem waiting for him, but for a few days he would be free again. "Tomorrow I'll sing for her the song I wrote after the first time I saw her. He hummed a few lines: "The winter is past, the rain is over and gone; the flowers appear on the earth." He was too tired to sing more. "Tomorrow I intend to tell Bessim that he can have the whole vineyard at Baal-hamon." With that he fell into a happy sleep and dreamed that he met a shepherdess dressed in thistle-gray. She looked just like Shulamit.

Epilogue

*T*he next day was a wonderful day for both of them. Dressed as his little shepherdess, she rode off with him to the villages with a whole retinue of courtiers.

It was spring, and everything was in bloom: pink flax, daisies, white mustard, cistus, and blue lupine. In the clear sky overhead flew sparrows, swifts, and every so often a vulture or an eagle. Great numbers of storks could be seen feeding in the marshy places or flying in groups to their far-off destinations.

Finally, leaving their companions with the warning that they were not to be disturbed, they rode to the watchtower at the edge of the vineyard. "Under the apple tree where [her] mother conceived and gave birth to [her]," she gave him her love, and he, we are told, "awakened" her.*

"Until the morning dawns and the shadows flee away," he said, "I will go to the mountain of myrrh and to the hill of frankincense. You are so beautiful, my love, in every part of you."

"Oh, feed me with your love," she said. 'Your 'raisins' and your 'apples'— for I am utterly lovesick."

"What a lovely, pleasant thing you are," Solomon said, "lying here upon the grass, shaded by the cedar trees and the firs."

It almost seems that what was lost in the garden of Eden was regained in the relationship of Solomon and Shulamit. In the Song of Solomon, theirs is pictured as the perfect love, and we're led to wonder what happened that we never hear of Shulamit again. We're especially curious since we know that Solomon did marry the princess of Rabbath-ammon, Naamah, and her son, Rehoboam, was the next king of Israel.

There are two other children mentioned, both girls: Taphath married Abinadab and lived in the region of Dor; Basmath married a man named Ahimaaz from the tribe of Naphtali, which was also in the north. I like to think that these were the daughters of Shulamit.

Perhaps here is the answer to our mystery, as happened so often in those days, Shulamit probably died in childbirth. It may have been at that time that Solomon wrote his great love song.

---

* Quotations in this Epilogue are taken from the Song of Solomon, as translated in the Living Bible.

There was no such thing as a photograph in those days. If people wanted to remember something, they had to picture it in words as Solomon did. Every memory was written down—not in the order events happened, but as he remembered them. The Song of Solomon starts in the present but covers the past through flashbacks with his conclusion coming at the end.

Solomon is known for his many wives. I imagine he may have thought that in them he could find again the love he lost with Shulamit's death. He obviously didn't, but he did make the discovery that "love is as strong as death."

And how is it, we ask, that the Song of Solomon found its way into our Bible, is read at Passover every year, and has been called by many rabbis the most beautiful poem in the world?

Someone, perhaps Nathan, realized its uniqueness and saved it as a special treasure. It's the story of a young girl's love that withstood every trial and temptation until she could say, "I am a wall and my breasts like towers: then was I in his eyes as one that found favor" (Song of Songs 8:10).

On the other hand, she was able to give herself freely when the time came. We see that she's in charge of her own vineyard, and she's ready to give it to Solomon without reservation.

There's also a political side to the preservation of the Song of Solomon. The north and the south in Israel were always divided, and it must have been a unifying element for the people to realize that while Solomon married the princess of Rabbath-ammon, he wrote his most memorable, lovely poem about a girl from the north who completely captured his heart.

The most amazing aspect of the poem is that it was written at a time when the differences between men and women often drove them apart. Men fought battles, and women raised children; men read, prayed, and pondered, and women cooked, planted, and sewed. Life was hard and serious. The idea of romantic love hadn't been discovered.

People reading or hearing the Song of Solomon received the first hint of the kind of relationship that was possible between a man and a woman. Solomon was perhaps the first romantic. He was the first to write about human love as God intended it to be.

MORE FROM
ROBERTA KELLS DORR

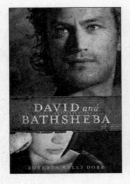

978-0-8024-0956-0   978-0-8024-0958-4

978-0-8024-0955-3   978-0-8024-0957-7   978-0-8024-0959-1

Also available as an ebook

IMPACTING LIVES THROUGH THE POWER OF STORY

www.RiverNorthFiction.com | www.MoodyPublishers.com

river north

IMPACTING LIVES THROUGH THE POWER OF STORY

Thank you! We are honored that you took the time out of your busy schedule to read this book. If you enjoyed what you read, would you consider sharing the message with others?

- Write a review online at amazon.com, bn.com, goodreads.com, cbd.com.

- Recommend this book to friends in your book club, workplace, church, school, classes or small group.

- Go to facebook.com/RiverNorthFiction, "like" the page and post a comment as to what you enjoyed the most.

- Mention this book in a Facebook post, Twitter update, Pinterest pin or a blog post.

- Pick up a copy for someone you know who would be encouraged by this message.

- Subscribe to our newsletter for information on upcoming titles, inside information on discounts and promotions, and learn more about your favorite authors at RiverNorthFiction.com.

www.RiverNorthFiction.com | www.MoodyPublishers.com

midday connection

Discover a safe place to authentically process life's journey on **Midday Connection**, hosted by Anita Lustrea and Melinda Schmidt. This live radio program is designed to encourage women with a focus on growing the whole person: body, mind, and soul. You'll grow toward spiritual freedom and personal transformation as you learn who God is and who He created us to be.

www.middayconnection.org

MOODYRADIO
Where you turn. For life.

the LAND and the BOOK

with Dr. Charlie Dyer

Dr. Charlie Dyer provides biblical insight into the complex tapestry of people and events that make up Israel and the Middle East. Each week he presents an in-depth look at biblical, historical, archeological, and prophetic events and their relevance for today.

www.thelandandthebook.org

MOODYRADIO
Where you turn. For life.